the Resolution

J. J. Sykora

 FriesenPress

Suite 300 - 990 Fort St
Victoria, BC, V8V 3K2
Canada

www.friesenpress.com

ISBN
978-1-5255-2308-3 (Hardcover)
978-1-5255-2309-0 (Paperback)
978-1-5255-2310-6 (eBook)

1. FICTION, HUMOROUS

Distributed to the trade by The Ingram Book Company

To my 'mom' whom I
love dearly
Thanks for enjoying
the book Andrey

'You say you want a resolution...
we all want to change the world'

—adapted from The Beatles (1968)

Love

JJ Sykora

CHAPTER 1

THE RESOLUTION

Wednesday, December 31, 2014

Over the din of multiple conversations, and Marvin Gaye crooning "Let's Get It On" in the background, Ron noticed his wife, Brandi, chatting with a group of friends across the room. *My God, she looks gorgeous tonight,* he thought. Unconsciously encouraged by Marvin's sensual tones, Ron was feeling particularly romantic.

It was ten minutes to midnight at a house party in Nepean, on the west side of Ottawa, and with the year's end approaching, the partygoers were now more frequently glancing at their phones and watches in anticipation of the countdown. The various gender-segregated clusters would soon start to dissolve, and the attendees would begin an instinctive drift towards their respective spouses and partners, as if drawn back together by an invisible fundamental force in charge of the hierarchical realignment of relationships. The exact scene would be played out at New Year's Eve social gatherings across the country.

The wine had certainly left its mark on Ron by this time of the night. Normally conservative and politely engaging, he was, at this moment, better described as unreservedly outgoing. Sporting a wide blue tooth-tinted smile tastefully accentuated with a red wine mini-mustachio, Ron initiated a shuffle across the congested room towards his wife. Like a happy-clown heat-seeking missile, he deftly parried his way through the crowd until he had wrapped his arms around her.

"Do you know how much I love you?" Ron whispered in Brandi's ear.

"I hope more than that goofy T-shirt you're wearing."

Ron looked down at his *Kiss Me I'm Irish* shirt, and stated, with a *faux*-hurt expression, "It's in your honour. Besides, I've always thought I was part Irish, especially when I've been drinking. And yes, I love you way more than this admittedly overstated but well-intended T-shirt."

As Ron nibbled on Brandi's neck, to the sound of her muted squeals and her feigned repulse, he considered what the next year would bring, and it occurred to him that he hadn't thought of a New Year's resolution yet. He snapped back to reality and asked her, "Hey, are you planning to 'resolve' anything for next year?"

"You know I don't go for that stuff, Ron."

"Ayyh, I can attest that ye already be perfect. Now kiss me, and give me Blarney Stone a wee rub perhaps."

Brandi gagged, suppressing a laugh. "That's the worst Irish accent *ever* in the history of mankind."

"To be sure, to be sure. But you know I do like a good resolution, and I just realized I haven't thought about this year's theme yet. Everyone can find a way to fine-tune themselves a bit, and it's a tradition. I love traditions! And," he added seriously, "I never break my resolutions."

Brandi guffawed. "That's because you always make them so easy you could do them in your sleep. Or else you alter them to make them more manageable."

"Not true. Remember the triathlon? I spent nearly seven months getting in shape for the summer triathlon! That one was *not* easy, and the race damn near killed me."

"OK, there was that one, but how about the one a few years ago about biking to work every day for a year? We live one kilometre from your office!"

"I needed snow tires for that winter, I'll have you know."

2

"Or how about spending one hour of quality time with the kids every day? You started banking the extra hours spent with them, as I remember. Summer essentially took care of the rest of the year. Or the year you promised not to wear your undies for more than one day. You stopped wearing underwear altogether to get around that one! What could you possibly do to top that?"

Ron started giving that some thought, but was instantly distracted by Brandi's proximity and the thought of *her* underwear. At the same moment, Pharrell Williams'"Happy" started playing, someone shouted,"Five minutes to midnight!", and a small alcohol-infused light bulb lit up in Ron's head. Now displaying an ear-to-ear smile, and with a twinkle in his eye, he faced Brandi squarely.

"What is it, Ron? Are you having a stroke?"

In response Ron turned up his smile a notch, raised his eyebrows *a la* Jack Nicholson, and angled his head a bit.

"Ok, now you're scaring me."

More smiling and eyebrow waggling by Ron.

"*What?*" Brandi blurted.

Calming his enthusiasm, ever so marginally, he explained."Ok, well, you know I've always wanted you to join me in a resolution."

Brandi rolled her eyes."Yes, but I, unlike you, already both wear and change my underwear daily."

Ron put on his most reasonable expression. "Wait, wait, wait, and hear me out. With our twentieth anniversary coming up next year, and us sliding—ever-so-imperceptibly, mind you," he added in a conciliatory manner, "towards our comfortable middle age, I think we should reinvigorate our marriage. Half of marriages end up in divorce, you know. The average length of a marriage is around fourteen years."

Suspiciously, Brandi asked,"Do you have a point here?"

Ron hardly missed a beat."We've already beaten the odds, and I want to keep it that way. So, my thought is…for our resolution…"

"Yes?"

"So, for our resolution…," Ron hesitated as he gave the idea a final quality-control assessment, "…for *our* resolution, I propose we make love every day of the year."

CHAPTER 2

GENIUS

Thursday, January 1

Ron shuffled around the kitchen, shifting his attention between coffee-making duties and his toast. Aside from the dull background cranial throbbing that signified overindulgence the night before, Ron was feeling pretty good this first morning of 2015.

He chuckled to himself, recalling the events of the previous evening, leading up to and immediately following midnight. When he'd made his proposal to Brandi for a shared New Year's resolution, she'd laughed it off as if it were a joke. But when Ron didn't respond accordingly, she had frozen in place and, after a heartbeat or two, gave him a shove and asked incredulously, "You're serious?"

At that point, and with about two minutes to plead his case before midnight, Ron had kicked it into high gear. Drawing upon all his skills of persuasion (honed through years of high-school debating), he launched his case. "Honey, we've always had a great sex life, but you have to admit, we're not at each other like we used to be in the early days," he had begun.

Brandi had suggested that was because they were in their late forties now. "We're not horny teenagers anymore," was the way she put it.

Ron had pressed his case. "What you did during your teenage years is irrelevant to this discussion. I'm talking about recapturing the sexual energy of our twenties, when we first met. That unquenchable, three-times-a-day, no-problem, I'm-ready, scha-wing, get-those-panties-off-before-I-eat-through-them, all-encompassing, I've-got-to-have-you-now state-of-mind thing." He delivered this argument in a single breath, since it was about a minute to midnight.

Brandi had stood motionless for a couple of seconds, Ron responding similarly until a wry smile began growing on Brandi's face. At that moment Ron knew she was softening. When she said, "Well, you can't be faulted for your good intentions," he knew she was considering it.

After that it was the typical caveats and cautionary warnings that always accompanied Brandi's assessments of his resolutions. "I hope you've thought this through, Ron," to which he remembered nodding vigorously in response. "You know how you are with these resolutions." The usual admonishments.

When Brandi got around to discussing *herself* in context with Ron's proposal ("This is my first resolution, and I'm going to hold you to this as a matter of principle"), Ron knew she had agreed, and his wine-stained smile had broadened. He had pulled Brandi to him and kissed her as hard as he dared, given their current public venue.

Just then someone shouted, "Ten! Nine! Eight! Seven! Six!..." and Ron had hugged Brandi through the countdown, and repeated the kiss following the eruption of reverie at midnight.

After being dropped off by some friends at about 2 a.m., Brandi checked on Samantha, their fourteen-year-old daughter, who had spent the lead-up to midnight at her best friend's house a few doors away and, from her text messages, had sleepily returned home before one o'clock. When Brandi returned to their bedroom she found Ron stripped down and lying in a Burt Reynoldsesque pose on their bed, quite ready to embark upon this 365-day odyssey. He had the starter pistol in his hand, and it looked ready to go off. Brandi laughed, and commenced a striptease, slowly and exaggeratedly removing her clothes, while sporting a Kardashian facial pout.

They were both fast asleep by a quarter after two.

Now, as Ron crunched his toast and sipped his coffee, his mind drifted to the prospect of completing the resolution over the following year. While most of his friends complained about not having enough sex as their relationships "matured," Ron had a full year of guaranteed sex-du-jour with his raven-haired beauty. He smiled smugly at the sheer brilliance of his resolution, and looked forward to sharing it with his best friend, Scott Hartwell. Ron imagined himself humbly absorbing his friend's praise at the inherent genius of the resolution. Even more so, Ron anticipated and looked forward to Scotty's animated envious groans, borne of his own sexual frustration—delivered periodically throughout the year in response to Ron's irrepressibly effervescent and, clearly, sexually satisfied persona. Ron typically didn't discussed details of his sex life with Scotty, but he foresaw plenty of opportunity for gloating through his exaggerated personal contentment and innuendo. Sex was even more enjoyable when you could make your buddy jealous of your good fortune.

Ron heard stirring upstairs. It was about 9 a.m., and neither Brandi nor Sam had yet made an appearance. Shortly after the girls joined him at the kitchen island, he and Brandi wished Sam a "Happy New Year!" Only their son, Tommy, was absent. He was home for the holidays from the University of Toronto, but had texted his mom last night that he would be staying over at a friend's house, so when he would show was anybody's guess.

It was a fairly relaxed atmosphere in the kitchen, with everybody off until January 5, and glad for the break. Other than today's meal with his parents, a supper at a friend's house on Saturday, and hockey on Sunday evening, Ron only had his immediate family to focus on for the next few days—during which he would steadfastly advance their resolution. This thought infused him with a warm feeling that spread through his body, settling squarely in his nether region. *This is going to be the best resolution ever!*

Monday, January 5

The weather had turned sharply cooler on the weekend, and Ron had a brisk walk to work on Monday morning. Still, re-invigorated from the break and feeling buoyant from the successful start to his year-long resolution, he really didn't notice the cold. Ron had been born and educated in Ottawa, earning his engineering degree at Carleton University, and as such, had long ago accepted winter as just another season. Ron had signed on with EllisDon right out of school, and had spent his entire career with them, working his way from junior assistant in the Buildings Department to his position as Project Manager in Procurement and Estimates. EllisDon was a great fit for Ron. A well-respected, employee-centric, and community-minded construction company, they had been named Canada's best employer three times. With their progressive corporate culture, they were a desired destination for Canada's best and brightest graduates. Ron knew he had played his part in building EllisDon into the company it was today, and took pride in that accomplishment.

His best buddy, Scott Hartwell, also worked at EllisDon, as an engineer in the Emerging Markets Department. Married but without children, Scott could more easily accommodate the travel requirements for this position, and had naturally gravitated to the business-development aspect of the job. Scott swung by Ron's office mid-morning for a catch-up over coffee.

After a quick download regarding their New Year's celebrations and the subsequent few days off, they agreed to get together Friday after work at the Bassline Pub for a drink and a more complete session.

Friday, January 9

As Ron walked into the Bassline Pub at five-thirty Friday afternoon, he quickly spotted Scott at the end of the bar, with an extra seat beside him.

"Good thing I got here about a half hour ago, or we'd be standing," Scott offered.

Ron looked around, and nodded in agreement.

The Bassline Pub was a local hole-in-the-mall venue that, in its eight years of existence, had become a bit of a neighbourhood hit—a cozy venue with decent live music six nights of the week, cheap draft beer, edible pub food, and a mature mixed-collar clientele. Friday evenings were rush hour. Since there had been more than a week of healing time since the New Year's parties, business was almost as brisk as usual, and patrons were pouring into the ever-more-crowded venue.

"Thank Christ it warmed up a bit today," commented Ron. "My house was making cracking sounds last night. I think it was shrinking." It had gotten down to -30 C the previous night, and in Ottawa's humid climate, that was arctic cold.

As Ron was attempting to get the bartender's attention, Scott asked, "Well, what's new?"

That was the invitation Ron had been looking forward to for about ten days. Ron calmly started to methodically list off the status of items contributing to his personal sphere. "Kids are good. Tommy headed back to TO on Sunday. He's loving his first year in engineering. Sam periodically emerges from her teenage satanic possession and actually acts human now and then. We may be able to skip the exorcism after all. Mom's still kicking Dad's ass around the roost. She was particularly feisty and entertaining when we had them over for supper on New Year's Day. Brandi's amazing as always, and, oh yeah, I'm nine days into this year's resolution."

Scott took the bait and tiredly inquired, "What is it this year?"

"Well, Brandi and I have decided to make love every day of the year."

Unfortunately for the bartender serving Ron his beer at that exact moment, Scott performed a textbook shock-and-gag reaction, hitting the unsuspecting suds server with a high-velocity mouthful of malty mist. The bartender's smile evaporated as he barked, "What the fuck?" followed by, "You alright man?"

Following some further sputtering by Scott, backslapping by Ron, and eye-watering apologies to the bartender, Scott gathered himself, and stared at Ron with an emphatic "Are you kidding me?" look.

Ron basked in Scott's over-the-top reaction, and recounted the events of New Year's Eve.

"And so far?" asked Scott.

"We're right on target."

"That's likely Elise's and my output for the first quarter this year!" moaned Scott. But then, after a brief pause and some further consideration, he added, "You know, this might not be as easy as you think."

Taken aback, and annoyed that his friend would attempt to diminish the pure and inherent joy of the moment, Ron's smug smile faded, and he asked, "Why do you say that?"

Scott paused a bit, and took a sip of beer. "A number of things come to mind. Firstly, you're not twenty-two any more. Secondly, life gets in the way. And thirdly, you're not twenty-two any more. Agreed, Brandi is one hot mama—and I mean that in the most un-lecherous way possible—an epic combination of beauty, brains and body, which raises the question of what she's doing with *you.*" After a short paused he added, "What I mean is, you're only human."

"What the heck is that supposed to mean?" asked Ron.

"Well, I know your depth of experience in this field is a bit limited," Scott stated, knowing Ron had had few girlfriends before meeting Brandi, "but there is hardwiring in every man that...how can I say this?...that overprints what we do and why we do it. Let's call this our *yang.* On the other hand, there is our *yin,* which balances us and directs us to spiritual enlightenment. Together they interact to create balance in life. Our *yin* and *yang.*"

"What the hell are you on about? You're just jealous of my new-found studiferous life, and are attempting to throw cold water on my gloataceous moment."

"Two interesting new additions to the English language," complimented Scott, "but my spidey-sense is tingling on this one. That said, I am a bit jealous."

Content with Scotts' confession, and pleased at his admission of envy, Ron turned back to the business of enjoying his evening, getting a light buzz on, and bullshitting with his buddy.

Meanwhile, in their nearby Centrepointe community home, Brandi was chatting with her good friend Charlene Tran, augmented with a decent bottle of Cabernet from the Trius Winery in the Niagara region. They were onto their second glass, and the conversation was beginning to loosen up. Brandi had endured a stressful week back at work, and was ready to decompress.

She had worked as a property sales and acquisition strategist at the Kanata Research Park for the last year and a half. The research complex was the brainchild of the telecommunications entrepreneur Terry Matthews, Chairman of Wesley Clover. The high-tech billionaire philanthropist had, fortunately for the citizens of the Ottawa Valley, fallen in love with the city during his successful time as co-founder of Mitel, and had made Ottawa the global headquarters for Wesley Clover operations. This was not Brandi's first job—she'd done a brief stint as a business analyst at Hewlett-Packard in Ottawa after graduating with an MBA from Queen's University—but it felt like it was, following her sixteen-year motherhood sabbatical.

Conversation between Brandi and Charlene darted around from work to family, then back to work and mutual friends, and eventually landed on the topic of special plans for the new year. Brandi considered this an acceptable segue into the topic of her and Ron's resolution, and cautiously embarked on telling the tale to Charlene. Together, they laughed their asses off as Brandi shared the story of how it came to be. Both, having been married for about two decades, knew how ambitious and patently ridiculous the resolution was, but on the other hand, both also recognized that Ron singularly possessed an extraordinary stubbornness when it came to the successful completion of his yearly resolutions.

"How's it going?" asked Charlene.

Brandi paused pensively for a few seconds, and then said, as she slowly nodded, "You know, not so bad, really. I thought Ron might have overextended himself with this resolution, but so far, I have to admit, I'm enjoying it. Family life has certainly been our priority over the last quite a few years, and our personal relationship has been for the most part relegated, out of necessity, to the mezzanine section of the bigger show. I'm not exactly sure what Ron's motives behind this were—we haven't really talked about it yet—but I'm genuinely touched that he thought this up. This resolution, in effect, structures some 'us' time into our lives, and gives us a chance to rediscover our relationship. I think it's romantic."

"Well, *I'm* very interested to see how this one turns out," Charlene said, with a mischievous smile and raised eyebrows.

Unbeknownst to her, she was sporting a jaunty Salvador Dali-like red-wine mustachio, which made the comment even more comedic. The visual was enough to send Brandi into a further laughing fit.

Upon composing herself, and while wiping the tears from her eyes, Brandi added, "So am I."

Thursday, January 15

Brandi was oscillating around the kitchen when Ron came downstairs for breakfast. He hadn't made it back from work last night until after ten, and the house was already asleep. Work related to EllisDon's biggest project, the downtown Ottawa Confederation Line LRT, had ratcheted up in the new year, and Ron had started to put in some long days. While this in itself wasn't unusual, it was the second time this week that it had happened, and it put him and Brandi into arrears on their resolution. Not that he had anything left when he actually got home. *That frickin' Scotty and his prediction that life gets in the way,* Ron thought. He knew there would be some "I told you so" going on the next time they talked.

Ron had now accepted that there would be short-term interruptions in the completion of the resolution, and this necessitated minor restructuring of the rules of engagement to maintain its integrity. He had realized earlier in the week that short hiatuses were inevitable, with a guys' golf trip to New York State planned in May, and Brandi's not-uncommon weekend trips to visit her mother and sisters in Toronto. While Ron was thinking this through, he also realized, much to his embarrassment, that he had not yet, not even once, considered the impact of Brandi's monthly menstrual cycle on the resolution.

He smiled at Brandi as she zipped by on her way to the base of the stairs to call up to Sam that breakfast was ready and to hurry up. The morning routine with Sam had simplified itself considerably since she had moved to the nearby Sir Robert Borden High School as a minor-niner, and could now walk to school. Once she was rousted and force-fed breakfast, her emerging spirit of self-reliance usually took over, allowing Brandi to allot more precious morning time to herself.

Upon Brandi's reentry into the kitchen, Ron asked, "You home at a normal time tonight?"

"Should be, why? How about you? You seem to be avoiding me these days."

Ron fought back the surprising bloom of heat in his face, which he knew would be accompanied by reddening cheeks. "We've been busy as hell this week on the Confederation project, but I should be home for supper tonight," he said as cheerily as he could manage at the moment.

"In addition to further advancing our resolution," he added as his composure returned, "we should agree on some rule clarifications in light of recent events and, in hindsight, recognition that we'll both be taking some solo trips this year." After a short pause he sheepishly added, "And also in consideration of your monthly cycles."

"I was wondering when we'd be having this discussion," Brandi commented with a smile then quickly and coyly added with pursed lips. "I'm available this evening for whatever you have in mind."

෯

Lying post-coital in bed that evening, Ron gently rubbed Brandi's shoulders as he brought up his proposal for the minor rule change concerning the resolution. "First of all, are you OK with altering the resolution from 'every day' to '365 times in one year'?"

Brandi smiled and chuckled.

"What?" asked Ron.

"You and your resolutions make me laugh. You know you don't have to go through with this if you think it's impractical, Ron. I'd understand."

"Come on. Who are you talking to? Have you ever known me to quit on any resolution? That was a rhetorical question, by the way. This is still on, my girl. With an agreed minor rule adjustment, we're back on track again."

Brandi smiled without saying anything, implying her agreement to forge ahead.

"Good," said Ron. "Since we're only one day in arrears, would you care to continue with this and balance the books, so to speak?"

"I'm up for it if you are."

Ron wasn't quite there yet, and requested some pre-multi-coital cuddle time to allow for a recharge. He suddenly realized that they had experienced a role reversal in their sexual dynamics. *Christ, I remember when it was Brandi who required a bit of foreplay!* he quietly bemoaned, while Brandi displayed her expert manipulation of Chinese baoding balls.

Saturday, January 17

Ron had spent most of Saturday at work. His reward was a quiet night at home with three of his favourite things: pizza, a decent movie, and his wife (not necessarily in that order). Sam was at her girlfriend's for a sleepover, so they had the house to themselves. Without formal discussion, they defaulted to the pizza/movie to kick off the evening. This sequence of events was driven by the fact that Ron hadn't eaten all day and was ravenous when he got home. Regardless of his emaciated state and low blood sugar, the fact that they didn't use this opportunity to immediately stamp another DONE concerning this year's resolution hadn't escaped Ron.

He and Brandi had used the time accessorizing, cooking, and eating their pizzas as an opportunity to catch up on the week's events. Brandi's mom, Megan, had recently been diagnosed with diabetes, so Brandi was constantly checking up on her. She felt better that her sisters where both in TO and in physical contact with her mom, but Ron could tell Brandi was feeling a bit guilty about not being there herself. Her mom now lived alone, since her dad had passed away from ALS a few years back at the age of sixty-seven, after a righteous four-year fight.

Mr. Fuller had been a smart, scrappy, and completely charming Irishman, one generation removed from the southern Irish city of Cork. The root cause of his family's immigration to Canada was Ireland's declaration of neutrality at the start of World War II. Although spared the devastation the rest of Europe suffered, Ireland was also left out when the capital flowed back into Europe for the rebuild. Sensing commercial opportunity lay elsewhere, and aware of Canada's favourable leanings towards immigrants from the UK and Ireland, the Irish Fullers, all seven of them, shuttered the shop, weighed anchor, and floated themselves over to Toronto on the *Queen Mary*, via Southampton and New York City. Thus, at the age of five, Grampa (Sean) Fuller had become a Canadian, during the golden years following World War II. His charismatic and genuinely affable nature had been passed on to all his children, and Ron had, for more than two decades now, been the long-term benefactor of this familial trait.

Further discussion over supper circled around to the whereabouts and current health of various uncles and aunts who were still amongst the living—all on Brandi's side, since Ron parents were both only children. Two Uncle Fullers were still kicking around—one back in Ireland and another in Arizona. Brandi had not seen either since she moved to Ottawa. Of her two remaining aunts, Aunt Colleen—Megan's only sister—was closest to their family. Colleen was an effervescent and genuinely eccentric soul who had often visited Toronto during Brandi's childhood, and had periodically surfaced in Ottawa in more recent years. As far as Brandi knew, she was still living a meager reclusive rural life somewhere in the Eastern Townships of Quebec, raising chickens, growing vegetables, and reading palms and Tarot cards. On her last visit to Ottawa, a few years ago, she had stayed for only one night, and made a point of reading everyone's palm and conducting a private Tarot-card reading for Brandi. For Ron, the most memorable event of that evening was Aunt Colleen emerging from the Tarot session in the office ashen-faced, and heading directly to bed. When they awoke the next morning she had already departed without saying good-bye. Brandi recalled that Aunt Colleen's demeanour had changed markedly about halfway through her reading. Upon turning over the last Tarot card, she had looked up at Brandi with a stunned look, and muttered, "You have the gift," before wordlessly hurrying out of the room. They had not seen or heard from her since that night. Ron now commonly used the phrase "you have the gift" to compliment Brandi for a nice meal, or when she mixed him a drink.

Their conversation eventually shifted to office gossip. Rumours of marital affairs and breakups abounded in both their offices. They toasted in appreciation of their enduring relationship, and soon moved downstairs to select a movie and settle in for some passive viewing.

As the movie neared completion, Ron sensed a feeling of discomfort rising within him. Given the checklist of tonight's activities was rather short, the completion of the movie would naturally lead into the last of the items on the night's agenda—some carnal delight with his bride. What surprised Ron, however, was that the prospect of this act tonight was not associated with the normal stirring anticipation and growing excitement. Instead, disconcertedly, he found himself getting progressively more anxious. As he sat, now only partially focusing on the movie's denouement, this initial anxiety grew, and morphed into a sense of dread. He knew that Brandi was also acutely aware of the next item on their evening's to-do list, and this thought only added to Ron's anxiety.

Brandi sensed something was up and asked, "Ron, are you OK?" She looked down at Ron's hand, held in hers, and added, "Your hand is sweating." Looking closer at him, she remarked, "And your face is, too. I can feel your pulse in your hand."

Ron was hoping to breathe through the event without Brandi becoming aware, but her raised alarm really wasn't helping the situation. "I'm fine. Just feeling a bit lightheaded and weak. I'm sure it'll pass in a few minutes."

Brandi's concerned face was now squarely focused on Ron, as she gently stroked his hand. After a few minutes, the wave of anxiety subsided, and Ron began to feel normal again. "Well, that was interesting," he said. "I must be getting run-down from the long hours at the office."

Since Brandi's father had died and her mom had been diagnosed with diabetes, she had become a bit more, if not paranoid, then certainly awakened to the spectre of disease, and the firm grip on Ron's hand and concerned look spoke to her concern.

After a few minutes Ron had sufficiently recovered to start laughing about the episode. Trying to deflect her attention, he talked her into replaying the movie's finale, so they could watch it again. With a pasted-on smile and determined nonchalance, he pretended to focus on the movie, while he started to process what had just happened to him. He concluded there was a direct correlation between the onset of the anxiety attack and his anticipation of their love-making post-movie. *What the hell's up with that?* he wondered.

When the movie ended, Brandi turned her attention back to Ron, suggesting they go upstairs and get him some water and into bed. With those words, Ron could feel another plume of anxiety well up within him. He effectively countered it by popping up from the couch in an exaggerated nonverbal agreement with Brandi's suggestion, and setting off to the kitchen.

While he sat at the kitchen island with a glass of cold water, regaining his composure, Brandi proceeded to tidy up the area up, part of her nighttime ritual. "Is that the first time that's happened to you, Ron?" she softly inquired.

Still in deflect mode, Ron replied, "It was nothing, Brandi. I'm just overworked and a little tired. I feel absolutely fine now." Ron emphasized this point with an open armed "ta-da!", accentuated with his best goofy smile. This evoked a smile from Brandi and successfully served to allay her immediate concerns, much to Ron's relief.

Later, while upstairs brushing his teeth, Ron further de-constructed the disturbing event. As best he could tell, the anxiety he had just experienced was a product of a leading edge of doubt creeping into his consciousness, cultivating some uncertainty as to whether he could keep up the resolution. Was his sexual desire concerning Brandi beginning to flag, and if so, why? He had never, pre- or post-marriage, experienced anything but a complete and effortless connection to her sexually.

As he heard Brandi enter the bedroom, he suspended his self-interrogation and slipped back into a carefree, nothing happened, denial-is-what-guys-do-best persona for Brandi's benefit. Lying in bed, waiting for her, Ron allowed himself a few more minutes of introspection before his wife appeared for bed, uncharacteristically sporting a long T-shirt. Ron followed her approach to the bed and watched as she climbed in. "What's up with the T-shirt?" he inquired. She almost always slept in the nude.

Looking at him somewhat sympathetically, she said, "I didn't what to pressure you tonight, since you weren't feeling good."

"You mean what happened downstairs?" Ron remarked, feigning surprise. "It's going to take more than a sweating fit to keep me from providing my sweetheart with the physical pleasures that she both deserves and is due under the accepted 2015 resolution proclamation."

Brandi cast him a look. "Are you sure?"

"As sure as eggs is eggs," Ron countered in an Irish accent, as he worked to release Brandi's T-shirt from her silky torso.

Friday, January 23

It was Ron who made it to the Bassline Pub first. Looking around, he saw that it was already starting to fill up, although it was only four-thirty in the afternoon. Ron had skipped out of work a bit early, and in doing so had resigned himself to the fact that he would be putting in at least four hours at the office tomorrow. Given the events of the last week, he had prioritized this BS session with Scotty over a relaxing Saturday at home. He needed to talk to someone and get an objective take on recent developments. And other than Brandi, he could only trust Scott with this personal subject matter.

He grabbed a small table near the back of the bar, and ordered a beer. As he sat waiting for Scott, he settled into people-watching mode. The crowd at this time of day was an eclectic mix of young and old and blue- and white-collar, and so far was mostly men. He surmised that the majority of patrons who were intermittently exiting to top up on vitamin-N were not office workers. Too early for that. The closet-smoking professionals in attendance would typically require a higher alcohol blood level before abandoning rational thought. Ron suspected that City of Ottawa workers were disproportionately represented in the current bar population.

He watched a few middle-aged ladies enter. They paused to allow their eyes to adjust to the dimmer light, while demonstrably enjoying the contrasting warmth of the bar and scanning the crowd for their acquaintances. Ron couldn't help but notice the exceptional figure on one lady in particular – noticeable even through her heavy coat. Unconsciously, his eyes followed her as she found and joined her friends at the other end of the bar, disrobing from her winter wear as she went. During her animated greetings and air-kiss session, his buddy Scott entered the bar, and Ron's drifting attention snapped back to the moment, his arm shooting up to wave his friend over.

As Scott arrived at the table, he started removing his coat and gloves, shaking off the cold as he did. "They say it's going to be a frigid rest of January and February."

"Who are *they?*"

Scott thought for a second. "You know—the Farmer's Almanac and the weather forecasters. The Almanac has an accuracy rating better than eighty percent," he added officiously, "so that's nothing to guffaw at."

Ron guffawed anyway. "It's the middle of winter in Canada. No one should expect anything else. Besides, it's just weather."

"Let's see if you still maintain that position come mid-February, my friend," chastised Scott.

Introductory jabs out of the way, Scott, using his much-practiced technique of wild gesticulations perfectly timed to intersect a server's reconnaissance glance, managed to quickly get the attention of the lone waitress. He ordered a beer, turned to Ron, and inquired, "Well, how's it going?

"As you know, the Confed project is taking on a life of its own. The company is getting its money's worth out of me these days, I can assure you."

"Good to hear," interjected Scott. "My bonus is dependent upon your hard work, so you can count on me for moral support during this challenging time. And while you're toiling away at full capacity, you can take some solace knowing that I'm doing what I can to have the next major project, complete with both an unattainable and unrealistic cost structure and delivery timeline, seamlessly ready for you when you get this one over the line."

Ron chuckled despite himself. "I wouldn't expect anything else from you, Scotty."

With the beer delivered, Scott swallowed a healthy gulp, and then asked, "How's the resolution going?"

Ron inhaled, pursed his lips, and slowly raised his eyebrows, at which point Scott, reading the restrained nature of Ron's reply, reflexively responded with an, "Oh-oh!"

"No, no, not *that* bad. Just a few bumps on the road."

"Ok, let's hear it," said Scott.

"Well, there's been some minor rules clarification," Ron began, to a growing "I knew it" smile on Scott's face. "Minor, I said. I've already had to work *très* late on a number of nights, and Brandi was in bed asleep when I got home. And we both realized that we'd be going on a number of individual trips this year, including our golf trip in May." Ron paused for emphasis, implying that somehow Scott shared the blame there. "And you know how close Brandi is to her mom and sisters, and her weekend visits to TO are only going to become more frequent now that her mom's been diagnosed with diabetes. And," he added embarrassedly, "I completely forgot about her periods."

At the last point, Scotty dropped his shaking head in disbelief.

"So, we agreed that instead of 'every day', the resolution would be 365 times this year."

After a couple of beats Scott muttered, "Jesus. Putting it that way makes it sound more like work than pleasure. Don't you think?"

Ron hadn't actually thought about it before, but now that Scott brought it up, it sort of did. But not willing to fully agree with this perspective quite yet, Ron countered, "No, not really. The primary intent of mutually re-affirming our spiritual bond through revitalizing the physical aspect of our relationship remains intact."

Unfortunately for Scott, he was drawing another healthy portion of beer from his mug just as Ron delivered this statement. Although Scott managed to effectively seal his lips, the force of his involuntary gag response sent a portion of the beer residing in his mouth through his sinuses and out of his nose. To his credit, however, he did manage to get his hand up quickly enough to meet the high-speed stream of suds departing his body through an orifice typically unfamiliar with dispelling beer, processed or otherwise. The stream hit his hand much like a storm-driven wave would slam into a fortified breakwater, and deflected radially outwards.

Given they were located against the wall, the collateral damage was limited, but all the same, not appreciated by the unlucky young couple sitting about three feet to his left. While Scott recovered from his spontaneous alcohol-infused carbonated neti-pot flushing, and headed off to the washroom, Ron did the apologizing to the adjacent couple on his behalf.

Under the suspicious gaze of the bartender, Scott returned a couple of minutes later, layered on some additional apologies to the resurgently indignant young couple, then turned to Ron and remarked, "You've got to stop doing that to me!"

Shaking his head in disbelief, Ron asked, "Does that happen to you anywhere else and with anybody else?"

"Actually, no," responded Scott, as he settled into his seat, wiped away the last remnants of his nasal incontinence, and composed himself. "So, other than this fundamental breach of the rules concerning this resolution, how's it going?"

"As well as can be expected I suppose. It's…," Ron checked the calendar on his watch, "the twenty-third of January, and I'm happy to report that the books are currently balanced on the matter of this year's resolution."

"Impressive. You've likely already eclipsed my total for the first half of this year." After a slight pause Scott added, "You know, although it seems like a big number, especially to me," he shook his head in a resigned fashion, "but in context with the size of the mountain to climb here, you're barely in the foothills." He did a quick calculation in his head as engineers are wont to do. "Assuming you haven't completed today's task yet…"

Ron involuntarily shook his head before he realized it wasn't meant as a question.

"…you've completed about six per cent of your resolution. Congratulations!" Scott raised his glass in a toast, with a cheerful air Ron instantly realized he didn't share.

Ron unenthusiastically met the toast, then emptied his mug and called out to the nearby waitress for another jug of draft and a dozen hot wings.

After a bit of a pause Scott neutrally asked, "There's more, isn't there?"

"Yup," admitted Ron.

"Well, let's have it. We've got another jug of draft to get through."

Back in Centrepointe, at Ron and Brandi's house, Charlene and Brandi were engaged in a full download of the events of the past two weeks. Both were enjoying an agreeable Pinot Noir from the Penticton East Bench in the Okanagan Valley. Charlene was getting the skinny on how the resolution was progressing. Brandi had just shifted to a volume just above a loud whisper, since Sam and her friend were goofing around in her bedroom upstairs. "You know how stubborn Ron is when it comes to these resolutions?"

Charlene nodded receptively.

"With his workload picking up, and the long hours he's got to put in, I know it's not easy, but…"

Charlene's nodding frequency picked up a touch.

"We're still right on target."

"Wow, that's friggin' awesome," Charlene commented, sounding honestly impressed. "And how are you …well…umm…you know, dealing with it?" she added more cautiously.

"To tell you the truth, I'm enjoying it. I actually look forward to it as the best part of my day!"

Both girls giggled as they brought their glasses up for a clink.

Back at the Bassline Pub, Ron had started rolling out some further details. A little embarrassed, he quietly recalled, "It all started last weekend while Brandi and I were watching a movie. We had the house to ourselves, so there certainly was an expectation of sex somewhere during the evening."

"What was the movie?" asked Scott.

"What?" Ron snapped back, a bit annoyed. "Why is that relevant?"

"Hey, buddy, a little soft porn can go a long way to set the mood. I'm just saying."

Ron shook his head in irritation.

"You mean you and Brandi have never watched a little porn together?" Scott asked.

"No!" Ron defensively replied.

It was Scott's turn to shake his head, in disbelief. "Never?" he said incredulously.

"Of course not. We've never even thought of doing that." Even as he said it, Ron immediately worried that he sounded a bit more prudish than he would have liked.

"Well I can tell you, as a mature couple, you are in the minority. Not every couple is blessed with endless youthful vigor and unfading sex drives like you and Brandi. Long-term relationships are hard work, and keeping your sex life a relevant part of your relationship can be…" Here he paused. "No, *usually is,* the toughest part of maintaining a healthy marriage. What do you think the number-one cause of divorce is?"

"I don't know, but I guess you're going to say sex."

"It sure is," agreed Scott. "Sex with people other than your spouse! And that usually comes about due to physical and/or emotional boredom with your partner. And to avoid, or remedy, this creeping sexual ambivalence, everything, and I mean *everything*, should be on the table. And part of the top shelf of your toolbox is a little couple's porn."

"You're serious?"

"Serious as chain sawing in the nude, my friend."

Ron sighed. "How about we get back on topic?"

"OK, OK, sorry. So, you were watching a Disney movie with Brandi last weekend and for some reason thinking about sex…?"

"Nice." Collecting himself, Ron picked up where he had left off. "As I was saying, there was an expectation of sex somewhere during the course of the evening, and as this thought crossed my mind, I had an anxiety attack."

"Sitting there beside Brandi while watching the movie?" asked Scott.

"Yup. Complete with cold sweat, lightheadedness, and rapid breathing. Brandi noticed straight away."

"Jesus. What do you think brought that on?"

Ron deliberated for a second, and then said, "My best guess was Brandi's expectation of sex. I was feeling the pressure and choked. I think it was performance anxiety."

Scott sat back in his chair, exhaled audibly, and steepled his hands. After a few seconds, he asked, "Did it last long?"

"A couple of minutes at most."

"Did you 'fully' recover before the end of the night?" Scott asked, making obvious his line of inquiry.

"Initially Brandi was worried about me, but I was fine. It's hard to keep a good man down, you know," Ron said, with the first bravado he had mustered in quite a while.

"Well, most likely it was an isolated event and not to worry. On the other hand, this quest of yours may have unlocked some deep-seated psychological pathology which will insidiously destroy your life as you know it." Scott smiled. "But *probably* the former."

Ron didn't smile back.

Scott's own smile faded. "There's more?" he blurted.

"Not that night, thank God, but a few days ago…" Ron hesitated, embarrassed about broaching the next topic. "A few days ago…" he said, as he gathered his nerve, "I had trouble, you know …keeping it up."

He said this a bit too loudly. The young lady Scott had earlier showered with beer overheard the comment and looked over, a smile growing on her face. Ron could feel his face reddening, and was thankful for the dim lighting of bar in helping to preserve what little remained of his dignity.

When Ron lifted his head he was met with Scott's smile. "What's so funny about that?" asked Ron, again a bit too loud, and again to the amusement of the young lady at the next table.

Giving the universal two-handed "settle down" signal to Ron, Scott asked, "How long have you guys been married?"

"I think you know we're having our twentieth anniversary this July."

"So do you think that's *unusual* for a man who's been in a relationship that long? Don't answer that, I can tell you. It isn't. Maybe this is the first time it's happened to you, but you're not alone, my friend. It's happened to me, it's happened to that guy," Scott pointed at a middle-aged man a few tables away from them, "and," he swung around and pointed at the slightly younger bartender, "it's probably even happened to that guy. So don't overreact. Keep in mind you're running a marathon here, and it'll take a while before you get into a rhythm." Scott punctuated the comment with an open-armed "come on, don't be so hard on yourself" expression.

That move was enough to get Ron to smile. "Yeah, you're probably right. Thanks, buddy. In any case, Brandi's as regular as the German rail system, so I expect starting Sunday, I'll be taking a three- or four-day break."

"Sounds like you could use it to recharge your 'double-T' batteries."

With that, Ron slipped off his chair and weaved his way through the tables to the washroom.

As his friend disappeared into the can, Scott wondered if Ron had given any thought as to how he was going to make up the three or four days that he was about to fall behind on. As he sat waiting for Ron to return, he thought it would probably be best if he didn't bring that up tonight.

Sunday, January 25

Ron was grateful for a day off. The planned four hours of work the day before had ended up being closer to six, and he was ready for some down time. They had woken late, had a relaxing chatty breakfast around the kitchen island, and then headed down to the Rideau Canal for a family skate.

Following a quick change and a welcome warm-up, they had headed over to Ron's parents' house, located in the older west-end Glencairn community. Ron's family had moved into the single-story unit when he was a teenager, and his parents hadn't yet found reason to leave. Fairly mobile, and in possession of most of their faculties, they could still manage most of the upkeep on the modest house and yard. With his younger brother Stewart out west, Ron was his parents' sole source of familial support in Ottawa, and he was constantly coming over and helping out with the heavier chores, as well as being on-call for emergencies like appliance break-downs and major snowfalls. So far this year he had only infrequently been called upon for his snow-shovelling skills. He was hoping the trend would continue.

He cleaned up the walk and driveway when they arrived, bringing back memories of his forced labour when he lived at home, before moving out for university. The current dusting looked like nothing compared to the one winter when Ottawa had experienced about seven feet of snow and he, by his recollection, had single-handedly kept the walk and driveway clear. Towards the end of that winter, he recalled the difficulty in heaving the snow onto the banks lining the drive.

They were now sitting at the familiar ancient dining-room table, dishing out the various courses his mom had prepared for their early Sunday supper. Attendance at these Sunday suppers could be painful at times. Ron's parents had been married for fifty-two years, and with that territory came an inevitable mutual weariness and impatience, which manifested itself in a habitual and near-incessant bickering. Ron's family was used to this, but all the same, as the gatherings became less gratifying, they became less available for these Sunday suppers. Today, however, was different. His parents appeared to be on their best behaviour, interacting civilly and cheerfully, and constructively contributing to the conversations. Ron wasn't expecting this, and it all made him a bit suspicious that there was an ulterior motive hidden amid the comestibles.

Ron's parents had been social trailblazers throughout their lives. His dad, Tommy, was a first-generation Canadian, born to Chinese immigrants who had made it their life's goal and financial priority to educate their child. Strictly raised in a family that never stopped moving, Tommy Lee had inherited a first-class, take-nothing-for-granted, don't-expect-anything-for-free work ethic. He had enjoyed a long and tenured career as a professor of physics at the University of Ottawa, retiring about five years ago in his early seventies.

Ron's mom—Abigail Pearlman—had been born into a secular Montreal Jewish family, and had been educated in law at McGill before making a career move to Ottawa, where she met Tommy in the late 1950s. Neither of their families were happy with the relationship, but love and intelligence prevailed over antiquated cultural prejudice and, after an extensive period of socializing the concept within their respective families, they were married in 1962. Ron and his brother had unwaveringly been brought up atheistically, but his mom had always considered herself a Jewish person. This privileged status, she constantly reminded her boys, was passed onto them, whether or not they actively practiced Judaism. She emphasized that fact when the boys were growing up by, not infrequently, reminding her husband that he was the only one amongst them who wasn't one of the chosen people.

As the meal pleasantly progressed, Ron's suspicions grew. When there hadn't been a single unkind comment made by the time dessert was served he was positive something was up.

"So," his mom began, during an extended pause in the conversation.

Here it comes, thought Ron.

"Your father and I have been thinking it over, and we think we're done."

Ron could feel an upwelling of heat spreading into his face in response to the comment. She wasn't talking about their marriage, was she? "What are you and dad done *with* exactly?" Ron asked, as calmly as he could.

"We're done with this old house, Aaron," his mom said, using his birth name for emphasis. "It's become too much for us. We need to get into a retirement community. We've decided to fix this place up and put it on the market this spring."

The upwelling of heat to Ron's face began subsiding. Relieved, he inquired, "Are you guys sure? You've been living in this house for about thirty-five years. Won't you miss it?"

His mother replied, "Of course we'll miss it, but there comes a time for everything dear. We were hoping that you'd help us fix it up—you know, get it market-ready."

Ron sighed. He could only imagine the amount of time and effort this help would involve. The house was more than forty years old, and there was no shortage of potential upgrades and remodelling projects.

"Tell you what, Mom, if you guys are sure you want to sell, I'll sit with you and Dad and we can come up with a timeline and budget that you both agree with. From that, we can put together a realistic to-do list that should maximize the resale value of this old shack. How does that sound?"

Ron regretted this offer before the words left his mouth.

"Oh, that sounds perfect, Ronny," his mother gushed.

With his dad in the washroom and his mom clearing some dishes, Ron turned to Brandi, who was sporting a telling deadpan expression, and gave her a "What the hell was I supposed to say?" look and shrug. As she was getting up to help clear the table, she just smiled back at Ron and shook her head in disbelief, clearly sending a "Now you've stepped in it!" message of her own to her husband.

Wednesday, January 28

Ron got home from work at a reasonable time, and quickly shovelled off their small driveway before he went inside. Brandi was on her cellphone, and she called out to Ron that she and Tommy were FaceTiming. He chatted with his son for a while before handing the phone back to Brandi. *All good on that front. One less thing to worry about.*

Ron was feeling the pinch at work, and his sleep was starting to suffer for it. He was, more often than not, waking up in the middle of the night and having trouble falling back to sleep. Consequently, he was heading to work tired and less effective than usual. He found himself, uncharacteristically, a bit on edge these days, and easily distracted—not great when you were making multi-million dollar decisions on a daily basis.

After supper, he and Brandi nuzzled up together on the couch over glasses of a full-bodied Cabernet Franc from the Stoney Ridge Winery in Niagara. "By the way, I've reopened the shop and I'm accepting customers tonight," Brandi said, indicating her monthly cycle had run its course.

Normally that announcement would have been met with a cheer and a high-five from Ron, but tonight he responded with *faux* exasperation. "What's it been? Ten days?"

The comment didn't garner a response from Brandi, nor was one expected.

After a few days of abstinence Ron was also physically looking forward to the resumption of resolution activity, but mentally, something didn't align. As they cuddled up a little tighter, and hurriedly finished their wine, Ron noted this disconnect, but he did what guys do best—ignored it. The growing promise of imminent intercourse had effectively handed over control of Ron's actions and thoughts to his sex drive. With Captain Libido now steering the Good Ship Ron, the single-minded pursuit of sex had no room or time for introspective contemplation or brooding on issues not immediately relevant to the task at hand.

About an hour later, while watching *SportsCenter* downstairs, Ron was quietly bemoaning his inability to execute. Starting to second-guess himself, he pondered if for some reason he was becoming emotionally disconnected from the process, or if he was just getting old. Whereas a younger man, it had not been unusual for him to climax four or five times in an extended session, tonight, after churning butter for a good twenty minutes, bathed in sweat and breathing like he'd just skated hard, he had barely squeaked out a second offering of his man-seed. Frankly, he had expected more from himself tonight after the multi-day hiatus. He had fully recharged physically, and had hoped he could close the gap on his debt to the resolution tonight. Unfortunately, the reality was he was sexually spent, and still behind on the resolution. He realized menstrual pauses would be a recurring problem through the course of the resolution, and he needed to find a solution.

Remembering what Scott had told him last week about the dangers of creeping sexual ambivalence and putting everything on the table in your effort to fight back against it, Ron started to devise a battle strategy. He was starting to accept the fact that he wasn't as young as he used to be and that he was over his head with this resolution; sex, like hockey, was a young man's game. It was going to push him to the limit, and he needed to pick up his game both physically and emotionally to have a chance at successfully completing it. Sitting there, he decided he would make an appointment with his doctor the very next day, and try to get to a bookstore on the weekend to get assistance with both pieces of the equation.

CHAPTER 3

THE GLOVES COME OFF

Monday, February 2

Ron had managed to get the last appointment of the day with his doctor at the nearby Centrepointe Medical Centre. Dr. Kaur had become the Lee family's general practitioner about a decade ago, and he had effectively guided them through the array of medical issues any growing family would typically encounter. Other than a particularly nasty bout of strep throat that had spread through the household three years earlier, the issues had thankfully been minor, and the visits, infrequent. All the same, given their similarities in age, family, and intelligence, Ron had developed a reasonable rapport with Dr. Kaur, and was comfortable enough with him to discuss just about any topic: a good thing, since today's subject was Ron's wilting sex drive.

Ron had perused the internet during his lunch hour, and had learnt that about four percent of men his age experienced erectile dysfunction. *That's not too bad*, he thought, but when he read that early manifestation usually consisted of difficulty in maintaining an erection *or* difficulty orgasming, he was hit with a wave of nausea and full body sweats that incapacitated him for about five minutes. *Christ*, he fretted, *I have both of the early symptoms!* As if that wasn't bad enough, he was horrified to see that the percentage of afflicted males rose to about one in four poor bastards by their mid-fifties. Clearly, Ron inferred, fifty was a threshold into the gates of hell, punishing all survivors with accelerating physical infirmity and sexual impotence. *So little time left,* he fretted. He was turning forty-eight next month.

The walk from his office to the clinic was about a mile. Normally not a big deal, but ever since the weather had turned cold about ten days ago, it had only become more bitter and snowier with every day. He was dressed as warmly as possible, and he was still thoroughly chilled. It had been snowing hard all day, and the wind had picked up that afternoon, so he was essentially walking through a blizzard. The adjacent traffic on Baseline Road was crawling along, and with the rush hour building and the snow deepening, he expected he'd soon be outpacing them—especially now that he had picked up his pace to avoid frostbite.

Turning off Baseline onto Centrepointe Drive, he saw the lights from the Medical Centre emerge from the snowy curtain. With the finish line in sight, he jogged the last stretch.

Dr. Kaur was running particularly late, and finally saw Ron about forty minutes after the office was supposed to have closed. On the plus side, it was only Dr. Kaur and himself left at the office, which made Ron a bit more comfortable, given the sensitive topic he was there to discuss.

The door to the patient room swung open, and Dr. Kaur shuffled in, visibly exhausted after a long day. "Evening, Ron," he said. "Sorry about the wait, but it's been a crazy day. And this weather! It's days like this I wish my parents had had the foresight to emigrate to the Caribbean instead. And it's only Monday!"

"The cold's supposed to last all week, as well," Ron told him.

In response to this comment, Dr. Kaur slowly shook his head in disbelief, while narrowing his eyes and puckering up his face: possibly, Ron thought, in a silent curse on his parents.

With the greetings completed, Dr. Kaur asked Ron to follow him into the closest examination room. "So, what can I do for you today, Ron?"

Ron took a deep breath. "Well, I think I've been experiencing some early signs of sexual dysfunction."

With eyebrows raised and a slight tilt of his head, Dr. Kaur said, "Tell me more."

Ron went on to explain that he had experienced some difficulty maintaining an erection and ejaculating.

"And how often, and for how long has this been happening?"

When Ron had explained that there had only been a single event of each, both confined to the previous month, Dr. Kaur immediately retorted that this was nothing to worry about. "It may feel like the end of the world to you Ron, but believe me, it isn't. You're getting older, and isolated incidents like this are, more likely than not, related to your state of mind, as opposed to physiological reasons. You're in good shape, and physically active, so I would say relax, and don't panic," his head bobbling as he spoke.

He turned away to his computer, where he entered some notes in Ron's open file. "Typically, how often are you and your wife having sex?" he casually inquired.

Ron paused. He hadn't wanted to bring up the resolution with Dr. Kaur. It would likely sound idiotic to an outsider who didn't understand Ron's predilection for his annual challenges.

"Every day, actually," he finally responded.

That comment stopped Dr. Kaur mid-keystroke. "Pardon me?" he countered as he turned to face Ron.

Now embarrassed, Ron repeated, "Every day."

"Why?…how?… Is this normal for you and your wife?" the doctor asked, his full attention now on Ron.

Feeling trapped, and fighting back the urge to get up and run out of the office, Ron knew he had no other option except to come clean about his annual resolutions, and this year's ongoing challenge.

Having finished with his explanation, Ron sat quietly looking at Dr. Kaur, who stared back with incredulity at Ron. Not attempting to temper his reaction in consideration of Ron's feelings, Dr. Kaur exhaled, closed his eyes, and gave his head a quick shake. "That has to be the most foolhardy, misguided attempt at relationship building I've ever heard of."

With this comment aired, Ron felt an explosion of heat on his cheeks, his embarrassment finally manifested.

"Still, if you're determined to go through with this...?" Dr. Kaur half-stated, half-asked.

Ron nodded yes in response.

"Then you're going to need some serious help," Dr. Kaur added, apparently now fully recovered, and resigned to help Ron out in this "foolish quest of biblical proportions."

Dr. Kaur asked for some further details concerning the resolution, following which he decided upon a three-pronged approach. He prescribed a low dose of Viagra for times when Ron was feeling his sexual desire wane. "Think of it as a partnership like you've seen in those WWF wrestling matches. When the stronger of the two has given his all, courageously and expertly representing the team with a Herculean effort, he has barely enough energy remaining to limp to the ropes to make the tag. But after a brief respite, he's back in the fight, stronger than ever."

Ron thought the last part of the narration was delivered in an incongruently upbeat tone.

"Try your best not to overuse it, or it will usurp you as the hero," Dr. Kaur added with a grin.

Ron didn't see the humour in the situation.

"Secondly, I'm going to prescribe you a low dosage of Cialis. Consider this your weekend support team for those special occasions. From what you've told me, there will be countless times this year when you're going to be significantly in arrears and could use more prolonged assistance. Cialis should allow you to perform like the good old days, my friend. You may even want to break out your favourite '80s tunes for these special times." Dr. Kaur laughed out loud at his own joke.

Ron thought he was enjoying this a bit too much at Ron's expense, but politely smiled in return, given he was currently at the mercy of the doctor.

"Again," Dr. Kaur added, momentarily serious, "do not overuse these medications. And never use them together."

As Ron sat there, hoping for this visitation to end, Dr. Kaur continued, apparently as an afterthought. "How is your wife, Brandi, adapting to this increase in sexual activity?"

Ron informed him that she was absolutely fine, and had actually told him that she was enjoying it and looked forward to it as the best part of her day.

In response to that comment, Dr. Kaur smiled broadly, bobbled his head, and turned back to his computer to enter some further notes in Ron's medical file. Ron imagined him typing "lucky bastard is married to a nymphomaniac."

After Dr. Kaur collected the prescriptions off his printer and signed them, he started to hand them to Ron, but paused without relinquishing them, clearly intending to extend the consultation. Ron steeled himself for the next assault on his dignity.

"You know, there's more to sex than just effectively functioning equipment," Dr. Kaur said. "As an educated and intelligent man, I know you're aware of this. Sex and romantic love are not the same thing, but in a marriage, they are inextricably intertwined. Your quest, although folly of the highest order, may have the unintended consequence of providing you with a greater understanding of this relationship than most people could ever hope to attain. For that reason, it has captured my imagination. That, and who doesn't like watching a good train wreck? Just joking Ron, don't look so grim."

After a beat, he continued. "You will also require some spiritual assistance. And for this, I'm going to recommend that you and Brandi read and experience the *Kama Sutra*."

Ron had of course heard about the *Kama Sutra*, but it had never occurred to him that he and Brandi should make it a part of their life's curriculum. Things were not perfect, but the *Kama Sutra*?

Doctor Kaur launched into a brief history of the treatise. "It is well known that India is unique in the way it has approached, appreciated, and evolved sexual relationships. My liberal ancestors realized that sex is a gift from the Gods, and should be cultivated, to most effectively extract all the enjoyment it has to offer. Towards this end, the *Kama Sutra* was written as a summary of the collective understanding of sexuality and interpersonal relationships, with the purpose of optimizing the sexual and human experience. Everybody could use a little more of that. Am I right, or am I right, Ron?" he added, his head bobbling enthusiastically.

Ron was by this point a bit numb, and on the verge of speechlessness. After a throat clearing and a couple of false starts, he responded, "Are you sure it'll help?"

Doctor Kaur slowly took his glasses off for added effect and responded, "Indubitably, my friend."

ॐ

About ten minutes later Ron was walking home in an increasingly intensifying blizzard. Now, however, he was walking *into* the howling wind. Mercifully, it was a short walk.

As Ron approached his house, he found some comfort in knowing he was now appropriately prepared and fortified for the task in front of him, and was actually looking forward to utilizing the pharmaceuticals Dr. Kaur had provided him. Without getting into the specifics that Dr. Kaur had discussed, he would of course inform Brandi of the medical assistance he was enlisting. More troubling to him was the future discussion and subsequent exploration of the *Kama Sutra*, assuming Brandi was on board with that.

While he was pondering why he was feeling some apprehension over the *Kama Sutra*, he turned into his drive, and was distracted by the not-insignificant amount of new snow that had fallen and continued to accumulate on his driveway and walk. Exhausted from his visit with Dr. Kaur, all he wanted to do was warm up, have a nice meal with his wife, and put his feet up. The shovelling would have to wait for tomorrow morning, before Brandi departed for work. As he entered the house and announced his arrival, an enthusiastic greeting by Brandi reminded him that his "duties" for the day were not quite over yet.

After removing his protective winter wear, Ron made his way over to the small bar, and remarked to no one in particular, "I'd kill for a decent glass of wine."

Brandi cheerfully called out, "Would you mind pouring me one as well, honey? Thanks!"

Ron had to immediately calm himself in an attempt to suppress a wave of anxiety growing in his belly. He knew Brandi always got a bit hornier after a drink or two.

Ron delivered Brandi's wine to her in the kitchen, and parked himself at the island. "How was work?" he asked.

"Crazy as always. This weather isn't helping!"

Ron closed his eyes as he sampled the wine. He had selected one of his favourites—a 2009 red blend from the Painted Rock winery adjacent to Skaha Lake in B.C.—and he wasn't disappointed. The smooth deep berry- and spice-flavoured oenophilian delight transported him away from the blizzard outside to a perfect 30-degree day in the Okanagan.

When he opened his eyes, Brandi asked, "Tough day?"

"Actually, the toughest part was my visit with Dr. Kaur," he admitted.

"Oh, yeah, what was that all about? Are you not feeling well?" asked Brandi, with a concerned look on her face.

Ron, now fortified with that decent glass of wine he had fortunately obtained without resorting to homicide, thought this was as good a time as any to initiate the awkward discussion. After a quick check to make sure Sam wasn't around, he began. "Since we really haven't talked about the resolution yet, you may be surprised to hear that I feel like I could use some 'assistance' with it." Searching Brandi's still-concerned face for her reaction, he continued, "I think I've been feeling some performance anxiety."

Etchings of concern on Brandi's face deepened, but she stayed silent.

"I explained our situation to Doctor Kaur and asked for some 'pharmaceutical' help."

Here he paused, and waited for a response from Brandi.

Picking up on the cue, she said, "Ron, you know I've been enjoying the resolution so far, but I'm not prepared to continue this at the expense of your health."

Shit, Ron thought. *This isn't going very well at all.*

"Hey babe, no, don't think of it like that. There's nothing wrong with my health, and these drugs are only for those *rare* times when I'm not feeling up for the job. There are no side effects worth mentioning," he added the half-truth to calm her further, "and after today's conversation you won't even know when I'm using them. It was just in the spirit of full disclosure that I even brought it up."

He offered a "no-biggy" smile to finish reeling her back in. Seeing she remained suspicious, he continued with the second part of the discussion. "Additionally, this endeavour has made me realize just how important the romantic aspect of our relationship is."

He saw her expression relax markedly with this comment. Encouraged, he continued. "So, in parallel with, and in support of, the physical element of the resolution, I think we should actively work on rediscovering the spiritual and romantic parts of our relationship."

As he waited for her response, he worried he had laid it on too thick. But Brandi's face relaxed and her eyes softened. "That's one of the loveliest things I've ever heard you say, Ron." She paused, and then looked Ron squarely in the face. "Okay, I'm still on board for the resolution, but do *not* do anything stupid. Promise?"

Ron nodded, not at all sure he could comply.

She hugged him, and cast him an unmistakable lusty look.

Great, thought Ron, *now she's even keener! I'll be popping Viagra like skittles before too long.* "As well, tomorrow I'm going to acquire some 'couples' reading for us."

"What do you have in mind?"

"How about the *Kama Sutra?*" Ron blurted, perhaps a bit too unreservedly.

"I've heard about it. Isn't it the ancient Indian sex book?"

"Indeed it is. I haven't read it either, so I thought we could start exploring it together. What do you say?"

She shrugged. "Why not? Might even be fun."

Friday, February 6

Scott and Ron had met up at EllisDon after work and walked over together to the Bassline Pub. The weather had only gotten colder throughout the week, and it had been snowing hard all day. It was less than a kilometre to the bar, but the bitter cold, wind, and snow made it feel considerably longer. Along their route traffic was moving agonizingly slow. At times their pace matched that of the cars. Given they were both encased in their arctic wear and not inclined to yell above the wintry din enveloping them, speaking was limited to curses periodically muttered at no one in particular. As they rounded the last corner and the Bassline Pub came into view, the wind and snow picked up a bit, and they jogged the last hundred metres in response. To keep the storm outside, they entered the pub as quickly as possible, involuntarily smiling upon reaching their objective.

Although it was almost 6 p.m., the weather had kept away, or at least delayed the arrival of, a good portion of the usual crowd. After shaking the snow off themselves in the entrance, they made their way to an open table.

"So," Scott began, "do you *still* think it's only weather?"

Ron had forgotten about the comment he had made to Scott in this very bar two weeks earlier. However, not at all surprised that Scott hadn't missed an "I told you so" moment, he defended his position out of principle. "A couple weeks of crap in the middle of winter? No big deal. Just think about the long hot summer around the corner," he said, sounding way cheerier than he actually felt.

"Well, according to the Almanac, this is supposed to last all February. I'll check in with you closer to the end of the month and see if you're still all sunshine and rainbows then."

After getting the attention of the waitress and ordering a jug of beer and a dozen wings, Ron asked Scott how things were going at work. Even though they were employed by the same company, the building was large enough that they could go days without running into one another, and when they did, they were typically in the middle of something else and there wasn't time for anything other than a brief salutation.

"I'm heading out to Penticton next week for technical qualification meetings for the regional hospital expansion job," replied Scott.

"The weather should be more to your liking out there."

"Now that you mention it, they've been having a bit of a warm spell, and weather permitting, I should be able to get in a game of golf." Scott glanced outside, and laughed out loud at the thought of it.

After they'd caught up on each other's families, Scott broached the topic that he was clearly *really* interested in. "And is the resolution still a going concern?"

"Absolutely!"

Exaggeration was the norm in just about every aspect of their communication outside of work. Ron had long ago realized that the dynamics of their communication was a form of escapism from the drudgery of everyday living, and he had grown to enjoy and look forward to their sessions, seeing them as a form of therapy. And he sure could use a little therapy tonight.

"Outstanding," replied Scott. "I had expected nothing less from you, my obsessive buddy. With confirmation that this most holy and noble of resolutions has been satisfactorily executed…" Here Scott paused to get confirmation that Ron was on target with the numbers. Ron nodded smugly. "You are officially 9.9 percent complete," he finished with a flourish.

"Not quite correct," added Ron.

Scott halted his mini-celebration in response to the comment, and looked inquisitively at Ron.

"Brandi and I had a bit of a lay-in this morning. Consequently, we're over the ten percent mark."

"Whoo-hoo!" Scott cheered. "A milestone!"

Scott offered Ron an imaginary microphone and assumed the role of a reporter with a British accent. "So, Mr. Lee, how do you feel about having just passed the ten-percent point of this absolutely epic and life-changing journey?"

Ron paused, adopted a slack-jawed stunned visage and replied with a questioning intonation. "Err...pretty good I guess."

"Surely you can offer our listeners some insights into the moments of elation you've experienced during the first month of this impressive challenge?"

The air mike once again was positioned at Ron's chin. With a hyper-focused, serious face, Ron offered his insights. "Well, you know, sometimes I got tired. And sometimes the old lady got tired, eh? But you know, it feels pretty good, so we just did it."

"Truly amazing!" Scott exclaimed, further clipping his affected accent to that of a haughty British-public-school elocutionist. "Do you have any trepidation going forward in your effort to complete this quest, Mr. Lee?"

"Not really, eh? I'll just keep doing it, you know. I just got to get through winter, and then spring, then summer, then fall and then to New Year's Eve. So not too bad, eh."

"There you have it, folks, a brave man if I've ever seen one. Scott Hartwell signing off for now. Until next time, I know I speak on behalf of all your fans, Mr. Lee, in wishing you all the best in the completion of your resolution. May the wind always be at your backside and the lead never leave your pencil."

With food delivered, the boys tucked into the wings and discussed the resolution further. "So, no more 'speedbumps'?" Scott delicately inquired.

"Well, yes and no. I certainly underestimated how difficult it would be to catch up on the days lost when Brandi was *indisposed*. For some reason, I had this image of myself when I was twenty-something. Not the case, as it turns out. Catch-up took the better part of the week, and.....well, let's just say I'm pretty much a one-trick pony now."

Here Ron paused, and collected his thoughts. "And there was a bit too much down time." Waiting until Scott had finished swallowing the beer in his mouth, he continued. "So I went to see my doctor for some pharmaceutical assistance."

"You waited for me to swallow for that?" Scott responded incredulously. "In all honesty, buddy, you shouldn't be surprised about needing some help in that department. There's a laundry list of physiological causes for losing the groove with age, but even more potentially problematic is your head. Listen. I'm thinking if there's any real problem here—I mean a *real* problem that has the potential to derail your resolution—it's going to be in your head. If a pill or two now and then makes you feel better, then by all means do it. Whereas broader physical issues can be symptomatically remedied with a pill, the brain is far more problematic. Without going into too much detail here and now, the entire process is driven by our primal pursuit of pleasure. And simply put, pleasure is what our brain tells us is pleasure. So with propagation as a priority, it's spent a disproportionate amount of time and energy evolving to encourage sex with a heroin-like reward system."

Scott noted the surprise on Ron's face with that comment, and continued. "Yes, my friend, you are essentially feeding your heroin addiction with this resolution."

He paused to let that sink in. Ron had never even tried marijuana, so the thought of being a heroin addict was quite disconcerting to him.

"So two things happen with age and marriage," Scott continued. "As you get older, the body naturally produces less testosterone. Having children has always been a young person's game. Procreate early and often, because there's a good chance you'll be dead tomorrow. Remember, we humans have only started typically living past forty years very recently, and our physiology hasn't had a chance to catch up with the new reality. The brain is adapting as quickly as possible, but really, it didn't expect to be around and sexually viable at your age, so it's functioning well past its warranty period. You're fighting both the naturally diminishing production of testosterone as the starter pistol for the whole sexual process, and more remarkably, I think, the longer you've been married and a father, the lower your testosterone becomes—regardless of your age. I think *that* change is an example of active evolution, with your brain reprioritizing and directing you to focus on your existing children, who have a better potential to effectively propagate than your sorry old wrinkled-ass body."

Here he paused to wet his loquacious whistle. "On top of this, you've got the everyday distractions and stresses of work and family overwhelming your brain and distracting it from your primary objective of rallying your tired, brittle, and dried-out gonads to produce a few more drops of testosterone to kick start the sexual act. The point is, everything is stacked against you on this resolution, my friend."

Ron caught himself smiling despite himself.

"Now that I think about it," Scott concluded, "you have to be pathologically optimistic and/or delusional to even attempt this resolution. But that said,"

Scott quickly added, "I have to give you credit. The fact that you've made it this far is truly remarkable."

"Thanks, man," Ron replied as they clinked beer mugs. "There's a certain amount of ignorance and naivety required at the outset of any difficult feat, and I agree with you, there's no exception here. I'm starting to see that I can't complete this resolution with my not-unsubstantial brawn alone. As you've so delicately pointed out, the boys are, not unexpectedly, a wee bit tired these days, and could use all the help they can get."

Ron paused, sipped his beer while pondering a thought, and then continued. "I actually caught myself becoming a little mechanical and routine a while back. That's completely out of character for me, and made me realize I was fighting an uphill battle. I figured the best way to do this was to enlist my intellectual side to rediscover and reinvigorate 'romantic Ron.' So towards this objective, I've opened up a new battle front. We've started to read and explore the *Kama Sutra* together."

"Isn't that the Indian sex manual?" asked Scott.

"More accurately, it's the ancient Hindu *love* manual. Brandi and I have just started into it, but besides the fact that it's hilarious and gives us an opportunity to share a laugh, it's a pretty extensive summary of the social, spiritual, and physical aspects of love and sex as seen through the eyes and social context of ancient India. I think it's truly amazing that two thousand years ago, society was more sexually advanced than our present-day 'civilized' world! The fact that most cultures have regressed, or more likely, not even tried to bring sex out of the shadows, just confirms to me that modern man has forever struggled with the complexities of love, sex, and relationships. I haven't had much time to think about it, but it may be our current society's prudish approach to sex that's, at least in part, responsible for the epidemic of dysfunctional marital relationships. One of the things that struck me about the *Kama Sutra* is its objective and 'matter-of-fact' approach to sex. The *Kama Sutra* sees sex as a tool to be used to find happiness, and the exploration of sex should be conducted unashamedly and competently to maximize the effectiveness of this doorway to happiness. I can tell you that when I realized this, that made me more determined than ever to finish this resolution."

"Shit," muttered Scott, again impressed with his friend, "that makes me want to do the same thing with Elise. God knows my tool could be better utilized. Give me one of the better gems you've come across in the sacred manual."

ॐ

Back in Centrepointe, Brandi and Charlene were weathering the blizzard in the comfort of Brandi's living room, having fortified themselves against the elements with the assistance of a delicious 2013 Monster Vineyards Merlot from the Lower Bench in Penticton. The floral notes and berry flavours had effectively distracted them from the maelstrom raging outside, allowing them to focus on the conversation at hand, which at the moment concerned the specifics of the *Kama Sutra*.

Wiping the tears from her eyes as she recovered from her most recent laughing fit, Brandi continued talking about her initial impressions of the Indian love treatise. "I have no idea what these Sixty-Four Arts have to do with love and sex, other than making the maiden more adept at everything else when she's not having sex."

"What are some of the other 'arts' recommended for these fair maidens?" Charlene asked encouragingly.

"How about, 'creating musical sounds with water.' Or 'preparing drinks' and 'fixing coloured tiles on floors?' Oh, yeah, there's also 'reciting tongue twisters,' 'carpentry,' and the 'art of impersonation.' " Brandi barely got that last one out before they both erupted in an uncontrollable gale of laughter.

Mostly recovered, Charlene caught her breath and commented, "You can sure tell this was written by a man. He didn't just expect sex, he wanted a Suzy Homemaker who would not only build and maintain the house, but could also effectively entertain him."

"And the passive looks on all their faces in the illustrations are hilarious. The woman looks like she's thinking about cleaning off a spider's web she's just noticed on the ceiling, and the guy is definitely thinking about sports," Brandi added.

This sent the girls into another laughing fit.

After a few seconds Brandi continued, "But honestly, it's fun to work our way through the book and share some giggles. The section on enlarging the penis through repeated stinging by wasps over a ten-day period surprised Ron. 'That guy *really* wants a bigger dick!' He was a little uncomfortable with the discussions on group sex, but he turned pale and clammed up completely during the chapters on pinching, scratching, biting, marking, striking, and shrieking as acceptable techniques for maximizing sexual pleasure. I can guarantee Ron has never—not even once—considered any of those activities as sexual in any way.

I could almost hear him worrying about what he would do if I were to request some rough sex. I'm almost tempted to ask for some well-placed nibbling just to see what his reaction would be."

"You know, that's not a horrible idea," suggested Charlene. "Given the marathon you two are grinding your way through, you may need to resort to some extraordinary measures. A girl can't be expected to survive on a diet of white rice alone."

"I can assure you it's not so bad, but you do have a point. Still, I have to be careful with Ron. He's not naturally adventurous, and I wouldn't want to make him think I'm bored or need to fill some sort of sexual void. As you know, men are remarkably fragile creatures."

"You got that right, sister," Charlene chirped, the wine making her progressively more agreeable.

"Well, we're only about half way through the book, so I'm sure there are some more treasures still awaiting us…"

Back at the bar, Ron had been telling Scott about his first impressions of the Indian love manual. "Seriously," Ron said, "ten days of having your pecker repeatedly stung by wasps, and get this—to make the effect permanent you have to sleep on your stomach with your swollen member hanging down through a hole in the bed to keep the blood pooled!"

Scott chuckled. "The advertising would be like, 'In only ten days you, too, can have a completely numb, permanently swollen dick that'll be the envy of every guy in your village. Hurry and order your treatment while the wasps are still in season!'"

"I've got to ask you, though," Ron said, "have you ever considered rough stuff like slapping or biting or scratching during sex?"

Scott screwed his face up and pondered the question. "Can't say I have. Why? Don't tell me that's part of the 'teachings' from *the Kama Sutra?*"

Ron nodded. "Brandi's interest in those chapters was a bit disturbing. What if she wants to experiment with those genres? And why? Is she getting bored with the status quo?"

With a resigned shrug, Scott said, "Well, considering the potential for monotony in the ongoing quest—no insult intended, of course—who could be blamed for wanting to introduce a little variety into the deed? Think about it. Who likes routine? That said, the repetition of this particular act has typically never been an issue in the past, either for myself, personally speaking, or, judging from global population growth, the human species in general. But—and this is the key difference—you are conducting the carnal act with an unnatural frequency and with a single partner. I would hazard a guess that this has never been achieved in the history of mankind—by a man of your age, that is. So, in that context, does a wee bit of nibbling, pinching, and light ass-spanking seem so ridiculous?"

Ron had to agree it didn't. But that didn't change the fact he was uncomfortable with the whole concept. "I guess I'll bring it up with Brandi this weekend and see what she thinks."

"Why not?" asked Scott. "The whole point of the resolution was to bring you guys closer, and getting you guys out of your comfort zone and sharing new experiences is definitely part of getting to know each other better."

"You make it sound as normal as morning coffee. But you're not the one contemplating spousal abuse."

Both guys chuckled and took another swig of beer. Ron looked at his watch and the weather still raging outside, and suggested he had time for one more if Scott didn't have to rush off. Scott agreed he had time for a quick one, and proceeded to order it while Ron made his way to the can.

Sitting alone, waiting for the beer to arrive, Scott couldn't help but worry that his friend might have unintentionally opened up Pandora's Box with this resolution of his. As he spotted Ron returning to the table, he knew that Ron was heading into uncharted territory, and as with every explorer before him, there would be unexpected surprises.

The beer arrived just before Ron, and when the mugs were refilled, Scott raised his in a toast. "To sex!" he called out.

"To sex!" Ron enthusiastically replied as he met the toast.

Saturday, February 7

Ron spent most of the day at his parents' place, digging them out, planning their house renovations, and setting a timeline for the sale of their house. After a couple of hours of sometimes difficult discussions, Ron sat at the kitchen table, waiting for a light lunch his mom was making for him. He felt beat-up. He and Scott had overdone it last night, and shovelling both his and his parents' driveways and walks had physically drained him. And that was before he had moderated the two hour bicker-fest with his parents. Now, he could use a nap.

He chit-chatted with his mom's back as she made him a sandwich. Glancing outside, he couldn't help but feel a little despondent seeing that the snow was still falling as heavily as ever. "So, Mom, I'll help as much as I can, but you're going to have to bring contractors in to do the roof at least."

"I know you have a life and family, Aaron," his mom replied. "As you've suggested, your father and I will set a budget and decide where the money can best be used for the renovations. We're just happy for *any* help you can offer us."

Ron wasn't about to let his guard down when dealing with his mom. He knew she would have no compunction conscripting him for an extended period of slave labour if he didn't firmly lay down the rules of engagement early and not waver from his position.

He continued, ignoring his mother's placating overtures. "I mean it, Mom. I'll help you whenever I can, as always, but I simply won't have the time to act as your general contractor."

"I understand completely, Aaron. Now eat your sandwich. And dear, can you please give the driveway another scrape before you leave? That snow is really piling up."

Ron made it home about mid-afternoon, following a painfully slow drive. He noticed the additional snow awaiting shovelling in his own driveway, and wondered how he could have ever marveled at winter's novelty. The forecast was for more snow and even colder temperatures over the next week, and that prospect only added to his glum mood. He was thankful the house was empty, and he decided to take the opportunity to crawl upstairs for a nap.

In the middle of a dream where he and Scott were golfing in the tropics, he woke to the touch of his wife in bed beside him. His first reaction was that of annoyance at having been woken up, especially since he had just hit an approach shot to within a few feet of the pin; but as his head cleared, he realized naptime was over. She warmly and moistly nuzzled into the crook of his neck, sensually whispering that Sam was at a friend's for the day, and they had the house to themselves. That scenario typically would have inspired him to suggest some sexy time with his bride, but here she was in his role, taking control of the process.

Afterwards, while distractedly working the Saturday crossword, Ron thought about their encounter earlier that afternoon. It was totally out of character for Brandi to initiate their sexual session, and as much as Ron would have relished it a few months ago, it now, conversely, caused him some angst. She had even grabbed the *Kama Sutra* and opened it back up to an illustration of an impassive couple in a contorted coital pose, suggesting that they "give this one a go." If that wasn't bad enough, she also requested that Ron pinch her bum as she was beginning to climax. In full control of their current union, Brandi had passionately and loudly urged Ron to pinch harder as she came. What the hell did *that* mean? Should he be worried? Was Brandi adapting better to the resolution than Ron? OMG, was she becoming a sex-addict along the lines that Scott had mentioned the night before? Would she start to look elsewhere if Ron couldn't continue to satisfy her?

While sitting in the kitchen and lost in his progressively darkening thoughts while he picked away at the weekend crossword, Brandi draped her arm around his shoulder, glanced at the mostly uncompleted crossword and commented, "Looks like a tough one today."

Suppressing a startled twitch, Ron recovered quickly and responded, "Another one of those guys who likes to show he's cleverer than everyone else by using foreign languages and making his clues as vague as possible. What ever happened to crosswords that required knowledge to complete?" vocalizing his frustration.

"Do you want some help?" asked Brandi.

"Sure, I'm a bit brain dead today after last night's session with Scotty and clearly I could use the help," he said gesturing at the puzzle.

"Oh, yeah, I was going to ask you, how are Scott and Elise doing?"

"As far as I know, everything's good. And you know Scotty. He just plugs along without any drama in his life. The lucky bugger is heading off to Penticton on Monday for work and will likely get a game of golf in while he's there."

"Hard to believe that's in the same country," Brandi replied as she glanced out the kitchen window, the snow continuing to fall outside. "You know, we should grab the kids and head down south *somewhere* this spring break. This winter is turning out to be a bit of a beast, and I think we could all use some time away in March. Do you think you can get the time off?"

Ron mulled the possibility over. No question he would love to get away for a week, but he would have to check with his boss, Nigel Hewitt, to see if it was doable. "Let me check with Nigel on Monday. You think you can get time off?"

"I should be able to. And I've already been casually looking into it; how about the Dominican Republic?"

"If it's not snowing and there's cold beer, I'm in," added Ron, now feeling considerably more cheery than a few minutes ago. As he turned his attention back to the crossword, watching Brandi fill in the blank spaces at an astonishingly quick pace, he allowed himself to relax, tucking away the distressing events of that afternoon into one of his man compartments, to be dealt with at a later date.

Friday, February 13

As predicted, the weather had turned colder, and it was snowing hard again. Ron was wondering why bad forecasts more often than not turned out accurate, and good forecasts had a way of worsening the closer you got to the date. The week had become so bitter that Brandi had started driving Sam back and forth from school as a survival tactic. He himself had nearly frozen to death during his relatively short walk home. The thought of that shuttle service sounded pretty good.

When he arrived home Brandi had greeted him in the hallway with the information that the current wind chill was around minus forty, and offered him congratulations on making it home alive. She wrapped herself around him as a warming instrument, and told him supper would be ready shortly. She also used the opportunity of proximity to whisper in his ear, so Sam, who was sitting at the island in the kitchen, wouldn't hear, that she had a surprise in store for him that night. "I'm sure you'll love it," she added, with waggling eyebrows to emphasize the point, as she receded back to the kitchen.

As Ron finished removing the multiple layers of high-tech thermal insulation that allowed Canadians to actually venture outside during the winter months, he began worrying about what exactly this "surprise" was. Brandi's new found sexual confidence had been growing since they first cracked that God-forsaken hard-covered porn mag passing itself off as a sex treatise. With every new chapter, Brandi's interest in the various erotic aspects explored in the *Kama Sutra* seemed to grow, and with it, her interest in sex. Ron had realized that Brandi was slowly replacing him as the dominant sex partner, and he was having some trouble adjusting to his new subservient role. They had already made it through the chapters on sexual aids, deviant (his word) forms of sexual foreplay, and techniques for love making. Mercifully, the extended chapter on marriage courtesies, nuptials, and empowerment of the bride had been more in line with his conservative personality, and likely hadn't given Brandi any more aberrant ideas on how to spice up their apparently quite boring sex life. But Ron believed the damage had already been inflicted with the previous chapters, and the metamorphosis of Brandi into this orgasm-addicted sex-crazed beast had already begun.

They had left off at the start of a new chapter called *extramarital love*, the reading of which Ron was absolutely dreading. Even more disconcerting to Ron, however, was Brandi's interest in that topic. She had actually said, far more enthusiastically than he would have hoped, she was "looking forward to seeing what they had to say about that." It was in this context that Ron's imagination whirred, thinking about Brandi's imminent surprise. Could it be a sex toy? A vibrator? Or, even worse, a massive dildo, which would soon replace him; his own relatively diminutive phallic to be relegated exclusively to anal penetrations, a fetish Ron was sure that Brandi would soon embrace. Or maybe it has something to do with alligator clips and nine-volt batteries, or that auto-asphyxiation thing you heard about with singers and actors.

Progressively more panicked he thought, *God; there was no telling what she's got up her sleeve.* Just about then Brandi called upstairs, "Pasta's ready!" snapping Ron out of his paranoid musings.

His mood brightened markedly over some light conversation around the dinner table. Sam might be a hormonally deranged, cellphone-addicted, invariably irreverent teen with the attention span of a newt, but she sure did know about some of the goofiest videos ever made. Soon, everyone at the table was laughing.

Brandi had decided to reward Ron for his successful arctic excursion by opening a 2013 Sumac Ridge Cabernet Merlot. Sipping the wine, Ron closed his eyes and shivered—his body involuntarily adjusting to the sixty-degree temperature contrast between his current outside and the wine's summery provenance.

Observing this, Brandi surreptitiously smiled; pleased the first part of her plan had been successfully executed.

Ron and Sam were cleaning up, and Brandi called over to him that she'd be upstairs when he was done. Sam looked over and gave her sheepish-looking father a "you're in for it now" look. Ron thought that indeed he was, but wasn't quite sure what the *it* was.

A few minutes later, as he entered the bedroom and closed the door behind him, he was enveloped by a floral scent and humidity that intensely contrasted with the dry, stale, hot air of the rest of the house. He turned the corner towards the ensuite and did a double take. Brandi was already in the tub, surrounded by bubbles. A few scented candles were aglow, and two glasses of wine were poured and ready for consumption.

"Well, heavens to Betsy," Ron exclaimed in his best southern accent. "What have you gone and done, little lady?"

Brandi countered in her coyest southern drawl. "Well, I'm sure I don't know what you're talking about, mister. I'm just here minding my own business, and having a little soak to ease my tired bones."

Peeling off his clothes, Ron countered, "Now, don't you go acting all naive and innocent-like, missy. I do believe you are up to something here."

As Ron slowly lowered himself into the hot tub, the floral scents of the candles and bubble bath intensified, and he exhaled slowly as he hit bottom. When he was fully immersed, he allowed himself a full-body shiver that seemed to wash his mind clean of all stress.

Brandi, now again herself, asked, "Bathgasm?"

Ron's eyes slowly opened, and he nodded positively, "Oh, yeah, baby."

"Something tells me that that won't be the last member of the 'gasm' family you'll be meeting up with tonight," Brandi added, with just the right amount of naughty in her voice.

"So what's the occasion?" asked Ron.

Brandi cast him an "are you kidding?" look, but didn't say a word.

Oh-oh! Ron thought. He conducted a lightning-quick mental check of all possible calendar events: anniversary (nope), birthdays (nope), first dates (nope), basmitzmah (d'oh, wrong family). *What the hell could it be?* he wondered.

Feeling pity for her now distressed-looking husband, Brandi revealed the answer. "Tomorrow's Valentine's Day."

Seeing the opening, Ron ret orted in a *faux*-flabbergasted tone, "I know, but what's today?" In truth he had completely forgotten about Valentine's Day, and was pleased he had now escaped the oversight.

"Tomorrow evening Elise and Scott are coming over for dinner, so I thought we'd celebrate Valentine's tonight."

Although Ron had also been clueless about their social plans for Saturday, he went along with the emerging theme, nodding. "Ah, it all becomes clear."

"And you've been trying so hard to add more romance into our relationship that I thought tonight I'd *give back* a little."

Usually he would have been highly excited about that proposal, but tonight he couldn't help thinking, *I hope she doesn't have a strap-on in mind.*

As it turned out, and much to Ron's relief, she didn't.

Saturday, February 14

Following a lazy start, during which Ron and Brandi advanced their studies in the *Kama Sutra*, Ron had spent the rest of the day shovelling snow, at both his parent's house and his own home. Now, with daylight fading, he looked out his living room window towards the street, expecting Scott and Elise's imminent arrival.

No doubt he'd be back on the shovel first thing tomorrow morning. His one consolation was the winter reprieve planned for next month in the Dominican. Once he had confirmed he could get the time off, Brandi had directed her considerable planning skills towards arranging the trip. Tommy, their son, couldn't make it, but the rest of them were enthusiastically all in, and the four-week countdown had begun immediately. While Ron was lost in the imagined sounds of surf and warm breezes on his face, Scott and Elise pulled into the driveway.

"Happy Valentine's Day!" Scott and Elise trumpeted upon entry.

"You guys too," Ron and Brandi answered in unison, as the mandatory hugs and air kisses were traded.

"This is the first Valentine's Day I can remember Scott being excited about," Elise said sarcastically. After a short pause, she added, "Brandi, I'm worried our husbands are having a bromance."

Scott and Ron suspiciously turned towards each other with stern expressions. Their grim looks quickly melted away, replaced with adoring gazes, as they slowly walked towards each other, arms extended, eyes closed and lips fully puckered.

"That can wait for later," laughingly added Brandi. "Come in the kitchen and let's get this party started."

In celebration of the special evening, Scott had brought over one of his favourite reds from the Colaneri estates from the Niagara area—the 2012 Visione Shiraz. The smooth and complex wine was sampled to the collective audible approval of the group.

The girls hadn't seen one another for a while, so while they caught up, the guys discussed work and Scott's trip out west. The technical-bid clarification had gone well, and Scott thought they had a good chance at winning the contract, given their planned construction was to a LEED (Leadership in Energy and Environmental Design) Gold Certified Standard, which EllisDon was more familiar with than their competition.

He had also been able to sneak in a game of golf before he flew back to Ottawa. When pressed by Ron about how he shot, Scott prefaced his answer with a number of excuses, including rental clubs, wet and cool conditions, and an unfamiliar course with too many trees, narrow fairways, and low lighting.

As Scott paused, preparing to reveal the final tally, Ron interrupted. "So, shitty, right?"

"Ninety-four."

"Not *too* too bad."

"With three mulligans."

Ron now looked visibly less impressed.

"And from the white tees," Scott confessed.

"Ouch," commiserated Ron. "But still way better than being stranded in a blizzard in Ottawa."

"True dat," Scott concurred, raising his glass in agreement.

Conversation around the dinner table was more inclusive and dealt with family, the ongoing brutal winter, summer holiday plans, and recent stories concerning workplace dramas. Scott and Elise had been married about twelve years, but hadn't been able to have kids, so Brandi, understanding this had always been a painful issue for Elise, provided only a brief update on their kids, and then tactfully moved on to a discussion of their upcoming vacation plans. With the wine still freely flowing, conversation became progressively more raucous, until, after a pause, Elise commented that she was totally impressed that Brandi and Ron had been able to stick to this year's resolution. Scott had gotten the green light from Ron to discuss it, in general terms, with Elise, and Brandi was also aware she knew.

Ron was silently going through the list of who now knew about his resolution in his head when Brandi responded, "We've been having fun with it. I was initially very wary about the whole thing, when Ron first brought it up on New Year's Eve, but to be completely honest, we got into a rhythm in January and since then, it's just been part of our daily routine." Brandi paused and smiled. "We've been reconnecting in ways we never would have considered, especially since we started reading the *Kama Sutra*."

Ron shook his head.

"As well as providing some of the best laughs we've had in a while, it reminded us that relationships are hard work, and you shouldn't ever become complacent about your partner's needs."

Scott and Elise both looked at Ron. After a beat or two, he concurred. "What she said."

Brandi continued, "And it's OK to be adventurous with your partner. Anything, really, is acceptable, as long as it's mutually consensual."

Ron's alcohol-infused mind was starting to wander now. *Mental note. Remember to bring up that mutual consensus thing if Brandi ever suggests a strap-on.*

"For example," Brandi added, "if either Ron or I were to ever be in need of a mistress or lover to complement our lives, the *Kama Sutra* has some helpful suggestions for what we should be looking for. While I should be on the outlook for a handsome, well spoken, confident, and liberal fellow, Ron would need to track down a poor, lonely, physically disadvantaged, ill-smelling, and somewhat obsessive lady to see to his needs."

"Sounds like a fair trade-off to me," Elise suggested. "You'd better pick up your game, mister," she added, glaring at Scott.

"Why would I *ever* think of looking elsewhere?" Scott responded sincerely. "It sounds as if I've already found the woman of my dreams."

Elise responded with a solid elbow to his ribs.

After a few seconds, Elise commented, "You know, I think we could all put a bit more effort into our relationships. It's so easy to fall into a daily rut and become bored with sex." She looked at Scott and deadpanned, "Present company excluded, of course."

Scott shook his head, and countered in his best Rodney Dangerfield, "If it wasn't for pickpockets I'd have no sex life at all."

&

Later, with the guys in the kitchen and the girls in the living room, Scott, sitting across from Ron, quietly asked, "So...everything good on the southern front?"

Ron quickly confirmed that the girls were fully engaged, and turned back to Scott. "Truth is, I'm having trouble keeping up with Brandi. All these years I've been living under the misconception that I'm the libidinous one in the relationship, but as it turns out, Brandi is."

"My friend, you have chosen wisely," replied Scott, nodding in admiration.

"She's actually hijacked the resolution from me. I'm thinking now that Brandi has developed a taste for the dominant role, I'll never get it back."

"From where I'm sitting, that sounds a bit like a first-world problem."

Ron had to laugh. "Yeah, you're right, but still it's taken me a bit by surprise, and honestly, I'm finding it hard to adjust. You know, I think dominance in the sexual process is part of the turn-on for guys, and from what I've seen recently, probably for girls as well. Who knew?" Ron shook his head disbelievingly. "With Brandi now the new alpha, or, more accurately, me demoted to the beta, I've found myself having to distract my brain so it doesn't focus on the change of roles and the dominance thing. The *Kama Sutra* has helped so far, but we're just about through it, and I'm worried. What's next? Brandi has become so 'adventurous', she's got me nervous that she'll be breaking out the toys pretty soon."

"And what's wrong with that?"

Ron gave him a "Really dude? Are you serious?" look.

"Seriously. Have you forgotten what we talked about at the Bassline already? Everything should be on the table for this resolution. Take that pickle out of your bum"

Ron winced at the thought.

"And open up your mind to the possibilities, man. How many guys would *kill* to be where you are right now? A beautiful, intelligent, sexy, extremely keen wife who instigates daily sex with her somehow saddened husband. Think of the global ridicule you'd have to endure if that ever got out."

Ron glared at Scott.

"It never *will*, of course," quickly added Scott. "But can you imagine the razzing you'd get at Sunday hockey?"

Ron did, and cringed at the mere thought of it. The ridicule would be remorseless and relentless.

"Now, I'm not familiar with the *Kama Sutra*, but from what you, and now Brandi, have told me, it's all about parking your inhibitions, and honestly and holistically exploring the endless possibilities of a healthy sexual relationship. You know, people in modern North America are generally a prudish product of our ridiculously conservative Catholic religious roots. No premarital sex, no birth control, no masturbation, no pornography, no condoms, not even for protection. And that's just with respect to relationship issues in a run-of-the-mill heterosexual relationship. How out of touch with modern society is that? The church has always used sex as a tool to control us; banishing it to a cloistered corner in our human house where all the other unspeakable baser tendencies reside; only held up to the light of day and railed at when the church decides a refresher course on guilt and shame is required. Consequently, we've been programmed to feel guilty about any sexual thought, let alone sexual pleasure. Even as we culturally evolve, there is a residual pall of guilt that follows us everywhere we go, and to a certain degree, determines our actions."

Ron looked at Scott skeptically.

"Yes, even in our so-called 'modern' and educated society," Scott responded. "For the church it's about being stuck in their old ways to some degree, but it's also about their addiction to power, and them not being willing to relinquish control over the general population, and in doing so, lose relevance. Having established themselves as our moral compass in all matters sexual, they have intentionally attached themselves to the single most ubiquitous physical need, aside from sustenance. Each of those forty or fifty times a day when you think about sex, the church is there on your other shoulder tsking disappointedly at you. But even the church realizes that we need to procreate, so if we *must* have sex, it is to be pursued with religious intent, and an understanding that the climax really is a divine moment—as close as we'll ever get to God. The church wants God to own the moment so they can take credit by proxy for that small reprieve from reality, that one glorious euphoric moment. It's like a pyramid scheme. The good Lord may receive only a subconscious glimmer of appreciation with each sexual event, but there are plenty of people out there having lots of sex, so the praise adds up, and ultimately they stay relevant—even in today's society." His voice then deepened, with a hint of New England pilgrim in it. "Time for us to shake off the religious yokes of yesteryear and rise up, says me. Time to reclaim sex for what it really is: a damned fine way to spend time with someone you love—or even someone you like."

As Scott finished his rant, the sound of slow clapping and cheering from the living room snapped both their heads around. Scott's tirade had progressively picked up in volume and had, a while back, attracted the attention of the ladies, who now, much to the embarrassment of Scott, stood in vocal appreciation of his opinion. "Honey, I had no idea that you felt so passionately about the subject," Elise stated, somewhat ironically, but with an inescapably serious overtone that everybody registered.

Ron looked at Scott, and whispered out of the side of his mouth farthest from the ladies, "It looks like you're going to get lucky tonight, my friend."

Scott responded similarly out the side of his face, "So it appears." And gave Ron a "well, what do you know" look. "Do you think I can borrow the 'manual' when you and Brandi are finished with it?"

Wednesday, February 18

Near the end of the workday Ron made it to Scott's office, and plunked down into a chair, clearly exhausted. He had an IGA bag with him, and conspiratorially slid it and its contents across the table to Scott.

"Here it is. Sorry if there are a few pages stuck together," he said with a smile.

"Excellent, I'll try my best to get it back to you without gumming up the pages any more than they already are."

After slipping it partially out of the plastic grocery bag and giving it a quick perusal before replacing it, Scott said, "I'm thinking you may be onto something here, buddy. Elise has been acting like a different, younger version of herself since last weekend. We've talked about sex more in the last few days than we have in the last year. And she's very keen to start expanding her horizons on the subject, beginning with the 'book of love.'" He looked down and patted the plastic bag. "And tell you the truth, so am I. I haven't been this keen for years. How goofy is that? All we needed was a little discussion on the subject and voila! I, too, have my own wanton woman.

"Of course," he added, "we have no intention of attempting anything as patently idiotic as your resolution. We're content to just use you and Brandi as role models." He laughed. "I guess you guys are the cult leaders. We're just the disciples."

"We're glad to help the flock out anyway we can," Ron said graciously, sporting an exceptionally serene look on his face. Then he asked, "Hey, how about a more fulsome update right after work on Friday? I can't stay long. Brandi's heading down to TO this weekend to see Tommy and her family, and Sam has a school thing Friday evening. Also, Sam and I are going to use the opportunity for some father-daughter bonding, and head out skiing early on Saturday morning—so only a couple on Friday."

Scott gave him a "should be good" look, and then verbalized it. "Let's start a wee bit earlier to give us more time. I'll swing by your office between four-thirty and five so we can head down together."

Ron answered with a thumbs-up.

It was about six-thirty, and Ron was walking back home. It was still bitterly cold, and snowing intermittently. Unfortunately for Ron, he was currently walking directly into the blustery wind. Whereas his usual walk home would have put the afternoon westerly winds at his back, he was making the short walk home from the nearby adults' store, *Aren't We Naughty*, located less than a kilometre to the east of Centrepointe.

Until he had googled the location of "sex shops" in the Ottawa area last Sunday, he'd had no idea that one was so conveniently located adjacent to his community. Still, it had been so bitterly cold today he had wimped out and used UberX to get dropped off about forty-five minutes earlier.

His experience in the adult store—his first—had been nowhere near as painful as he had earlier feared. He had become somewhat emboldened after the expanded discussion on sex with Scott and Elise on Saturday, and decided on Sunday morning that he would embrace Brandi's sexual metamorphosis, and become a more active participant in his own resolution, by introducing some toys into the mix.

He had spent about an hour online on Sunday assessing the extensive, and sometimes perplexing, range of options out there, to give himself a general idea of what might be appropriate for Brandi and him in advance of his anticipated-to-be-very-uncomfortable visit to the actual store.

Much to his relief, however, the patrons hadn't appeared to be overtly alternative-lifestyle practitioners. The demographics had been pretty much what you'd see walking down the street on a summer's day, just currently with a lot more clothes on. He'd also been very relieved that no one stared at him as he walked the aisles and pondered both the uses and the possible outcomes of the various sexual aids on offer. That was, until this one Rubenesque thirty-something lady with an unnatural purple coif had spotted him and slowly closed in on him. Her lack of outerwear suggested she was an employee. He'd initiated subtle evasive actions in an attempt to avoid an encounter, but he was no match for the seasoned retail veteran in hot pursuit.

Edging uncomfortably close beside him, she broke the ice, the distraction of her nose and ear piercings eclipsed only by her brilliant genuine smile. "First time?" she asked.

Ron responded, "Is it that obvious?"

She nodded, and offered, "My name's Cassandra—my friends call me Casey—and I'd be glad to help you out."

Normally, he would have responded to the offer with a polite version of the "I'm a guy and can quite capably complete any task anywhere at any time without assistance, thank you very much" reply, but he surprised himself by actually thanking Cassandra, introducing himself, and accepting her offer.

"OK, then, what can you tell me about your situation, your expectations in augmenting your sexual experience with some aids, and you and your partner's tolerance for experimentation?"

Holy shit, Ron thought, standing dumfounded beside Cassandra. *Did I just hear what I thought I heard?* As a naturally conservative person, just a couple months ago the mere thought of discussing any of these issues with a complete stranger, especially in a public retail setting, would have been utterly inconceivable. So when Ron opened up his mouth and began seriously responding to Cassandra's inquiries instead of running screaming from the store, the old Ron sat isolated and marginalized in a corner of Ron's brain, watching in disbelief. The *new* Ron lowered his voice and responded, "Well, my wife and I are trying to strengthen our relationship and, I guess, better understand ourselves using sex."

Cassandra, now intrigued, nodded encouragingly at Ron.

When she didn't say anything, Ron continued. "We've been happily married for about twenty years and, as you can see, I'm no spring chicken."

Here Ron paused, looking for some engagement from Cassandra, but when he only received an understanding smile in return, he went on, now committed to the narrative. "And after about a month and a half, I thought it couldn't hurt by spicing it up a bit."

Cassandra jumped in. "A month and a half?" she asked, puzzled.

Oh, shit, Ron thought, immediately realizing his mistake. There was an extended pause, and reluctantly Ron continued. "OK, Cassandra, I'm going to trust you with this only if you promise not to mention a word to anybody."

Further intrigued now, Cassandra nodded agreeably.

"I mean it," added Ron.

"Cross my heart," she replied, tracing the shape of the cross on her ample bosom, attempting to dispel the last of Ron's apprehension. "And you're protected under our client-confidentiality obligations."

Not without some trepidation, even under the iron-clad legal assurance proffered by Cassandra, Ron detailed the nature of his resolution, and gave her a brief summary of events. She stood in silence for a few seconds, and then reverently replied, "Ron, that's the most incredible thing I've ever heard!"

Ron stood dumbfounded while she quietly enthused, "I'm honoured to even be a small part of this epic endeavour. You and your wife can *absolutely* count on me for anything, and I'd be glad to offer a woman's perspective for you at any time along the way. And I'm going to give you the employee discount on everything you purchase. And," she added with an officious flourish, "as an added incentive, because I think your resolution's so kickass, if you and your wife successfully complete it, you'll get that employee discount for life!"

Ron had been appreciative of Cassandra's unexpectedly enthusiastic support, and now fully incentivized, they'd gotten down to the business of improving Ron and Brandi's sex life.

Now, walking home, he still couldn't believe just how comfortable he'd been with his new best friend, Casey. They'd shared stories and debated sexual issues as Ron shopped, only interrupting this primary conversation when they needed to engage in a specific discussion of an 'aid', its purpose and its effectiveness. His thoughts went to the purchased objects he currently had tucked up under his arm.

Ron had confided in Cassandra that the more his wife got turned on, the more he got turned on, so to help keep Ron fully invested in the process, she suggested a vibrating u-shaped thingamajig, calling it the "ultimate couple's toy. Understanding the benefit of creating a positive feedback loop to encourage going "the extra mile," she guaranteed that this unit would bring his wife to repeated and stronger orgasms, while simultaneously stimulating him. He could hardly wait to try it out. She'd also supplied him with various lubricants, and a couple of different penis-rings in recognition of his "mature" status.

He recalled Cassandra's wistful comment as she cashed him out. "Your wife is a lucky woman for having a guy like you who's willing to do this for her."

He hoped she was right.

Friday, February 20

It was just after five in the afternoon. Ron and Scott had snagged a table at the back of the Bassline Pub, ordered a pitcher of Keith's and some wings, and were settling in. The walk over had been bitterly cold but, thankfully, today it wasn't snowing, the wind was negligible, and it was still daylight out. The lengthening days provided a reminder that this vicious winter would eventually end, and had infused Ron with a sense of optimism.

"So what's different about Elise since last weekend?" he asked Scott.

Scott shrugged, exhaled loudly, and said, "I think she's unconsciously made this some sort of competition. There's no other explanation. She's gone from zero to a hundred during the last week, and since we've had that bloody *Kama Sutra* in our possession, she's kicked it into overdrive! I honestly do not know how you do it. I'm already starting to avoid her. I tried staying up past her normal bedtime on Monday, but that didn't work. I just ended up more tired for work on Tuesday. Last night, I went to bed real early, and she woke me up. There's no escaping it."

"From where I'm sitting, that sounds like a first-world problem." Ron relished the opportunity to throw that comment back at Scott, and he did so with an ear-to-ear smile.

"*Touché,*" replied Scott. "I'm hoping the novelty of her newfound sexuality wears off pretty quick, or I'm going to have to follow in your footsteps and head to my doctors for some help."

"Well, I can tell you those little blue pills have certainly come in handy so far. And starting sometime next week, when Brandi's finished her monthly cycle, I'm planning to enlist the full force of both the pharmaceutical and pleasure industry to execute an efficient catch-up session."

"Pleasure industry?"

"Yup. I made it over to the local sex shop this week and beefed up the arsenal a bit."

"Nice," effused Scott. "You beat Brandi to it. Brilliant."

Ron absorbed the praise for a couple seconds, and then continued. "And you know, an unintended consequence from that move has been me regaining my confidence. I feel like I'm on equal standing with Brandi. I've been promoted back up to alpha."

"Well, Mr. Alpha, I can tell you that as of today you have completed… fourteen percent!" Scott said, finishing with a "hey how about that?" look and two thumbs up.

Ron hadn't really thought about this for some time now, and was surprised at just how little progress he'd actually made. Or more accurately, he was hit with a wave of worry about how much further he still had to go.

Scott registered the dejected look on Ron's face, and said, "Sorry, buddy. I know it doesn't sound like much given what you've gone through; believe me, I now understand your pain—but think about where you are. Almost two months of the resolution completed. You're reinvigorated, having reclaimed your alpha status. You and Brandi have got into a rhythm, so to speak, and… spring's coming!"

Ron remained motionless and pensive, so Scott added seriously, "Come on, you knew this would be a long climb. The good news is now you're in game shape and well into the foothills."

A resigned smile slowly grew on Ron's face. "Of course you're right. This resolution was always going to be one day at a time." He paused briefly. "I just can't help but worry about what other surprises are in store for us, and if this resolution is ultimately going to do more harm than good. Sex is the most intimate core of every marriage, and it's turning out to be a little exhausting to expose and play with it on a daily basis. I've recently realized that if there are any hidden problems in our relationship, this resolution is going to expose them."

Scott knew that to be true, and considered his response while he chugged a portion of the beer in his mug. "Well, worry all you want, it won't help you. In fact, it'll likely hurt you. You know there's no turning this ship around. So put your dumbass head down and keep plowing forward."

Just as Ron shrugged and raised his beer to his mouth, Scott asked him in his best deadpan, "So have you and Brandi tried anal yet?"

While wiping the beer from his face Scott added, in the same deadpan manner, "I'll take that as a no."

Thursday, February 26

Brandi waved to Charlene, who stood at the restaurant entrance searching for her friend. Charlene smiled when she saw her, and started towards the table.

Out of the blue Charlene had texted Brandi that morning and said she'd be in the area on an errand, and would she be available for lunch? Brandi had decided she could skip her lunch-hour workout, and suggested the restaurant in the Brookstreet Hotel, located within the Kanata Research Park where she worked. Brandi got the employee discount, and the lunch menu was excellent.

As the ladies traded hugs and air kisses Brandi said, "Well how nice it this? Squeezing in some girlfriend time over lunch."

"So weren't you in Toronto last weekend?" Charlene asked.

Brandi nodded. "I was checking up on my mom and got to see Tommy, and my mother and sisters. I decided I'd go down on that weekend since it coincided with my period, and I didn't want to overwhelm Ron. You know, having to make up even *more* skipped days."

Charlene nodded. "That makes sense. And how is everybody there?"

"Thankfully, everyone's great. Mom's adapting to her new medical regime, and both Mags and Debbie are happy as clams."

"Have you mentioned your resolution to anybody in your family?"

Brandi laughed. "You know, I had to think about that just last week before I headed down to TO. In the end, I only had the guts to tell Mags, since, you know, we've always been close. I was too embarrassed to tell mom or Deb."

"What did Mags think about the resolution?"

"Well, I actually had to convince her I wasn't kidding, and when I finally did, she was really interested in the details. She thought it was a very cool idea, and said she and her hubby could use a bit more 'romance' in their lives as well. She suggested that I keep her updated and jokingly suggested I should post my progress on Facebook." Brandi laughed. "Can you imagine?"

"It's funny that Mags was as interested as she was, because I was going to ask you the same thing today," Charlene said, a bit self-consciously. "You know, about how you guys are coping and some of your 'techniques' that you've found useful."

Brandi giggled, and responded, "You know, Charlene, I'm beginning to think that most couples our age *are* struggling with intimacy in their marriage, and could use some tips on how to reinvigorate it. That said, I'm not going on Facebook anytime soon to discuss this. Can you imagine the reaction at work? At Ron's work? Our kids? Good grief. They would be mortified."

"Well, you can worry about the world later. How about tossing a girlfriend some advice on spicing up her love life right now?"

Charlene sat giggling and transfixed through Brandi's recollection of her and Ron's progress so far. She mentioned Ron's trip to the doctor, their continuing journey through the *Kama Sutra*, and most recently Ron's initiative to introduce some "toys" into the process.

After Brandi finished, Charlene said, "You know, Mags is right. What you and Ron are doing could be inspirational. And to avoid the potential for embarrassment," Charlene continued, "maybe you could do it anonymously?"

While Brandi pondered the implications, Charlene brought her back to the present by asking, "And hey, if you guys are done with the 'love manual', could I borrow it for a while?"

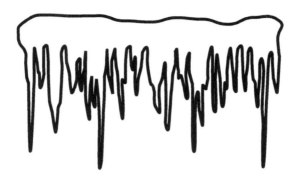

CHAPTER 4

EVERYTHING IN MODERATION

Monday, March 2

Ron sat alone in Dr. Kaur's waiting area, again the last patient of the day. He had walked over to the clinic after work, and regretted doing so about halfway over. Although it was still light out, and only about minus five degrees, it was snowing hard and, counter-typically, the wind had been blowing out of the east and directly into his face the entire distance.

As he sat alone in the waiting room, he wondered if he was becoming a wimp. He remembered the winter days spent outside when he was a kid—outdoor hockey, skiing, building snow forts, and endless ball hockey on the street out in front of his house. Now, more often than not, he dreaded even going outside when it was really cold.

His winter reveries were abruptly interrupted by Dr. Kaur's salutations, as he emerged quickly and loudly from around the corner. He looked wiped-out again after his long day. The dark circles around his eyes, barely noticeable during Ron's last visit, had since darkened considerably. "Ron, I'm so sorry to keep you waiting again. Everybody seems to be sick these days, and I just can't keep to my schedule. I tell you, it must be this vexatious weather. Did you hear that February was the coldest ever on record? Global warming my hairy patootie, I say. If it really is warming somewhere, then I need to move there."

He motioned for Ron to follow him into an examination room. "Come in, Ron let's hear what's up in your life, go ahead have a seat please." Still not finished complaining about the winter weather, he added, as he sat opposite Ron, "I truly don't know how you ever survived growing up in this climate. And look—you still have all your fingers!"

After a short pause, and a rolling slide over to the computer to bring up Ron's files, Dr. Kaur sighed, and asked, "So, what can I do for you today, my friend?"

Ron refocused himself. "Well, you remember the medication that you pre-scribed for me last month?"

"Yes, I'm reading your file and it's all coming back to me now." Dr. Kaur inter-rupted. "I've been seriously thinking about your resolution, my friend. It's been a topic of much interest between my wife and me."

Ron's eyes opened in a "WTF, you're talking to your wife about my sex prob-lems" look.

Dr. Kaur noted this, and calmly added, "Don't worry, Ron, not even the smallest bit. She is also bound by my physician-client confidentiality obligation. Some-times I need to discuss ideas and patients to help with my diagnoses, and she's all I've got and she's a very intelligent woman. And she's intrigued about your resolution. Let me tell you, if my wife is interested in something to do with sex, that subject has now got my full attention." He accompanied the last comment with a waggle of his eyebrows, and a purposely lecherous smile.

"So," he continued more seriously, "how *are* things progressing?"

Ron took a couple of seconds to recover from Dr. Kaur's last comments, and restarted. "Things are generally OK. The pills you gave me are doing exactly what you said they would."

Dr. Kaur smiled, his head bobbling with satisfaction. "So you are still on target concerning the resolution?"

Ron got the distinct impression that the doctor was inquiring more out of personal rather than professional interest. It would likely be the first question Dr. Kaur's wife would ask him tonight. "Yes, more or less, we're still on target," Ron replied.

"Wonderful!" Dr. Kaur exclaimed, clapping his hands together joyfully.

"Wonderful perhaps, except I've recently experienced some 'side effects' from the Cialis."

Dr. Kaur, now quite concerned, asked, "What kind of side effects, Ron?"

"Well, I decided to use it following my wife's last menstrual cycle, and the pills themselves worked very well. *Really* well, actually. So I just kept on going, if you know what I mean. I wanted to make up for the previous days when we couldn't—you know—have sex."

"I'm a little confused here, Ron," Dr. Kaur interjected.

"Concerning what?"

"You're telling me you couldn't have sex while your wife was menstruating?"

Ron nodded.

"Does she have an aversion to having sex during this time of month, or possibly finds it painful?

Ron shook his head.

"So why are you not having sex during her period?"

Ron could feel the heat rising into his face, his embarrassment silently signaling the answer for the doctor's inquiry.

"Ah. Now I see, Ron. It's you."

Ron nodded his crimson coconut.

"Ron, this is not uncommon. We instinctively associate blood with physical trauma, so the majority of couples will naturally and unconsciously avoid sex during this time of the month. That said, I do know there exists a minority of men—menophiles, I believe they are called—who embrace it, due to their partner's heightened arousal, or the enhanced sensory experience related to the act. Who knows for sure?" The doctor shrugged. "The point is, you're not alone. But given your task at hand, you may want to reconsider your mensal hiatus to make it easier on yourself." He smiled. "After all, a warrior should expect to bloody his sword every now and then. But I digress. Please continue."

Ron took a few seconds to reconnect with his previous narrative. "So we had an unusually long session." Ron paused. The doctor nodded encouragingly. "And I got a little raw. Friction burn, I think." Ron felt his face starting to re-redden.

Still the doctor silently nodded.

Ron pushed on. "I think it may have been caused in part by the material."

"The material? What material?"

"Well, the material on the 'toy' we were using," Ron replied, his face now hot and a deep red. "I may be a little sensitive to it."

With the problem finally identified, Dr. Kaur said, "Well, let's see what's got you so uncomfortable."

Ron stood up, undid his belt, and slipped his pants and his underwear down to his thighs, presenting his penis to the good doctor, who was just turning back to him after donning a pair of latex gloves. "Good God, man!" Dr. Kaur exclaimed. "Was your 'toy' a cheese shredder?"

Ron could feel his ears get even hotter as he looked down at his aching member. As Dr. Kaur turned it in his hand, inspecting Ron's pride and joy from every angle, Ron started to imagine the conversation the doctor would be having with his wife tonight.

"Well, it looks worse than it is," he finally opined, much to Ron's relief. "It's probably just a superficial fungal infection, which would make your skin very itchy and very sensitive. I've got a cream for you that should quickly clear it up. Let me get it for you."

As the doctor left the room to retrieve the cream, Ron hurriedly pulled his pants up, glad *that* was over. When the doctor came back and handed Ron the tube of cream, he dispensed some verbal advice as well. "Ron, I'm going to suggest that you use that 'toy' of yours a little more sparingly, and possibly with more lubricant when you do. And try not to overwork the old boy. You're not twenty-two anymore, you know."

Here he paused for effect, while he pointed at Ron's crotch. "I know that there will be times that you have to 'redouble' your efforts to make up lost ground, but I would suggest that you spread it out over a couple of days instead of getting the job done in one session. This is most certainly a marathon, not a sprint." He chuckled at the obviousness of this statement. "So apply the cream three times a day for a week. You will see the effects almost immediately, but take a few days off to let it heal—OK?"

Ron nodded his agreement.

"I want you to know that my wife and I are rooting for your successful completion of the resolution, my friend. Now tell me, what exactly is this 'toy' you're using, and how does it work?"

Thursday, March 5

The doctor's diagnosis had been spot-on, and Ron experienced a quick recovery. Today he was back in game shape, and physically ready to carry on with the resolution. They were five days behind now, and Ron wanted to be at least caught up by the time they left for the Dominican Republic the following Saturday.

Brandi, on the other hand, was not as keen. It had worried her that Ron had caused himself physical harm in pursuit of their resolution, and she had voiced her concern for his wellbeing, even asking him to consider abandoning the resolution. He would have no part of that, and although it took a while to convince Brandi, she ultimately consented to continue, on the condition that he use condoms for the next day or two to give him extra time to heal before going bareback. He agreed without hesitation.

It had been so long since he had used a condom - having been "fixed" immediately after Sam was born - that he had forgotten how much he disliked them. Although fortified with one of his blue pills and more than ready physically, having been sidelined for almost a week, the condoms had quickly dulled his enthusiasm, making his second, and final effort, of the evening more work than it should have been.

Lying beside Brandi, breathing heavily after this extended second effort, he had recalled a saying concerning condoms: "The only time you think you're going to use all three of the condoms in the package is before you use the first one." But he *was* glad for the protection that they had provided him today. He couldn't afford to re-injure himself and suffer any further setbacks to the resolution. It would be a slow and steady climb back to par over the next week, but he, and probably Brandi, were OK with that. Dr. Kaur would also approve.

Still intertwined with Brandi, he kissed her on the shoulder, and noticed she looked distracted. "You OK, sweetie?"

She turned to face him, and with a soft smile replied, "Yeah, I'm fine. It's just the resolution has got me a bit worried. This is turning out to be harder work than I expected; not so much physically for me, I'm enjoying that part," she said, offering Ron a genuine and purposefully promiscuous smile. "I'm more concerned about the changes I'm feeling in my head. I've been experiencing some very unusual 'energy', for the lack of a better word, during my orgasms. I think the resolution may be rewiring my brain."

Ron contemplated her last comment. That hypothesis would explain quite a few of the personality changes he had seen in himself over the last couple of months. "You may be right, Brandi," he concurred. "I've seen changes in myself, as well, but is that necessarily a bad thing?"

Brandi considered that question for a moment, and then replied, "Not so far, I guess. I'm just a little worried about *why* this is happening."

"Yeah, I've been worrying about that as well, to tell you the truth. But I'm also glad we're talking about it."

Brandi smiled, leaned into Ron, and passionately kissed him.

The kiss unexpectedly reinvigorated Ron. He felt his soldier get off the bench and start to stand at attention.

Then he remembered the condom, which had the equivalent effect of an ALS Ice Bucket Challenge.

Friday, March 6

"Yyyuuuuck," Scott spontaneously commented.

Ron had just relayed some details about his "infection" of the previous week.

"So essentially, you were growing mushrooms on your pecker?" Scott added, not in the least sympathetic.

Ron silently stared back, deadpan.

"You're lucky Brandi let you go near her with that thing. Hey!" Scott suddenly exclaimed, "Now I know why they call it your *root*."

The guys were sitting at a small table near the stage at the Bassline Pub. The crowd was gathering in celebration of the end of another work week. Ron recognized a few of the regulars, and was thinking it a bit strange that, although he had shared a small space with these people on numerous occasions, he had never actually spoken, or even introduced himself, to any of them—an urban anonymity that all city dwellers unconsciously accepted.

"It's almost over," Scott exclaimed, shaking Ron from his musings.

"What's almost over?"

"Winter. It's supposed to break next week, and then we should be done with it. Just in time for your trip to the Dominican," he added with a sardonic chuckle.

"You know it doesn't really matter. Sure it would be best if we departed in a minus-thirty blizzard, but I'm just happy to get away from winter and spend some time away from work with the girls."

Scott nodded in agreement. "Yeah, this winter has made me realize that our crappy climate is the price we pay for enjoying everything else about Canada. But enough already—Uncle! I'm ready for spring."

"To spring!" Ron lifted his mug in a toast.

As they gulped a bit of beer, Ron's attention was again drawn to the adjacent crowd, particularly a table of thirty-something ladies settling in for what looked like a full-evening session.

"So what's on your mind?" Scott asked. "You look preoccupied tonight."

Ron pondered the answer for a few seconds before replying. "Well, I've got to tell you, I'm worried about Brandi. She's probably the most positive, resilient person I know, and she's beginning to feel stressed from this resolution. After our close encounter of the fungal kind, she even suggested we ditch the resolution."

"And?"

"We decided to carry-on. It's not just about me being stubborn, either. We've both gained a healthy respect for what we're attempting here. And although we're a bit concerned about how it's changing us, we're also curious as to how we're going to hold up as a couple and what's still yet to come."

"You know, I've been looking into the physiology of the brain and sex, and I can tell you, you're a braver man than me."

"What do you mean by that?" asked Ron.

"Well, there's so much we don't really know about the brain, but we do know that it's evolved over a billion years to maximize its chances of survival. The pleasure thing was very likely an integral and early part of the brain developed to condition the organism to repeat positive survival experiences - like food for sustenance and sex for propagation. Now fast forward a billion years, and this most primal of neurological programming has remained pretty much unchanged at the core of the human brain. Sex is, essentially, placing the instincts of an ancient worm at the controls of a supercomputer. So what could *possibly* go wrong? The human mind has, for all intents and purposes, evolved *around* this basic instinct as a priority. So although we *can* think about other things when we're not actively pursuing or having sex, it exists as hard and cold as an olive seed, dominating everything just below the surface. It is the old man in the brain."

"And what does that have to do with our resolution?" asked Ron.

"Pretty much everything. When you engage the primal core as often as you have, the rest of the brain probably undergoes some sort of rewiring."

These comments got Ron's attention. "You know, both Brandi and I have seen changes in ourselves since we started the resolution. We've actually used the term 'rewiring' to refer what's going on in our heads."

"I'd be surprised if things weren't changing," Scott said, as he got up and headed to the can. Ron sat there alone thinking about the "rewiring" that both he and Brandi were possibly experiencing, getting more and more worried. By the time Scott returned he was a bit agitated.

"So what do *you* think is going on our brains?" asked Ron.

Scott took a hefty pull from his mug. "Now, that's the sixty-four-thousand-dollar question. We know *something's* going on, but I bet you there are only a handful of people on this earth who could provide you with some real insight into that question. The good news is that both of you are not naturally impulsive or compulsive. Those two traits are directly connected. Impulsiveness usually leads to compulsiveness, and compulsiveness is what leads to addiction, and addiction leads to some serious, and commonly irreparable, rewiring in the brain. Thus the saying, 'Once an alcoholic, always an alcoholic.' You can exchange alcohol with nicotine, or heroin, or cocaine—whatever; the rewiring occurs with any addiction."

Here Scott paused and took another sip of beer. "Anyways, you guys have decided to use the reward system in your brain for one of its designed purposes—sex. And the human reward system associated with sex is pretty sophisticated, and is very familiar with self-abuse. You see, the more sophisticated parts of our brain knows that the 'pleasure-seeking worm' in us has control issues, so it's introduced buffers and internal checks and balances to decide if a dose of dopamine, the pleasure chemical, is warranted, and when you do get the green light, it doles it out sparingly, and throws in a number of other chemicals that effectively work to help avoid addiction. 'Unnatural' drugs bypass the internal checks and balance system of the brain, go directly to the synapses in our pleasure centres, and get them to dole out dopamine like Hallowe'en candy. And they don't come with the other chemicals, like serotonin and oxytocin, which limit the high's intensity and timeline.

"That's not the worst of it, however. For some reason—and unfortunately for all addicts—the brain's reward system invariably reduces the number of dopamine receivers in response to the constant flood of dopamine an addict's behaviour is generating. Consequently, the addict needs to provide ever more of the drug to get the desired high—and the process escalates to an unhappy conclusion.

"So, to answer your question about what's going on in your heads—I don't know."

Now it was Ron's turn to hit the can. Still mulling over what Scott had suggested, he checked out his manhood at the urinal for any sign of a fungal resurgence. Much to his relief, there was none. But he did notice a slight redness and itchiness that hadn't been there yesterday.

When he sat down again, he found Scott had become uncharacteristically quiet. "What's up, buddy?"

Scott responded seriously now. "I'm worried if it's even *possible* for you and Brandi to complete the resolution. There is a chance that once you get past the honeymoon period—who knows how long that's going to last for you two freaks?—this hormone, prolactin, can act as a sex block for both the man and woman. I'm talking about, 'not tonight, honey, I've got a headache' serious stuff. Completely normal in all animals apparently, and part of the ingrained programming that encourages the broader spreading of your seed to promote diversity in the population. I thought you should know this. You know—go into it with your eyes open."

Here he paused for a sip of beer. "My guess is this is going to get harder than linear algebra, and you and Brandi are going to have to be pretty creative to have a chance at getting through this. And the thought of you guys not succeeding is strangely sad to me. It could be because when Elise and I started talking about your resolution, our sex life markedly improved. So it's probably all about me."

Ron replied, "I'm glad you brought this up, actually. Given my problems of the last couple of months, I knew this was coming. And it doesn't hurt to start thinking about some coping strategies. I suppose we may have to revisit the *Kama Sutra* as more than a novelty sex guide." He grinned. "So don't gum it up!"

"You guys have already beaten the odds," Scott said in a more upbeat tone. "Who knows? Maybe your honeymoon will last all year."

He affected a "could happen" pose...but he didn't believe it for a second.

Friday, March 13

Everybody had finished packing, and was chatting excitedly around the kitchen island. Sam was particularly excited about getting a chance to model her new bikini, and parade her newly boob-bearing body in public. They were going to an all-inclusive in Punta Cana, and the thought of soft sand, warm breezes, and endless piña coladas sounded like just what the doctor ordered. Work had been getting progressively busier for Ron, so he was lucky to get this break. It would likely be his last for a couple of months.

During the week since Scott and Ron had talked at the Bassline, he and Brandi had had a number of discussions about how the resolution was changing them. Both of them thought that they felt healthier, and intellectually a bit sharper. On the other side of the coin, Ron had admitted that his need for sex was less urgent than he remembered it being. He'd also had more difficulty in achieving orgasm during the previous week when they were making up lost ground due to Ron's medical issue. He also thought that he was starting to experience a sex-hangover that lasted into the next day.

Most disturbing to Ron, however, were his actions of a couple of days ago. He had exhausted himself, unsuccessfully attempting to climax for a second time, and upon realizing that he wasn't going to get the job done, had actually faked an orgasm when he realized he wouldn't be able to hide his waning interest for much longer. That was a first for him. In fact, the thought had never even crossed his mind until the moment he had started to feel the wind go out of his sail. He wasn't sure he'd gotten away with it, either. The experience had eroded his confidence.

It was under the pall of these two concerns that Ron prepared for his week away from the normalcy and predictability of his life.

Saturday, March 14

With the tropical sky dimming, Brandi and Ron lay in beach chairs by the pool, drinking in both the humid air and their diluted alcoholic beverages. Sam was beside them, enjoying a virgin equivalent. The sound of the nearby ocean and upbeat merengue music echoing in from somewhere in the complex fused to create a perfect moment of non-Canadian tropical bliss—exactly what they had been looking for. Ron and Brandi held hands, listening to Sam speak excitedly about her agenda for tomorrow, which included morning volleyball, sun bathing, swimming in the ocean, shell collecting, a wide sampling of tropical drinks and seafood, shopping, trampoline, and the nightly cabaret. Brandi smiled, and reminded her that they were going to be here for seven days, so she could, if she wanted, spread her activities out a bit.

After another cocktail, they all headed off to the room to fully unpack and shake off the travel with a good night's sleep. The apartment layout had them in a separate private room, adjacent to the living room where Sam's pullout bed was located. Sam had always wanted a TV in her bedroom, so the sleeping arrangements worked for everybody.

Sunday, March 15

Although the irrepressibly energetic merengue beat lasted well past their normal bedtime and into the night, over breakfast Sam commented that she had fallen asleep right away and hadn't heard a thing. The parents, on the other hand, had had plenty of energy left for each other, and had commenced the tropical vacation with an extended lovemaking session for which Ron was fully engaged and enthusiastic, and which had left him looking forward to the resumption of activities the following day. The disconcerting memory of the previous week, and the darker thoughts concerning his evolving sexual dysfunction unconsciously receded deeper into his mind.

After a full day in the sun, the three of them gathered back in the room to shower off the sunscreen and sand. Brandi and Sam were both much pinker than they had started, and although Ron's browner complexion gave him a little more protection from the tropical sun, his skin still felt a bit tender after a few hours of direct sunlight. They washed and dressed for the night's entertainment, looking forward to enjoying it much more close-up-and-personal than the previous night.

As Ron was showering, he recognized an enthusiasm and vigor in himself that he hadn't felt for some time now. *How long has it been?* he wondered. Was it the physiological changes caused by the resolution, or just winter wearing him down? All he knew for sure was he felt like his old self, and was going to make the most of every day down here, and try to carry the feeling back to Canada when they returned in a week.

Just then, Sam knocked on the door. "Dad, you asleep in there?"

Thursday, March 19

Over the week they had effortlessly settled into a hedonistic routine consisting of late breakfasts, some light exercise at either the gym or in the pools, daily beach time, great lunches and suppers, happy hour, and a surprisingly entertaining and different stage show every night. The weather had been as perfect as advertised. Ron suggested that he wouldn't be able to handle the monotony of this lifestyle for more than a couple of years. Three years, max.

The three of them had spent more quality time together in the last five days than they had in the previous five months in Ottawa. Ron's birthday was on the Wednesday and they seamlessly built the celebration into the day's activities. They were all missing Tommy, and had Skyped him yesterday to remind him that they were thinking of him, allow him to wish Dad a happy birthday, and do some old fashion weather gloating. He couldn't believe how dark they were and, conversely, Tommy looked ridiculously pale to them.

Ron and Brandi had effortlessly advanced their resolution in this idyllic, stress-free, tropical setting. It had infused them both with a youthful sexual energy that translated into longer and more exuberant sessions, usually performed against a cacophony of background sounds, including the incessant merengue beat, balcony conversations in both Spanish and English, and the TV in Sam's room. Their muffled love-making sounds were efficiently absorbed in the white-noise ambience that enveloped the resort.

While they were enjoying another late breakfast on Thursday morning, Brandi abruptly left the table. Sam and Ron, fully engaged in a spirited conversation concerning whether or not they should take the evening dancing lessons offered later that day, hardly noticed her departure. Sam was explaining a number of possible scenarios where her dad could publicly humiliate, not only himself, but his entire family for generations to come. Ron was defending himself with stories of his fabled dancing prowess from his earlier days. They were still happily volleying their good-natured remarks back and forth when Brandi returned a few minutes later, looking a bit distracted. After Ron had offered a fanciful story of him winning the national Cuban-Canadian dance competition when he was in his twenties, Sam barked a laughing guffaw and headed out for some more food.

Ron turned to Brandi and asked, "You all right, honey?"

Brandi offered a small conciliatory smile, and said, "Well, wouldn't you know it. The one time that my period comes early," and left the comment hanging.

Ron reflexively groaned. The onset of the monthly curse was never welcomed; on vacation even less so.

But, as usual, the wave of disappointment passed quickly, and Ron replied, more positively than he felt, "Well, it could have been worse. We got to enjoy five days of tropical delight."

The day progressed pretty much as all the previous ones had. After another great supper and an outstanding Michael Jackson-themed stage show, they went for their nightly nightcap at one of the many open-air bars around the complex. Over icy drinks they enthusiastically discussed their favourite parts of the show, and cooled off for bed with the early night breezes.

Even before Brandi had finished her first drink, she said she was whooped (code for cramping), and was going to head back to the room. Sam said she was tired as well, and would go back with her. Ron had just ordered a second cocktail, and indicated he'd be up shortly.

About three hours later, despite his best efforts to the contrary, Ron banged, knocked, and thumped his way into the room, through his disrobing and bathroom process, and finally into bed.

Friday, March 20

When Ron awoke to a painfully bright morning, the room was empty; the girls were already at breakfast.

He attempted to recall the events of the prior night. Although he had fully intended to down his drink and head on back to the room, a small group of similarly aged Americans had taken up residence beside him at the bar and struck up a conversation, believing him to be a fellow American. When he had corrected them as to his Canadian origin, they announced, "Close enough!", and offered to buy him a drink. Since it was an all-inclusive resort, that wasn't much of a carrot, but they did offer to spring for the undiluted higher-quality rum. That was all the arm bending Ron needed, and he accepted their offer.

Consuming a few of those stronger rums had completely released Ron from his normally conservative cocoon, and let loose the party butterfly. Before too long, he was embedded in the group, telling jokes and backslapping as if with best friends. A single lady from Michigan latched onto him, and they had talked for about an hour and a half, all the while getting progressively drunker on the stronger rum. By about one in the morning the bar was packed with boisterous inebriated tourists, one of whom was Ron. The lady from Michigan had been giving him some not-so-subtle suggestive glances, laying her hand on his arm to accentuate a point, or rewarding him for making her laugh by throwing her head back. The noise level had increased to the point where, at times, she had to talk directly into Ron's ear to be heard. A number of times her lips had fluttered against Ron's ear while she spoke.

All of this had had a doubly intoxicating effect on Ron. At about two in the morning he had glanced at his watch. Shocked at the time, he had waited until his "friend" was distracted, and then had beaten a hasty retreat back to the room, his tail wisely between his legs.

As Ron recalled the specifics of the encounter, he remembered he had definitely been attracted to the Michigan lady. He also recalled that he had been sexually aroused while talking to her, although he hadn't remembered ever seriously considering acting upon those urges.

He had never even thought about cheating on Brandi in their relationship, which was well over twenty years old now, so his newfound sexual desire for another woman had caught him off guard. As he lay in bed, his head aching, he realized that the great week he and Brandi were having was in part due to *his* increased interest in sex. No doubt the relaxed tropical setting had contributed to this, but in context with his unconscious response to the Michigan lady last night, he realized that being around scantily clad, and not uncommonly topless, women was stoking his sexual desires. As a man who prided himself on self-control and fidelity, this realization unsettled him profoundly.

Showered and accessorized with his largest and darkest sunglasses, Ron set out to track down the girls. He found them at their favourite breakfast spot, chatting comfortably and unaffectedly like good friends would. He sat down at the empty chair at the table, and smiled sheepishly. Both girls stopped talking, and stared at him with "I hope you're happy with yourself" looks.

"You were snoring so loudly, you woke me up," complained Sam. "You were so loud," here she paused for effect, "mom had to sleep with me in my bed. *And you talk in your sleep.*"

Cripes, Ron thought guiltily. *I hope I didn't say anything incriminating!*

Brandi just sat there with a placid look on her face, letting Sam act the part of chief berater, doling out humiliation with impunity.

Sam leaned in and took a big sniff of her dad. "Yeeeew! You smell bad, too."

"OK, enough already. I'm sorry for waking you guys up last night. At least I was quiet when I got home," Ron said, attempting to quell the onslaught.

Here Brandi spoke up. "If you call the banging of doors, knocking over of lamps, singing in the bathroom, and swearing when you stubbed your toe on the foot of the bed 'quiet', then yes, you were *very* quiet when you got home last night."

Ron sighed, and lifted his arms in surrender. "Really, guys, I'm sorry. It just… happened. You know—spontaneously."

As they sat there holding onto the last vestiges of their indignation, but starting to soften, Ron unwisely added as justification, "I *am* on vacation, after all." He regretted the comment before it was out of his mouth.

After a short pause, Brandi leaned in and said, "Actually Ron, *we're* on vacation."

Finally beaten, Ron's let his head drop, nodding slowly in agreement with the indisputable clarity of her statement.

"Come on, Sam, let's get ready for the beach," Brandi suggested, pushing away from the table.

After Ron had picked away at a greasy breakfast and drained a couple of cups of decent coffee, he regained some semblance of normality, and headed back to the room to catch up with the girls and continue his penance. When he got there, they had already left, so he put the *"No molestar por favor"* sign up on the door and went back to bed for a quick nap. He quickly fell into a fitful sleep, his erotic dreams filled with images of the Michigan lady naked and in numerous coital positions. He awoke with a start, covered in sweat. He was fully aroused and just about as horny as he could remember being for quite some time. He resisted the urge to masturbate, and went about distracting himself by slathering himself with sunscreen, then heading out in search of his family.

He found Brandi and Sam on the beach. An unoccupied lounger beside them suggested the door to atonement had been opened.

It wasn't the first time he had been in the dog house. He knew this initial olive branch was the first step on the path back to the main house, but he also knew he had to be on his best behaviour for the remainder of the day. He and Scott called it a "snakes-and-ladder day." A lot of hard work climbing back into the fold, but just one slip and *wham!*, you're starting all over again.

Soon after he arrived and lay back in the lounger, Sam went out with a boogie board into the light surf. Brandi got up and followed her into the ocean, up to about her knees, keeping a watch on Sam and shouting encouragement to add to her joy. As Ron lay there, he couldn't help but notice the array of bronzed and beautiful women around him. He caught himself staring more than once and, try as he may, couldn't stop himself from sneaking a peek at, and physically assessing, just about every woman who paraded up and down the beach in front of him. *Thank God for the sunglasses,* he thought as Brandi and Sam retreated from the ocean back to their lounge chairs.

After they had dried and settled into full sunbathing mode, Ron reached over, gently grasped Brandi's hand, shifted his sunglasses down on his cheek so his eyes were visible, and gave Brandi an "I'm a shithead. Sorry you married a shithead" look. She softened, smiled and squeezed his hand in response.

Ron lay back and thought, *OK, I'm on row two now. Don't do anything stupid.* Just then a knock-out Latino-looking girl in a thong bikini walked past them. Ron could feel Brandi's focus shift peripherally onto him, gauging his reaction to this visually enticing stimulus. Cognizant that Brandi would register the smallest of twitches, Ron remained completely relaxed and fought the urge to swivel his head, keeping it unmoving, cemented front and centre. Still, unable to resist, and once again very grateful for his sunglasses, he tracked her sandy-saunter with squinted scanning eyes.

After a long lunch, where Ron was pleased with the surprisingly full body-and-spirit regenerative effects that a couple of cold *cervezas* provided, the group headed back to the pool area to relax and splash around in the freshwater. They made it back to the room about an hour before sunset, the air temperature already cooling, and the audible buzz of the masses collecting on the grid of balconies surrounding them already beginning to rise in volume.

After complaining that her bed hadn't been made—Ron had forgotten to remove the "Do Not Disturb" sign—Sam grabbed a chair on their balcony, and hungrily dove back into a novel she had been reading. Brandi and Ron receded back into their room, and had their first one-on-one discussion about the previous night.

"So how much trouble did you get into last night?" asked Brandi.

Ron figured the fewer specifics the better, so he answered non-verbally, with a sheepish look.

"You were fairly pissed when you got back last night. I don't know what time it was, but I imagine you had been at it for some time, judging from how stumbly you were."

"Yeah, I know it's not like me to get like that, and around strangers too! I'm wondering if the resolution's not partially to blame."

"What do you mean?" asked Brandi.

"Like we talked about earlier, with our brains being rewired. Maybe it's starting to affect my behaviour." He threw this out, in part, as a deflection, but he was also honestly curious as to her response.

Brandi sat pondering the comment longer than Ron had expected her to. "I'm going to preface this by stating that you are culpable for your actions regardless—but I do know what you're saying. I think I've been enjoying the sex and cocktails on this trip more than usual, and although we've only lost one day concerning the resolution, I'm already missing my daily orgasm."

Ron wondered if Brandi was also being unconsciously influenced by her proximity to the well-muscled, good-looking, testosterone-charged young men present in high density around the resort. He'd leave that discussion for another day. But he did pick up on Brandi's comment concerning "missing" it. His hangover and near encounter of the extramarital kind had aroused his passions, and he cautiously suggested to Brandi, "If we're true addicts, then we should feed the beast."

Brandi reminded him, "I'm only on day two, my dear alcohol-addled husband," pointing at her crotch.

Not to be deterred, Ron pressed on. "It's not an unreasonable expectation that every warrior will bloody his sword from time to time," he said, shamelessly plagiarizing Dr. Kaur's line.

Brandi knew that Ron was no bloodhound, so she instantly realized that he was feeling it. "So what do you have in mind?"

"I would suggest we clean up in the shower and discuss it further there."

In a few minutes they were erotically engaged within the stream of tepid water from their shower. The unusual venue had excited both of them, and their session was uncharacteristically short and passionate. As Ron approached climax, his focus unintentionally drifted back to the events of the previous night, and he caught himself fantasizing about the Michigan lady. Brandi's soft groans quickly brought him back to present, but he couldn't completely shake his sexualized image of the stranger for the rest of the day.

Even though he was still muddled from his hangover, Ron knew that a threshold of sorts had been crossed this vacation and there was no going back. He had no idea what the implications for both the resolution and, possibly, his marriage were likely to be, but he did know with certainty that everything from now on would be different.

So Ron did what he did best when dealing with deep emotional issues. He boxed them away to be dealt with at a later date.

Sunday, March 22

Ron, Brandi, and Sam had arrived home Saturday to an early spring evening in Ottawa. The snowbanks had shrunk considerably since they had left and, although it was still cool, the air had an indisputably organic scent to it, indicating the seasonal thaw had commenced. There was only a one-hour time difference between the Dominican and Ottawa, but the entire travel experience had nonetheless left them wiped-out, so today they were lounging around the house, catching up on chores, and enjoying the familiarity and incomparable comfort of their own home and surroundings. Brandi had phoned both her mom and sisters in TO and provided them with a firsthand account of highlights from the vacation. Ron had driven over to his parents' place first thing that morning and checked on them, scraped the driveway and walkway clean of snow and ice, and had a quick chat about progress on their house renovations and sale.

Since he had returned home, he had been remotely and half-heartedly picking away at his work inbox. He could already see that tomorrow at the office would be a bugger, and his interest in work issues dwindled as the afternoon progressed.

Anxious and distracted, Ron stared at one email for about five minutes before he realized he hadn't yet actually read it. Feeling thoroughly unmotivated, he went onto the internet and checked the weather, the market, sports, and recent news, and unconsciously drifted into some celebrity gossip clickbait. He settled on one story concerning a wannabe mainstream soft-porn star who had become famous for her clips on a site called *YouPorn*. As Ron glanced at her photographs attached to the article, he thought that she certainly had career potential, at least with her clothes off. Ron had never heard of the *YouPorn* site, and assumed it would be a seedy internet rip-off requiring your name, SIN, and credit card number to gain access to. To his surprise, when he entered the web address into his search engine it popped up without barriers or requests for payment. He went one click further, and cautiously entered into the "porn categories" window. Ron almost fell off his chair. Unbelievably, here online, at his fingertips, was an unedited visual presentation of every possible sexual preference, every imaginable sexual act and genre, encompassing every body type, race, fetish, hair colour, group size, situation, and age. Thankfully, Ron realized, all participants appeared to be adult, and there were no animals involved. Ron counted sixty-nine categories and sexual preferences.

After about twenty minutes of skimming through the seemingly endless website, Ron signed out, completely overwhelmed and, undeniably, sexually excited. As a teenager, porn to him had been the very private viewing of well-used crumpled and dog-eared girly magazines like *Playboy*, *Penthouse*, or *Mayfair*. During those early exploratory years, there had been an informal and highly secretive cooperative made up of trusted, same-minded boys who respectfully shared a limited number of highly prized mags amongst themselves. The rules were clear and immutable. Do not get caught, and if you do, do not squeal on your friends. And do not get the pages stuck together. They had operated under these guidelines for a number of years until life's unyielding progression introduced real girls into the equation.

When he moved out during university, Ron had found a long-forgotten *Penthouse* in a disremembered hiding spot in his room. Before he chucked it deep into the garbage, he flipped through the dry and curled pages, fondly recalling the many moments fantasizing about the nude models who had bravely and shamelessly posed in them. He had endlessly dreamed about actually seeing, with his own eyes in person, a nude girl—preferably beautiful, but not being too ugly would have been OK as well. In his boldest moments, he imagined touching her breasts, the possibility of having sex not even crossing his mind.

But after seeing how ubiquitous and available sex now was, Ron realized those days of innocence were well and truly gone. Apparently, now teenagers were growing up with an unrestricted exposure to the widest imaginable range of sexual possibilities. What type of person would that create, he wondered? Would the society-wide loss of innocence at a young and tender age create a sexually jaded population, living in their parents' basements, with no need for intercourse, social or otherwise? Ron couldn't help but think that, overall, the development of social skills would suffer, and that indifference to real relationships would be increasingly more common. Whereas sex had always been a private and intimate thing for Ron, he thought it unlikely he would have developed into the man he was today in an overtly promiscuous environment without boundaries and controls. *No wonder kids today are so different—how could they not be?* His head hurt just thinking about it.

But the resolution had been slowly but surely changing Ron and his views on sexuality. The new Ron started to think about this shifting attitude towards sex from a different and more progressive perspective. His generation had placed so much emphasis and energy on the time-consuming pursuit of sex and relationships. Could unlimited early exposure to the full spectrum of carnal possibilities in life encourage some sort of positive evolution in society? Would the current generation reallocate all the time, passion, and energy saved from not pursuing sex, in the classic manner, to effecting positive change elsewhere in society?

In that moment, something clicked in Ron's head. *We're evolving into a culture that treats the hedonistic pursuit of sex in the same manner that the* Kama Sutra *preaches. Different times, to be sure, but with the same intent—demystify sex and treat it like a gift to be explored, developed, and used to better understand yourself and your relationships, and most importantly, to enhance your human experience.*

Just then Brandi called out from the kitchen, "Supper's ready!" abruptly disconnecting Ron from his musings.

Friday, March 27

It had been a few weeks since Ron and Scott had gotten together, so there was a lot to catch up on. Work had become even busier, and it was all they could do to have a quick coffee earlier in the week and set up their Friday bar therapy session.

As it turned out, Scott was able to get out of work a little after five and grab a couple of stools at the end of the bar. After fending off a number of inquiries as to the availability of the unoccupied seat beside him, he was relieved to see Ron enter the bar just before six. The weather had now settled into early spring, with rain showers more common than snow and, consequently, there was a much-reduced chance of frostbite while venturing outside.

Ron peeled off a thin jacket when he reached Scott. "Packed in here again," he said, stating the obvious while looking around. Immediately after he parked himself he started pouring a beer from the half-filled jug.

"I've had a few offers from some ladies who were far more attractive than yourself, so I hope you're appreciative of the seat," Scott said.

"Thank you for concerning yourself with my well-being," Ron volleyed, "but we both know that they would have gotten up and left after talking with you for a couple of minutes. I am, sadly for you, your best bet tonight for a conversation of substance lasting more than ten minutes."

Scott chuckled and agreed. "You're probably right there, buddy. Cheers." After a perfunctory clinking of glasses, he asked, "Well, how was the Dominican? Judging from your colour, the weather must have been pretty good."

"We loved it," Ron said. "I'd definitely recommend it for a week's vacation. As with all these kind of places, after a week the food and repetition of the venues start to become tedious, but for a week—perfect. Direct flight from Ottawa, reasonably priced, real nice people, great weather and beach, and no hassles. Just what the doctor ordered."

"Christ, I'm sold already. I'll book it as soon as I get home," Scott said with mock conviction.

After about ten minutes of office talk Scott broached the subject that was at the top of his "not work" list. "So, how's the resolution going?"

"Well, we're still on track."

"Congratulations!" Scott raised his glass in a toast. "Well done. You're now," he quickly calculated, "about twenty-three-percent complete."

Ron blew his breath out through his pursed lips and replied, "It sure feels all of that and a bit more, I can tell you."

"Oh-oh. Some further 'challenges'?"

"You could say that."

"OK, let's hear it."

Ron told Scott about the disconcerting desires for other women he had experienced while he was on vacation. He neglected to mention his close encounter with the Michigan lady. As he sat there, waiting for a response from Scott, he realized that he was a bit embarrassed.

Scott picked up on this. "That's nothing to be ashamed about, Ron. The amazing thing—to me, anyways—is that it's never happened to you before now. Honestly, Ron, every guy is hardwired to automatically sexually assess women. Amongst all the mammals on earth, only about three percent are monogamous. Humans are not part of that group. We're hybrids. We've evolved into a socially monogamous species as a way to protect our offspring, but physiologically we're still sexually polygamous. Now there's the real *yin* and *yang* of the human spirit."

He let this sink in for a couple of seconds, and then asked, "Have you ever heard of the Coolidge Effect?"

Ron shook his head.

"It's a term developed by a behaviourist named Frank Beach in the 1950s to explain the near-ubiquitous mammalian phenomenon of sexual ambivalence towards an established mate, and extra-pair promiscuity. As the story goes, while American president Calvin Coolidge and his wife were visiting a farm, Mrs. Coolidge was told about a rooster who would mate with the hens all day, day in, day out. She was so impressed by this she asked the farmer to tell the president about the famed rooster. When the president heard about this, he asked if the tireless cock did this with the same hen. The farmer answered that it did not. President Coolidge then asked the farmer to 'please tell that to Mrs. Coolidge.'"

Both guys laughed out loud at the punchline.

"The point is," Scott continued, "that sexual desire outside of a relationship is normal. It's our challenge to control those desires. The fact that you're just dealing with it now shows that you most certainly are an exception. You and

Brandi have an incredibly unique relationship, and the two of you are probably so balanced and matched for each other that it's taken both the unrelenting stress of the resolution and twenty years of marriage to develop an issue that most married couples have to deal with before they're even married."

Ron looked at Scott, raising his eyebrows in a "like you and Elise?" query.

"Absolutely," confirmed Scott. "We're just a normal couple, forced to be content with the odd crumb of joy sparingly meted out by life. Our sex life is hard work. Always has been. We struggle with boredom and ambivalence, like the majority of couples out there."

Ron replied, "I honestly didn't have any idea. Or if I did, I ignored it because I didn't have to think about it, given how happy Brandi and I have been."

"That's why Elise and I are so interested in your resolution. Is there a magic pill, mindset, or specific practice that can help us rediscover the passion and sexual satisfaction we had in the beginning of our relationship? I'm hoping—no, *we're* hoping—that you and Brandi are going to stumble across something while completing your resolution that'll provide both insight and remedy."

Scott paused for a mouthful of beer. "So now that you are starting to experience what just about every other man who has ever lived on this earth has experienced, from my perspective I think this is great news. Because *you* need to have the disease before *you* can find the cure."

"Well, I'm glad that my troubles are reason for your optimism."

"I'm your friend, Ron. I'm here to help. So as long as you don't act on your urges, and you rule them and not vise-versa, this can be managed." Scott lifted his mug. "And welcome to everybody else's world my friend."

During the break in the conversation provided by beer, Ron mulled over how he would bring up the next topic. He was staring down at his lap, nervously debating how to broach the subject, when he suddenly blurted out, "I've discovered porn."

"What the hell does that mean?"

Ron recounted how he had stumbled across the *YouPorn* website the previous weekend, and asked, "Did you know this stuff was out there?"

Scott stared at him for a second, and then replied, "Duh, yeah. Are you telling me you had no idea these online porn sites existed?"

Ron shook his head that he hadn't.

"Once again, you are proving yourself uniquely unprepared to manage adult life," Scott said with disbelief.

"Do you know the extent to which this site covers every aspect of sex?"

Scott nodded affirmatively.

"And that it's all free and unrestricted?"

Once again, an affirmative nod from Scott.

Ron paused, and asked no one in particular, "Where do all these people come from?"

Scott assumed that Ron knew he couldn't answer that question, so he treated it rhetorically. "And there's another one called *PornHub* that you want to check out. Pretty much the same as *YouPorn*, but with different videos and its own cast of aspiring actors."

"Unbelievable," muttered Ron.

"So what's the problem, other than the loss of both your innocence and your faith in mankind?" asked Scott.

Ron took a deep breath. "You know how I had been engaging in a little female fantasy in the Dominican to help me along with the resolution?"

Scott nodded.

"Well, since I've found the 'site', I've been using it in the same way. You know, to get me a bit fired up so I can perform a little better with Brandi."

He waited for Scott's response, which was an uncomfortably long time in coming. With a serious face, Scott said, "Not good, Ron. That's a slippery slope, to be sure. Online porn is like any other addiction. It'll give you a quick and uncomplicated high, and have you coming back for ever more outrageous sexual activity to find that heightened level of excitement."

Ron came to his own defense. "I'm not using it to get off. God knows I haven't got any to spare these days! I'm just using it to…you know…get my engine started."

Scott just stared at Ron.

"What?" Ron asked.

Scott replied, "Are you fantasizing about these women when you're with Brandi?"

Ron could feel the heat rising in his face, and knew his reddening cheeks were providing Scott with the answer.

"That's just the start, Ron. Pretty soon you'll start associating your sexual desires with these online women and, well…it's only a matter of time before you won't be able to get and stay aroused by Brandi."

After letting that comment sink in, Scott asked, "Have you got to be home anytime soon?"

"I've got time. I'm bachin' it for the weekend. Sam and Brandi have headed down to TO to see her mom and Tommy, but I had to hang and catch up on my workload after the Dominican."

"Good," said Scott. "Because I've been looking into this subject since you drew me into this resolution with the *Kama Sutra*, and things may be about to get real tough for you, my friend."

"Tougher than it already is?" asked Ron incredulously.

"Unfortunately, it looks that way. Your current sexual regime with Brandi is causing something called 'self-induced anhedonia.' That's a neurological phenomenon that reduces your sensitivity to pleasure, and is the primary cause of compulsive behaviour and addiction. What's particularly dangerous about these online sex sites, compared to scoping out girls on a beach, for example, is you can search out and find *exactly* which erotic idiosyncrasies lie at the core of your own sexuality. These are unique to every person, a product of your life experiences and, probably, your inherited genetic make-up as well. You'll know which erotic idiosyncrasies work for you, because these are the sexual elements that excite you the most, reward you with a flood of dopamine, and will beckon you back with ever-increasing frequency. Unless Brandi embodies these exact idiosyncrasies, she won't stand a chance against the rest of the world. So, that's a long-winded bit of advice for you."

"So what do I do now? Do you think the resolution is dust?"

"Not necessarily. Since you've got some time, let's order another pitcher and see if we can't work out a strategy," suggested Scott.

Once the beer arrived, Scott refilled his mug, and said, "Let me start by quoting the unflappable Miss Rose Sayer."

"Who is Rose Sayer?"

"Rose Sayer was the Methodist missionary in *The African Queen*, played by Katharine Hepburn, who starred opposite the hardened and unrefined Canadian-born Charlie Allnut, played by Humphrey Bogart. In the movie, Rose tells Charlie, 'Nature, Mr. Allnut, is something we were put on this earth to rise above.' And that, my friend, is exactly what you need to do."

"And how do I do that?" Ron pleaded.

"What the hell do I look like? A sex therapist?" retorted Scott. "All I can do is give you some general advice and provide someone to bounce the ideas off. To have *a chance* at getting through this resolution, you're going to need some professional help."

Ron gave him a "WTF" glare, and responded, "Are you nuts? We don't need to go to a friggin' therapist."

Scott calmly responded, "Well, apparently you do. You're up against millions of years of neuroprogramming, and frankly, you're unprepared. You have very little sexual experience, an inclination for porn, and you've started to fantasize about other women while you're having sex with your wife. The fact you haven't sought out professional help already may be construed as emotional and marital indifference at best."

Ron sat there silent, a look of disbelief painted on his face.

"Do what you want, buddy, but you're only a quarter of the way through the resolution. You've got to ask yourself the question—can I reasonably expect to succeed by doing *nothing?*"

It was close to nine when Ron got home. The emptiness of the house instantly hit him. While at the Bassline Pub, he had resisted Scott's advice to seek out counseling, but agreed to talk with Brandi about the developing issues on Sunday when she returned from TO.

He warmed up some leftovers, grabbed a glass of wine, and went downstairs to watch some sports. The Sens had been having a great March, and it looked as if they'd make the playoffs this year, so he had started following them a lot closer. As Ron settled in for some mindless viewing, he was feeling a bit antsy, and couldn't get comfortable. He went through a mental checklist of what it could be—thirsty, no; hungry, yes, but dealing with that; have to go pee, no; sports, check; missing Brandi, yes, but not desperately—and froze mid-chew when the brief consideration of visiting the porn site instantly alleviated his anxiety.

Sunday, March 29

Ron had used his work all weekend long to distract himself from the disconcerting thought that he might have become a porn addict. Brandi and Sam weren't planning to get back into Ottawa until about eight o'clock Sunday evening, so Ron had an early supper and went to hockey as per usual. He planned to skip the post-game beer so he'd get back home early enough to talk with Brandi. The prospect and subject of the conversation with Brandi had been bothering him all weekend, and at hockey he was so distracted and ineffective that a couple of the guys asked if he was feeling all right. One guy asked if he had his skates on the wrong feet.

When he walked into the house he could hear the girls talking in the kitchen, and was filled with the warmth of familiarity that reuniting with loved ones brings. After catching up on the news from the family in TO, he and Brandi poured themselves glasses of wine. They typically didn't drink at home on Sundays, but Brandi needed to relax after the road trip, and Ron was missing his post-hockey beer.

As the wine relaxed the two of them, and they slid towards each other on the couch, Ron nervously started into the discussion. "So...I had a nice session with Scott Friday after work."

"Oh, yeah? How are he and Elise doing?"

"I think pretty well. He remarked again that our resolution has improved their love life. How about that?"

"I think the thought of it captures the imagination of couples looking to revisit the glory days. From the woman's perspective, it could even be considered a romantic initiative."

"I think the guys just want to get laid more often," Ron said.

Brandi playfully elbowed his ribs.

"You know that we've been dealing with some 'changes' during the resolution," he continued. He paused long enough for Brandi to nod in agreement, and then said, "I think it may be changing me more than you."

"What makes you say that?"

"Well, ever since the Dominican, I've been..." He paused, then decided to point the finger directly at the real culprit. "My *brain's* been attempting to direct me towards other women."

He left that comment hanging.

After a few seconds, Brandi asked, "So you've been looking at other women?"

Checking for any concern in Brandi's eyes, and not seeing it, he continued. "You make it sound creepy, but yes, down in the Dominican I found myself *unintentionally* checking some of them out."

Ron waited for a response from Brandi, and felt a wave of relief wash over him when a smile grew on her face. "I know every guy does that, Ron. I think it's adorable that you feel guilty enough to have to tell me about it." Brandi leaned over and kissed him. "I check out guys as well," she added matter-of-factly. "I'm just better at it than you are, and I don't feel guilty when I do." She pursed her lips in a "so there" look.

Ron liked the way the conversation had gone up to this point; well, except the part about his wife lusting after other men. But he knew it was just the beginning of their chat.

Brandi's coy smile faded when Ron didn't respond in kind. "There's more, isn't there?" Brandi asked.

Ron nodded sheepishly and replied, "A bit, yeah. You see, after the Dominican, I stumbled across a porn site, and out of curiosity had a look, and I think it may have ruined me."

"How do you mean, 'ruined you'?"

"Well, I can't get some of the images out of my mind, and I've been using them to…well, get myself 'psyched up' for our daily sessions." He smiled and nodded, adding, "And that's been working pretty good so far."

His smile quickly evaporating as he met Brandi's stern gaze. He coughed and continued. "But I was starting to worry that these images could be replacing you in some ways. Scott and I talked about this."

Brandi asked, "You've talked to Scott about this?"

Ron froze, and sheepishly answered, "Yes?"

Brandi sighed, but didn't say anything, so Ron continued. "And he suggested this behaviour was not going to be productive to either the resolution or our marriage, and I should talk to you about it."

Ron waited.

Brandi finally replied, "Well, I'm liking that Scott more every day." She paused a moment. "I'm not pissed at you, Ron. In fact, I'm glad you decided to discuss this. I've been worried that the resolution was causing you some problems, and

I'm not surprised we've got issues. I think the first decision is whether to ditch the resolution, or figure out some coping mechanisms to manage it going forward."

Ron grabbed Brandi's hand, and looked into her eyes. "I've been thinking about that all weekend, and you know we've already made it a quarter of the way, and I still think we should stick with it to make us stronger, individually and as a couple. The fact that I've been having troubles tells me it's doing just that - even though it doesn't feel that way at the moment." He paused briefly. "I want to keep going."

"OK, then, what do you propose?" asked Brandi.

Ron pensively inhaled, and replied, "That part I haven't figured out yet. Scott suggested going to a counselor, but…"

Brandi jumped in. "That sounds like a great idea."

Ron stared back at her. "Really?"

"Sure, why not? If we've got nine more months of this, we're going to need all the help we can get. You're committed to the resolution, aren't you?"

Ron knew he was negotiating from a very weak position, and recognized he was beaten. After a couple of seconds, he gave her a resigned look and answered, "OK. I'll try and book something next week."

Brandi squeezed his hand, and commented, "Now that we have that out of the way, how about we go upstairs and continue this resolution of ours?"

Ron smiled back.

"Will you be requiring a few minutes with your computer beforehand, or can we head upstairs directly?"

CHAPTER 5

A HELPING HAND

Tuesday, April 7

Ron procrastinated for the better part of a week, until Brandi's more frequent and increasingly firmer reminders finally drove him to peruse the internet for a therapist or counselor. He had no idea where to look, and he certainly wasn't going to ask any of his friends or family.

The array of help on offer was impressive. There were marriage counselors, psychologists, pastoral counselors, couple psychotherapists, psychiatrists, hypnotherapists, reflexologists, EFT practitioners, naturopaths, holistic therapists, and a whole suite of alternative and spiritual healers.

But Ron didn't contact anybody from any of those professions. To Ron, his problems were born of sex, and had evolved because of and through sex. In Ron's mind there was only one professional who could help him, and that was a sex therapist. Even this relatively narrow vocational search revealed more than forty qualified sex therapists in the Ottawa region.

As he looked over the available professional help, he initiated a discriminating filtering process. *Not a guy-check; taking new patients-check; available evenings-check. Hey—she's cute. And look at those qualifications!*

So it was through this clinically discerning approach that Ron happened to find and arrange an appointment for himself and Brandi the evening of Tuesday, April 7, with Dr. Fiona Xanthopoulos, Ph.D., LPC, CST, and a member of the AASECT. Ron thought if she couldn't help them, their situation was likely hopeless.

Brandi and Ron showed up at Dr. Xanthopoulos' office just after six o'clock, both of them a little nervous about this initial session. After checking in with a tired-looking receptionist, they quietly sat by themselves in the dimly lit waiting room, awkwardly holding hands. Both were avoiding making inadvertent eye contact with each other. After a couple of minutes, Brandi removed her hand from Ron's, wiped his sweat from her palm, gave him a quick smile, and refolded her hands in her lap. This only added to Ron's angst. His hands were now sweating copiously.

After a few more minutes, the silence got to Ron. He had just leaned in towards Brandi to get her attention when Dr. Xanthopoulos slipped into the waiting room. A petite lady of about fifty years of age, she exuded a peaceful and professional aura that instantly put Ron at ease. As he and Brandi rose, Ron wiped his palms on his jeans, and started to offer his hand to the doctor, whom he recognized from her website.

"Fiona Xanthopoulos," she said cheerily beating Ron to the punch. "But please, call me Dr. Fiona."

When the three of them got settled into Dr. Fiona's office, she grabbed a pad of paper and a pen, lay them on her lap, smiled brightly at Ron and Brandi ,and asked, "Is this your first time at sex counselling?"

Since Ron had selected both the type of counselling they were currently considering and this particular doctor, he answered. "The first counselling of any kind, actually."

Dr. Fiona paused. "So a fairly good, stable relationship?"

Both Ron and Brandi nodded affirmatively.

"Good to hear," said the doctor, meaning it more than they could possibly know. "How long have you been married?"

Here Brandi spoke up, stating somewhat proudly, "We'll have been married twenty years this July."

Dr. Fiona nodded encouragingly. "Any kids?"

Brandi told her about Tommy and Sam.

Dr. Fiona continued gathering more background on the two very normal people in front of her, until, after about twenty minutes of filling in the blanks, she looked at them quizzically and asked, somewhat rhetorically, "So you two have had a long and solid marriage?"

Ron and Brandi nodded in unison.

"Everybody in the immediate family healthy and well-adjusted?"

More nodding from Ron and Brandi.

"Active sex life, no infidelity or major relationship conflicts?"

The nodding continued.

"So," the doctor paused and took off her glasses, "What exactly brings you to my office today?"

Brandi filled her in.

The three of them sat quietly while Dr. Fiona, scribbling notes on her pad, sorted the information that she had just heard. Ron noticed his hands were sweating again.

After a few moments, Dr. Fiona stopped writing, removed her glasses, took a deep breath, and searched for the right words with which to respond. "Whose idea was this?" she asked, a little too seriously for Ron's liking.

Brandi silently and slowly pointed her index finger at Ron.

Ron offered his best, "sure, I'm an idiot, but I mean well" look to the doctor.

She wasn't affected by his charm. "So what was your objective with this resolution, Ron?"

"It's pretty straightforward, really. I like having a resolution every year to challenge myself. I love my wife. I've always wanted to involve her in one of my resolutions and ….voila!" He added the final flourish to see if he could get Dr. Fiona to smile. It didn't work.

"Ron, this resolution is…'wrong' is too harsh a word. Let's say 'ill-conceived', for a number of reasons, too many to go into in this session. The most disconcerting thing is that you've hijacked *the* primary mechanism that you and Brandi use to demonstrate and re-affirm your love to each other as a *daily goal*."

"Daily-ish," Ron interjected, raising his index finger as a prop in correcting the doctor. "We can make up the days that we missed."

Dr. Fiona silently stared at Ron.

Believing her silence a request for further clarification, he added, "You know— for the 'time of month' thing—or if one of us is off traveling alone."

After a few beats, Dr. Fiona removed her glasses again, and look directly at Ron. "You're playing with fire here, Ron."

Brandi then interjected, coming to Ron's defense. "*We're* playing with fire, doctor." The tone caught Dr. Fiona a bit off guard: she appeared to be surprised by Brandi's complicity.

"It may have been his idea, but both of us decided to attempt this resolution, Dr. Fiona. We knew it was going to be a challenge when we started." She looked at Ron. "And we haven't been disappointed so far." She turned her gaze back to the doctor. "We've come to you looking for help in completing the resolution, not for you to talk us out of it. So can you help?"

Dr. Fiona sat, looking serious and uncomfortable, obviously mulling over the pros and cons of taking on the unique challenges of this couple. After the better part of a minute, she looked up from her lap, leaned forward, and spoke her thoughts out loud. "Well, I can honestly tell you that you two are about as well-adjusted as any couple that's ever walked through that door. Given your unified determination concerning this resolution, your personalities, your commitment to each other, and the fact that you've made it this far, I think there actually is a *chance* that you could complete it without doing irreparable damage to your marriage. *Maybe.* And with some serious assistance. What you're attempting is, in essence, a social and physiological experiment. And if you're both OK with it, I'd be willing to take you on *pro bono if* I can publish a paper about your resolution at the end of it. You would both remain anonymous, of course. I'll let you two discuss my offer. I'll be right outside."

Dr. Fiona left the room, while Ron and Brandi stared at each other with "WTF was that?" looks on their faces.

ॐ

When they got home, Sam was in the living room, lying on the floor on her back, feet against the wall, with her earplugs in, doing math homework. She pulled one plug from an ear when she saw them, and asked, "How was date night?"

Brandi looked at Ron, smiled, and said, "Romantic, as always."

Concerning Dr. Fiona's proposal, Ron and Brandi both agreed being regarded as an experiment made both of them uncomfortable, but the offered anonymity helped mitigate that issue. The thought of having to do this all over again with another doctor was unappealing, and the *pro bono* offer from Dr. Fiona was also attractive. Ultimately, though, it was Dr. Fiona's affable and genuine personality, and her awareness and conscious protection of their marriage that convinced them to accept her offer.

Saturday, April 11

After Ron and Brandi agreed to Dr. Fiona's proposal, it was decided to set aside an hour every Saturday morning for counseling. In advance of their inaugural session, Dr. Fiona asked them to complete and email her back a questionnaire she had given them dealing with their family, education, and their sex lives, along with some personality-related questions. When they got to the otherwise empty office at nine on Saturday morning, Dr. Fiona cheerfully greeted them at the door, ushered them into her office, and offered them some coffee. As they settled onto the couch, sipping the coffee, Dr. Fiona sat a few feet away at her desk, shuffling pages containing, Ron assumed, the personal details he and Brandi had forwarded to her the previous day.

Thank God for doctor-client privilege, Ron thought. It was difficult enough for him to talk about these details in this environment. The mere thought of any broader dissemination made Ron feel ill.

While he was actively suppressing these nauseating thoughts, Dr. Fiona spoke. "Thank you both for forwarding this information to me. I know a lot of it was very personal, but with this background material we can make the most of our time together."

Both Ron and Brandi nodded.

"The information you have sent me corroborates my initial thoughts concerning you two. I think that while we're tackling the primary challenges caused by the resolution, and further enriching your marital environment, at the same time, we may be able to gain some profound insights into brain function and human sexuality and, perhaps, help some people down the road. That's my working hypothesis, anyway."

Ron said, "You know, Dr. Fiona, of the small group of people that know about our resolution, all of them are supportive, and finding it an inspiration for their own love lives."

"That's good to hear, Ron, and not surprising, really. As you guys know, marriage is hard work and, as someone active in this profession, I see a general malaise or fatigue amongst most couples that suggests there are, typically, fundamental difficulties in every marriage. No one ever gets married to get divorced, so if couples are forewarned, they can be forearmed to deal with the inevitable issues that arise in long-term relationships.

"Your resolution is likely triggering these typical marital issues that you've escaped to this point because…well, because of who you both are—and it's likely accelerating their development, given the intensity of the resolution. I believe we can causally relate your recent and ongoing physiological and interpersonal changes back to the effects of the resolution. I'm expecting that, over the course of this resolution, you guys are going to experience all the challenges one would typically expect to encounter through the course of an entire marriage.

"Our goal is to not only identify them, but find remedies for them that we will be able to use as a template to help the broader population; who'll, by the way, be typically experiencing them at a much slower rate. More of a creep, as opposed to hitting it on the head with a hammer like you guys are doing. Any questions?"

Ron and Brandi sat silent, somewhat overwhelmed by Dr. Fiona's insights and enthusiasm. Any hopeful view that they were not going to be an experiment had been dispelled. For the next eight months, they would be living in a Petri dish of sorts, with Dr. Fiona as the observing scientist.

Brandi asked, "No issues if we decide that we want to withdraw from the 'experiment'?"

"Of course I'll be disappointed," replied Dr. Fiona, "but there are no strings attached here. Keep in mind, my first obligation is to your marriage, the second is to the resolution, and the third is to the publication of my findings."

Both Brandi and Ron were relieved to hear these words. Rubbing his hands together, Ron then suggested, "Well, let's get on with it then, shall we?" in an indistinct faux-posh accent, possibly of midtown Toronto provenance.

Dr. Fiona started by asking for some further clarifications. Looking at Brandi, she asked, "So I see that the frequent sexual activity has, at times, been painful?"

Brandi nodded affirmatively, but when she realized that the doctor had directed the question to her she clarified, "No, not me, Doctor. That's Ron. I've been physically fine throughout this so far."

"Oh, sorry," Dr. Fiona muttered, as she shuffled a page from one pile to the other.

Ron could feel the heat rising into his face, and was sure that he was nicely blushed by the time the doctor finally refocused her attention on him. He explained. "It was because we were trying to catch up after Brandi's period. And we were using a new toy. And I was having trouble, you know, climaxing more than once. Oh yeah, and I was trying out one of the 'male-assistance' drugs that my doctor had given me."

Dr. Fiona commented, "Under those circumstances, it's probably fortunate that you didn't do yourself serious damage, Ron."

With his cheeks still warm and flushed, Ron yielded. "In hindsight, I guess I was pushing myself. It was the first time we had used either the 'toy' or the pharmaceuticals, and we probably should have phased them in. We've gotten better at using them since then."

"Two things really interest me about this," added Dr. Fiona. "Why did you think the 'toy' was needed, and why do you think you were having trouble climaxing?"

As the blood finally started to drain from Ron's face, he exhaled and replied. "Well, the toy was for Brandi." He explained its construct and intent. "But really, it was for me. Brandi has no trouble orgasming."

Dr. Fiona looked over at Brandi, and sporting a grin, Brandi gave her a "what can I say?" look and shoulder shrug.

"And I've realized that her pleasure was my pleasure. So the more she orgasmed, the more turned on I got. So although the toy was for Brandi, it was for me as well."

"Sounds like the perfect toy to me," commented Dr. Fiona. "Sorry, go on, Ron."

"So, we were just getting used to it, and I was having trouble orgasming." Ron paused thoughtfully, and added, "It actually wasn't very long into the resolution when I had first experienced this difficulty—sometime in mid- to late

January—and I got really concerned about it. I really didn't know how to deal with it, so, on the advice of a friend, we started using the *Kama Sutra* to 'spice things up.'"

"Did it work?" asked the doctor.

"Yes, for a while," responded Ron, "but then the problem reoccurred and I went searching for other remedies—thus the pills and the toy."

"And did those work?"

"Yes, again for a while, but it all seemed…how do I put this? Like band-aids on a deep wound. Temporary fixes—if you know what I'm trying to say?"

Dr. Fiona was scribbling furiously. After a few seconds she looked up and replied, "I most certainly do, Ron. Please continue."

Gathering his thoughts, Ron said, "Then I started checking out other women when we were on vacation, and then, when I returned from vacation, I progressed to porn and thinking about those visuals to 'get up' for the task. It was when I realized I was craving porn that I realized I either had, or would soon have, a problem, and I talked to Brandi, and we decided to seek out some help."

The doctor finished taking a few notes, then took off her glasses and said, "Well, Ron, you don't have a problem, and you should be congratulated for recognizing these earliest signs of sexual fatigue and acting upon it as you have."

Now sporting a smug smile, Ron sat back in his chair, quite prepared to accept any praise the doctor was doling out.

"What you're experiencing is a progressively worsening sex hangover. When you orgasm, your body releases a hormone called prolactin. Prolactin is *the* satiation chemical that immediately suppresses your sexual desire after orgasm. Prolactin not only makes it difficult to orgasm a second time, it starts to build-up in your system over time with over-stimulation—which is exactly what you and Brandi are doing with the resolution. This hangover can last several days or more before your system totally equilibrates. Your resolution doesn't allow your body to ever recover, and the sex-suppressing hormones continue to build up. And that's not the worst of it. With excessive stimulation," here Dr. Fiona opened her hands to take in both Brandi and Ron, "your brain's ability to feel pleasure is diminished due to overuse of the receptors in your pleasure centres, and, probably, concomitant reduction of dopamine production in your brain. Since dopamine acts as a suppressor of prolactin, when you start producing less dopamine, prolactin production increases. You get a negative feedback loop that gangs up to work against you."

"If my sexual pleasure centre is becoming numbed, what's with me looking at other women?"

"That's the interesting part. It appears that we humans retain primitive hard-wiring which devotes a limited amount of pleasure circuitry to any one partner. To encourage maximum genetic diversity, the polygamous mammalian brain comes over-engineered with ample pleasure circuitry in reserve, and sex with a new partner will utilize fresh pathways, delivering—reminiscent of the good old days—high doses of dopamine to fresh pink receptors.

"Consequently, when you look sexually at women, you're unconsciously, instantly, and holistically, creating a relationship with them and having glorious and gratifying sex. All of this in a fraction of a second! If this front-end experience is satisfactory, you may even start to fall in love—love at first sight. And it can be repeated over and over again *ad infinitum*; there's plenty of redundant circuitry for sexual rewards built into our brains. In this context, the wonder isn't why men look at other women; it's *how do they not?*

"From your history, Ron—if you're telling me the truth and you've only started experiencing this phenomenon recently—your newfound wandering eye is, in all likelihood, a direct result of the degradation of your *marital* pleasure centre, brought on by overstimulation during the resolution. Very cool, right? Now you understand why I'm so interested in what you guys are doing."

Ron nodded, recalling what he and Scott had discussed earlier. "The Coolidge Effect," he said.

"You've done your homework on this, Ron," the doctor responded.

Ron smiled as he proudly and shamelessly took the credit for Scott's research.

"Yes, that's the terminology that captures this phenomenon," replied the doctor. "But again, that's where it gets interesting. I'm not looking at spending my valuable professional time with you and Brandi to confirm that you embody the willpower of a chicken or a bull. No, I'm interested to see how we, as sentient human beings, separate ourselves from the less evolved and less cerebrally advanced organisms on this Earth. Ron, I'm looking to explore your *humanity* over the next few months."

Oh my God, the humanity, thought Ron. After a few seconds, he asked, "What about Brandi?"

"What do you mean, Ron?"

"I mean, why isn't she as affected by the resolution as I am?" asked Ron.

Brandi jumped in. "That's true, Dr. Fiona. My orgasms are becoming more frequent and more powerful."

"No question, Brandi, the woman's brain is wired and programed differently than a man's. Your chemistry is biased towards stability for the family and, consequently, your pleasure pathways are more durable than those in a man's brain. You are much better suited to this kind of resolution than Ron.

"That's not meant to diminish the significance of *your* challenges during the course of the resolution, Brandi—and there likely *will* be some for you—but I expect Ron will be more challenged over the next few months. Sexually, the woman's brain is made for marathons, while the man's brain is best suited for sprinting."

Ron thought that comment was apropos, given how exhausted he was suddenly feeling. "This has been a lot to absorb, Dr. Fiona," he said. "Can we call it a day?"

"Sure, Ron. But first, let me give you and Brandi an exercise to practice over the next week."

Sunday, April 12

"I don't see what this has to do with anything," complained Ron.

"Shhhh. You're ruining the ambiance, Ron. Just keep massaging. And don't forget to get in between the toes."

Dr. Fiona had told Ron to massage Brandi's hands or feet every day for at least fifteen minutes, alternating between them, one day before, and the next day after, their coital encounter. Today, Ron had chosen feet for *after* their lovemaking. "Am I even doing this right?" he asked.

"You're doing just fine, my sweet. Now less talking and more massaging. You may want to use a bit more lotion. In between the toes now. Yeah, that's good."

After a few minutes, Ron settled into the moment and relaxed. *She does have lovely feet,* he was thinking. It had been a long time since he'd spent this much time on a part of her body that didn't engorge with blood, have a mucous membrane, or secrete bodily fluids. When he thought about it, he actually couldn't remember spending this much time on her feet—ever. He'd been with this woman for more than twenty years and was just now exploring her feet. He found that curious.

What other unexplored domains were waiting for discovery, he wondered. After ten minutes Brandi fell asleep, but Ron kept massaging until she woke up about a half hour later.

Monday, April 13

As Ron walked home, he felt an optimism that had been evading him for the last while. It could have been the brilliantly sunny warm day; it was currently twenty-one degrees—the first day this year that the temperature had risen above twenty degrees. It could have been the rejuvenating feeling the budding leaves and song-singing birds were providing. It could have been that work was going great. It could have been all of this, but Ron knew these factors were playing backup to the real reason he felt so positive today. It was the resolution. Since he and Brandi had met with Dr. Fiona on the weekend, he again believed that he could actually finish this damned resolution. Now with Brandi fully on board and Dr. Fiona helping, he felt a confidence that he hadn't felt since early January. He now knew that completing the resolution was far more than not failing. He knew that he was going up against the nature of things, and the odds were against him. This thought made him more determined than ever to complete the resolution; hopefully with his marriage intact.

Closing in on his house, he turned onto Baseline Road and thought of the Bassline Pub. He wondered if Scott would be available for a beer on Friday.

Friday, April 17

"A sex therapist, eh?" Scott said. "She any good?"

"Brandi and I really like her. And get this—she's offered to take us on *pro bono.*"

"No kidding? Why is she doing that?"

"Well, she thinks our resolution is a bit of an experiment, given we've been together as long as we have, and we've had such a solid relationship. She figures that any issues that are now occurring in our marriage can be directly attributed to the resolution—so we're now officially being 'observed.' And she may want to publish the results—anonymously, of course. We've only had one working session with her, and the first therapy she suggested was for me to massage Brandi's hands and feet every day."

Scott chortled. "Sounds like Brandi's getting some preferential treatment."

"That's what I thought as well, but as I got into it, I found that I didn't mind it. I normally don't spend any time on Brandi's hands or feet—she has far more interesting bits to explore—but the massaging does something for me. I think it builds a stronger emotional connection."

"Sounds like you're being duped," Scott joked.

"That's exactly it, Scotty. My friggin' brain is trying to vote Brandi off the island, and we're looking at ways to trick it into accepting her back into the inner circle. I have a feeling the brain-level skullduggery and deception has only begun." Ron raised his glass to the prospect of successfully fooling himself.

"You'd like this doctor too," he continued. "She spoke of the neurochemical mix that you mentioned to me last month. When I brought up the Coolidge Effect, she indicated that this was our—as in us guys'—cross to bear, and our challenge was to use our humanity to rise above the instinct of a cow."

"I thought it was a chicken?" queried Scott.

"Apparently the same phenomenon exists in cattle as well."

"Well, that changes everything. I probably had a reasonable chance of out-thinking a chicken, but all bets are off if I have match wits against a cow. So how are you guys actually feeling about the resolution now?"

"After meeting with Dr. Fiona, and this first week of 'light therapy', as she calls it, I'm feeling reinvigorated. Not only about the resolution, but also in general. I think I may have turned a corner on this."

"Christ, maybe Elise and I should go see Dr. Fiona. Better yet, I'll just keep picking up pointers from you for free. Hey, speaking of which, do you want your *Kama Sutra* back?"

Ron nodded. "I think so." He thought about it again and added, "Do I?"

Scott ignored him, and continued. "You know, the more I think about it, you and Brandi should really consider starting a blog, or more appropriate these days, a Twitter account, where people could follow your progress. You can dispense unsolicited advice-bites based on your own experiences, and save marriages in the process. If just one marriage can be saved…!" Scott added, *faux*-seriously, stabbing the air with his index finger, reminiscent of their safety manager speaking of accident avoidance.

Ron guffawed. "There is no way that either Brandi or I would ever go along with that. Can you imagine what the kids would think? Our families? Everybody at our work? It would be torture. Poor Sam would likely have to change schools... and her name! Besides, I'm not even sure we could help anyone," Ron added with finality.

Scott grabbed a wing and let Ron cool down a touch, then suggested, "You know you could do it anonymously."

Ron sincerely asked, "Why would we want our personal details in the public eye?"

Scott paused and searched for the right words. "Look, Ron, I think you and Brandi are in a very special time and place right now, and are uniquely positioned to help some people out. I wasn't kidding when I mentioned that I thought you guys could provide a little inspiration for struggling couples. Tell me. What's the downside if you could do this anonymously?"

"Whatever...."

"Don't make up your mind now. Just talk it over with Brandi and think about it."

After a few seconds Ron said, "Can we talk about something fun, like our golf trip for the long weekend in May? How's the booking going?"

Scott, looking very happy with himself, replied, "I'm pleased to report that the rooms are booked, tee-off times reserved, and kitchen passes secured. All systems are a *go.*"

Saturday, April 18

Ron and Brandi were back in Dr. Fiona's office to continue their counseling. Ron had surprised himself with his enthusiasm. His zeal, however, was short-lived.

"Before we get going," Dr. Fiona spoke, "I'd like you both to independently fill out this short survey for me."

The survey dealt with their sexual preferences, fantasies, and turn-ons, as well their sexual turn-offs. They were also asked if their spouse embodied this characteristic, and if so, to what degree. The second part of the survey asked them to list what they thought their spouse's turn-ons and dislikes were, as well, and again, if they embodied this characteristic, and if so, to what degree.

Ron saw the potential for some embarrassment here since, in the twenty-some years they'd been together, he couldn't remember—not even once—discussing his turn-ons with Brandi. Additionally, Ron realized that he didn't have a good understanding of Brandi's full "off-limits" list. Day-to-day situations and events had evoked discussion of specific objectionable third-party behaviour, but nothing more substantive than that.

He noticed his hands were starting to sweat again.

They took about twenty minutes to complete the paperwork, at which time Dr. Fiona asked them to relax and have a coffee while she compiled the information. Ron noticed that Brandi was looking a bit nervous as well. While they waited, they made some small talk concerning subjects as far removed from the current topic as possible. After about fifteen minutes, Dr. Fiona announced that she could now provide her initial comments on the results of their survey.

She sat calmly at her desk, casting a serene gaze towards the couple. "The purpose of this survey is twofold. Firstly, Ron has started to look elsewhere for his sexual gratification—not physically, but conceptually. His brief excursion into internet porn has likely awakened some of his deep-seated erotic idiosyncrasies, and I need to see what these are and if Brandi is currently providing, or is even capable of providing, an outlet for these desires. The same goes for you, Brandi, and Ron's part in satisfying them.

"Secondly, I wanted to see how much commonality there is between your lists. You've both indicated that you've never talked about this subject specifically, so the commonality we do have in your lists is likely because of the unconscious matching that occurred when you were developing a relationship and assessing each other as a suitable mate during early field testing. Although it's more likely than not that your individual sexual and erotic idiosyncrasies were *mostly* set earlier rather than later in life, your evolution as a sexual being doesn't ever stop. In a long-term relationship it's all about accommodation of your core erotic idiosyncrasies, and adaptation to your *evolving* erotic idiosyncrasies, to maintain a healthy and mutually gratifying relationship."

Dr. Fiona noticed Ron looking a bit bemused. "Yes, sex is a complicated business," she told him, nodding sagaciously.

"Let me comment first on the commonality of both your lists. There is a significant amount of overlap on both the desirable characteristics and the negative ones. This isn't surprising to me, since the length and stability of your relationship suggests that you have a lot in common, from both a sexual and a sociological perspective. As you already know, you guys are a good match for each other. What we're doing here is looking for the sexual disconnects between you two so we can 'fine-tune' your relationship. And there are some. Probably more than you realize."

Brandi and Ron looked at each other, mildly surprised.

"That's nothing to be worried about. It just gives us more avenues for enhancing your already healthy relationship. If everything was perfectly aligned and in complete harmony, our work here would be done. As it is, however, things are about to get interesting for you."

Both Brandi and Ron simultaneously felt trepidation and anticipation.

Dr. Fiona said, "I'm not going to get specific right away, however. And I'm going to ask you both to not to discuss the details you've written down today. We'll gradually roll those out so as not to overwhelm either of you. For now though, I'll start introducing some more exercises to directly and indirectly address those issues that I can most effectively remedy. You'll have to trust me that, regardless of how ridiculous some of these exercises seem, they will address some fundamental issues in your relationship—if you'll dutifully complete them."

Dr. Fiona waited for agreement from both of them. When that was obtained she added, "Good. Well, can I ask how the massaging exercise went this last week?"

Ron looked at Brandi. "Surprisingly, I liked it. It felt soothing to touch Brandi in a non-sexual way. At least, it was non-sexual when I massaged her *after* having sex."

"So you know, Ron," Dr. Fiona responded, "that first exercise was solely for your benefit. This week, we're moving onto the next level."

Brandi added, "Can we have more exercises where Ron has to obediently massage me on a daily basis?"

"Actually, yes," answered Dr. Fiona. "But this time, Ron will also be the recipient."

Ron blurted, "Yeah baby!" in response to that information, and added, "My feet are feeling particularly sore these days," while nodding sincerely at Brandi.

"As I understand, Brandi, you're expecting your period any day now?" Dr. Fiona inquired.

Brandi nodded, and replied, "Probably today, the way I'm feeling."

"Good. That'll help, since you're going to be exercising a non-sexual technique over the next few days. It's called *sensate focus*, and it's all about building up your mutual level of trust and improving your emotional intimacy. It's really an extension of what you were doing last week, Ron, but as I stated, it's reciprocal now. I want both of you to touch each other for a half hour a day. One of you lie down and the other will touch and stroke, not massage, *touch* the person lying down for fifteen minutes on the front, then fifteen minutes on the back. No sex, no kissing, no sexual provocation, no orgasms. Stay away from the genitals. Just touching and stroking. Can you do that?"

Both Ron and Brandi nodded.

"Good. Additionally, I don't want you to talk to each other about your experience. Not before, during, or after. Understood?"

Again Brandi and Ron nodded.

"Excellent. Do this for as long as your period lasts, Brandi, and then resume normal activities. And Ron, be careful you don't hurt yourself when you re-engage. You can't afford to be out of commission. OK?"

Ron sheepishly nodded his understanding and agreement.

Sunday, April 19

Brandi's period began right on cue Saturday night, and on Sunday they set aside an hour for their sensate therapy session after they returned from family supper at Ron's parents'.

Ron's parents now had their house up for sale, and were planning to move into their "mature couples" living arrangement by July. It seemed the closer they got to the reality of moving out, the more agitated they became, and the faster Ron wanted to get out of the house when he did visit. He hoped and reasonably assumed they'd revert back to their normal only slightly irascible selves when they finally sold the old house and moved into their new living arrangements. It couldn't come quick enough.

After a few hours with his parents, Ron was even looking forward to that night's inaugural sensate session. Truth be told, he would have preferred a full-body wax to spending any more time with his parents. He wasn't overjoyed with the absence of an orgasm, but it was what it was. He was going to try to enjoy it all the same.

Friday, April 24

Ron and Brandi had been invited over to Scott and Elise's place for happy hour and supper. They drove over with the intention of taking a taxi or Uber back, and Ron jogging the five kilometres back on Saturday morning to collect the car. The themes for tonight's gathering were springtime, and good Canadian wines under thirty dollars. Although the forecast was for increasingly warmer temperatures for next week, today had been cool enough to put the kibosh on any outdoor plans Elise had for happy hour.

Undeterred, the couples gathered in the kitchen to sample their wines of choice. Ron and Brandi led with the 2012 Merlot from Kraze Legz Skaha vineyard, located south of Penticton. Both couples groaned their approval as they tasted this wee bit of bottled sunshine. The layers of berry and plum base beautifully paired with the caramel and clove finish to create a work of art.

Conversation centred on their parents, and the increasing burden they were becoming as they aged. Ron and Brandi led with their narratives, followed by Elise. Both of Elise's parents were still alive, and the situation with her wasn't much different than Ron, except without the ongoing renovations that Ron was suffering through—Elise's parents were determined to die in their current house. Everybody knew that would come with its own unique set of challenges. Both of Scott's parents had already passed away, so all he could offer was gallows humour concerning the joys of being an orphan. Elise was quick to remind him that it was his good luck then that he would have even more time to dote over *her* parents as they continued on their journey towards infirmity. With an exaggerated joyful expression, Scott exclaimed, "Now that's *grrreat* news!" in a thick Scottish accent.

After about twenty minutes, Scott suggested that they open their spotlighted bottle before their collective taste buds became numbed into indifference. On his recent trip to Penticton, he had had the opportunity to visit a number of smaller vineyards in the area, and had brought back some gems that, according to him, were unobtainable anywhere outside of the actual vineyard. He fetched a decanter of a 2012 Mosaic from the Hillside vineyards adjacent to Penticton. The group unanimously agreed that it was a winner with its subtle mingling of dark fruits with a chocolate palate and a tobacco finish.

"Did you know," Scott said, "that the Okanagan region has about one hundred and thirty wineries, and has been ranked amongst the top ten wine destinations in the world? In a recent *Huffington Post* article, it was ranked number-one in the world, ahead of Bordeaux, Tuscany, California Napa and Sonoma, Spain, and Australia." He sipped his wine and let that sink in.

"The four of us should take a vacation there," suggested Elise.

Brandi almost blurted out that they needed Sam to finish high school before they could do any of that stuff, but caught herself in time and replied, "That does sound wonderful."

Ignoring the cool weather, Scott started the BBQ for the lamb chops they had planned as the main course for tonight's meal. Ron came outside and chatted with him as he scraped and prepared the grill, leaving the girls chatting and sipping their wine in the kitchen.

"Elise sometimes forgets that other people have children," Scott commented.

"The worst part is Sam's in that in-between age—too young to set out on the streets to fend for herself, and too old to sell to science," added Ron.

"So, what shenanigans are you and Brandi up to these days?"

Ron laughed. "Never a dull moment with Dr. Fiona. She's had us doing something called *sensate focus* where we just touch each other. Nothing else. And I mean *nothing* else."

"What do you think the objective of that was?" queried Scott.

"I think it was an extension of the hand/foot massage therapy she had us doing the week before. The difference was that this week, both of us shared in the labour."

"Did it have any positive effects?"

"Hard to say. I don't think it did any harm, but Brandi and I were instructed not to talk about it until we meet with the doctor tomorrow. I haven't really thought about it much, but I'm sure the doctor will have some things to say about it."

In the kitchen, Elise was talking to Brandi about the resolution, as well. "So she had you guys doing a bunch of non-sexual touching?"

"Yup. I didn't mind it, but I don't know about Ron. He seemed a little distracted at times. We're going to talk about it tomorrow with the doctor, but it may have been a bit boring for him. I think he's all about the orgasm. Not that there's anything wrong with that, but it may not be what the doctor wants to hear. We'll find out tomorrow."

"Have you and Ron talked about going public with the resolution?"

"We have and we're both really uncomfortable with the thought of that. Maybe I should bring it up with Dr. Fiona to see what see thinks?"

Elise nodded encouragingly. "I'm interested to see how that discussion goes. Scott and I have been a lot more 'active' since we last met and had some time with the *Kama Sutra*. In and of itself, it really is a goofy manual, but it did get us thinking, and opened us up to talking about and exploring our sexuality—and even our fetishes a bit."

Brandi responded, "We haven't started talking about our fetishes yet with Dr. Fiona. I'm pretty sure we will soon, and when we do, I think Ron is going to be quite surprised. He really is a conservative old soul."

Both ladies giggled, and sipped their wine.

Saturday, April 25

Dr. Fiona sat at her desk with her first coffee of the day and cheerfully asked Ron and Brandi, "Well, how did the week go?"

Ron deferred to Brandi, who said, "I enjoyed it thoroughly. I absolutely love having my own toucheuse. Mind you, the last part of the week wasn't so bad either."

"The last part of the week was my favourite," Ron said, shooting a lustful look at Brandi. He suddenly remembered where he was, wiped the smile off his face, and refocused on the doctor.

Dr. Fiona pursed her lips and asked, "So can I assume that the touching was less enjoyable than the last part of the week for you, Ron?"

Ron gave her a sheepish look and replied, "Well, if I were to be completely honest…"

"That's what we're all expecting here, Ron."

"Then yes. It's not like I didn't enjoy the touching, because I did. But the sex is really what I'm craving. I understand the value of just touching Brandi in a non-sexual manner. It did help me re-connect with her on an emotional level, not just as my sex partner, but in my brain it's only one side of the same coin. Physical contact, then sexual gratification. Peanut butter and jam. Laurel and Hardy. Bow and arrow." Believing he had gotten his point across, he paused.

Dr. Fiona quickly added, "*Yin and yang*, Ron. That's what you're describing. They exist together, and together they make themselves possible. Your feelings are completely normal. Just as the beast in you must eat, Ron, your soul has to be nourished to keep everything in balance. You've gained some rejuvenation and rebalancing from the touching exercises I've had you do over the last couple of weeks, but you're still biased towards the orgasm as a goal. Ideally I want you to see the orgasm not as a goal, but only part of the broader process associated with connecting to Brandi. From what I can tell, Brandi is pretty well balanced in this department, so before we can get into the really interesting stuff focusing on elevating your sex lives to the next level, I'll need you do a bit more work on balancing yourself."

Ron sat there looking a bit deflated. He wasn't used to not excelling at anything he did, and having a small yang, compared to his larger yin, anyway, felt a bit disappointing.

"Ron, you look saddened," Dr. Fiona said with a laugh. "Don't be. You're actually much better balanced than the majority of men I see in this office. All we're doing here is a little fine-tuning, for the lack of a better description. Before I bring you two to the next level, I just want to be confident that you can handle it."

Ron felt better, and he nodded that he understood.

Dr. Fiona continued. "I realize you need to pay attention to your sexuality in parallel to developing your spirituality, so I've got an interesting exercise that I'd like you two to introduce into your daily lovemaking to strengthen the non-sexual bond at the same time. Before you start making love, I want you both to get completely naked and either sit cross-legged or stand directly in front of each other. For at least five minutes just stroke and touch each other's face while staring into each other's eyes. Focus just on the eyes and the face, nothing else. After that, anything goes. Should be easy enough, right?"

Both Ron and Brandi nodded affirmatively.

"Good," added the doctor. "Do this all week and I'll assess Ron to see if he's ready for the next stage next Saturday."

Again more nodding by Ron and Brandi.

"OK, then. In preparation for the next stage, I'd like you two to have a look at this list I've put together of sexual preferences, kinks, fantasies, turn-ons, and fetishes. It's extensive—about two hundred examples—but it's by no means complete. The human spirit and imagination truly have no boundaries, and this list will hopefully help demonstrate that to you.

"There're two reasons for looking at this list. Firstly, Ron, your list of sexual preferences was woefully short and unimaginative. I have yet to encounter an individual as sexually uncomplicated as your list would suggest you are. I want to tease out some more information as to what your inner sexuality *really* looks like. Secondly, Brandi did demonstrate, how do I put this…a materially more sophisticated embodiment of sexuality than yourself, Ron, and I want to explore and attempt to quantify the depth and breadth of that sexuality—if that's OK with you, Brandi."

"I'm here with Ron to discover my sexuality as well, doctor. Full speed ahead," Brandi replied.

"Excellent. Here are two copies of the list I just referred to." And she handed it out to Ron and Brandi. "I'd like you to separately look at the list, and as with your previous list, highlight the preferences, fetishes, etc., that you can relate to, and mark those that you really respond viscerally to – both positively and negatively. OK?"

Ron and Brandi absently nodded back at the doctor, already being drawn into the list, their eyes widening with amazement at the nature, variety, and often, bizarreness of the examples in front of them. And they were still on the A's.

After about fifteen minutes, both Ron and Brandi had completed the lists and handed them back to Dr. Fiona.

"Now, I don't want you to discuss this list and your reaction to the specific fetishes on it just yet. I can appreciate that the majority of them will have sounded strange to you, but let me collate the information and combine it with your previous list first so we can have an honest, unscripted, and revealing discuss sometime in the near future—depending how quickly Ron progresses."

She quickly went through the list and spoke. "But I can see there is some broad commonality as to what neither of you are sexually interested in." She chuckled to herself again, and said, "Neither of you are interested in alien sex, agalmatophilia (aroused by statues), bestiality, coprophilia (attraction to feces) or urophilia (golden showers), human furniture, emetophilia (arousal to vomiting), incest, formicophilia (aroused by insects), necrophilia, avisodomy (sex with a bird), sadism, eproctophilia (arousal by flatulence), vorarephilia (arousal by eating other people), or children."

The doctor paused and took off her glasses, and added, "Far be it for me to judge, but personally, I'm happy to see that!"

As the session came to a close, Brandi remembered she wanted to ask the doctor's opinion on whether or not she thought it was a good idea if they were to anonymously discuss their journey through the resolution as a public inspiration to struggling couples.

When she brought this up, the doctor replied, "You and Ron are, of course, free to do anything you want. But intuitively speaking, playing marriage fixer on the internet sounds dangerous. Let me think that one over and we can talk about it next week, if that's OK with you and Ron?"

Brandi replied, "Sure, thanks, Dr. Fiona."

Ron just looked stunned.

When they got to the car, the first thing on Ron's mind was Brandi's comment to the doctor about going public with their resolution. (Well, it was a close second, behind the residual astonishment brought on by the range of fetishes, preferences, and kinks they had just seen.) Ron asked, more calmly than he actually felt, "So you're seriously thinking about going public with our resolution?"

"We'd have to agree on that, Ron, before anything like that happened, but I was just floating the idea with Dr. Fiona since she's the expert on sex and marriage. We're just the lab rats."

Ron nodded, somewhat calmed by her comment. "I'm not against it," added Ron, "it's just that there's lots of opportunity for unintended consequences when you're dealing with sex, and we should tread very carefully."

Ron left that last comment hanging, and started imagining some of the more positive reactions to the resolution if it were to be made public. At the front of that daydream was an article in the *Ottawa Citizen* with a flattering photo of Ron, and the caption "Sex Guru Aaron Lee Discusses The Resolution."

Sunday, April 26

This was the final hockey night of the season. That, plus the promise of an extended drink session afterwards, had generated an excellent showing. Typically there were only two or three subs in total, and everybody was sucking wind and gliding around the ice after about fifteen minutes. But tonight there were two and a half lines per side, and the pace had been good for the entire hour. This meant the guys were especially thirsty by the time they got to the bar.

The group of guys was a disparate collection of middle-aged men from all corners of Ottawa society. They either knew the original organizer—an old buddy of Ron's from university—or were within one degree of separation as a friend of a friend. The significant common thread that ran through them all was their love of hockey and beer.

Conversation became considerably more boisterous once everyone got a bit lubricated, and because of the quality of play that night, focused mainly on their lives wasted in non-professional hockey careers. A couple of the guys sitting near Ron eventually started bitching about how their wives had "forgotten how to have sex," or "had probably found a younger, better-looking guy," which Ron assumed was barely veiled code for not getting laid enough. The comments were delivered in an offhand sardonic manner meant to make light of the matter, but Ron recognized the real core of angst the guys were poorly concealing.

There was absolutely no way Ron would presume to know these guys well enough to offer some unsolicited advice, nor did he want to expose his resolution to this broader group, but he strongly felt that he now possessed some insights into the marriage-sex dilemma that could at least get these guys and their wives thinking about the subject a little differently and, possibly, provide some remedies for them.

After about an hour, the group started breaking up, and wishes for a great summer and at least one decent golf game this year resonated around the table. Ron made it home just before ten, and Brandi was still awake.

"What are you still doing up, little lady?" asked Ron in a deep-south drawl.

Brandi put down her book and replied in her best southern belle, "Well, I was just waiting up for my little ol' face-touching session."

Ron laughed, and replied, "Look at what we've become. Asexual sensate practitioners in quest of spiritual enlightenment."

"And in the spirit of full disclosure, you should know I'm feeling a wee bit 'lusty' tonight, so get your gear off and come stare into my eyes," Brandi said to Ron, making it sound like an order. He did as he was told.

CHAPTER 6

SECOND WIND

Friday, May 1

Brandi sat in her backyard with Charlene, basking in the early-evening warmth and sunshine. Summer had arrived, brash as a bully, and had declared itself now in charge. The subjects of Ottawa had surrendered without a fight, faithfully sworn their allegiance, and hoped for a long and fruitful reign.

Speaking of fruits, the warm weather had encouraged the ladies to make an early seasonal change from red to white wine as their beverage of choice for the evening. The succulent apple and pear base and lemony finish of the 2013 Pinot Gris from the Arrowleaf winery outside Kelowna nicely complemented the evening's warmth, providing them with reminiscences of late-summer ripened orchards.

Charlene had quickly directed the conversation to the topic of the resolution, both curious about its progress and looking for further insights with application to her marriage. "So what did Ron think about all this touching, massaging, and eye gazing?"

"He didn't *not* like it. But he didn't love it, either. It's helping him deepen his bond with me—which is good. And it's helping him refocus on me during sex—which is good. And it's helping him with being more in the moment during sex—which is also good. Really, it's all good, except guys are goal oriented when it comes to sex. It's not the journey for them, it's the destination. So excess foreplay and massaging has to be learnt; it doesn't come natural for young guys. Concerning older guys, I think they *can* be re-conditioned to a certain degree, simply because their chemistry is less intense, but it's also not natural for them to embrace a sexless physical encounter."

Charlene responded after a few seconds. "Yeah, different animals, that's for sure."

"But be that as it may, that doesn't mean they're without hope. Dr. Fiona acknowledges that progressive rewiring of the brain is real, and she's working with us to fight against these natural processes, and allow our 'humanity'—as she puts it—to take back control of our will, thoughts, and, ultimately, our actions."

"That doesn't sound easy, girlfriend."

"It isn't, or there would be significantly fewer divorces and every marriage would be an unending lovefest—which we know isn't the case."

"So, I think I understand how the non-sexual couple exercises could help, but why do you think the doctor's looking at yours and Ron's kinks and sexual preferences?" asked Charlene.

"That I'm not so sure about," replied Brandi, "but I think it may be an attempt to fool the brain into allowing us to look at each other with fresh eyes. Like in the good old days."

"I'd kill for those good old days," said Charlene, with a look of exaggerated anguish on her face. "That's a good segue into my next question. Did you bring up going public with Dr. Fiona?"

"We talked to the doctor about that last week to see what she thought. She didn't immediately counsel against it—which is positive, I guess—but she wanted some time to think about it. Maybe she'll have something to say about it tomorrow. Social media is so fickle and anonymous and potentially cruel, you have to be pretty sure that you're going to do more good than harm, to both yourself and your audience, before you'd be willing to take that chance. And I know we're not there yet. The resolution is tough enough on its own. Do we really need the added pressure of keeping a social media site up to date with our most intimate information?"

"When you put it like that…not so much," added Charlene.

The girls chatted for a few minutes, until one of the first bugs of the season made a suicidal rush for the bewilderingly magnetic draw of the liquid in Brandi's wine glass. The kamikaze critter plunged into the glass with such ferocity that both ladies jumped at the plop created by the impact.

As Brandi fished the stunned, but likely somewhat sated, thrashing wayward pest from her glass, Charlene recalled their earlier discussion on the fetishes the doctor had recently had them look at. "Can you imagine being sexually aroused by bugs? How weird is that?"

Meanwhile, Scott and Ron were in a similar, but decidedly more irreverent, discussion over beer and wings at the nearby Bassline Pub. They were having a pre-golf trip meeting with two other friends, who were expected any minute. Ron had filled Scott in about his last week of "therapy," and the unusual focus on fetishes by Dr. Fiona. Ron had figured that the doctor was trying to better define his and Brandi's erotic landscape so she could use their sexual idiosyncrasies to amplify their sex life by fooling the brain's pleasure centre into pumping up their—and by *their*, Ron meant *his*—neural-reward system associated with sex.

"So, do you think you'll be allowed to pass to the next stage?" Scott asked in a condescending tone.

Ron replied with his best hockey persona. "Well, I've been giving it one hundred and ten percent every day, and I've been putting in extra time as well, and you know, I've been really, really, trying hard not to think about sports when I'm touching Brandi's face and gazing into her eyes."

"So probably not, then?"

"I don't know. I'm just a little apprehensive about the results, to tell you the truth."

"What's up with that?" Scott asked.

Ron mulled over his thoughts a bit. "It's probably because I'm pretty simple when it comes to sex, and I think Brandi might not be. We haven't talked about our 'preferences' in a long time." Here he paused. "In a *very* long time, actually. And I'm worried about what I may find out about my wife. The doctor actually said that Brandi was 'materially more sophisticated' than I was sexually."

"Ouch," responded Scott.

"Yeah," said Ron as he nodded, grateful his buddy thought the same as he did.

Both of the guys pensively sipped some beer, following which Scott added, "But regardless of what you find out, I'm pretty sure that it's going to spice up your love life and help with the resolution."

Ron nodded in agreement. "Most likely. I just hope not too much, if you know what I mean."

Scott actually *didn't* know what he meant, but let the comment slide.

After a pause in the conversation, Ron asked, "Did you know that you could be sexually aroused by just about anything?" He didn't give Scott a chance to answer before continuing. "Big people, small people, statues, urine, shit, bugs, disease, amputees, caves, falling down stairs, cannibalism, bees, noses, stone, wood, and the congenitally deformed."

"Good grief," replied Scott. "Is there nothing sacred?"

"No, in fact. I forgot about religious objects. They're also on the list. And that's just the tip of the iceberg. God, I hope that Brandi doesn't have a suppressed desire to hump a giant," he added in a despairing tone.

Just about then, the previously absent pair from their golfing foursome entered the bar wearing shorts and Hawaiian-shirts, obviously having gone home first to change. When the guys got to the table, Scott prodded, "Already on vacation, gents?"

These "gents" were long-time mutual friends Ian and Gerry. The four had been golfing together for as long as they could remember, and had been taking this May golf trip for almost twenty years now. Ian was married, with a couple of kids of similar age to Sam and Tommy, and ran his own business as a master carpenter. Gerry was a real estate agent, and recently divorced. His one child had already moved out of the house, and he was currently "dating." This was code for sleeping with as many desperate women as would have him. And given that Gerry was not the picture of good health at close to two hundred and fifty pounds, one would imagine there was a certain level of desperation involved in even considering Gerry as a candidate for coitus. *But given there are people out there who find being urinated on sexy, Christ, anything is possible,* Ron thought.

After a round of man-hugs and some backslappery, the drinking began in earnest. Strangely, Ron always felt particularly thirsty around these guys.

Scott started in on the formalities. "Fellow golfers—departure to Turning Stone Resort as early as possible on Friday, May 15—two weeks from today. Ian will be driving this year."

A confirming nod from Ian.

"Two suites with two queens each booked, three tee-off times booked, one at each of the three courses—Atunyote, Kaluhyat, and Shenendoah. Golf Saturday, Sunday, and Monday morning, returning afternoon on Victoria Day. Everybody good with that?"

A chorus of "you betcha," "yup," and "yeah, baby" followed, signaling all were good to go.

Ron had no intention of bringing up the resolution with either Ian or Gerry, but after about a half hour of general chatter, Gerry recalled Ron always had a resolution and innocently asked what this year's quest was. Ian heard the question and, curious, quieted to hear the answer.

Scott held his breath.

Ron hesitated. He didn't want to lie to Gerry, but, alternatively, he didn't know Gerry and Ian as well as Scott, and didn't feel comfortable with full exposure of the resolution either. "Just a little thing between Brandi and me," he offered, and then quickly sipped his beer while looking around nonchalantly, hoping his brief explanation would suffice.

Gerry sensed something was up from Ron's response, and instinctively pressed on. "Sounds interesting. But aren't your resolutions just a *your* thing?"

Ron's face started to heat up. He knew he was a terrible liar, and being aware of that caused his face to redden more, which made it more obvious to Gerry that he was hiding something, which made his face even more red, and so on.

Gerry smelt blood. "What kind of 'thing' are you and Brandi up to?"

Scott was looking away now, smiling at Ron's pathetic attempt at concealing the resolution from Gerry and Ian.

When Ron didn't answer, Gerry goaded him on, "Rooooooooonnnny. Come on, you can tell *me*."

Resigned that there was no dignified escape from the current line of questioning, Ron said, "OK, I'll tell you guys, but you have to swear secrecy."

Their interest now truly piqued, Gerry and Ian abundantly and unconditionally agreed to Ron's insistence for confidentiality.

"Well. We've resolved to make love every day of the year."

Both Ian and Gerry instantly erupted. "No fucking way!" "You're kidding!"

When it became apparent that Ron was indeed serious, Ian inquired, "How's it going so far?"

Gerry lecherously added, "Brandi *is* pretty hot."

Ron calmly replied, "Thank you, Gerry. Yes, she *is* hot. And I'm happy to report we're currently on target."

"That's pretty impressive," replied Ian. "I'm jealous. I wish Kelly and I would do a tenth of that. You've got to give me some pointers, Ron. I could use the help these days, if you know what I mean?"

Ron thought that comment out of character. Ian was quiet to begin with, and never talked about intimate issues, so when he engaged enthusiastically about the resolution, it got Ron's attention.

Scott saw his opening. "See, Ron!" He turned to Ian. "I've been trying to talk Ron into making the resolution public, to help out couples like you and Kelly. You wouldn't believe what he's been up to. A lot of it could be helpful if the couples were willing to listen and try some things out. Elise and I have tinkered with a few techniques they've been using, and I can tell you, our sex life has definitely improved."

Gerry now spoke up. "So Scott has been part of the inner circle and we've been kept in the dark," he said, more as a statement rather than a question. "As you know, I'm not married anymore, but I'm always looking for ways to please as many ladies as possible, so if there's advice for 'impermanent' couples, I'd be interested as well."

Ron rolled his eyes, shook his head, and reached for his beer. He knew this was a bad idea.

Saturday, May 2

Ron and Brandi had just finished discussing how their week of therapy had progressed. Dr. Fiona, nodding positively, took off her glasses in preparation for her commentary. "So what we've been trying to achieve with the touching therapies of the last few weeks has been to further strengthen your already strong personal bonds. The constant physical proximity and non-sexual contact increases production of your 'cuddle hormone', oxytocin. Unlike dopamine, oxytocin actually increases with more frequent physical contact, so we've been creating a positive feedback loop that is essential to everything we'll be doing over the next few months. Without high oxytocin levels, your neurochemistry will experience intolerable swings that will cause significant emotional fluctuations that will destabilize your relationship. Am I clear on that?"

Both Ron and Brandi nodded.

"Sticking with the neurochemical theme, Ron, I've got some bad news for you." The doctor paused for dramatic effect, and after a few beats continued. "Your testosterone levels have been dropping for the last decade, at least, and with that comes an increase in the hormone prolactin—which you'll recall is the satiation chemical released immediately after sex. A good thing, yes, but as you both are realizing, you can have too much of a good thing. With higher levels of prolactin building in your system, caused by your constant sexual activity, your desire for sex wanes. Combined with your falling testosterone levels—your T-levels—your sexual urges have been, or soon will be, receding as fast as your hairline."

Ron unconsciously rubbed his head.

"An additional bad bit of news is the increased prolactin in your system decreases your dopamine levels, which, when combined with your progressively less effective dopamine receptors, that we talked about earlier, creates a negative feedback loop discouraging sexual activity—simply because it just isn't that fun anymore. All this is obviously counterproductive to the completion of your resolution."

Ron's face became grimmer as the doctor rolled out the negative prognosis. He was still rubbing his head.

Dr. Fiona noticed the growing darkness on his face and said, "Ron, you knew there were issues. That's why you and Brandi are here, remember? Lower T-levels are part of the challenge, but it's one we can try and manage. Your T-levels are probably high for your age, since you're still able to engage in regular sex, Ron, but with the neurochemical battle that's currently raging in your brain, that won't be enough. So I'm going to give you and Brandi some natural ways to increase your testosterone levels."

Brandi nervously looked over to her husband.

"Brandi, your sex drive will also surge with an increase in your testosterone levels, so I want you both to introduce some lifestyle changes that will help raise them."

Dr. Fiona handed over a summary of ways to naturally raise your testosterone levels. Ron quickly perused it while the doctor was shuffling around her desk looking for something else. The list included heavy-weight strength training, weight loss, stress reduction, reducing sugar and alcohol intake, and zinc supplements.

Dr. Fiona spoke, bringing Ron's attention back to the discussion. "I'm also going to give you some very effective daily testosterone supplements. I want you both to keep a log over the next month as to how 'energized' you are sexually, so I can track the effectiveness of this program."

Ron felt a bit more positive. He wondered if the program would help restore his hairline as well.

Dr. Fiona gave Brandi and Ron a large container of testosterone supplements, and continued with the session.

"For the next week, I want you both to focus on introducing these lifestyle changes, while taking the T-supplements and continuing with the sensate therapy. Fifteen minutes a day minimum. If Ron continues with his progress, we'll move onto the next stage next Saturday. How does that sound? Any questions?"

Brandi responded, "Have you had a chance to think about what we briefly discussed last week—concerning going public with our progress - as inspirational assistance for struggling couples?"

Dr. Fiona took off her glasses, and drew in a deep breath. "That's a tough one for me. Officially, I can't approve of anyone offering therapeutic advice that isn't professionally qualified. That said, I am professionally and personally interested in the public reaction to what you're doing, and if your resolution can actually be inspirational to other couples. As such, I'm neither going to encourage or discourage you—if you're picking up what I'm dropping." She winked, and left it at that.

Sunday, May 3

May was birthday month for the Lee family. Abigail was on the second, Tommy Jr. on the third, Brandi's on the sixth, her mom's on the sixteenth, and Sam's on the twenty-fourth. As was tradition, Ron and Brandi held a group birthday party on the Sunday closest to the early bunching, and today was the designated party day for 2015. The weather had cooperated, and everyone was outside soaking up the sunshine and warmth. Tommy Jr. had just finished his exams, and was home for the summer. Ron had pulled some strings at EllisDon and secured him a summer job at the firm. Both Tommy Jr. and Ron were thrilled with that arrangement, but not nearly as thrilled as Brandi, who had badly missed Tommy while he was away at school that year.

Ron took a break from talking with his dad, and looked around at the familial joy surrounding him. He recalled a recent Indiana University Medical study he had come across that suggested that children conceived during the summertime had considerably lower IQs than the general population. He chuckled to himself, and mused that there must be some real smart people out there.

Although it was a genuine celebration that his mom had now made it to seventy-eight years of age and Brandi was soon to be forty-seven, the big deal this year was Tommy turning the legal drinking age of nineteen. He wasn't a big partier, so his decision to hang with the family didn't surprise Ron. He likely had missed the family as well this last year. Ron and Brandi had pressed him to invite some of his closest Ottawa friends over to today's event, and by the permanent smile he was currently sporting, he looked like he was enjoying himself. One of his friends was a pretty petite blonde who, Ron was fairly certain, had dated Tommy before he headed off to U of T last fall.

Ron tried to recall when he was nineteen. He could remember the details of specific events, but he had trouble remembering how he'd actually *felt* when he was that age. For some reason he did remember how insatiably horny he had been. Without the grace and good looks that his son Tommy possessed, Ron had stumbled through late adolescence and early adulthood clueless, and usually without female company. The rare encounters of the coital kind were like the proverbial opening of the flood-gates.

"What are you smiling about?" asked Brandi, as she wrapped her arm around his shoulder and kissed him on the cheek.

"Just reminiscing about being Tommy's age," replied Ron. "There wasn't a whole lot of joy back then until I met you, but it's still fun to think about it."

"Hopefully you can absorb some of this youthful energy around us for later," Brandi said. She nipped his ear and departed to chat with his mom.

He and Brandi had just started with the lifestyle changes and supplements to increase their testosterone levels, but the mere *thought* of elevating her libido had gotten Brandi all worked up. Ron had a hard time imagining how ravenous she'd be if the T-therapy actually worked on her. Dr. Fiona had certainly been keeping them busy with her staged therapies, and Ron realized that, on a couple of levels, it was working. They were already in May, and the angst that he had felt as far back as January had disappeared. Sure, some apprehension remained, but both of them now looked forward to the weekly sessions with Dr. Fiona. She was making sex fun again, and with the fun came an increase in their all-essential primal energy.

Wednesday, May 6

Ron, Brandi, Sam, and Tommy were having supper at Travola's—Brandi's favourite neighbourhood restaurant. Normally they would have driven the three kilometres, but the weather this evening was so lovely they'd decided to walk over. Their reservations were for six-thirty, so they left just before six, and marched over at a brisk pace. This longer-than-usual walk aligned nicely with the lifestyle changes that they were introducing as part of Dr. Fiona's program to boost their T-levels. They had only been on the program for a few days, but Ron thought he was feeling a surge in his sexual energy. Brandi was *sure* she was feeling an increase in her sexual energy, as well. That didn't surprise Ron at all.

Since they'd already celebrated her birthday the previous weekend, this meal was a bonus for Brandi. But only part of the bonus plan. Brandi had requested a fulsome love-making session when they returned home, and Ron was looking forward to delivering the "B is for birthday" in the annual obligatory lethargic ABC sex program that most longtime married couples joked about adhering to. A was for anniversaries, and C was for Christmas. Ron mused that would be a very bad week for him and Brandi these days.

Supper was a boisterous affair. The family-run restaurant was firing on all cylinders tonight, and the unseasonably fine weather had not only brought out the local restaurant-goers, but also the best in the restaurant staff. Conversation ranged from the great weather to summer vacation plans to Tommy's first impressions of his work at EllisDon to girlfriends and boyfriends (which Sam denied having and didn't want to talk about in any case) to friends and family.

As part of Dr. Fiona's lifestyle program, Ron and Brandi had decided they would limit their alcohol consumption to the weekends—at least for now—and uncharacteristically avoided the wine.

Holding hands on their way back home, Ron and Brandi walked behind Sam and Tommy, and thoroughly enjoyed watching them enthusiastically engage in a sibling-style rough-house conversation for the duration of the walk.

Back at home, and having made stock excuses to the kids for an early bedtime, both knew that they were not really fooling anybody, but were still grateful they played along.

The kids were growing up. Ron recalled that when Sam was about three years old she had burst into their bedroom while Brandi was riding cowgirl. With hands on her hips, Sam stated with precocious indignation that whenever they were finished doing whatever they were doing, she needed help with her colouring, and stomped out without a second look, while they remained frozen in place like deer in the headlights. They'd made a habit of routinely locking the bedroom door after that.

When Ron entered the bedroom, Brandi was already in bed, displaying a come-hither look and pose. Ron knew he was about to get into it, so he went to the bathroom and fortified himself with a Viagra. Probably unnecessary, but he wasn't taking any chances tonight, with Brandi in full-heat. As he slipped into bed and lay beside her, his manhood suddenly aware of where it was and its call to duty, Ron asked Brandi, "Well, my birthday girl, what's your preference tonight?"

About two hours later, Ron, grateful for the Viagraian fortification, looked over at his sleeping wife. He realized they had passed some sort of threshold tonight. Brandi had relegated her normally prim tendencies into the background of her rapidly evolving sexual mindset, and cast aside the veil of her socially ingrained sexual modesty. To his surprise, Ron wasn't as uncomfortable with it as he thought he would be, and certainly as he would have been in January when they had just begun the resolution. One thing he knew for sure—when they discussed their fetishes and various kinks with Dr. Fiona, biting and pinching would definitely be on Brandi's list. If they weren't near the top, then there were some big surprises in store for him in the very near future.

Saturday, May 9

Brandi and Ron had just finished updating Dr. Fiona with their progress on the various "therapies" she had assigned to them the previous week.

"Now that's more like it, guys. Well done, Ron. It sounds as if you're making real progress. And I'm glad to hear that the T-level therapy is having some early positive results. That improvement should continue over the next few weeks. We'll keep that and the sensate therapy going for the next month or so and re-evaluate then."

Ron piped up. "Can you help me understand again the point of these sensate touching exercises from a therapeutic perspective?"

Dr. Fiona looked at him. He couldn't tell if the look was cogitative in nature, or simple exasperation.

"Of course, Ron. We know that sex is typically more than just physical release. It also satisfies complex emotional needs. But what's lesser known is that the emotional component of sex is intrinsically tied to our human need for social interaction. The sensate therapy you're currently practicing strengthens your emotional bond with Brandi by satisfying your need for intimate social interaction.

"The American sociologist Randal Collins believes that all humans crave social contact and our sexuality can only be understood in this social context. That may sound self-evident to you—we all know the limited metallic relief provided through masturbation—but I assure you, the study of human sexuality in its social context is surprisingly complex. The extreme position in this camp believes sexual desire is not driven by either physical pleasure or procreation, but our need to connect with others. I agree with Collins that there is a strong social component to our sexuality, and we have to ask ourselves *why* we crave social interaction."

She paused to further collect her thoughts, and then continued. "I believe that, as part of our survival strategy, our brain has evolved to actually reward us for our social interactions, in the same way that it rewards us for performing acts like eating, making copies of ourselves, and then nurturing our children. You have to agree that having sex is the most social thing we humans do, and we do it on a regular basis. Some *very* regularly." Dr. Fiona emphasized this last comment by glancing back and forth from Brandi to Ron, eyebrows raised. "So, during sex we're combining two reward systems into one act; effectively doubling up on the dopaminergic reward and reinforcement process. No wonder we can't stop having sex! Although non-sexual social encounters are rewarded neurochemically, that reward is typically not as intense as it is with sex. While this social reward is like sipping tea, orgasm is like drinking from a fire hose. In a sexual relationship, when the firehose gets choked off, the incremental neurochemical reward from a stronger social bond will *usually* not completely fill the pleasure void. Typically, couples will then avoid any remedial actions and either accept their permanent state of sexual dissatisfaction, find a lover, or let the relationship fail.

"While the sexual component of *your* relationship is strong, it's the perfect time to reinforce the social aspect of your relationship. That's what the sensate therapy is attempting to do. A stronger non-physical relationship will enhance and further entrench your entire neurochemical reward network, and expedite our journey to…well, to wherever we're going."

She paused and went back to her notes. After a few seconds she continued. "Now…I think with the progress that you've made," she said to no one in particular (but Ron knew she was talking to him), "we can move to the next stage of our therapy. My theory is that once we've achieved a balanced neurochemistry, we will be better positioned to attempt to *fully* satisfy your primal core, and enable the transfer of control of your *will* over to the uniquely human and sentient regions of your brain, creating a spiritual harmony that should benefit your relationship. But the primal core is a voracious, nearly insatiable beast, and demands to be continuously feed the sweetest and finest of diets. That's where your fetishes can help. I've been looking at your list of sexual preferences, fantasies, and kinks, etcetera, and I think it's time we had that discussion."

Ron could feel his anxiety rise. His palms started to moisten, his heart started racing, and he could feel his face reddening. He had amazingly never, in twenty-some years, had this conversation with Brandi. There were probably a multitude of reasons for that, but the fact remained—here they were now about to embark onto these dangerous grounds for the first time, and in *his* mind, embarrassingly belatedly, given how fundamental to the well-being of their marriage this discussion was.

Dr. Fiona could see the growing discomfort on Ron's face, and said, "Ron, if you're not comfortable with this, we can delay this discussion until later."

Ron replied, "Thanks, doc, but I think the sooner we have this discussion, the better. It's probably already twenty years late."

The doctor laughed, put her glasses on, and replied, "Alrighty, then. I'm not going to be talking about your normal sex practices. These will focus on desires and practices outside of your everyday off-the-shelf sexual activity. I've had a look at your lists, and am glad to see that both of you have very manageable, and not atypical, desires.

"OK, let's start. Brandi, Ron enjoys the sounds of sex and vocalizing and moaning during orgasms. He prefers the pubic area free of hair, is a bit of a voyeur—especially concerning female masturbation and lesbianism—and fantasizes about female ejaculation."

She took off her glasses and stared at Ron first, then Brandi. "That's it," she added. "Oh, yeah—Ron is also attracted to redheads. Nothing even remotely unusual on that list, but I figured that would be the case with Ron." She looked directly at him, and asked, "Anything else to add?"

Ron sat with his wet hands folded in his lap, while a strange cathartic feeling flowed over him. He looked at Brandi and she smiled broadly back at him. His most private sexual desires had just been laid bare before his wife and a relative stranger, and he felt fine. Better than fine—released—*finally*. Ron shook his head no.

"Good," said Dr. Fiona. She then turned to Brandi and asked, "So Brandi, how do you feel about Ron's list?"

"Honestly," Brandi said, looking at Ron, "I knew all of this about Ron except for the female ejaculation thing."

"How are you going to react after hearing his list?"

Brandi pondered for a couple of beats, and then replied, "I want to talk with Ron about them and try to accommodate him."

"Very good. Let's leave that for now and move on to your list, Brandi."

Ron's feeling of anxiety started to resurface, but he fought it down. Speaking to Ron, Dr. Fiona said, "Brandi has a more extensive list of desires, but still very much within the realm of normalcy. She fantasizes about pinching and biting during sex."

Bingo! Ron had known that was coming, and was thankful it was at the top of the list.

"Enjoys shower sex, outdoor sex, tickling and is not averse to trying analingus." Ron noticed he was holding his breath. "She fantasizes about being tied up during sex, having sex in public places, and threesomes, and is turned on by the thought of anonymous sex. Is that about it, Brandi?" asked the doctor.

Brandi nodded that it was.

"Can I ask if you have a preference for the gender of the third person in the threesome?"

"Even though I'm not repulsed by the thought of a woman, my preference would be a male."

"Thanks, Brandi. Ron, can I ask how you feel about Brandi's list?"

Ron wiped his hands on his jeans, sat up in his chair, and responded. "I knew about the first parts of her list," he looked at Brandi and smiled, "but nothing about the last part. Which bugs me more than anything else, really."

"Why is that Ron?" asked the doctor.

"Because we've been together for over twenty years. There shouldn't be any aspect of her sexuality that I'm either unaware of, or surprised by, at this point."

After she realized Ron wasn't going to add anything more, Dr. Fiona asked, "And what are you going to do about Brandi's list, Ron?"

"I'm going to talk to my wife about them, and see what I can do to continue pleasing her," replied Ron, as he smiled at his wife.

"Excellent. This exercise can be difficult for some people, but I know you two can handle it. The purpose of it is to both expose yourself—your full and true sexual self—to your partner, and, just as importantly, work together to use these innermost individual sexual idiosyncrasies to grow together. When you work on your lists over the next week or two, I want you to see if and how you can work to expand your sexual horizons together. You may not want, or even be able, to accommodate all of them directly, but both of you *can* do more." She let that comment sink in.

"Initially, talk about the items on your lists that you're both comfortable with, and make a plan to do what you can to incorporate them into your sex curriculum. Start slowly. Most important—above all else—any expansion of your horizons must be done together, and with full compliance from both of you. Do you understand?"

Both Ron and Brandi nodded they did.

"Good. Your plate is getting very full, Mr. and Mrs. Lee. Work on introducing some more range into your sex life in parallel with the other therapies, and we'll meet again in two weeks. Good luck," she added enthusiastically. "I'm sure you'll have fun."

Sunday, May 10

Brandi and Ron had a 'sleep-in' on Sunday to talk about what they had revealed to each other the day before at Dr. Fiona's office. Brandi propped herself up on an elbow. "All these years, and now I find out you're a pervert?"

"If I'm the pervert, then you're the sexual deviant," countered Ron, as he started tickling her. When the tickling subsided, he said, "I really had no idea. Being tied up? Sex in public? Threesomes!? If I'd only known earlier."

Brandi leaned in and gave his nipple a pinch.

"Hey, that's your fetish, not mine," Ron said, and more seriously added. "There's no going back now, Brandi. Now that I know you're thinking about these things, my instinct is to do what I have to do to make sure you're happy. I guess what I'm saying is, you're not only the mother of my children, you're my soulmate and my best friend, and if this is what you want, I'll do my best to accommodate you."

Brandi cupped Ron's face and came in for a deep kiss, after which she replied, "I bet some of that was pretty shocking to hear, but honestly, if there's anything that you can't stomach, I'm fine with that. Really. The priority here is our relationship, and these desires are add-ons—nothing more. If the risk of doing our relationship damage is greater than the potential benefits gained in having them bring us closer, then let's forget about them right now."

"I'm glad to hear that, Brandi, but I say we go through our list and talk about each one. How does that sound?"

"That sounds perfect."

"Good," added Ron. "I think we can get most of the way through my list today. Shall I get a razor for you and quietly nestle into my front-row seat?"

Friday, May 15

It was about three-thirty by the time Ian had collected all the eager golfers and they could hit the road. Brandi was still at work when Ron got picked up, but she, Tommy, and Sam were planning to head down to Toronto for his mother-in-law's birthday as soon as she got home. The timing for the golf weekend was ideal from Ron's perspective. As much as Ron loved his mother-in-law, he really didn't mind missing her birthday celebration. Additionally, Brandi's period was due any day, and although it had become less of an issue over the last couple of months, he was delighted about it coinciding with the golf trip.

They had finally lucked into beautiful weather for their golf weekend, with the forecast calling for hot and sunny conditions for the entire trip.

It was a three-and-a-half hour drive to Turning Stone Resort in upstate New York, but you could add another half hour or so for the border crossing at Hill Island near Gananoque. Traffic along the way and at the border was heavier than usual because of the Canadian long weekend, so the guys didn't get to Turning Stone until close to nine o'clock. There was a common feeling in the group of arriving home when the resort finally materialized on the horizon. They had been coming down here since 2011, when the Oneida Indian Nation had at last settled its feud over alcohol licensing with the State of New York, and every year had been more fun than the previous one. With Gerry freshly divorced and on the prowl, the weekend was shaping up to be another memorable event this year, and the guys were keen.

Following check-in at The Inn, the boys met in the lobby, and walked over to the Over/Under Sports Lounge for some warm food and cold beer. The place was rocking, with half the clientele consisting of Canadians doing the same thing as the four of them. After a couple of quick beers, the conversation moved away from each of them recalling their dominance during past golf weekends and the inevitable victories each would embrace over the next three days, and on to Ron's resolution. Gerry was again the instigator.

"So, Ron," he asked, "are you and Brandi still doing the resolution?"

Ron nodded.

Gerry pressed on, "And still on target?"

Ron nodded again, realizing he wouldn't be able to shake him in this setting.

Gerry pursed his lips and nodded, looking impressed. Unexpectedly, Gerry then remarked, "You know, I sort of miss being married. I wonder if Karen and I had tried something like this we'd still be married."

It was an uncharacteristically introspective comment from a normally narcissistic individual, and it caught the guys off guard.

Scott was the first to come to Gerry's aid. "But look at you now, Gerry. 'Dating' whomever you want, and beholden to no one's whims except your own. You're living the life, my man."

Gerry responded despondently, "Yeah, it was good in the beginning, but all those women remind me how desperate and sad I probably look to them."

That comment landed with a thump on the table. No one dared comment.

After a brief pause Gerry continued, "I know I'm not getting any better looking, or even richer, these days, so I'm finding myself dating progressively older and more anxious woman, who don't want to spend the rest of their lives alone and die that way. The conversations after sex can be a little stifling at times." He looked around and smiled ironically. "Shit, sorry, guys. You guys don't need me bringing you down with this stuff on this weekend."

They simultaneously spoke over themselves assuring him not to worry about that.

Ron added, "Look, Gerry, I know it's been a tough year for you, and I'm glad you brought this up tonight. Now we know, that as your wingmen this weekend, we have to focus on younger and less-anxious women for you." He finished with a "no problem" pose, with hands open, to emphasize the comment, which brought a smile to Gerry's face and started turning the conversation around.

Scott jumped in, now looking serious. "I would suggest, however, that we focus on blind and/or deaf women. We only have three nights to work with here." He quickly looked around and added, "With the sausage party going on here tonight, make that two. Even God needed six days for a miracle of this magnitude." A chorus of laughter completed the mood change, and moments later the guys were back to their old selves, with talk now refocused on tomorrow's golf game and negotiation of their respective handicaps.

As Ian, Scott, and Gerry kibitzed, Ron pondered Gerry's comments further, and quietly thanked his good fortune to have met Brandi, and, more importantly, to have had the wisdom to marry her. He was snapped out of his pensive state by the sound of Ian yelling his name in his ear. "To the handicaps!" Ian toasted, his beer raised high. Automatically Ron raised his mug of beer and toasted, much to the delight and howls of laughter from the other three guys.

Scott explained. "You just agreed to a ten handicap for the weekend. Sorry, buddy, you snooze, you lose."

Saturday, May 16

Tee-off on Saturday was late morning at the Shenendoah course. A large part of the appeal of coming down to the Turning Stone Resort was the proximity of all three golf courses to the resort. This, not coincidentally, promoted a no-driving-and-excessive-drinking atmosphere. In support of this strategy, the Shenendoah and Kaluhyat courses were all of a three-minute walk from their rooms.

About four and a half hours after tee-off, the guys were sitting on the outside patio adjacent to the clubhouse, having a post-game drink. They rehashed the day's best and worst shots, the conversation working itself around the table a number of times until all the stories of athletic genius, barely missed opportunities, and inexplicably lucky and unlucky bounces were exhausted. Somewhere in this initial period, the drink of choice moved from beer to rum, as was par for the course with this group. The conversation became progressively louder and more animated, with the guys partaking in comedic one-upmanship.

After a particularly funny remark that had the guys wiping tears from their eyes, Ian asked, "Why can't life be like this every day?"

"First of all," Scott replied, "we'd die from cirrhosis of the liver. Secondly, I couldn't stand being around you guys for more than a few days at a time. And thirdly, if you didn't have to work for your joy and suffer through the tough times, you probably wouldn't enjoy these times nearly as much."

"I know what you're saying, but I'd be willing to take the chance," retorted Gerry.

Ron replied, "I think the key to happiness in life is variety, and the satisfaction that comes with successfully dealing with challenge and change."

Gerry said, "You may be right, but how do you reconcile your marriage, and monogamy in general, with the need for variety and change? Which, by the way, in my opinion, makes your resolution with Brandi even more amazing after twenty years." He lifted his drink in toast.

"Thanks," Ron said, meeting Gerry's compliment with a raise of his own glass. "That's the key to making it work right there, Gerry. The two—change and monogamy—they aren't mutually exclusive. Think of it as two circles overlapping. The more you overlap them, the healthier the relationship. You have to keep a relationship dynamic or you'll get bored. You know that's true. How else could something as magnificently gratifying as sex ever become uninteresting? Still, it does. That's really one of the great ironies of marriage."

"Well, you're probably the best person I know to tell me—now possibly a bit too late—how you actually do that?" inquired Gerry.

Ron spent the next fifteen minutes giving Gerry the *Reader's Digest* version of the challenges, changes, and remedies that he and Brandi had so far dealt with, and resorted to, to keep the resolution on track.

Afterwards, Gerry asked, "Let me see if I've got this right. The resolution is, in effect, compressing issues typically experienced through the entire span of a relationship into a one-year timeframe?"

"Yes and no. The one-year period is arbitrary, being the intended length of our resolution. And although we had experienced some marital issues already, what the resolution has done is reset our marriage back to day one. I can tell you early January was a honeymoon all over again, and it was over by about mid-January. The resolution's like a marriage on steroids, with everything sped up. The doctor expects that, at about five months in, we're at a stage most couples don't ever even get to in their marriage, because they're either content with where they are, they lose interest in their partner and sex and the relationship ceases to evolve further, they divorce, or they don't live long enough."

Gerry asked, "So what's your best advice up to this point?"

"The key to getting through the resolution and the issues that come with it is, most importantly, understanding and talking about why the problems are arising. Brandi and I did what we could in the beginning, but it wasn't long before we—meaning *me*, really—were overwhelmed, and went for help with Dr. Fiona. Who, by the way, has been brilliant so far."

Ian asked, "And all this because of your resolution? Seems like you got more than you bargained for."

"Listen, I had no idea what I was getting into when we started the resolution. In all likelihood, Brandi and I would have blissfully continued 'as is', or slowly and unconsciously evolved our relationship, quite happy with its relative stability, and just left it at that. I think that's what most people do. And when sexual problems arise—and they will—they don't know how to deal with them, and the relationship deteriorates. I look back knowing what I know now and wonder how, without doing the things we've been doing over the past few months, Brandi and I made it this far without having some major issues. Probably a mixture of the fact we're a solid natural match, and dumb luck. Brandi's the luck part of that, and I'm the dumb. I expect that if we make it through the resolution, we'll be bullet-proof."

Scott commented, "You aren't out of the woods yet, son."

"You got that right," replied Ron.

Ian jumped in. "So what are you planning for the rest of the year?"

"For the rest of the year, I have no idea, since we're reacting to issues as they arise. But for now, in addition to the other 'therapies', the doctor has us exploring our sexual preferences and fetishes. I imagine the next month is going to be quite interesting."

In unison, the three listeners at the table hooted their approval of Ron and Brandi's next stage in the resolution. Ron took note of their enthusiasm.

Gerry said, shaking his head, "The fetish thing seems like a no-brainer now. I can't believe I didn't try that with Karen."

"I think I'll discuss it with Kelly," Ian said pensively.

After a pause Scott added, "I already have with Elise." His Cheshire-cat smile signified to the group that the tactic had been successfully implemented.

"What about creating some sort of public log of your techniques and progress?" asked Ian. "I'm sure people would be interested."

"Yeah, we've been debating what to do there. It does sound like a lot of extra work, and we have concerns that our identities could slip out. Imagine the shit storm that would cause. Just think—work, kids, and parents."

All the guys grimaced, and nodded understandingly.

"On the other side of the coin, it might be inspirational, and possibly helpful, to struggling couples." Ron shrugged with a "what the hell do I know?" look on his face.

After a few seconds, Scott spoke. "Enough with this marriage stuff. You guys probably want to hear about my chip-in on fifteen again. Let me start with a detailed re-telling of the event from my perspective and *then*, we can get each one of you to share your take on the shot."

With only a break for a quick shower and change of clothes, the guys continued seamlessly into the evening and early night. They knew that ballast was required for these heavy drinking days, so a perfunctory meal was ordered and consumed at the Upstate Tavern, directly after which they revisited the Over/Under Sports Lounge to continue the drinking in earnest.

The theme tonight was "get Gerry laid." Not an easy feat, given his age, sorry state of physical fitness, and progressive inebriation—but the guys liked a challenge, and execution of this theme had the highest probability for some good laughs. The hometown New York Rangers had beaten the Tampa Bay Lightning in an afternoon game, and the entire game was being replayed at the sports bar. Though they were typically ambivalent concerning playoff games without a Canadian team playing, the infectious hometown atmosphere had them boisterously cheering for the Rangers before the first period was half over.

The unseasonably warm temperatures and the Ranger's victory earlier in the day had brought hockey fans out in droves, attracting locals from as far as Rome and Utica, as well as a number of nearby smaller towns. Although males dominated the demographic, mature ladies were surprisingly well-represented, as well. The friendly alcohol-infused atmosphere made it easy for the more gregarious Gerry and Scott to strike up conversations with the surrounding tables, at one of which was a group of not-unattractive hockey fans who played on the local "cougars" team. By the end of the second period, introductions had been made, personalities and characters assessed, and tables joined into an impromptu multi-nation pro-Rangers tribal unit. It was game on.

The third period was a thoroughly entertaining affair, capped by a late Rangers goal that sent the crowd into a euphoric celebration, during which one of the ladies actually hugged Gerry. It was shaping up to be a memorable night—especially for Gerry, who was responding to this bit of good luck by doing his best stand-up routine (while he was sitting down). The two other ladies in the group had turned their attention to Ian, who didn't wear a wedding ring because of his line of work. Apparently the fact that he was married hadn't yet come up in the brief-but-vigorous conversation. Both Ron and Scott knew that they themselves would be overlooked, or at least not targeted, by the ladies because of their advertised marital status. There was no question that Ian, who was modestly good-looking, was being aggressively competed for by the two "uncommitted" ladies at the table because of his apparent unmarried status—and he didn't mind the attention in the least.

Ron realized what was happening on both sides of the ongoing encounter. Ian was allowing his brain to reward him with ever increasing doses of dopamine from proximity to a new potential mate, and from stimulation of the pleasure centres by the alcohol itself. Additionally, the alcohol had effectively slowed down the failsafe parts of his brain in his cerebral cortex and frontal lobes, responsible for full-cycle critical thought processes, consequence assessment, and psychological inhibition. The endorphins being released in response to the laughter-filled conversation were also adding to the pleasure cocktail swirling around in his brain.

The effect of his apparent availability and the alcohol on his newest best friends was even more amplified. In addition to experiencing the same effects on the brain as Ian, alcohol increased their testosterone levels, turbo-charging their interest in sex. If that wasn't enough to encourage a blind sexual rage, woman typically had more intense orgasms with some alcohol in their systems—a fact Ron figured the ladies talking to Ian were aware of.

Physiology aside, the ladies had apparently respected the sociological norms of leaving married men alone, and it was this humanistic side of what was transpiring that really interested Ron. From what he had observed of male behaviour, this aspect of the collective social conscious was disproportionately borne on the shoulders of women. He wondered if these ladies themselves had endured a philandering spouse, or maybe they were acting out of a broader adherence to the unspoken rules of the sisterhood. What he did know was that Ian was looking progressively happier, and becoming more physical with the two ladies on either side of him. As if Scott were reading Ron's mind at that moment, he looked over and gave Ron a quiet "should we do anything?" look, while gently jerking his head towards Ian. Ron gave him a little nod, and subtly signaled that he would talk to Ian.

After another round of drinks, the entire crew decided to meander over to the adjacent Lava Night Club, to extend the night with some music and dancing. Once they had settled at a table, Ron followed Ian into the washroom, and took up position at the urinal beside him. He asked Ian, "So buddy, you thinking about taking either of those girls home?"

Breaking focus from the task at hand, Ian looked at Ron, smiled, and replied, "Both would be better, don't you think?"

Ron involuntarily imagined that scenario, and felt a warm and pleasant wave of dopamine infuse *his* brain, encouraging those actions, especially since he had been drinking. Memories of that night in the Dominican came flooding back. He consciously pushed away those thoughts and responded, "I have to admit, that does sound pretty good right now, but I can guarantee it won't feel so good in the morning."

He gave himself a shake, and left Ian wobbling at the urinal. Ian eventually returned to the table, much to the exaggerated relish of the two ladies. After about an hour, during which Gerry and his date didn't leave the dance floor, and Ian, Scott, and Ron rotated as dancing partners with the other two ladies, Scott signaled Ron he had had enough and was going to call it a night. He glanced at Ian and unsuccessfully tried to get his attention. Ron also decided to call it a night. On the way out went over to Ian, put his hand on his shoulder, and whispered, "Be careful, buddy." Then he walked over to Gerry, who was in an animated conversation with his date on the dance floor in-between songs. He informed him that he and Scott were heading back to the room, gave him a wink, and told him to enjoy the rest of the night.

About forty-five minutes later, as Scott and Ron were just hitting their snoring stride, they were awakened by a knock on the door. It was Ian. He had his pillow and a blanket in hand, and asked, "Is there room for one more? Gerry could use a little privacy at the moment."

Ron ushered him in, pointed at the softest place on the floor, and replied, "Absolutely. You just have to abide by the house rules of no snoring, no farting, and visitors are last to use the bathroom in the morning. Have a good nap." He then proceeded to fall back into his bed, to a chorus of burps and farts emanating from Ian's corner of the room.

Sunday, May 17

Tee-off on the Sunday of the golf weekend was at noon, due to the expected intensity of festivities on Saturday night. That turned out to be good planning this year. Ron was the first to stir, just after nine-thirty, and when he emerged from the shower, Scott and Ian were awake and talking.

"Morning," Ron said, and then crimped his face, sniffing the air. "Christ, it smells like a toilet in here." He went over to the balcony door, and slid it open to let in some air.

Scott said, "Well, you and Brandi can add Ian to your 'salvation' list."

Ron turned around with a confused look on his face. "Say what?" He glanced from Scott to Ian.

Ian replied, "I can tell you that if I hadn't listened to your brief download yesterday afternoon after golf, last night might have had a different conclusion."

"What do you mean?" asked Ron.

"You said if you're mindful of what's happening to you physiologically, you can control it."

Ron nodded.

"Well," Ian continued, "about way past midnight last night, as I was imaging what those two ladies looked like without their clothes on, for some reason I recalled *that* comment and had something like an out-of-body experience. I saw myself all boozed up, and realized my brain was in the latter stages of duping me into 'spreading my seed' around. I sobered up on the spot, told myself I was in control here, made my apologies to the ladies—who by now were expecting more than a kiss on the cheek, I can tell you—and got myself out of there."

"Yikes," interjected Scott. "They must have been some mad."

Ian nodded his head in agreement, red eyes and all. "Let's just say that the odds of me getting run over while walking the streets of Oneida are a lot higher today than yesterday."

"Well, I know that wasn't an easy thing to do, given the circumstances, Ian. And Kelly will also be impressed when I remind her of what a stand-up guy you are." Ron delivered the last comment with an evil smile.

"Fuck you very much for that, Ron," replied Ian.

Scott asked, "So, can we assume that Gerry is with his date in your room as we speak?"

"As far as I know," Ian answered.

Picking up the phone, Scott dialed room-to-room, and said, "Well, it's about time you got up. We have to golf in less than two hours, and I'm assuming you didn't get that physique of yours by skipping breakfasts."

The day was hot and sunny, and even with the cloud of alcohol-induced dullness felt by all four guys, their round at the Kaluhyat course was as fun as the day before. Most annoying was Gerry's irrepressible jolliness and uncharacteristically good golf. He shot close to his personal best, and despite themselves, the guys couldn't help cheering him on near the end of the round.

On the patio after the game, still sporting the smile he had brought to breakfast with him, Gerry fished for further praise from his three friends, while nodding enthusiastically. Notwithstanding their *faux*-resentful veneers, the guys were collectively happy for Gerry, and jumped in right on cue to keep the conversation going. They all knew that the last twenty-four hours had been good for him, and they were glad to extend the event for his benefit.

Ian, however, tired of stroking Gerry's golf ego after a while, and directed his line of inquiry towards what he considered the more interesting narrative concerning Gerry's inaugural encounter with his Oneidaian friend last night. "You haven't thanked me for sleeping on the floor in Scott and Ron's room yet," Ian prodded.

"You're right," answered Gerry. "Thanks a bunch for that. You know I'd do the same. Like before you were married, I mean," He added with a sardonic smile. Then he clasped his hands to his chest, rolled his eyes, and presented his most cherubic expression. "Her name is Trish, and I think I'm in love."

That comment was automatically met with groans by all three listeners, whose bowed heads, shaking in unison, emphasized their incredulity.

"We really hit it off. We like the same music, same movies, hockey, and dancing, and she golfs!" Gerry exclaimed, as if the proverbial cherry had been added to a Black Forest masterpiece. "And although we spent the night together, we didn't have sex."

That comment froze the rest of the guys mid-whatever they were doing.

"You're kidding!" said Ian.

"Nope. I'm not saying there wasn't some jiggery-pokery going on, but we decided that we'd get to know each other better before we got too intimate."

Ian responded by shaking his head in disbelief. "You mean I slept on the floor for *that?*"

"Every journey starts with a single step, grasshopper, and we decided to make ours a baby step. Besides, I've been knee-deep in insincere and superficial relationships for coming onto a year, and after listening to Ron yesterday, I realized that I wanted to 'rediscover my humanity', as Ron put it; as opposed to letting the 'dirty dog' in me rule the roost." He searched their faces for understanding. "Besides, she's planning to come to Ottawa next weekend for a visit. I can let the dogs out then."

Ron realized that that was the second time today that one of his friends had quoted him and his newfound understanding, born from the resolution.

Scott said, "Well, I say good luck to you, Gerry," and raised his drink in salutation. The rest of them did the same.

"By the way, it's your round, lover-boy," reminded Ian.

After a few drinks, the guys headed back for a hot tub. Gerry mentioned that he had forgotten his bathing suit, and if they didn't mind, he would go naked. Ian responded, deadpan, that although the thought of Gerry transferring his pubic hair directly onto his body without containment by some sort of fabric covering had always been a hot-tub fantasy of his, he fortunately had an extra bathing suit with him. And good luck squeezing into it.

Sunday evening was typically a quieter affair than the alcohol-fueled dementia of Saturday night, and after showering up they headed down to the Upstate Tavern for some basic eats and a couple of cleansing beers. Ron sensed that Gerry purposely sat beside him at the restaurant, and wasn't surprised when he started conversing, close and confidential-like, soon after they had ordered their food and gotten their beers.

"You know, Ron, I was skeptical about your resolution when I first heard about it, but last night I found myself actively managing my emotions and urges when I was with Trish, and it felt…well, really good to be in control—if you know what I mean?"

Ron felt he wasn't finished, so he just nodded encouragingly.

"I really think there's something to understanding the whole brain chemistry process, and rising above it and controlling it. Basically, I just wanted to thank-you for sharing some insights from your resolution with me."

Ron nodded and said, "No problem, Gerry. Glad it could help."

Gerry added, "Trish was impressed with what you and Brandi are doing with this resolution and…"

Ron interrupted and asked disbelievingly, "You told *her* about the resolution?"

Gerry, seeing Ron's reaction, fumbled a bit with his response, eventually saying, "Well, yeah? I told her that it wasn't public knowledge and to keep it to herself."

He hesitated, looking at Ron, who had his head in his hand and was shaking it in continued dismay. "She doesn't even know who you are, Ron. Well, other than last night."

"Gerry, Ian pissed off two of her friends last night. If they find out, they may use it against us."

Gerry sheepishly absorbed Ron's perspective with his best "well I can't un-ring that bell" look, adding, "I'm sure it'll be OK, Ron. I wouldn't be paranoid about it."

Ron replied, resigned at the ingrained stupidity of the majority of his friends, "You don't have to be paranoid about it—*I* do. Let's hope you're right about Trish. Please make sure she keeps it to herself, OK?"

Gerry nodded vigorously, happy to end the exchange.

A few minutes later, while the other three guys were talking, Ron pondered just how many people now knew about his "secret" resolution. He figured the number must be getting close to twenty now. And those were the ones he *knew* about. He could feel the anxiety rising in his belly, thinking about the old saying, "It's only a secret if you don't tell anyone else." When Scott suggested they head out to the Over/Under Lounge to catch the Chicago-Anaheim game, Ron was glad for the distraction.

Monday, May 18

It was close to 8 p.m. when the guys got back into Ottawa. The final day of golf had been a warm and far less boozy affair. Gerry had lost his form of the previous day and, having themselves in the past experienced the vexing phenomenon of inconsistent play from one day to the next, his friends helpfully offered possible reasons for Gerry's poor performance.

Taking a scientific approach, and focusing on what was different between the two days, they suggested the likely factors affecting today's quality of play included:

1. The need to dance publically the night before the game like a blind spastic imagining no one was watching;
2. The need for giggle-filled, cuddly pillow-talk sessions with a first date to enable the softer, emotional element of his game;
3. Resumption, on Sunday night, of his life-long habit of farting in bed;
4. Having made the mistake of looking in the mirror this morning.

In conclusion, they unanimously decided it could have been a combination of any or all of these factors.

Ron got dropped off just after eight-thirty. Brandi met him at the door, waving at the guys in Ian's truck as it reversed out of the driveway. She gave Ron a big full-on kiss and asked, "How was it?"

Ron responded, "Always fun. Always eventful."

"Well, it's good to have you back." Brandi kissed him again. "But now you've got some work to do to catch up, laddo. And I've been giving some thought to my 'list', and have an idea or two for tonight."

Although Ron was tired from the weekend and the drive home, he was looking forward to resuming the resolution and making up a bit of ground over the next few days. "So you've got a tall handsome well-hung young man tied to our bed upstairs?' asked Ron.

Brandi giggled, and replied "You've got part of that right, but I haven't found a young guy who can measure up to you—yet." Then she beat a hasty screaming retreat as Ron launched a tickle attack.

Saturday, May 23

It had been two weeks since Brandi and Ron had met with Dr. Fiona. Consequently, the doctor was anxious to get down to business. "Nice to see you both again. How are you two feeling?"

"We're good," answered Brandi. "Still on track and still enjoying each other's company."

"That's important. It would be extremely difficult to accomplish this resolution if you two didn't like each other." She chuckled. "Have you been sticking to the exercise and sensate regime?"

Ron replied. "Yes and no. Brandi has been exercising like crazy, but I've been slacking off a bit." Here he looked down at his growing belly, and gave it a grab. He surprised himself with the amount of fat he now had in his clutches.

While he was momentarily lost in pondering his bloated physique, Dr. Fiona asked, "And the sensate therapy?"

That snapped Ron back to the present, and he replied, "Every day we're together, doc."

"Good. And still taking the testosterone supplements?"

Both of them nodded positively. Ron hadn't been all that regular with them, but didn't feel like receiving a lecture at the moment.

After a few scribbles, Dr. Fiona looked up from her notes. "Ron, you're going to be testosterone-challenged very soon if you aren't already. I'd recommend enhancing your exercise routine, not reducing it."

Ron nodded sheepishly, and was thankful he hadn't brought up his delinquency concerning the testosterone supplements.

"Now, tell me what actions you two have taken concerning your 'fetish' list."

Brandi responded first. "We've been working away at it, Dr. Fiona. I've been keeping myself shaved, and allow Ron to watch while I go through the process."

Ron couldn't help but smile as he visualized Brandi shaving herself. He felt his penis involuntarily thicken.

"For me," she continued, "Ron ties me up, face down on the bed, and penetrates me without talking. We also have a variation on this, where I'm blindfolded and Ron remains quiet through the love-making."

"That sounds like you're both getting the hang of this. Do these actions excite both of you?"

Ron nodded affirmatively, covering the bulge from his semi-erection with his hand.

Brandi replied, "Absolutely."

"That's precisely the point," said Dr. Fiona. "Acting out your fantasies together is a very powerful bonding tool. As well as reinforcing your physical and spiritual bond, when you partake in these fantasies, the pleasure neuropathways associated with these sexual idiosyncrasies grow and become reinforced. No surprise there, but indulging in your sexual fantasies *together*—and the key word is *together*—actually assigns those pleasure pathways to your partner. This results in a chemical rejuvenation during sex with your long-time partner to levels similar to your initial honeymoon period, or even levels which you'd experience with a new partner." Dr. Fiona made the last point sporting a "how cool is that" look on her face.

"Here's the other interesting aspect of this exercise. We have no idea if there is a limit to this 'reinforcement' process. Can you max out on sexual pleasure with the same partner? What happens when you stop these activities? How permanent are these neurological changes? What other neurochemical changes will transpire in your brain? How will these changes manifest emotionally, holistically, and intellectually in each of you?" Dr. Fiona took off her glasses, and stared excitedly at both Brandi and Ron.

Ron noticed that he had become completely flaccid.

After a short-but-uncomfortable few seconds, Dr. Fiona added, "I believe that we're going to go places that very few individuals have ever gone, and I for one am looking forward to the journey. I hope you two are half as excited as I am."

Speechless, Ron looked over at Brandi who, to his surprise, was looking back at the doctor with a growing smile on her face. *Oh-oh*, Ron thought to himself.

After a few seconds returning Brandi's smile, Dr. Fiona went back to her notes, replaced her glasses, and commented, "Since you've made good progress on your 'list', I want you to keep up with those new activities that you've already introduced into your sex lives, and keep increasing the breadth of these new activities. Towards this end, I have a couple of suggestions."

Ron noticed his hands had begun sweating.

"Ron, I see that you have 'female ejaculation' on your list." She waited for Ron to respond.

Ron nodded. His could feel the sweat pooling in his hands. His ears were heating up. He realized that no matter how long they did this he would never, *ever* get used to discussing these issues with anyone else but Brandi.

"Ron, when did you know you were turned on by female ejaculation? I assume that Brandi has never ejaculated during orgasm? Is that correct, Brandi?"

"Not even once." She slowly shook her head, with a dejected look on her face.

Ron rolled his eyes in response.

Dr. Fiona's attention went back to Ron as she waited for his reply.

Sporting a sheepish grin on the crimson background of his face, Ron replied, "On the internet, I guess."

Dr. Fiona nodded neutrally, and asked, "What do you think it is about that phenomenon that turns you on, Ron?"

Ron didn't miss a beat, replying, "It's the intensity of the orgasm that seems to be related to the ejaculation. I've read that it is, by far, the singular most intense orgasm that a female can have, and I guess I want Brandi to experience it and for me to be part of it."

"Although there are some who adhere to the belief that all women are capable of ejaculation, the majority of sex therapists are of the opposite opinion," Dr. Fiona said. "I fall somewhere in between. I believe that most women who are sexually 'unconstrained' and normally capable of multiple orgasms can also experience ejaculation upon orgasm with proper technique. That, in my mind, makes Brandi an ideal candidate."

She had Ron's full attention with those comments.

"Ron," she continued, "you should be aware that the fluids involved are, in part, diluted urine."

Ron's face morphed into a scowl. *Oh God. Not the urine thing again. Maybe I should just get it over with and ask Brandi for a golden shower.*

Dr. Fiona, picking up on his change in demeanour, responded, "Nothing good comes without a price, Ron. Messy business, to be sure. Are you still as keen?"

Ron sat there dumbstruck, doing his best guppy imitation.

Brandi replied for him. "I know I am." And she smiled at Ron, who looked wide-eyed back at her.

Dr. Fiona took in the exchange, scribbled some notes, and replied, "I'm sure you are, Brandi, however, the technique for stimulating female ejaculation during orgasm is quite intricate, and requires a high level of finesse. I wouldn't expect that Ron would have much of a chance on his own."

A feeling of inadequacy washed over Ron.

"There is some literature available on the subject, but if you two are determined to explore female ejaculation, you may want to use a 'surrogate' to assist you through a hands-on demonstration of proper technique."

Ron sat frozen in his seat. Although horrified that they were even having this conversation, Ron couldn't help but hope the suggested surrogate was female.

"With this instruction, Ron should be able to replicate the effect, assuming, of course, you're capable of ejaculation, Brandi."

After a few seconds Brandi spoke up. "I have a couple of question, Dr. Fiona."

The doctor nodded.

"What gender would this surrogate be, and would the session be held here or at our house?"

"It can be either in both cases," Dr. Fiona replied. "Personally, I use a female surrogate for these hands-on sessions…"

Ron realized he had been holding his breath, and audibly exhaled upon hearing the doctor's last comment.

Both ladies glanced at Ron, but Dr. Fiona continued without pause. "…and we can conduct the session here, or in the privacy of your own bedroom, if that's more comfortable for you."

Brandi nodded, and replied, "Let Ron and I discuss this further, and we can talk about it next time we meet."

"That sounds reasonable. She's in high demand these days, so there's a two-week waiting list. I'll cover her costs, so don't let that be a factor in your decision. In the meantime, I'd like you two to start building some pornography into your love life, and independently record your responses for me." Looking directly at Ron, she added, "I want you to experience this visual stimulation *together*. The point of this exercise is to *share* the experience, and in doing so, have your brain associate this sexual stimulation with your partner. It's an extension of what you've started doing by exploring your fetishes and reinforcing the pleasure neuropathways assigned to your partner. Talk about and agree upon the theme of the pornography beforehand. I would suggest that you focus on your fetish lists, and try and capture as many of each of your turn-ons as possible. Are you both good with that?"

Brandi and Ron both nodded affirmatively.

"Good. I'm away next weekend, so let's plan to meet again in early June. Until then—good luck, kids, and don't forget to enjoy the journey!"

Sunday, May 24

Ron was grateful for the distraction of Sam's birthday party. He was feeling a bit overwhelmed by the growing number of daily therapies that he and Brandi were implementing, and since their session with Dr. Fiona the day before, he had been worrying about building couples' pornography and a "surrogate" into the mix—all this on top of an increasingly busy work environment and helping his parents sell their house.

Speaking of parents, the backyard was replete with them today. Brandi's mom, Megan, had travelled up from Toronto to spend a few days with her daughter and family, and timed her visit so she could be at Sam's party. Both of Ron's parents were also in attendance, and because of the public venue, were on their best behaviour. Especially Abigail, Ron's mom, given Brandi's mom, Megan, was present. For some reason, there was a subtle competition between these ladies whenever they were together. After all this time, he still didn't know if they actually liked each other.

Ron looked over at them in conversation, and marveled at the adroitness with which both ladies engaged in this civilized verbal backyard combat. Ron wasn't quite sure what the rules of engagement were, but the sparring was manifested through reciprocal frozen perfunctory smiles, mutual hyper-attentiveness, and purposely understated recitals of the dustiest of family stories, delivered with the common denouement of overcoming the greatest of odds that clearly, but tacitly, demonstrated the depth of character and quality of familial lineage. *Either lady would be a fine candidate for Canada's diplomatic corps*, Ron mused.

A number of Sam's friends were over as well. The weather had cooperated again, and despite the cold rainy day on Saturday, today was hot and sunny, so the entire crew was spread out over the backyard, clustered in various conversational groups, soaking up the sunshine.

Ron was sitting with Brandi, both Tommies, and Charlene and her husband, Kevin. Their daughter, Sarah, was at the party as one of Sam's invited friends. For about a half hour, conversation had focused on topics foremost on everyone's mind. Tommy Jr. talked about his summer job and friends. Tommy Sr. was all about selling his "ancestral" Ottawa home and moving to the raisin farm. The middle-aged adults were focused on family, politics, and taxes.

Given Tommy Sr. was in attendance, Charlene couldn't resist asking about his secret to sustaining a long and happy marriage—a theme her current interest in the resolution had inspired. Ron had never had this discussion with his Dad, and was unusually interested in the response offered by his typically reticent father.

Tommy Sr. chuckled, and slowly replied, "First of all, long doesn't necessarily mean happy." He let that comment hang for a few beats, and then continued. "Sure, Abby and I have been together for over fifty years, but I'd be lying if I didn't admit some of that was more like surviving the moment so you could live to fight another day. There are phases in every relationship, and the truth is, we're all experiencing and dealing with them for the first time. Even me, now. I imagine Abby will do something brand-new today that'll either exasperate me or make me smile. A relationship is always in motion."

He paused and pondered for a couple more seconds. "It's like a river, with the adrenaline-filled turbulent headwaters representing the early days of a relation-ship; the slowing and warming waters of middle age representing progressing security and stability; and the stagnant, slow-moving, and predictable waters of the lowlands—just fine for us old folk. The point is, every relationship begins at the same point in the headwaters, and journeys downstream from there. Not everyone is made for the slower, warmer, and safer waters. There are plenty among us who are easily bored with warm comfortable waters, and would just as soon swim to shore, hike back up, and throw ourselves back into the frozen rapids. Just so happens that Abby and I were adaptable and, as it turns out, somewhat compatible. I attribute that to equal portions of luck and intelligence. And patience, humility, and the ability to walk away from an argument; and it's me doing the walking." He looked at Ron, and matter-of-factly stated, "To my knowledge, your mother has never walked away from an argument—so someone had to. I'm not complaining," he held up his hands in surrender, "I'm just saying."

Everyone around the table remained silent while he took a drink of his lemon water and looked around at the group. "As I sit here now, I can tell you that there's joy to be found at any point on the river. Sure, you have to sacrifice adrenaline for cerebral fulfillment, and then cerebral fulfillment for vicarious engagement, but I see that as a natural process. You can't fight it. It's going to happen. You can't ignore it, because denial works for only so long. You simply have to accept it, adapt to it, embrace it, and wake up the next morning and do it again. That's how you survive fifty years in a marriage."

He paused so long, Ron thought he was finished. Just before he commented, his dad threw out a concluding remark. "That, and lots of sex."

When everyone in the small group stopped laughing, Ron went over and gave his dad a big hug. His mom, hearing the eruption of laughter, had sauntered over. "What's so hilarious?"

Still smiling, Ron replied, "Dad's just entertaining us with stories of his sexual prowess," and walked away, leaving his dad to provide a more accurate and less incriminating explanation of events.

About an hour after everyone had eaten, Ron came out of the house with a beer in hand, and scanned the backyard. Most of Sam's friends had left; the grandparents were clustered in a small group chatting, and Brandi was standing with Charlene. He noticed Brandi was looking a bit ashen. Charlene was currently holding up her phone for Brandi to see.

Ron instinctively went over, and asked Brandi, "What's up, babe?"

Brandi looked at Charlene, who looked at Ron, and slowly shifted her phone so Ron could see the screen.

Ron felt the blood drain from his face. On Charlene's phone was a tweet from one of her friends. All Ron saw was the hashtag title at the end of the tweet: *#resolutionottawa*.

❧

Charlene stayed and helped with the clean-up after Kevin left. Ron drove his parents home, then hurried back to further investigate just exactly how much of the resolution had been leaked into the public domain. Brandi and Charlene were sitting in the backyard talking when he got back. He sat beside Brandi, and asked, "Well, how bad is it?"

Brandi replied, "There don't seem to be many background posts, and we couldn't find any specific reference to our identities in the posts we could track down."

Ron felt a wave of relief upon hearing that. He asked, "Can you tell where it originated?"

Charlene replied, "Actually, no. The furthest we can track it back is to an anonymous tweeter named *Marny@gogirl*. She seemed to be responding to a personal tweet, and came up with the hashtag *#resolutionottawa*."

"The good news," Brandi added, "is that there aren't that many posts, and it's certainly not trending, so it could just as easily wink out over the next while."

Ron rubbed his head and face as he pondered this news. After a few seconds he asked, "What's the general 'mood' of the posts?"

Charlene replied, "They seem to be split between supportive and mildly derisive."

"Like what?"

"We can look at them later, Ron," Brandi replied, "but a couple that come to mind are—in the support camp—'Kudos to the couple attempting this. The world could use some more love!' From the trolls—'Gross! These geezers should act their age.' There's more, but that sort of captures the spirit of what's out there."

Ron paused for a brief cranial re-rub, and then said, "I guess that's not as bad as it could be. Thanks Charlene. It's good we know about this."

Monday, May 25

After a rough night of *almost* sleeping, and a crazy day at work, Ron walked home, exhausted, at about six in the evening. He had eaten his lunch at his desk,

152

and assessed the extent of the resolution's online exposure. There was no doubt in his mind that the posts and discussions out there were referring to him and Brandi. It was the first time that he had ever been drawn into a media conversation, and he was bewildered by the categorical tone of the tweets. Opinions were thrown like beanballs. *Good God*, Ron thought, *can anything constructive come of this?* Although he appreciated the positive support, it seemed that for every encouraging post there was a contrarian view, with groups of tweets naturally flowing towards ever-more-extreme positioning before ebbing back to common ground, only to have the cycle repeat itself. As Ron closed in on their home, he concluded that this was not the way to create a meaningful dialogue on their subject—even if that was what they wanted.

After supper he and Brandi sat in the backyard, enjoying the warm high sun of late evening, and discussing how to deal with the "leak." Although the thought that someone in their inner circle might be betraying them was disconcerting to both of them, they eventually concluded that it wasn't important who had leaked their resolution to the public (although Ron couldn't help but have a short list of prime suspects). More relevant was—how they were going to deal with it?

Ron spoke first. "It's not really a conversation on Twitter, Brandi. It's either endorsement or opposition. Or, more commonly, overblown praise, or vilification and shaming. It comes across as snippets of cheering or booing."

"That's my feeling as well, Ron. If anything, this has made me less motivated to share our resolution."

Ron nodded in agreement.

Brandi said, "I'm not saying we absolutely shouldn't still consider going public, but *definitely* not via Twitter. I suppose I wouldn't mind commentary concerning the resolution, but on Twitter I can see us losing control of the message, with the 'conversation' being hijacked by the people who are posting and making it about themselves."

From what Ron had learnt over the last day, he couldn't disagree with of any of Brandi's comments. He added, "How about we don't do anything; deprive it of any oxygen, and let this Twitter thing die a natural death?"

Brandi nodded. "I'm good with that, Ron. We've got enough on our plate these days without having to worry about daily shaming from basement-bound virgins espousing their philosophies on marital sex."

Ron chuckled, and raised his glass in agreement. To help facilitate their discussion tonight, they had enlisted the support of a Jackson-Triggs Sauvignon Blanc from the Niagara region. Both of them now sat back quietly, enjoying the stress-relieving lemon and tropical fruit undertones of the chilled wine. Ron realized this was the best he had felt all day.

Friday, May 29

Sam was at a sleepover in the neighbourhood, so Ron and Brandi had made tonight "porn Friday." Earlier in the week they had discussed their preferences, and how to get their hands on said porn for Friday. Ron had visited his buddy Cassandra at *Aren't We Naughty* for some help in his selection. As expected, she was enthusiastically supportive and helpful.

As well as providing him with a medley of porn, which balanced intensity with his and Brandi's preferences, she sold him another vibrating toy, and some "stimulating lubricants." Discounted to wholesale, of course.

The porn experiment didn't go quite as planned. About a half hour into the poorly acted, but sexually well-represented "movie," Brandi disrobed and mounted Ron on the couch, reaching her first of a half-dozen orgasms that she would enjoy that evening. By the end of the evening, Ron's numbers were up as well. Their enthusiastic reaction to the erotic stimuli clearly indicated that they had both responded positively to this stage of Dr. Fiona's therapy.

Once time had been called, both Ron and Brandi admitted they were looking forward to their next porn-therapy session. Brandi had mentioned that "those female ejaculating orgasms look like fun." Ron knew where this was going before she got the words out of her mouth.

CHAPTER 7

WHAT WOULD MY MOTHER SAY?

Friday, June 5

Ron and Scott had grabbed a table at the back of the Bassline Pub just after five. Ron had filled Scott in about the Twitter leak the previous week, but hadn't talked to him since—almost ten days.

After they had settled and ordered a jug of beer, Scott commented, "Those tweets can sure be entertaining."

"More so for you than us, I'm sure."

"Probably, "Scott agreed. "How do you think they found out about the *Kama Sutra?*"

Ron froze with mug against lip. Slowly lowering his arm, he asked, "Say what?"

"The *Kama Sutra*," repeated Scott. "The recent tweets are talking about your use of the *Kama Sutra* as an 'aid' for you and Brandi in the resolution. Well, not you and Brandi, specifically. Rather, the two geriatrics indulging in age-inappropriate and deviant sexual behaviour. Not my words," he clarified.

Ron hadn't looked at any postings attached to *#resolutionottawa* for more than a week, and had assumed it was withering on the vine as they had hoped. "You're kidding me? Tell me you're kidding?" pleaded Ron.

Scott took out his phone, opened Twitter, punched in *#resolutionottawa*, and passed it over to Ron. After a few minutes of rolling through the stack of new posts, Ron returned Scott's phone, and sighed. "We have a mole."

"So it would appear," concurred Scott. "And just for the record, it isn't me or Elise." He immediately crunched his face introspectively, and added, "Well, not me, for sure."

"I thought this was behind us," lamented Ron.

"The good news is, it's not 'trending'...yet," Scott said. "So what *are* you and Brandi up to these days? These Twitter posts are *soooo* dated."

Back at Centrepointe, Charlene was updating Brandi on the new *#resolutionottawa* posts on Twitter. "It wasn't me," Charlene assured her.

"I know it wasn't you, Charlene. It was probably inevitable that this got out. I just never imagined it would be all over the internet. I suppose that if Ron and I aren't identified, then we can live with it."

She paused as she read a few more posts. "So mean," she exclaimed, an exasperated look on her face. "'Geriatrics?' 'Deviant behaviour'?" She scrolled on. "'Patently unbelievable?' I'd like them to have seen Ron and me last Friday when we had our 'porn Friday.' That would have shut up the skeptics."

"We'll get back to your 'porn Friday' in a minute, but forget the trolls. I want you to focus on the less ignorant, more positive posts." Charlene took her phone back, and scrolled for a second, then read out, "'Amazing effort. Love never dies.' 'We tried and got tuckered out after four days—haha.' 'Resolutionists—my husband and I would like to meet you.' 'The *Kama Sutra* is a riot!'" Charlene looked up with a "doesn't that make you feel better" look on her face.

Brandi nodded agreeably. "Thanks for some perspective, girlfriend," she said, raising her wine in appreciation. It was a fragrant and tangy 2014 Sauvignon Blanc from Bench 1775 in the Okanagan. As she sipped it, Brandi mused that she only had first-world problems. *Suck it up girl*, she thought.

Back at the Bassline, Ron had mentioned their introduction of pornography as the next stage of Dr. Fiona's therapy. He had decided against bringing up her proposal to engage a 'surrogate' to educate them in the subtleties of female ejaculation.

"I told you," Scott responded. "Your doctor is clearly a genius. I have to meet her when you're done with her."

"Does that mean you and Elise have 'regressed' a bit from the lofty heights reached during your recent sexual renaissance?"

"We're pretty steady these days, actually. But as you know," Scott replied with a defensive tone Ron was pleased to have extracted, "this constant sex thing is a lot of hard work. Even using all the add-ons that you guys have introduced. But I've already indicated, we've decided we're not going to pursue the daily coital sacrament with the same religious fervour you and Brandi have adopted, but instead shamelessly cherry-pick through your successful therapies with impunity and use them to entertain ourselves at our leisure. Now doesn't that sound like less work?"

Ron was thinking that it did. But approaching the half-way point in the journey, this wasn't the time to allow daydreams of sexual abstinence to leak into his consciousness. He recalled the intense training he had endured preparing for his triathlon. He missed the simplicity of those days. The mental game associated with this current resolution had turned out to be much tougher in comparison. "Don't be too hard on yourself Scott," he said. "Not all men are destined to be love gods."

"Apparently not," Scott concurred, with a resigned look of a mere mortal.

Brandi had just finished telling Charlene about their porn night the week before.

"Kevin and I are definitely going to see Cassandra over at *Aren't We Naughty* and get some porn flics, and maybe a toy or two. And by Kevin and I, I mean *me*. I think that would be a bit too far out of his comfort zone."

Brandi had debated whether or not to discuss Dr. Fiona's proposal concerning using a "surrogate" to demonstrate the sexual technique to achieve ejaculation during orgasm. Eventually, she decided she wanted Charlene's opinion, and broached the subject.

"I have to admit, it does sound weird as hell," Charlene replied, "but I can understand why you and Ron would be curious about it. I know I am! Still… bringing a third person into your lovemaking…" She exhaled, eyebrows raised and head shaking for emphasis. "What do you think about this?"

"With the right setting and in the comfort of my own bed I could see it happening. Don't get me wrong, I think it's weird as hell too, but now that we've been talking about it, I'm genuinely curious. It's not like Ron will be having sex with her or anything. Actually, now that I think about it, it'll be me having sex with her."

"What does Ron think about all of this?" asked Charlene.

"He's more than a bit overwhelmed, but I know if the 'surrogate' is a woman, he'll go along with it. He does harbour lesbian fantasies, after all, and this activity likely wouldn't be offensive to him. It's just so different than anything we've ever done, and I'm worried it may have unintended consequences."

"Like what?"

Brandi exhaled, and replied, "It could be anything. What if I like her touch more than Ron's? What if Ron really likes having another woman in the mix? What if I can have a gushing orgasm and nothing else will satisfy me? What if we get weirded out and we can't recover from that?"

"No shortage of possibilities there," Charlene agreed. "Why do you think Dr. Fiona is suggesting the surrogate? Surely she's aware of the possible downsides."

"You know, Charlene, that's the right question to ask her. And I'll do exactly that tomorrow."

Saturday, June 6

Brandi and Ron had recounted their positive response associated with introducing pornography into their lovemaking.

"Why do you think you both responded so viscerally to the pornography?" Dr. Fiona asked.

Brandi was first to reply. "For me, it was like having sex with other people watching, and that turned me on. Apparently watching other couples have sex arouses me as well."

"Ron," asked Dr. Fiona, "how about you?"

Ron pondered his response. "I think it was a combination of having Brandi so aroused and letting my imagination roam. We watched some female ejaculation, and that definitely helped augment the mood."

"On that topic, have you given any further thought on bringing in a 'surrogate' to assist you?" asked Dr. Fiona.

Brandi spoke up. "Actually, we're still feeling a little uncomfortable with the whole thing." She let that comment hang for a second, and then added, "We think there may be a good chance of unintended and unhelpful consequences."

Dr. Fiona nodded, and scribbled some notes. "You guys continue to impress me. This tells me that you put your relationship ahead of what both of you currently consider an apex sexual experience."

She removed her glasses, and while gazing at them professorially added, "I have to come clean. The truth is I was exploring your limits with the 'surrogate' proposal. You guys have consciously decided to keep your sexual intimacy to yourselves. I consider that a major step on the path to defining your humanity. Congratulations."

After a few seconds of smiling at them, she added, "That, however, doesn't mean you should be deprived of the experience. It does mean that you can work at it together at your own pace and ability. If you're still interested, I can suggest a couple of excellent guides on how you can experience ejaculation, Brandi. You can probably find them at your local adult store."

Brandi and Ron looked at each other. Ron was thinking, *Cassandra.*

After Dr. Fiona passed on the details of a couple of self-help books dedicated to sharing the female ejaculation experience, she said, "You guys have made good progress. To keep things moving along, I'd like you to introduce…"

Ron had to suppress a moan. The thought of adding to an already full plate of sex-enabling therapies seemed excessive at this point.

Dr. Fiona read his face, stopped her comment mid-sentence, and instead said, "Ron, I'm detecting some angst at this suggestion of adding further to your 'therapies' workload."

"I guess. We're already actively practicing sensate touching, using testosterone supplements, exercising with heavy weights at least three times a week, introducing various fantasies into our love life, and periodically watching porn, and today you've given us some homework dealing with female ejaculation. On top of all this, I've got to make sure I can get the job done—on a daily basis! That said, I am looking forward to your suggested reading," he added with a smile.

"That alone tells me you're not quite at capacity yet, Ron," commented Dr. Fiona. "I know it does seem like a lot, but let me clarify for you. I don't expect that you have to do all of these things every day. By no means. What I'm doing is opening up different doors for you—giving you options that you can use, whenever, wherever, and however you want. The point of this is to establish techniques to fight the most common destructive marital malady—boredom. Boredom leads to indifference, which leads to dissatisfaction, which leads to—well—nothing good. You guys are well past that, but I still have some tools to complete your 'tool box.' Once your tool box is fully stocked, you'll have a full menu of activities that you can draw upon, to not only keep your sex lives interesting and stimulating, but also, I'm hoping, to keep both of you truly looking forward to sex for the rest of your life—sex the way it was meant to be."

Ron had to admit that sounded pretty good. Brandi was also smiling in agreement.

In response to Ron's "I can't argue with that" look, Dr. Fiona continued. "Good. For the next couple of weeks, besides working on Brandi's heightened orgasmic experience, I want you both to take your love life out for a walk."

Confused, Brandi and Ron waited for clarification.

"Part of adding dimension, texture, and excitement to your love life is to get out of your comfort zone. Typically for couples, as I'm sure it is with you two, the comfort zone is your home, and more specifically your bed. For the next two weeks I want you two to experience—at least once in each setting—sex in..." she paused for a few seconds as she referred to her notes, "in a restaurant; in a grocery store; in your car; your backyard; on a golf course; and at a friend's house." She let this sink in for a while then clarified, "I'm not suggesting that you engage in publically obscene full-blown screaming bare-assed intercourse—unless you can do so without getting caught," she added with a smile. "I'm saying sex in the sense that Bill Clinton would *not* have sex. Use your hands and mouths and be sneaky about it. Keep your clothes on if you have to, but get underneath them if you can. From what I know about you Brandi, you'll find the introduction of various venues quite exciting."

Ron was thinking that if the doctor wanted to get him out of his comfort zone, this would certainly do it. He was not looking forward to this new 'therapy.' But judging from the broad smile on Brandi's face—she was!

He immediately started conjuring up a number of scenarios where he and Brandi had been caught and arrested for having sex in public, with the act captured photographically and displayed on the front page of the *Ottawa Citizen*. He imagined a look of guilty shock on his face, with his pants around his ankles and his genitalia pixelated so not as to offend the masses. The unedited version would no doubt be captured on the smartphone of a passerby, and be trending online before he had his belt done up.

He was visualizing the walk of shame to his boss's office the next day to receive his pink slip when his musings were interrupted by an incongruously cheery-sounding Dr. Fiona. "This therapy can be incredibly rewarding. The key to keeping it a positive experience is to be clever about it and not getting caught," she said, emphasizing the last statement.

As far as Ron was concerned, she needn't have bothered stating the obvious.

Sunday, June 7

It was a beautiful, warm, sunny day in Ottawa, so Ron and Brandi had decided to walk over to *Aren't We Naughty* to find the appropriate literature on female ejaculation. Although the store was only open for a few hours on Sundays, due to bylaw restrictions, the managers at *Aren't We Naughty* were astutely cognizant that the human requirement for sex superseded all seasonal, climatic, cultural, and calendar considerations, regarding them as nothing more than backdrops to the main human drama playing out on life's stage. Whether a day was one of worship or not was considered inconsequential to this primary sensual objective. The managers had consciously decided to serve the greater good of the community by staying open on Sundays, and business was typically brisk. Perhaps the Lord did work in mysterious ways.

Much to Ron's relief, Cassandra was working, single-handedly manning the ship late on Sunday morning. She was her typically effervescent self in greeting Ron, and proceeded to gregariously introduced herself to Brandi—the "resolution priestess," as she referred to her—with a deference that bordered on spiritual. Suppressing her embarrassment, Brandi graciously accepted

Cassandra's compliments, and before long, the two of them had struck up a comfortable rapport.

Once Brandi had explained her reason for the visit, Cassandra proudly exclaimed that fate had conspired to bring them together today, since she was in-fact the self-acclaimed "Queen of the female ejaculation."

Ron almost had to pinch himself upon hearing Cassandra utter those words. Here was his wife in an adult store on a Sunday morning in June, enthusiastically engaged in a discussion about female ejaculation with a purple-haired stranger she had known for less than ten minutes. *You can't make this shit up*, he thought.

After a general discussion on technique, and the "magnificence" of the experience when achieved, Brandi and Cassandra settled on a paperback called *Female Ejaculation: Unleash the Ultimate G-Spot Orgasm.*

Before they could escape, Cassandra decided to help Ron out, and passed on some "insider" tips on technique to complement the purchased literature. Much to Brandi's surprise, Ron wasn't embarrassed with the conversation, but instead listened intently, and asked a few questions. *We're going to have a busy afternoon*, mused Brandi.

Thursday, June 11

Today was designated as Brandi and Ron's inaugural venture into the realm of public sex. They had informed the kids that they were having a date night, and to forage the fridge for their own sustenance. On the walk over to one of Brandi's favourite restaurants, Ron's profusely sweating hands betrayed his nervousness concerning this evening's plan. They had been discussing it all week, and it had taken Brandi until last night to convince Ron to attempt it.

Approaching the restaurant, Brandi wiped his sweat from her hand again, and confidently assured Ron that their plan was solid, and it would all be OK. Neither of them was wearing any underwear, and Brandi was sporting a light mid-thigh length skirt that could be easily hiked up when the timing was right. Ron was wearing loose shorts.

This restaurant had been chosen, not for its great food, but mainly for its setting. Its overlong table cloths provided ample cover for their mission, and they had purposefully reserved a dimly-lit corner table away from the well-trodden corridors, which allowed them to sit with their backs against the wall. This table was an artifact of the restaurant's earlier days, decades ago. It alone had somehow escaped the series of renovations that the rest of the restaurant had undergone to stay in lockstep with the progressively more urbane population of its surrounding communities. From previous meals, they knew that the bench seats on this table were low-riders, with the table top coming up almost to mid-torso on Ron; higher on Brandi.

Brandi thought the plan was foolproof. Ron thought it might be foolproof, but it wasn't idiot-proof, and that was what worried him. Historically, this was exactly the kind of stressful and over-planned situation in which Ron found a way to embarrass himself.

Brandi repeated herself when Ron didn't respond at first. "So, you still good with this?"

Ron's mouth was so dry as they entered the restaurant that he could only offer a weak distracted nod that yes, he was. His expression suggested otherwise.

Ideally positioned in their amply clothed sunken corner table, and halfway through his first glass of red wine, Ron started to feel a bit more at ease. No one was watching them—and why should they be? A mature couple having a romantic meal and engaged in comfortable conversation in the quiet corner of the restaurant? Nothing could be more normal.

It was about that time that Ron felt Brandi's hand subtly snake over, unzip his shorts, and start groping around, while she didn't miss a beat in their ongoing conversation. Her search didn't last long. Much to Ron's surprise, his johnson rose to meet her halfway, and their operation started unfolding as planned. With her unoccupied hand, Brandi directed Ron's hand closest to her towards her crotch. The skirt had already been positioned to accept Ron's probing fingers, and Ron had to suppress a moan when they intersected Brandi's sopping wet nether region. From the outside looking in, their arms were casually angled towards each other, innocently augmenting the physicality of the ongoing conversation.

At that exact moment, the waiter popped into view and loudly interjected, "Excuse me!" snapping Ron back into the moment, complete with a stranger standing a couple of feet away from his public erection, firmly ensconced in his wife's grip. Ron immediately felt his face start to redden, and within a couple of seconds, his ears were burning. This blood had to come from somewhere, and his brain had instantly and involuntarily shifted priority from erection to protection.

Before he could respond with anything other than his best neon guppy imitation, the waiter continued. "Sorry to interrupt, but have you had a chance to look at the menu and decide what you'll be having tonight?"

Brandi smiled. "Yes, we know exactly what our pleasure is tonight, thanks for asking."

Remarkably—to Ron at least—they ordered with the waiter apparently none the wiser as to their covert jiggery-pokery, and the operation picked up where it left off. With ordering out of the way, and a period of uninterrupted "them" time expected, they moved into phase two of their plan. While outwardly quietly engaged in a private conversation, both managed to climax in a matter of minutes. While not surprising for Brandi, Ron was truly surprised just how physically stimulating the whole experience was for him. All bits were tucked away, hands wiped relatively dry, and items of clothing returned to their pre-masturbatory state by the time the meals arrived.

Their conversation and mood was electric during the meal, and Ron thought he noticed a dreamy look in Brandi's eyes that he hadn't seen since they were initially dating, more than twenty years ago.

The waiter returned, and asked if they wanted any dessert. Ron was winding up for a standard, "No thanks, just the bill" response when Brandi grabbed his hand, placed it back on her crotch, and indicated to the waiter that she *was* in the mood for a little dessert, and could he please bring some warm apple pie with vanilla ice cream and two forks. *Oh-oh*, thought Ron, as Brandi hiked up her skirt and repositioned Ron's hand.

Sunday, June 14

Ron's parents had just finished the paperwork on the sale of their house, with the move to their new living arrangements planned for three weekends hence. Ron, Brandi, and the kids were over at the Glencairn house for Sunday supper, and to discuss the details of the move.

After about ninety minutes of cycling through the minutia associated with their real-estate transaction, and logistics concerning their move into senior-community living, Tommy Sr. had had enough, and retired to his La-Z-Boy in the adjacent living room to watch the tube. Sam had already lost interest in the ongoing discussion, and had been watching some entertainment-related television for about an hour. Tommy Sr. talked her into watching the early news, while the rest of them remained at the kitchen table to discuss the move.

After about ten minutes, with the discussion winding up at the kitchen table, Sam exclaimed a loud "Gross!" and everyone's attention was drawn to the television. The local station had recently introduced a human-interest segment into their evening broadcast, dealing with "trending issues," which usually consisted of cute animals, misbehaving or pretentious children, improbable sports clips, or bizarre weather shots. Tonight, however, they had decided that a mature Ottawa couple's resolution to make love every day of 2015, currently trending on Twitter, was newsworthy.

As both Ron and Brandi stared in disbelief at the smirking broadcaster now discussing some of the details of their resolution, Ron slowly turned his reddening face towards Brandi who, for a change, was performing *her* best guppy imitation. He noted her cheeks were also looking a bit warm.

Mercifully, the soundbite lasted only about twenty seconds. Unfortunately, however, the background on the story was followed-up by the three broadcasters at the news desk trading witty innuendoes and thinly veiled sexual inferences in reference to the clip.

"They must be newlyweds." offered Broadcaster One (male).

"No, apparently they've been married about twenty years!" countered Broadcaster Two (female, empathetic type).

"Viagra must be making a killing off of these two," responded Broadcaster Three (male jock).

"I hope they can keep it up," quipped Broadcaster One.

"You're bad," replied Broadcaster Two.

"I want to meet these guys. I think the whole thing's made-up," returned Broadcaster One.

"Well, I don't, and I think it's romantic," mewed Broadcaster Two, signalling an end to this segment. She then immediately introduced a video about a beer-drinking Dalmatian who, after a couple of pints, danced an Irish jig, while standing on his hind legs and howling in tune to Irish Rover songs.

It was, officially, the longest forty seconds of Ron's life. Immediately afterwards, Sam offered up a final heart-felt, "That's gross!" as a punctuation to her previous comment, dispelling any possibility that she actually condoned sex by mature couples, either specifically in pursuit of this resolution, or, more likely, in general, just to expunge the thought completely from her mind.

Abby turned to Ron, who over the last few seconds had been performing a Zen Master-like biofeedback meditation to flush the blood from his cheeks, and ironically stated, chuckling, "That's something that you two would do, Aaron!"

With this final assault, Ron felt himself losing the battle to remain outwardly calm. As he mustered a weak casual smile in response to this comment, his mother's smile faded into the growing realization that these broadcasters were indeed talking about Ron and Brandi. Immediately coming to his defense, and instinctively protecting her grandchildren from permanent emotional damage and a lifetime of expensive remedial psychotherapy, she quickly added, "But even you guys wouldn't try that." And immediately asked the group, "Would anybody like tea?"

During the drive home, Ron and Brandi enthusiastically directed the conversation towards topics as far away from sex as possible to avoid any further discussion of the segment they had seen on television. Despite, or perhaps because, of their best efforts, Tommy Jr. sensed that the Danish Esrom cheese he was being fed was a bit too ripe, and casually asked, "What do you guys think about that resolution that they talked about on the news tonight?"

Ron looked in the rearview mirror, and saw both of his kids with their heads slightly craned, waiting patiently for a response. An extended pause ensued, during which both Brandi and Ron actively hoped the other would offer a reasonable reply.

Much to Ron's relief, Brandi eventually responded. "You have to ask yourself why they think that sort of thing is newsworthy? Normally something as private as marital sex would be anything but news. But make it a challenge and turn it into something epic, and it captures the imagination of the public."

After a couple of beats, Tommy replied, "If it's just a challenge then…whatever. But part of me is hoping there's something more to it."

Neither Brandi nor Ron had a response for that, and the comment hung in the air long after the words had been spoken.

Friday, June 19

Brandi and Ron were invited over to Scott and Elise's for supper, and it was there they planned to cross off the final venue on Dr. Fiona's "out of your comfort zone" sex list, before reporting back to her the following day.

Following their positive restaurant experience, they had regrouped, and headed off to the local Loblaws to scope the premises and plan their next "therapy" session. They had identified a secluded cubbyhole, just past the gluten-free section and out of camera shot, where neither customer nor employee visited for extended periods of time. They had decided that the best time to execute "Operation Sugar Muffin" would be an hour before closing on Tuesday, when the limited, exhausted, and indifferent staff were glued to their stations, waiting for the last hour to tick off the clock. Although out of view of the 360-degree cameras, the possibility that their tardiness in returning from the shadows could be registered in the security room allowed for only the briefest of coital encounters.

The golf-course endeavour was far less problematic. With Brandi working at the Kanata Research Park, she had twenty-four hour access to the complex, which included the adjacent Marshes Golf Club. She and Ron waited for a beautiful evening, headed down to her office, watched for the flags to be pulled from the greens and the dusk to deepen towards night, and then simply strolled onto the golf course. Ron thought the seventh green was exceptionally moist and accepting that evening. The operation was executed perfectly, the only blemish being the mosquito bites on Ron's *derrière*. The house was well asleep when they arrived home, so they used the opportunity to continue with the outdoors theme in their own backyard that night.

Later that week an excursion into the unpopulated concession roads west of Ottawa presented innumerable vehicular venues where the ride could continue after the car was parked. They enjoyed that outing so thoroughly it had been repeated twice more during the last week.

But tonight's effort was more challenging for its own reasons. Firstly, both Scott and Elise were very intimate with their resolution, and although they would understand if their friends' therapeutic requirements included short-term usage of their facilities, Ron and Brandi thought that it would defeat the intent of the exercise if their friends were complicit in the act. Secondly, it didn't feel right sneaking around in their friend's house, but they had agreed that they would assess the situation as the evening progressed and decide if, then how and when, they would proceed.

About half way through their first glass of a 2012 Sandhill Small Lots Syrah, Ron and Brandi simultaneously realized that they couldn't go through with it. With the change of plans communicated through the subtlest of eye contact between them, Ron relaxed, and actually began to enjoy the evening.

(During the ride home, when they discussed their change of heart, both agreed that their planned operation would have driven a wedge of secrecy between the two couples, and risk the relationship and the open and honest dialogue and counsel that they had grown to count on over the years, and especially the last six months.)

Later in the evening at Scott and Elise's, when Ron was in the toilet, he ruminated over the resolution. In particular, his son's comments concerning the reasoning behind the resolution still resonated with him. What *was* his rationale? It had been almost six months since New Year's Eve and his moment of inspiration, and he honestly couldn't recall if there *was* any rationale other than the baser drivers of fulfilling his annual resolutionary requirement, and his general enjoyment of sex. Was he really that shallow? He was embarrassed to think that he could be. He hoped that he had had, at least unconsciously, more noble motives. Somewhere over the past few months Ron had realized that sex was far more than a physical act—it was a portal into the human psyche.

As he was leaning over the sink washing his hands, he started to visualize sex as a high-voltage cable, sparking and writhing dangerously at its earthly terminus. But when he followed the cable back to its source, it unraveled into innumerable impossibly delicate strands drawn from every corner of the brain, each carrying the smallest of charge. By themselves, the strands were of no consequence, but together they grew into a force powerful enough to move mountains, mobilize armies, and create life. At that moment, Ron knew the resolution had a greater purpose.

When he returned to the living room, Scott spoke. "Brandi was just filling us in on your most recent therapy prescribed by Dr. Fiona."

Ron did a quick mental recall of what he and Brandi had been working on over the last couple of weeks. *Oh-oh*, he thought. *Nothing good can come of this.* "Which one was that?" he asked apprehensively.

"Golf-course sex? Are you kidding me? You guys are beasts!" Scott exclaimed, with open reverence for his friends.

Somewhat surprised by Brandi's candidness, Ron played along with the buoyant mood of the room. "My first hole-in-one!" he quipped ironically, with a "how about that?" look.

Scott chuckled. "I'm constantly amazed with you guys. What's next?"

Ron shook his head, and exhaled loudly. "I honestly have no idea, Scott."

Saturday, June 20

Ron and Brandi had just finished updating Dr. Fiona on their progress over the last couple of weeks. After she finished scribbling some notes, she looked up and asked, "So how did you feel before, during, and after your public encounters?"

Before Brandi could collect her thoughts and speak to the question, Ron answered. "There was certainly a sense of anxiety beforehand," he glanced at Brandi, "for me anyways. But I think I speak for both of us when I say that the actual act was exhilarating." He looked again at Brandi, who was nodding in agreement. "In fact, *that* was the surprising part to me. It was incredibly exciting. For me it was one part sex, one part successful deception, and one part rebellious behaviour, stirred into a single spicy dish. Not just the restaurant. All five venues."

After looking down at her notepad, Dr. Fiona commented, "My notes indicate I gave you six venues. Which one of those did you not complete?"

Brandi now spoke. "Having sex at a friend's place. We actually planned this for last night, but decided against it just after we arrived."

"Can you tell me why?" asked Dr. Fiona.

"We both *felt* it at the same time," Brandi replied. "These are our best friends and to do something sneaky like that in their home would have been a breach of trust. And we need our friends now more than ever."

Dr. Fiona started back at her notes. "Huh," she said absentmindedly, nodding her head. Then she took off her glasses and cast her now-familiar professorial gaze at them. "As we've discussed earlier, these exercises are attempting to rewire your brain. Instead of a withered, choked-off, and bored neurochemical pleasure delivery system, by using these therapies we've built up and created fresh neuro-pleasure pathways through fantasy, fetishes, and risky sex in your relationship, while fortifying the emotional and social connection with sensate and other touching practices. At the risk of oversimplifying things, we're trying to diminish the role of your primal core, or even take it out of the equation, so the more evolved, sophisticated, and truly human portions of your brain can operate in an unconstrained manner. And from what you've told me here today, I believe that these therapies in support of your resolution are starting to work."

"I have to agree, Dr. Fiona," Brandi said. "Ron and I are definitely sharing a more complex and complete pleasure during these experiences."

Dr. Fiona chuckled. "It's notable you stated that in the manner you did, Brandi. It's an excellent segue into my final and most profound observation. What I've observed in our sessions, and the fact that you both simultaneously and silently decided not to risk your relationship with your friends, suggests to me that you two are developing a shared consciousness."

Ron and Brandi looked at each other.

"That may sound unusual, but it's been scientifically documented, with varying degrees of frequency and intensity, in most couples, more commonly in sexually active and/or older couples. You've heard of members of couples finishing each other's sentences, or knowing what their spouse is thinking before they speak, or even 'feeling' something that only their spouse has experienced. These are real phenomena, and we've all experienced it."

"Telepathy?" asked Ron.

"That's one word for it," replied Dr. Fiona, "but not quite. Understanding of this phenomenon is far from complete, but its existence has been positively confirmed in numerous controlled experiments. Some people are naturally more sensitive and capable of this 'thought alignment', but most people experience it infrequently and completely at random—and almost never when they're actually *trying* to look into another person's mind. Similar to when you're searching in vain for an elusive name, only to have it pop into your consciousness all by itself shortly afterwards."

As Dr. Fiona paused to let her comments sink in, Ron started assessing the likelihood of this occurrence in the context of him and Brandi. Now that Dr. Fiona had mentioned it, he had been noticing that more frequently he and Brandi moved around the house with shared purpose, without having to verbally communicate intent. Over the last couple of months Brandi had, almost on a daily basis, known what Ron was going to say before he spoke. And specific to the resolution, he understood exactly what Brandi desired sexually, and was actually sharing in her orgasms with her. *Actually feeling real pleasure when she did.*

Coming back to the present, Ron turned his head to look at Brandi, and saw she was silently nodding her head at him.

Dr. Fiona noted this. "What just happened there?"

Brandi answered. "Well, Ron was pondering how he was 'sharing' in my orgasms and I *heard* him."

"Wow. This may be even more advanced than I had suspected."

After an extended pause, Dr. Fiona added, "There's a good possibility you two are starting to undergo an advanced neurophysical alignment of brain waves when you're in close proximity to each other. Your half year of frequent intimate bonding has very probably caused this event. As I mentioned, we all have this ability, to a greater or lesser degree, but I'm assuming that neither of you had previously considered yourselves possessed of a 'Kreskin-like' ability to read minds."

Both Brandi and Ron shook their heads.

"Then I suspect that this recent development is a consequence of your resolution. I can't say for sure what's happening, but it may be caused by your brain's unrelenting search for more pleasure."

Ron and Brandi stared back at Dr. Fiona, looking confused.

"Yes, your brains have figured out a way to tap into your spouse's reward system, and boost their own neurochemical reward as a result. An unintended consequence of this 'mutual alignment' is an ability to read each other's minds."

She paused and pondered further. "This doesn't feel like something the primal core could pull off," she muttered, almost to herself. "No, what we're seeing here is most likely the initial emergence of the more sophisticated, truly human parts of your brains."

"But what's changed?" asked Ron.

"I think there may have been an emancipation of sorts."

Another confused look simultaneously blossomed on the faces of Ron and Brandi.

"It's quite possible that the heightened levels of pleasure neurochemistry in your brain feeding the primal core may have concomitantly provided the more evolved, uniquely human regions of your brains some unprecedented freedom. Fully aware that the primal beast needs to be fed, with its sole sustenance being the neurochemical reward system, these more sophisticated regions of your brain are now doing what they can to further placate the needs of the primal core. And towards this end, your brains have figured out how to tap into each other's reward systems, introduce an additional layer of neurochemical pleasure for the primal core, and in doing so, encourage further freedoms. If this is an early product of the resolution, we may be in for some big surprises - if we can keep your primal core sated, and enable further engagement of your 'human' brain."

"And if this reward system isn't maintained or even stops?" asked Brandi.

"Then all hell will likely break loose, Brandi. The beast will flex its considerable muscularity and influence over your actions, and will direct you to fill the void as quickly and completely as is humanly possible. And nothing good can come of that."

"You make it sound as if we have no control over our actions, Dr. Fiona," exclaimed Ron.

"And here you have hit upon the very essence of our experiment, Ron. Every animal on earth, including ourselves, has this primal core directing or at least influencing its *every* behaviour—to a greater or lesser degree. What separates us from the rest of life on earth are the highly developed regions in our brains, responsible for our reasoning, emotions, abstract thinking, and self-awareness. This is what makes us humans, well... human. Our objective is to use the reso-lution to discover our true humanity—and its potential. And to do that, we, meaning you and Brandi with my assistance, will attempt to rise above your primal nature—your hardwired core—and place control of yourselves into the figurative hands of the uniquely human regions of your brains."

Any lingering belief that Ron may have had that the resolution was just about sex was completely dispelled at that moment. "So the fortifying of our relation-ship and brain chemistry is only the beginning?"

"Possibly, Ron. This is uncharted territory for me, as well. We have, in effect, primed the pumps, by introducing an optimal neurochemical reward cycle while maintaining healthy brain chemistry, and set the stage for whatever's next," replied Dr. Fiona.

"As you know, we're currently close to maximum capacity at the moment, doctor. Will our brain expect, or demand even, that we continue supplementing our neurochemical reward system? Where does it stop?" asked Ron.

"Not quite yet, but soon is the answer Ron. I'll get to that in a moment." She took a breath. "So, whereas previously, before the resolution, you had a solid relationship, now it's is pretty close to bulletproof. However, if you didn't know this before, I'll remind you now. Nothing, and I mean *nothing*, in life is ever static. We can adapt to routine and daily sameness, but sooner or later, we'll reject it. Introducing new facets of activity into your love life at a torrid pace has so far kept your brain's need for change and variety satiated, but we know that it's impossible to keep up this pace of change. The compromise that might just work is—and this is my theory—if the brain's core is *fully* gorged on a high neurochemical diet, and it's essentially content, then it may accept the status quo in perpetuity. My plan is, once we've peaked, we'll move into a 'plateau stage' where we can subtly transition control of your will and actions away from your primal core to the more sentient regions of your brain, which define your humanity. These recent developments suggest that the process may have already begun. But no one and nothing freely relinquishes power or control, and there'll be no difference here concerning your primal core. This process will have to be conducted with diplomatic subtly and patience to preserve harmony, since nothing happens in your brain without the full support of your primal core.

"Now, let's talk about that one remaining piece of the reward equation, which I suspect will likely make our work going forward a lot easier. Brandi: have you successfully ejaculated yet?"

Tuesday, June 23

Tommy and Sam were home before their parents. Tommy was perusing something on his laptop when Sam came into the kitchen. "What's for supper?" she asked, as she flung open the fridge door.

"Leftovers," Tommy answered absently, scrolling through an item of obvious interest.

After heating up a plate full of leftovers from the last few days, Sam sat down beside him and asked, "What're you looking at?"

"You remember the story about the older couple and their 'resolution' we saw on TV last weekend at Grampa and Grandma's house?

"Ooooooh! I've been trying to get it out of my mind ever since. Why would you be looking at *that?*" she demanded, with a look of extreme agony.

"I'll tell you why in a sec, but I've been cruising through the recent tweets for *#resolutionottawa*, and there're some real doozies. Want to see?"

"Do I have to?" pleaded Sam, her eyes already tracking towards the screen.

"I think you may like some of them."

"Well OK, show me," conceded Sam, already beside him and focusing on the tweets. Tommy turned the screen towards Sam and she read them out loud.

"'Now using testosterone and watching porn—whatever gets you through the night!!!' 'When I grow up, I want to be like these guys.' 'I hear the wife was a porn star when she was younger.' 'Look for the old guy with a smile in your office—that's him.' 'Why??????????????' 'Why not?' 'What about her monthly period?' 'I've heard she's post-menopausal.' 'If things don't work out at home I'd like to date her!' 'Ditto for me re: the husband.' 'Unbelievable!' 'Sex wasn't meant to be abused like this.' 'A beautiful testament to their love for each other.'"

Sam looked at Tommy. "Really? Just a bunch of bored people with nothing better to do. And now, *you're* one of them. Why are you so interested in these guys? You looking for a perfect wife?"

"Well, actually, I'm interested because I think these guys are Mom and Dad."

"No friggin' way!" exclaimed Sam. "Why do you think that?"

"Think about it. Dad's annual resolution thing." He held up his index finger. "An older couple." He held up his middle finger. "Married forever." His ring finger joined the other two. "They've been acting real strange for the last couple of months, since I've been home." His pinky sprang to attention. "And finally, did you see their reaction to the TV segment at grandma's place? I though dad was going to pass-out." His thumb joined the party to complete his jazz-hand. "Grandma thinks it's them too."

"How do you know that?" asked Sam.

"I saw it in her face when *she* put it together last weekend. It was the same serious look she had when she heard that Grampa Sean was dying of ALS. It only flashed across her face for a second, but I saw it."

"Oh my God," sighed Sam. "What are we going to do?"

"Nothing. Absolutely nothing."

"Nothing? If this gets out I'll be ruined!"

"This isn't about you or me, Sammy."

"It just creeps me out."

"Well then, get over it. You're missing the bigger picture, little sister. I know you're aware of how things work. And we should be thankful we have parents who not only get along, they still love each other enough after twenty years of marriage to give this resolution a try. Would you rather they not be interested in each other physically, and constantly bickering?"

"No. You know that. It's just so weird."

"We forget, or haven't yet realized, that they're people as well. As children we've only known them as parents looking after us, when all the while they were looking after us as well as themselves and everybody else in their families. Now they're doing something for themselves while they have time."

"What do you mean while they have time?"

"Well, from what I understand, these kinds of desires diminish with age."

"Thank God for that—I couldn't handle thinking about Grampa and Grandma that way."

"Sam, this need may diminish, but doesn't go away with age. It's part of what makes us human. Get your head around it. There's no avoiding it as long as you're alive."

"Then I would have liked to have remained innocent just a bit longer," she moaned.

"Don't think about the details. It's like making sausage. Just enjoy the results. In our case, two happy cool parents."

"Ha! Dad's not cool. And is making sausage gross, too?"

Thursday, June 25

After dinner Ron and Brandi retreated upstairs, and proceeded to engage in some good old-fashioned early-summertime bondage sex, with Brandi loosely bound to the four corners of the bed. She was also blindfolded. Both of the kids were out of the house, so a more intense lovemaking session had been planned out for this evening. Ron commenced the proceedings with some full-body tickling, toe- and finger-sucking, and light pinching, followed by some focused attention on Brandi's naughty bits, mixed with short periods of penetration.

With Ron executing recently learned techniques from *Female Ejaculation: Unleash the Ultimate G-Spot Orgasm*, Brandi parked whatever remained of her inhibitions and completely submitted to the moment. About twenty minutes into the session she started to experience a building pressure in her vagina, with warmth spreading throughout the core of her body like lava. It was a sensation she hadn't before experienced. An electric energy crawled up her spine, and began pooling at the base of her skull. Over the next few minutes the intensity of the sensation grew, and the glowing core in her genitalia seemed to link directly with the high-voltage knot of energy growing in her brain. The electricity spread to the extremities of her body like ink in water, its intensity growing towards a near-unbearable level, until her entire body shuddered with an explosive release of pressure, fluids and neurochemicals briefly sending her consciousness adrift into a void unburdened by either her senses or time.

Over the course of half an hour, and five such orgasms, both were completely spent. After a few moments, once the electricity had drained from her body, the ringing in her ears had dissipated, and her breath had calmed, Brandi broke the silence.

"That was incredible, Ron!"

Brandi leaned over and kissed him, while caressing the back of his head. "Those were the most intense orgasms I've ever experienced, Ronny. It was as if my spirit detached from my body...Does that sound too weird?"

Ron held her hand, looked at her, and said, "It doesn't. Remember, I'm sharing your feelings during sex. I felt it too, Brandi."

They quietly sat entwined for a few minutes, and then Brandi pensively whispered, "Ron. I think for the first time in my life I feel totally at peace."

Saturday, June 27

Dr. Fiona sat silently smiling at Ron and Brandi. They had just informed her of Brandi's successful orgasms, and their shared sense of complete serenity following the event.

"I'm still feeling fantastic, Dr. Fiona, and it's been over a day," remarked Brandi. She looked over at Ron, who was unsuccessfully trying to suppress a smile.

"Me as well," he admitted to the doctor.

Dr. Fiona removed her glasses, exhaled, pursed her lips, and spoke. "We've been working hard over the past couple of months to get ourselves to where we now are, and I want to congratulate you both on your progress to date. You've now reached a critical point in your quest. With your attainment of complete, possibly absolute, physical pleasure, it's time to move onto the next, and likely more challenging, phase in the exploration of your humanity. The primary purpose of these therapies and exercises and experiences has been to placate your primal core so you can more freely explore your humanity—that which separates you from the rest of life on this earth; to actually understand what it means to be human and, ultimately, appreciate and better utilize the gift that time and evolution has uniquely bestowed upon our species. Your real journey is about to begin my, friends."

Both Brandi and Ron felt their mood fade from one of elation and calmness to apprehension and trepidation. "What exactly do you have in mind, Dr. Fiona?" asked Brandi.

"Let me metaphorically paint the picture for you both. The beast—your primal core—is now well fed, and has contentedly receded back into its cave, allowing the rest of your brain to roam unrestricted over the landscape of your mind, without fear of molestation by the brutish overseer. Its hunger, although currently sated, will require periodic feeding, so you can't become complacent. You must now strictly adhere to your sexual regime so as not to awaken, agitate, or anger the beast. You have all the tools you'll require to successfully achieve this over the next six months, and as of this week, your toolbox is full. The one uncertainty that remains—given the lack of published material on this—is, will the beast remain sated under the current feeding program? Or does its appetite know no boundaries? If that's the case, all this has been for naught and you two are in for an extremely bumpy ride. Sorry."

After letting that comment hang for a few seconds, the doctor continued. "That said, from everything I've learnt, and based upon what I now know about your current state of mind, I don't think this is what's happening. Let me tell you why I believe this. Although the beast represents your more primal essence, it's still part of *you*. If *you're* truly feeling a state of complete peace, this means your primal core is also at peace. If *you're* feeling completely sated, it's because *your* primal core has been sated. There is no total peace without having *complete* harmony in your brain, and a neurochemical equilibrium that supports that harmony.

"So what is the next stage all about, Dr. Fiona?" Ron asked

"Yes—let me explain," replied the doctor.

Twenty minutes later, Brandi and Ron sat speechless in front of Dr. Fiona. The doctor had just summarized her forward strategy for the next six months.

"And what if we decide not to follow your suggested program, Dr. Fiona?" Brandi asked.

"Then I'm afraid our relationship will end here and now," answered Dr. Fiona. "You two have all the tools you'll require to complete the remainder of your resolution. That I'm sure of. You don't need me any longer to help you out on the physical side of this challenge. What I'm interested in—and I hope you will be, as well—is the spiritual component of what you guys can now achieve. Your brains are now as open and unburdened as they ever have been as adults, and I'm sure if we explore its potential, this will be a defining time in both your lives. Doors will be opened that you didn't even know existed. You'll experience emotions and clarity of understanding of what it means to be human that only the most devout typically experience. It is, quite literally, an opportunity of a lifetime."

Here she paused, and then added, "But it's up to you. If you want to keep it as a physical challenge, that in itself will have been quite an accomplishment."

Brandi spoke up. "Let Ron and I discuss this further, Dr. Fiona. We'll get back to you with our decision before the end of the weekend, if that's OK with you?"

"That's fine with me, Brandi. Let's call it a day and I'll talk to you later."

On their short drive home, Ron and Brandi privately considered the implications of Dr. Fiona's six-month program. After a few minutes, Ron turned to Brandi. "Makes you long for the days when I just had to change my underwear every day, doesn't it?"

Brandi just nodded her head in agreement.

CHAPTER 8

OVER THE HUMP

Wednesday, July 1

The skies had mostly cleared by the time guests started arriving, around three o'clock, for Ron and Brandi's annual Canada Day celebration. This year's fete was different, however. Today marked the beginning of the second half of the resolution and, with the cresting of the mountain, the finish line was finally in sight. It might still be as distant as an ocean horizon, but at least they could sense it was out there now. They had both awakened revitalized and manically optimistic.

All the regulars were in attendance, including a slew of Tommy's and Sam's friends, neighbours, Tommy Sr. and Abby, and, of course, Scott and Elise, and Charlene and Kevin.

Soon after his arrival, Scott grabbed a beer and tracked down Ron. Lifting it in salutation, he toasted Ron. "Congratulations, my man. In January I sure as hell wouldn't have bet that you guys would have made it this far in the resolution; but here we stand. Once again, you and Brandi have beaten the odds."

Ron smiled and returned Scott's toast, clinking his beer can with Scott's. "Thanks, buddy. There was nothing easy about it, though." After a brief pause, he added, "And it appears things are about to get more interesting."

Scott's brow furrowed, and he cautiously asked, "What exactly do you mean by that?"

"Too much to talk about right now Scotty. How about we catch up Friday after work?"

"Deal," replied Scott. "I can't wait to hear what's next."

Later, Ron sat with his mom, going over details concerning the imminent move and their new residence. The big day was in a couple of weeks, and he and his mom were discussing the minutia of how to store and distribute the redundant homeware, and the lifetime collection of memorabilia and keepsakes. It was an emotional time for both of his parents, and Tommy Sr. was especially feeling *verklempt*, displaying classic signs of denial; avoiding any discussions of the subject and walking around in a morose frump. As a result, all the heavy lifting had fallen to Abby and Ron. Abby had asked Ron's brother, Stewart, to help out, and he had been strong-armed into compliance. The truth was the move would take care of itself, and his parents really only needed Stewart for emotional and familial support during the transition.

Ron and his mom had decided to hold a garage sale on Sunday to help clean out the house. Ron and Brandi had agreed to 'store' most of their antique furniture and larger heirlooms, which they couldn't fit or find a use for in their more modest living space at the seniors' home. Anything left over would be off to the junkyard. Abby had a cache of their most intimate and personally valuable items that she wanted to divide between her two sons, and that was the primary reason she insisted Stewart come to town to help out.

Ron marveled at his mom's internal strength; her quiet grit and fortitude. He knew that this change of life was as hard for her as it was for his dad. Yet here she sat, calmly and happily discussing how to parcel up her life's belongings, disbursing essentially all of the items collected through her life that had been purposefully hoarded to provide context, continuity, and emotional security. *How tough must that be?* Ron asked himself.

"So how are you and Brandi doing?" his mom spoke, jolting him out of his musings.

"Uh, um…fine. Yeah, we're great, Mom. Thanks for asking."

His mom smiled back at him, shifted her glasses down her nose to afford herself an unobstructed view of her son's face, and quietly said, "You know what I'm talking about, Ron."

Ron could feel all the blood draining from his face, followed immediately by a tsunami-like hemoglobin resurgence, painting his ears and cheeks a bright crimson.

"Yes, apparently you *do* know what I'm talking about," his mom said, chuckling.

After a few seconds Ron collected himself, and sheepishly inquired, "But how…?"

"Ron. Never play poker for money. You have a face incapable of deception. The other day at our place when the news story about the resolution came on, you might as well have just blurted, 'Hey, Brandi, look. We're on TV!'"

Shaking his head in *faux* shame, Ron replied, "Well, without going into too much detail, we're doing great, Mom."

"Seems like a lot of work, if you ask me," she said in a sardonic tone. She stood. "I'm going to check on your father."

Good grief, Ron thought to himself. *Who* doesn't *know?*

Meanwhile, Brandi, Charlene, and Elise were having a chat in one of the quieter corners of the backyard. Brandi had been updating the girls on their progress concerning the resolution, and had been coerced into describing her most recent experience.

"Holy shit!" exclaimed Charlene. "I thought that was a myth."

"Me too," added Elise. "What was the name of the book you guys used?"

"We used *Female Ejaculation: Unleash the Ultimate G-Spot Orgasm*," replied Brandi, "but there are about a half dozen books available that would do the trick."

"So any woman should be able to have one?" asked Elise.

"Dr. Fiona believes that if you can already freely orgasm, then with a little practice, there's no reason why you shouldn't be able to achieve one. I was skeptical at first as well, but now I realize the key is to completely relax and submit to the experience.

"And as a minimum, you'll require a willing and dexterous partner who can read."

All the ladies laughed out loud. Ron looked over, concerned.

"From what you've described, I *definitely* want to give that a try," Charlene said exuberantly.

Elise, eyebrows raised, nodded her head in agreement.

❧

Later on, the cooling evening chased the last of the gathering inside. Tommy Jr. had just left to drive his grandparents home, and Sam had gone to sleep over with one of her neighbourhood friends. Charlene sat at the island with Brandi, absentmindedly scrolling on her phone. When she stopped and reflexively exhaled a "Jeez!" Brandi asked what was up.

Charlene hesitated, and then showed her the phone. It was a particularly mean tweet tagged to *#resolutionottawa*. "The demented duo have now taken their sex into public spaces. What's next? Schoolyard sex during recess?"

Brandi was not as much taken aback by the comment as Ron was when he saw it. She had gotten used to the ignorant and mean-spirited nature of anonymous trolls. So much so, she now rarely followed the comments, even though the positive and encouraging ones now outnumbered the negative ones by a large margin. What did surprise her was how they knew her and Ron had had public sex. Was it just a lucky guess? If not, who the hell was leaking this?

"They're just jealous, Brandi," Charlene said. "It seems there's no shortage of frustrated and bored people who don't have a life of their own and are envious of anyone else who does. That and the increasing number of people who are actively looking for a reason to be indignant. They walk around with their finger on the self-righteous trigger, just itching to pull it as an excuse to get themselves into the conversation. Sad really." She paused, and then carefully asked, "Are they right, though? About the public sex?"

Brandi exhaled, shrugged, and with a resigned look on her face, nodded yes.

"You're a friggin' rock star, girl!" blurted Charlene, as she moved in for a high five.

182

Thursday, July 2

Enough was enough. Brandi and Ron sat in their backyard after work and attempted to deduce who the mole was. The most recent tweets suggested it was someone with whom they had, over the last two weeks and before yesterday, discussed their sexual forays into the public arena. That was a small group indeed—only three people, in fact, as far as they could recall: Dr. Fiona, Scott, and Elise. It was inconceivable to them that Dr. Fiona would breach doctor-patient confidentiality, so that left Scott and Elise as the primary suspects. Or, barring that, a spurious and lucky guess by one of the more than twenty thousand followers of *#resolutionottawa*.

To get to the bottom of this, they agreed to press the issue further with their friends the following day.

Friday, July 3

"Tantric Buddhism?" Scott asked, truly perplexed, trying to make sense of what Ron had just told him.

The guys had arrived at the Bassline Pub about fifteen minutes earlier, and once the beer had arrived at the table, Scott had hungrily inquired as to what adventure Ron and Brandi were now embarking on.

"Listen," Ron answered, "we don't know exactly what this is going to entail, but Brandi and I thought, 'What the hell. Why not give it a try'?"

"But learning about Buddhism at this stage of your life? Doesn't that seem, well, a little...unusual? And what does Buddhism have to do with your rather sordid resolution anyways? I though all religions—even Buddhism—were fundamentally conservative, and hid their sex in the closet with all the other unspeakable human acts and shortcomings."

"Generally that's right," concurred Ron, "but not exclusively. It appears that Buddhism is not one large uniform entity. Just as Catholicism has evolved and sprouted branches born of dissention and circumstance, so has Buddhism. Geography, time, and individual ego have created a complex lineage, where now there are three main Buddhist 'schools', and within these schools there are a number of sects, each of which has evolved specific practices. To make a long story short, one of the primary schools is called 'Vajrayana' or 'Tantric' Buddhism. It evolved out of India in the sixth century, and quickly spread to Tibet, where it became the primary form of religious practice. I've looked into this, and it may have all started because a local king in India didn't want to give up his carnal pleasures, but still yearned for enlightenment. The local Buddha wisely found a way for the king to use tantric practices to transform his sexual proclivities into transcendence and enlightenment."

"How convenient. That behaviour does sound like King Henry VIII's subjugation of Christianity to accommodate *his* libido."

"Now that you mention it," Ron mused, "it does. I guess sex always wins out. I suppose the best outcome is to bend the system with the concession, not break it."

"So, what are 'Tantric practices' anyways?"

Ron audibly exhaled. "I honestly don't know yet. It probably has a different meaning for everybody, but it seems that, as with all other Buddhist schools and sects, it's a vehicle to enable us humans to reach that higher plane of awareness and spirituality. What *does* make it unique is that it appears to be the one Buddhist sect that can utilize sexual pleasure to get the job done."

"Most unexpected bedfellows when you think about it," suggested Scott. "It's like a union of demons and angels."

"That's your Catholic conscience talking, my friend. Fundamentally, why should sex and enlightenment be mutually exclusive? Sex has been vilified as a base urge—which of course it is; amongst the base urges it's certainly near the top of my list. But that doesn't mean it can't be used as a wormhole into self-enlightenment."

"Now I remember!" exclaimed Scott. "In the sixties and seventies, western style 'Tantric sex' was all the rage. It docked rather seamlessly with the growing acceptance of uninhibited sexuality and drug use, and quickly devolved into something carnal, with little or no adherence to true tantric traditions. It became the McDonald's fast food of religious practices. So why is your doctor directing you guys towards those practices now?"

"That's what we're going to find out, I suppose, but the basic premise is that Brandi and I can shortcut the endless years of meditation and self-deprivation with our current biochemical harmony to fast track our enlightenment. That is the point of all religion, isn't it? Enlightenment."

"So, what's Dr. Fiona's connection to this Buddhist approach?

"Much to our surprise, Dr. Fiona is a practicing Buddhist, and she has a close relationship with an actual Yogi here in Ottawa."

"No kidding? So, what's a Buddhist Yogi doing in Ottawa?"

"Funny you should ask. Dr. Fiona did give us a little background on him. His name is Yogi Kukuraja. He's fifty-six years old, and was actually born in Tibet—the heartland of Tantric Buddhism. He was born the same year that the current Dalai Lama, openly threatened by the occupying Chinese and fearing for his life, was forced out of Tibet and, with the help of the CIA, found political sanctuary in India. Apparently, Yogi Kukuraja was born into a big family on a small farm in western Tibet, and directed towards the monastery at puberty, to allow for the little his parents could provide to better sustain his remaining siblings. He remained at this monastery for about a quarter century until, in the mid-1990s, the Chinese state policy towards Tibetan Buddhism and the Dalai Lama grew progressively more belligerent. With an increasingly caustic and unhealthy environment at home, Yogi Kukuraja decided to join his brotherly diaspora and the Dalai Lama in India.

"It was there that he aligned with a tantric college, began focusing on 'esoteric' Buddhism, eventually evolved into a tantric master—and took the name Yogi Kukuraja. He immigrated to Ottawa in 2012. Dr. Fiona was a bit vague on why he immigrated to Canada, but she implied that there was a connection between the 2012 events in Tibet and his decision to come here. When he arrived, he immediately opened up a Buddhist temple on Bank Street, which has been steadily growing ever since. As a Buddhist herself, Dr. Fiona searched him out to welcome him when he arrived, and they've been good friends ever since. Apparently, better than good friends. 'Professional collaborators' is the exact wording she used."

"Sounds as if he's got a story or two to tell. When are you going to be meeting him?"

"Well, Dr. Fiona's set up an 'interview' with Yogi Kukuraja tomorrow."

"An interview?" queried Scott. "That sounds a bit formal, doesn't it?"

"According to Dr. Fiona, he's very particular about whom he takes on as 'students', and he's only even considering Brandi and me because of their personal relationship. And also, she mentioned, because of the highly unusual nature of our situation."

Nodding slowly, Scott commented, "Well, your situation *is* highly unusual. That I get. What I'm curious about is how this is supposed to help you and Brandi with the resolution."

"That thought also crossed my mind."

After a moment of silence, Ron took a deep breath. "Sorry to bring this up again, buddy, but I have to ask. You're not the 'mole', are you?"

Meanwhile, back in Centrepointe, Brandi and Elise were also discussing the resolution. Brandi had already asked Elise if she knew anything about the leaks that had shown up on Twitter, and Elise had emphatically and somewhat indignantly denied any knowledge. Brandi "felt" she was telling the truth, thanked her for her indulgence, and quickly moved on to more agreeable topics without permanent damage to their relationship.

Although pleased to confirm that Elise wasn't the source of the leaks, during the rest of the evening part of Brandi's consciousness still lingered on the issue of the mole. She thought that it was unlikely that Scott was the mole, and was sure Ron would confirm this later tonight.

Then who could it be? she pondered.

Saturday, July 4

Brandi and Ron felt like schoolchildren on the first day of classes. They clung to each other wide-eyed as they entered, through the innocuous semiopaque glass-door street entrance, a small hallway facing a dark, circular room with a candlelit gilded shrine on the far wall. As their eyes adjusted to the dim lighting, an intense sweet smell of incense enveloped them; both of them unconsciously drew deep breaths through their noses, allowing the floral and spicy scents to infuse them. Their tensions melted away, their shoulders relaxed, their grip on each other eased, and a smile simultaneously grew on their faces. The intensity of their visual and olfactory experiences progressively swapped places, and the temple revealed itself as a colourful, silk-festooned and gold-gilded chamber unlike anything that either had previously seen. On both sides of the short, colourfully rugged runway to the shrine were shoulder-high rows of bronze prayer wheels—four on each side. Against the opposite wall was a trio of golden Buddhas, sitting lotus-style in a gilded shrine. Below them, numerous large incense sticks burned, contributing to the heady atmosphere. Adjacent to that shrine, a framed portrait of a benevolent-looking Dalai Lama with his hands steepled under his chin in prayer stood out, encased by flickering candles. The ceiling was dominated by a brilliantly coloured circular mural, with a rectangular, maze-like centrepiece encasing a finely detailed core. There were pillows distributed around the perimeter, some of which were currently occupied by followers quietly engaged in prayer. It seemed that every square inch had been attended to with bright intricately woven tapestry or silk fabric, in celebration of an overt, fundamental understanding that confidently nodded, "Yes—you've come to the right place."

Removing their shoes and adding them to a small cluster of footwear to one side of the entranceway, Ron and Brandi timidly stepped into the main hall, and glanced both around the room and at their watches. The "interview" was scheduled for nine o'clock that morning, and they were about two minutes early.

At that exact moment a small, cheery-looking, barefooted man, sporting short grey hair and a white goatee, jeans, and a dark, short-sleeved plaid shirt, appeared in front of them. He more stated than asked, in heavily accented English, "You must be the Lees. I've been expecting you. Dr. Xanthopoulos speaks highly of you both. Welcome to our inner-city temple. I'm Yogi Kukuraja. Pleased to meet you."

Following introductions and a short but enthusiastic tour of the main hall, Yogi Kukuraja took them through a previously unnoticed door, next to the central shrine, which led into a narrow, curving hallway, ringing the core of the complex. They could see a few doors providing access to the inner sanctum. The Yogi opened up the one closest to the shrine, and invited Brandi and Ron into his office. The decorating theme displayed in the main hall extended to his office, complete with a golden Buddha shrine and smoldering incense.

"Please have a seat," the Yogi requested, gesturing towards a low bench in front of his equally low seat and table. "Before we start, please let us sit quietly for a few minutes." With that, his face relaxed, his lips released into a contented neutral line, his eyes closed, and he fell silent.

Ron and Brandi looked at each other, shrugged, and joined the Yogi in a bit of quiet meditation. About five minutes later, both of them were roused from their calm by the Yogi softly suggesting, "So, let us get to know each other a bit better, shall we?"

For over an hour, Yogi Kukuraja listened to Ron and Brandi take turns recounting their story, first of their life before this year, and then in more detail, their journey with the resolution.

Upon completion of their narrative, Yogi Kukuraja sat back, nodded his head slightly, offered a vaguely perplexed expression, and folded his hands in front of himself. He quietly maintained this posture for a few minutes, until he got up without saying a word and left the room, leaving Ron and Brandi confounded, looking at each other for an explanation neither had.

After a couple of minutes, Brandi asked, "Do you think we offended him?"

"I honestly don't know."

"Do you think we should leave?" she asked.

Ron answered with a "what the hell do I know?" shrug and facial expression.

Just at that moment, Yogi Kukuraja swept back into the room, sat back in his place behind the table, and, without explanation for his interlude, spoke to them as if the last couple of minutes had never happened. "Dr. Xanthopoulos was correct. Yours is a story that does interest me. I'll tell you why, but first let me offer some background about myself, to help put the intersection of our lives today into a broader context."

Two hours later, Ron and Brandi were having lunch at a downtown café, discussing the morning's events. Yogi Kukuraja had offered them the *Reader's Digest* version of his life thus far. He was born in 1959 as Tenzin Zhaxi—the eighth child in a poor nomadic family from the high plateau region of Ngari in Eastern Tibet. He suggested his position in this familial lineage was at best a guess, since he had personally witnessed the death of three of his siblings, subsequent to becoming sentient at about the age of three. He matter-of-factly stated other siblings might have met with similarly premature demises prior to his spiritual awakening, but there was no way to know, since family history had never been a topic of discussion at the dinner table. The total number of deceased siblings was made further speculative by the fact that, upon entering the monastery, he had never again communicated with his family. "All I know for sure," he had proffered with a smile, "is that all my siblings will, as will I, one day pass into the next life."

Childhood memories consisted of brief, cool summers herding yaks, sheep, and goats, and long, brutally cold winters huddled around smoldering piles of yak dung in large, wind-whipped tents, accompanied at times by the weakest and sickest animals in their herds. He had secretly given names to a number of his favourite animals, the majority of which died due to a combination of illness, starvation, and extreme weather conditions, all three of which were constant companions on the high-altitude steppes.

He was barely thirteen when his parents informed him that he was now going to live in the nearby monastery. To his question of "When?" his mother dispassionately indicated tomorrow morning at sunrise. Hugs were shared with his remaining siblings, his mother kissed him goodbye on his forehead, his father saddled up one of the larger yaks, and they trekked six days to the Tholing Monastery, near the Indian border. There his father delivered him into the arms of a waiting monk. Following some perfunctory bowing, where a single tear was shed (the number so precisely known because it was he who had shed it), the last memory of his father and the large yak receding into the distance was imprinted on his consciousness forever.

At the Tholing Monastery, he had quickly been absorbed into the daily cycles of meditation, chanting, theological dialogue, and, of course, contribution to the communal chores. He quickly learned to read, and excelled at debate. The teaching at Tholing, as in most of Tibet, was based on the third school of Buddhism—Vajrayana, or 'Tantric', as it was more commonly called in the west. While remaining true to the fundamental Buddhist quest for enlightenment, the Tantric school was considered the most esoteric of the three, focusing on mantra, visualization, and mental acuity to achieve enlightenment.

Yogi Kukuraja admitted there was far more in common among the three schools than there were differences, suggesting that the establishment of the three primary schools, and the numerous sects within each school, was due mainly to geography, and the accumulation of minute changes that inevitably occur over time and in isolation. "That, and the indomitable human need to create something new and unique," he said.

Tenzin remained at Tholing through adolescence and as a young adult. He became known as a gifted scholar, and a devoted and innovative practitioner of Buddhism. As he made his way towards the progressively brightening light of self-awareness, he was increasingly troubled by the growing oppression and anti-religious sentiment of Tibet's Chinese masters. The anti-Dalai Lama campaign was ratcheted up in 1994, and within a year, the Tholing Monastery was on the Chinese radar.

Denouncement of the Dalai Lama was unconscionable for Tenzin, as it was for every monk in Tholing, so after much deliberation, discussion, and consultation, Tenzin decided that he could no longer flourish and evolve spiritually in the negative repressed atmosphere of his homeland. He would follow His Holiness, the Dalai Lama, to his current residence in Dharamshala, India.

Consequently, in the summer of 1995, a group of four young monks led by Tenzin struck out from Tholing and walked along the high plateau until they reached the headwaters of the Langgen Zongbo/Sutlej River Valley. They walked, climbed, scuffled, and clambered their way along the river valley and through the Himalayan Mountains to the Shipki La Pass at the Indian border. This initial part of the journey, although only a hundred kilometres as the crow flew, took seven days. Yogi Kukuraja described this passage to them as "the most difficult physical challenge of this life….so far." The small group of monks skirted the high-elevation border entry, and when they were sure they were in India, worked their way to a road, tracked down an Indian official, and claimed political refugee status.

The Indian authorities had long ago positioned themselves as sympathetic to Tibetan monks escaping the Chinese regime, as an act of national-sovereignty defiance towards their aggressive northern bullies. "Thank Buddha the Himalayas separate the two countries!" Yogi Kukuraja commented.

Once on the travelled roads of India, the monks were benefactors of an obliging population, and over the next four days rode their way through about a half-dozen mountain passes, around innumerable precipitous hairpin curves, and over endless, impossibly steep wet roads into the Tibetan exile community within Dharamshala, arriving well-fed and mostly recuperated from their hike to the Indian border.

The welcome mat was always out and brushed off at the Namgyal Monastery in Dharamshala for any Tibetan who had dared to escape the oppressive yoke of the imperialistic Chinese—and who had survived the trek from the homeland; so much so that in 1993 the Dalai Lama had opened the Tibetan Transit School (TTS) for newly arrived Tibetan citizens between the ages of eighteen and thirty. After a few days of interviews, Tenzin was offered a position as a junior staff member in the TTS.

The years between 1995 and 2012 in Dharamshala were indescribably joyous and enlightening for Tenzin. Dharamshala, located on the steep, south-facing foothill slopes, with the Himalayas as a backdrop, presented a stark physical and spiritual contrast to his life on the high plains in Tibet. The warmth, forests, and view of the green Indus Valley falling away into the distant mist invigorated him on a daily basis, augmenting the nurturing theosophical environment in which he was now entrenched.

It was there that Tenzin, focusing on the esoteric Karmamudrā offshoot within the Tantric Buddhist lineage, transformed into Yogi Kukuraja. Amongst all the various Buddhist families, Karmamudrā teachings were likely the most unique of all schools. Born in India in the sixth century as sexual Tantric practices, it finally evolved into the Karmamudrā sect, through the pragmatic amendments developed for the libidinous medieval Indian king, where sex could be used as a quicker, more effective vehicle to attain enlightenment. Forget that everyone else had been spending their rote monastic lives clawing their way towards a spiritual peak shrouded in clouds miles above them, building on lifetimes of knowledge and learning filtered and concentrated for oral transference by the wisest amongst them. Forget all that. Here was mail-order enlightenment with benefits.

The strict tenet of celibacy was the only-paper wall that prevented a stampede of monks from entering this sect, but over the years many had given back their vows to find enlightenment in the physical arms of consorts. For all other monastic practitioners, "visualization" would have to do. Yogi Kukuraja confirmed that he was of the latter group.

Ron and Brandi silently contemplated Yogi Kukuraja's journey to that point.

"What amazes me is that in context with the typically conservative and ritualized Buddhist practices, a sexually oriented sect not only exists, but is sanctioned and supported by management," remarked Ron.

"What amazes me is that Yogi Kukuraja left Dharamshala," added Brandi.

"I'm sure he has his reasons. Maybe he'll share them with us if we decide to join his temple and get to know him better."

"So what are you thinking?"

Ron thought back to Yogi Kukuraja's assessment of what his tutelage could offer them: *"Clearly you are not of my physical world, and I am a newcomer into yours. Regardless, we do share the human need and ability to search out and find enlightenment. I have studied the nuances of the Tantric Buddhist lineage, and more recently Karmamudrā, and believe with all my being that this is a viable gateway to enlightenment and transcendence of our earthly bond, and you two are well positioned through your sexual relationship to attain it—if ever so briefly. I don't want you to be under any illusion that you will attain any permanent universal insight. That is likely reserved for a fortunate few who have committed their lives entirely to the teachings of Buddha, who are standing on the shoulders of the greatest gurus of the last twenty-five generations, and themselves stretching even further towards understanding their place and meaning in the universe. No, what I offer you is a back-door entrance, and a fleeting glimpse of Nirvana."*

"That was quite the pep talk," Ron finally said in answer to Brandi.

"It was probably best to lay it on the line right up front, Ron. What I find encouraging is that this highly educated and spiritual man thinks we may be able to use our resolution to gain entrance into the celestial peep show. Now *that's* what I call an unintended consequence of what we set out to do in January."

"But do we want to take on a new, and likely time-consuming, program at this time, just for a reverse bungee-jump into the heavens? Isn't what we have enough?" Ron said, almost pleadingly.

"Absolutely, Ron, but what we have *here* is a unique and once-in-a-lifetime opportunity to experience something that is virtually unattainable by the vast majority of people who have ever walked the earth. Aren't you curious? I think we should think about it and talk it over tomorrow."

Ron pressed his lips together, exhaled loudly through his nostrils, looked into Brandi's eager face, allowed himself a silent but heartfelt *oy vey*, and, with a resigned shrug, unenthusiastically agreed that that was probably the best course of action.

Sunday, July 5

Over Sunday supper at their house in Glencairn, Abby leaned over and quietly asked her son if something was bothering him. He had been acting distracted all afternoon, and she had chosen a moment when the kids, Brandi, and Tommy Sr. were otherwise engrossed in their own discussion.

Ron thought about deflecting the comment, but simultaneously realized that he had never been able to fool his mother, so why think today would be any different? "I guess it's mainly that this is the last meal I'll ever have in the house I grew up in," he forlornly confessed to her. It wasn't the only reason for his current state, but certainly it was contributing considerably to his sour mood.

"Change is never easy, Ron," his mother evenly replied, "but it is inevitable. I hope you're not worrying about your father and me? We'll be completely fine at The Redwoods. And we'll be closer to you and Brandi and the kids. It's all good."

"That's not it. I'm happy about that, Mom. What's really bothering me is the callous indifference time has for life and the brief moments of happiness. This move that you and Dad are making has shaken me awake a bit, and made me realize just how ephemeral everything we do and are really is."

"Well, you're not the first person to struggle with that, Ron, I can assure you," Abby replied with a wry grin. "I wouldn't let it get you down, however. My advice is to fully enjoy the actual moments, knowing that each and every one of them is a unique and fleeting gift, deserving of your utmost respect and attention. That really is the best we can do, Ronny."

"Is it really that simple, Mom? Can something as infinitely confounding and vexing as our lives be understood in the context of boundless appreciation?"

Unbeknownst to Ron and his mom, the others at the table had been drawn into the conversation, and were now listening intently. Unsolicited, Tommy Sr. answered Ron's question. "The short answer, son, is *yes*."

He let that hang for a couple of seconds before continuing. "If you want to make every day an unhappy conflict—you can do that. If you want to sit and stare in stunned amazement at the wonder of everything around you—that, too, is possible. It's completely up to you. Why not chose acceptance and happiness over struggle and angst? I guarantee that will enhance your human experience. As fleeting and inevitably bittersweet as it is." Tommy Sr. took a sip from his wine glass, looked around the table into everyone's eyes, then slowly got up and walked to the kitchen.

Abby chuckled, and softly commented, "Once a Buddhist, always a Buddhist."

Brandi and Ron simultaneously stopped breathing, and stared at each other. Ron calmed his pulse, took a deep breath, and asked his mother, "What do you mean, Mom?"

"Didn't you know?" she asked, looking a bit perplexed. "Your father and his family were Buddhists in China, but stopped actively practicing when they came to Canada. You know—to better assimilate."

Taken aback from the surprised looks on Ron and Brandi's face, she added, "Really? We mustn't have thought it was important."

Ron's eyes widened as he glanced at Brandi. He knew *exactly* what she was thinking.

Later in their backyard in Centrepointe, over a crisp glass of an exquisitely crafted Peller Estates Signature series Sauvignon Blanc, Ron looked up at Brandi, and asked, "You're thinking this is fate, aren't you?"

"Well, aren't you?"

Staring at his wine glass, Ron dipped his head, exhaled slowly through his mouth, then looked up with raised eyebrows. "I'd be lying if I said I didn't. So what do you suggest we do now?"

"I think we should sit down again with Yogi Kukuraja, get to know him a bit better, and ask him what his expectations are and what he has planned for us."

Ron nodded in agreement, and said, "I'll phone tomorrow and set something up," then immediately escaped back to the solace of his fermented fruit beverage.

Wednesday, July 8

"Buddhism doesn't search out its followers. Its followers find Buddhism on their own."

Those were the first words Yogi Kukuraja offered to Ron and Brandi, once they were settled in front of his modest desk back at the temple on Bank Street. With the spicy floral scent of incense thick in the air, Ron and Brandi waited for the Yogi's continuing parlance. Instead, he just sat, wordlessly smiling at them both, until Ron succumbed to the awkwardness and broke the silence.

"Thank you for seeing us again, Yogi Kukuraja. Brandi and I have further discussed us working together with you, and were interested in the specifics of how....um...exactly this would happen?"

Ron waited for a response from Yogi Kukuraja, but he remained silent, smiling passively.

"Good, then," Ron said, wearing a shit-eating grin, his head nodding. "Brandi and I were also curious about why you left Dharamshala. From what you told us, you were content and happy there."

Yogi Kukuraja's demeanour changed markedly upon hearing this question from Ron. His smile faded, and a neutral look of calm replaced it. "I have already shared with you what my greatest physical challenge has been. My decision to emigrate to Canada was equally challenging. Although in Dharamshala I had been immersed in a most hospitable environment, conducive to unobstructed growth and enlightenment, I felt that my spiritual development had—as you say here in Canada—'hit the wall'.

"Our obligation, as sentient humans, is to faithfully and honestly pursue a path that challenges and improves us each and every day. This was no longer happening for me in Dharamshala. In 2012, the plight of my Buddhist brethren in Tibet was weighing heavy on my conscious. It seemed that every day I would hear that another monk had self-immolated in protest of the oppressive Chinese rule. What was I in comparison to these men, and women, and their devotion to our shared path to enlightenment? I felt unjustly privileged and coddled, and ashamed that I had grown too comfortable in my life. I meditated for two days, and the answer came to me." He paused, and smiled again at both of them.

Their look must have begged for further details, since Yogi Kukuraja quickly added, with a chuckle, "Not specifically this temple on Bank Street in Ottawa. My revelation was that I must relocate to a setting where I could apply my learning and assess its universality. I had to challenge myself, and use this test to continue on my path to enlightenment." He opened his arms. "And here I am."

"Why Ottawa?" asked Brandi.

"Many reasons, but predominantly it was because the Canadian government has a very open immigration policy, especially when it comes to the Tibetan diaspora. Specifically, I looked at Ottawa since the seasons beautifully mirror the central tenet of Buddhist cyclicity, the population is educated and open-minded, founded in pluralism, and there already was a small, but thriving, Buddhist community. And I was hoping to meet you two." He added the last comment with a grin that startled Ron and caused Brandi to inadvertently titter.

Ron looked at her and, disconcertedly, saw she was mirroring Yogi Kukuraja's broad grin.

"Again, not you two *specifically*, but you two as a manifestation of what, I believe, the human spirit in general is capable of achieving under accommodating conditions. I believe there are no rules when it comes to personal enlightenment and development of our spiritual side."

After a few beats, Ron broke the silence. "So you're confident that our resolution can facilitate our enlightenment?"

"The *need* for personal enlightenment is in each and every one of us. As sentient beings, we are all intellectually driven towards a higher plain, with a clearer view of reality," Yogi Kukuraja solemnly replied. "Unfortunately, our quest for it manifests itself on a daily basis in our society with the excessive and commonly destructive use of drugs as an imperfect, but instantaneous, tool to deliver a form of enlightenment. As briefly efficient as drugs may be, in my opinion, the use of artificial agents to achieve bliss is essentially wrong and unsustainable. I see it almost every day in downtown Ottawa, and it saddens me.

"All religions tap into this need, and provide an 'opiate for the masses' with a socially acceptable, sustainable, and non-destructive vehicle that, at least partially, satisfies the fundamental human yearning for enlightenment. Unfortunately, the goals and tenets within each of the major religions are *intentionally* made unattainable in an absolute sense. This guarantees that even a full lifetime of devotion will progress the devotee, at best, only a few rungs on a ladder which metaphorically extends into the heavens without a destination in sight.

"Although this aspect of religion is, not unexpectedly, self-serving, the goal of enlightenment is real. Why not try to achieve it in a shorter timeline?" Yogi Kukuraja asked rhetorically. "There really are no rules. Everybody is making this up as they go along," he added, with his now familiar smile.

"Personally, I'm profoundly drawn to Vajrayana, and more specifically to the sect of Karmamudrā, and to your challenge, for their purity and simplicity. You two are merely using the tools Buddha has given you to enable your spiritual evolution. Think of me as your facilitator towards this goal. I will first, show you how to capture your energy, second, help remove your earthly hindrances, and third, prepare you to fearlessly accept your state of bliss."

And all this by having sex! Ron thought. *Sounds like a win-win to me.*

Yogi Kukuraja noticed the distant stare and spreading tranquility on Ron's face, and asked him, "What are your thoughts, Ron?"

Caught a little off-guard, Ron sputtered for a few seconds, brought himself back to the moment, and replied, "This all sounds great, Yogi Kukuraja, but how does all that actually happen?"

"It's a journey, Ron. It starts with you and Brandi attempting to non-sexually focus your considerable energies."

"And how do we do *that?*" asked Brandi.

"This can be achieved through a meditative and breathing technique we call *Tummo.* From what you've told me, you've both reached a level of spiritual sovereignty where you can freely access your humanity without inner obstruction. This ability *should* allow you to master *Tummo* fairly quickly; possibly within a year or two. *Tummo* will allow you to capture and control your considerable physical energies, using nothing more than your force of will."

"Are you saying that we'll be able to generate the same physical energy that we experience during sex *without* sex?" asked Brandi.

"It's more than that, Mrs. Lee," replied Yogi Kukuraja. "You'll not only be able to generate this energy, you'll be able to control and focus it at will. Imagine a malleable ball of energy in the palm of your hand that you can reshape at will. This is what a master practitioner of *Tummo* is capable of."

Brandi and Ron looked at each other, silently pondering how this would feel, and the implications of having this ability.

Yogi Kukuraja noticed their silent discussion, and interjected to clarify. "*Tummo* is only our first, but very necessary, step. If you are both able to master it, the journey will continue, with subsequent, progressively ever-more-challenging steps."

Their countenances instantly turned concerned at this comment.

"Do not become discouraged," the Yogi added with a smile. "Every journey of merit is earned, and all journeys begin with a first step. So let's focus our energies, for the time being, on developing you both as *Tummo* practitioners."

Friday, July 10

Ron impatiently waited for Scott to stop gasping, clear his throat of inhaled beer, and wipe his "you've got be kidding" grin off his face. "Are you done?" Ron asked, waiting for Scott to regain his composure.

Blinking and exhaling loudly, Scott slowly and *faux*-seriously resettled on his stool, straightened his back, and brought his gaze back to Ron—at which time his laughing fit resumed, and he sprang off his stool, bent over nearly horizontal, and proceeded to crack up uncontrollably, much to the delight of the adjacent patrons at the Bassline Bar.

It was another beautiful summer's day, and the compact accommodations of their local pub were filled to capacity. Ron and Scott had gotten there late from work, but had lucked into a small corner high table for two, just vacated by a couple of Ottawa City workers who looked as if they had wholly enjoyed the early and extended happy "hour" offered by the establishment.

Attempting, yet gain, to reconvene the conflab, Scott managed to fully return to his stool and make eye contact with his friend, while quietly sporting a smile that suggested he might not be entirely finished with his jocular convulsions.

Ron waited a couple of seconds after Scott settled before he continued. "As I was saying before you so rudely interrupted me…" Scott started shaking again, his hand firmly sealing his lips, barely containing his laughter as his shoulders pumped irrepressibly.

Ron again impatiently paused, while his friend wiped the tears from his eyes, shook his head, exhaled loudly again, and refocused on him. Ron gave him a "how about now?" open-armed shrug, complete with furrowed brow look. Scott returned the gesture, mirrored except for the slight smirk and concessional head tilt meaning that, as best he could tell, he thought he was done.

"Ok then, where was I?" asked Ron

"You were telling me that you've embraced Buddhism, are going to shave your head, take to wearing an orange robe, donate all your worldly possessions to the poor, and start begging, barefooted, for your daily bowl of rice outside of EllisDon's offices," glibly replied Scott.

Exasperated, Ron slowly exhaled through his nose while shaking his head, and wondered why he even tried.

Picking up the marked change in Ron's usual indulgent demeanour, Scott quickly backpedaled and said, "OK, OK. It's just when you told me you've started into Buddhist meditation, that's the mental image that came to me. You have to admit, *that* would be pretty funny!"

Ron commented, "Sometimes I worry about you, Scott."

"Don't worry about me, other than choking to death on beer while trying to get through *your* resolution this year. Let's get back to you. So you've started meditation. Why?" He added a sincere "tell me, I really want to know" look.

"Tough to fully explain at this time, but apparently, it's the first step in our journey to enlightenment."

"Using sex?" asked Scott.

Ron nodded affirmatively. "Yup."

"I'm still flabbergasted that you could do that. I mean, using sex."

"Who knew? This meditation will teach us how to capture and control our body's physical energy. The same energy we generate during sex."

"What? While *not* having sex?"

"Exactly. Now you're getting it."

"Not really," replied Scott. "How can you do that? And *why* would you do that?"

"Firstly, the how: Yogi Kukuraja has instructed us in a very specific and secret meditation technique that, he says, is proven to be able to capture and control your physical energy. It's called *Tummo*."

"It can't be all that secret if he's doling out this mystical knowledge to virtual strangers like candy on Hallowe'en!"

"We did ask about that. His view is that knowledge provides its greatest good when disseminated to those who can effectively and productively use it. He thinks Brandi and I are worthy." With a *faux*-apologetic look he added, "He specifically asked us not to discuss these techniques with anyone else, so sorry, buddy. You'll just have to remain unenlightened. *Sans lumière, mon ami.* That shouldn't be too hard. You know, to stay the course." Ron added a purposely hubristic chuckle as payment for Scott's recent fit.

The comment rolled off of Scott like water off a duck's back. Now intrigued, he asked, "What about the why?"

"*Tummo* is the first and necessary step on our journey to 'enlightenment.' We don't know what happens if and when we can effectively master it, but Yogi Kukuraja has informed us the next steps are even more challenging."

"Jesus," Scott exclaimed. "Is this really what you wanted to do for your summer holiday? All of a sudden, your resolution has gone from working hard, to hard work."

"I'm with you on that, buddy. I honestly could do without it, but Brandi is really keen on giving this an honest effort, and she's been far too supportive of this damned resolution for me to say no to this. Besides, we're still faithfully keeping up with the primary goal of the resolution—and you and I both know what extremes a man will go to to get laid."

Scott raised his mug in a toast, accompanied with a hearty "Hear, hear!" to second that thought. Immediately after the toast, he asked, "So your parents are moving into the raisin farm this weekend?"

Ron nodded affirmatively. "The Redwoods is about a kilometre from our place. In a lot of ways it's better for us with them being closer. We'll probably see more of them, but we're OK with that. After we move them in, as you know me and the girls are heading out to White Lake for a couple of weeks to enjoy the water and the weather. Tommy Jr. will join us on the weekend. Someone's got to work. Are you and Elise still coming up next weekend?"

"If we're still invited, you bet. We could use some lake time. Hopefully you and Brandi won't be on a higher plane by then, and we'll still be able to relate to each other."

Saturday, July 11

The move to The Redwoods turned out to be remarkably easy. Good planning, and a determined sleeves-rolled-up downsizing over the previous couple of weeks leading up the big move, had turned the experience into a non-event. Moving essentials consisted of their bed, a few tables, a television, the computer, clothing, and a few boxes of art, framed photos, and keepsakes. Since there wasn't that much furniture to move, most of the time was spent with paperwork, and unpacking and organizing their clothes. Claiming a crisis at work, Ron's brother, Stewart, had cancelled his trip out at the last minute, promising to come out as soon as he was able. As it turned out, he wasn't needed physically, but Ron was still annoyed that he had placed his work ahead of his parents' emotional needs.

Late that afternoon, Brandi and Ron sat in their backyard with Sam and Tommy Jr. Conscious of their new proximity to Ron and the family, and determined not to be a burden, Abby and Tommy Sr. had shooed them home after they got settled at The Redwoods. Although Ron knew they were just a cellphone call away, he was still uncomfortable with leaving them.

Sam noticed her dad agonizing over something, and rightly assumed it was about his parents. "Dad. Stop worrying. They're probably just getting acquainted with their new neighbours."

The sun was still high and hot, so they had all crowded into the umbrella's shade on one side of the table. Sam was at Ron's left shoulder. He looked down, smiled, and said, "Yeah, you're probably right. But it just feels weird leaving them there. It feels like I'm abandoning them."

"Are you kidding?" asked Tommy Jr. "Did you see the schedule of activities for tonight? Bingo, euchre, and a movie? That's a full program compared to yours and Mom's social life. That reminds me, I'm meeting up with friends this evening and I won't be here for supper."

"Me, too," chirped Sam. "I'm off to Caroline's for a BBQ tonight. That'll just leave you two alone tonight to get up to whatever you want." She couldn't completely suppress an eye roll as she delivered the last comment.

Tommy chortled, sprang up from his chair, and said he wouldn't be too late, leaving his parents looking guilty, with Sam squished between them.

After a few seconds of awkward silence, Sam mercifully slid her chair back, said she was going to get ready, and headed into the house.

"I think she knows," whispered Brandi.

"I think you're right," agreed Ron.

"How great is that?" added Brandi. "Just as we're heading out for a couple of weeks to a nice secluded lake setting. Just you, me, and our creeped-out daughter."

"Do you think we should talk with her?" sheepishly asked Ron.

Brandi exhaled. "Probably. But it should be me. I don't see your involvement in that conversation as being helpful."

Ron silently and thankfully accepted this, while nodding in agreement. He was quite relieved to not be part of that conversation, and didn't envy Brandi in the least.

"But on the positive side," Brandi continued, "as our daughter has pointed out, we do have the evening to ourselves." She delivered the last comment with an exaggerated lasciviousness that triggered an involuntary release of endorphins in Ron's brain, which in turn caused him to refocus solely on Brandi and the impending sexual act with her, which in turn infused him with an overwhelming sense of well-being that manifested itself outwardly in a growing look of tranquility on his face, framing a growing smile.

"I do believe you are the most wanton woman I've ever met."

"And don't you ever forget that," Brandi whispered, as she leaned in for a smooch.

Unbeknownst to them, at that very moment Sam was looking out the window into the backyard. "Oh gross!" she quietly remarked, and quickly turned away.

Later in the evening, after a cooling bubble bath, a *Tummo* meditation session, some reciprocal massaging, and an extended lovemaking session using their favourite toy, they sat in the now pleasantly cool backyard, discussing the evening over a glass of wine. Their post-coital selection tonight was a fruity and sensual 2012 Summit Merlot blend from the Mt. Boucherie Estate Winery in the Okanagan.

"What do *you* think about the *Tummo* meditation?" asked Ron.

"I think it enhanced my orgasm. Sorry, orgasms."

Ron nodded with an impressed expression. "How about the meditation itself? How did the visualization go? Did you feel any core warmth?"

"Actually, yes I did," replied Brandi. "I found it easy, as Yogi Kukuraja instructed us, to imagine myself as an empty vessel. Creating the glowing core of energy in my belly was a lot harder, but I think I did feel some growing warmth and I visualized a spark or two there. How about you?"

Ron did find the meditation relaxing, but had trouble calming his thoughts, and specifically couldn't derail his anxiousness concerning the imminent sex with Brandi. His visualization was too overcome with Brandi's expression during her orgasms to even attempt the "hollow body" *Tummo* thing. "Not so much success in the visualization department, but I enjoyed it all the same. The toughest part, I find, is calming my mind."

"You'll get it eventually, Ron," Brandi said optimistically. "If it was easy, everybody would be doing it. Well… everybody being tutored by a devoted Tibetan monk committed to Tantric meditation and prepared to ignore his sacred oath of secrecy for the benefit of mankind."

Ron chuckled, but inwardly, his trepidation concerning the addition of medita-tion into their daily "routine" was growing, especially with Brandi's enthusiasm and her apparent natural mastery of what Yogi Kukuraja cautioned would be a slow process requiring "a determined patience" to see results. They were less than a week into it, and already Brandi was glimpsing what the good Yogi had suggested would likely take months to achieve. *Still*, he mused, *the sex is getting even better.*

"I *can* read your mind, my dear." Brandi's comment snapped Ron out of his thought. "This is about something more than sex. Try to remember that. At least when you're meditating. After that, *then* it's all about the sex."

The tone of Brandi's final comment melted away any guilt he might have been feeling from her light admonishment, and the familiar flush of endorphins filled Ron again. "How about we finish our wine and head upstairs for a proper night cap? *Sans* meditation this time."

Brandi rolled the wine around her tongue, savouring the berry overtones and spicy finish, while she stared at her husband. "Now who's the wanton one?" she asked. Then she downed the remainder of her glass and led Ron by the hand back upstairs.

Tuesday, July 14

After checking in with Abby and Tommy Sr. at The Redwoods the next morning, Brandi, Ron, and Sam drove out to their rental cottage on nearby White Lake. Sam had only agreed to join them for the two weeks because the place had an adjacent bunkie, and her good friend Caroline would be joining them in a couple of days to occupy it with her for the duration of their stay.

After a relaxing day on the water, Brandi and Ron sat on the deck in Adiron-dack chairs, facing the lake, while sipping a chilled unwooded chardonnay from the Gray Monk vineyard in the Okanagan. Watching the finches jostling for posi-tion at the nearby feeder, Ron silently appreciated the expertly constructed fruity flavours of the wine. A loon calling in the bay signaled the start of conversation.

"Good grief, it's lovely here," Brandi commented.

"This place came highly recommended," replied Ron. "And it had enough bells and whistles to satisfy Sam."

Brandi nodded her understanding.

"By the way," asked Ron, "have you had a chance to talk to Sam about…you know…the resolution?"

"I did yesterday evening while you were burning the meat on the BBQ."

"And how did that go?"

"She doesn't want to talk about it, if she knows. We were chatting in the kitchen and while she was checking her tweets, I asked if there were any updates concerning *#resolutionottawa*. She made an *ughing* sound and asked, 'Why would anybody want to follow that?', and immediately changed the topic to how much she was looking forward to Caroline getting here on Thursday."

"Probably a coping mechanism. Way cheaper than counselling," he added. "Well, you tried. She'll talk to you if she wants, I guess. That said, let's be real discreet while we're here so as not to traumatize our baby."

"Absolutely. I may have to stuff a sock in your mouth," Brandi playfully added.

"Hey, how did your meditation this morning go?" asked Ron.

"Funny you should ask. It was weird. I actually did visualize a red-hot glowing ball in my empty core. Afterwards I realized that I hadn't been thinking about…. well…anything else when that was happening. And weirdest of all, when I finished, my stomach felt hot to the touch."

Conversely, *he* had used meditation time to run through his checklist of things to do today and what they were having for supper tonight, and made a mental note to supplement their wine reserves in advance of receiving their guests later this week. Guiltily, he also remembered leering at his motionless naked wife beside him, and checking his watch to see how much longer he'd have to wait until their daily coition could commence. It was a good thing Brandi was fully absorbed in her meditation at that moment. Otherwise, Ron's growing erection would have betrayed his meditative delinquency.

"Me, not so much," he said.

A few seconds later the significant of Brandi's milestone struck him, and he exclaimed to her, "Holy shit, Brandi! Yogi Kukuraja said that it would likely take months or even *years* of daily focused meditation to be able to pull that off. You've done it in a week!"

"Just a good student, I suppose. Compared to you, anyways. I bet you were thinking about the Blue Jays or something like that during meditation."

The Blue Jays hadn't popped into the basket of topics Ron had considered during meditation, but now that Brandi had brought it up, he *was* wondering how they'd done the night before.

Seeing Brandi's expectant look, he responded, "It's not that easy, Brandi. I think you're some sort of freak," he added *faux*-defensively.

"Nice. Now you're calling me a freak. It really isn't that hard, Ron. You just have to really commit to the moment, and follow Yogi Kukuraja's instructions."

Exhaling to demonstrate his exasperation, Ron yielded. "There are a lot of things in orbit in my mind Brandi, and it's tough to slow their momentum." He paused for a sip of wine. "Maybe the serenity of this place will help."

Friday, July 17

Scott and Elise had arrived for happy hour, and the four of them were well into it by six o'clock. Sam and Caroline were completely absorbed in teenage-girl things in the adjacent bunkhouse, and Ron could hear waves of exuberant giggles intermittently rising above the music the girls were playing. Ron briefly disconnected from the ongoing conversation to take in and appreciate the exquisite harmony that surrounded him at that moment. An involuntary blissful shiver then rolled through him, catching him by surprise, and leaving him with a frozen smile on his face.

"You wearing your Depends again, Ronny?" Scott commented, having noticed Ron's suddenly catatonic state. "Because you look as if you've just had a great dump."

"Just enjoying the moment, buddy. Does it get any better than this?"

"Maybe not, but I'm sure we're going to give it a try again tomorrow," said Scott.

Just then, Elise broke into their discussion, asking her husband, "Did you know that these two are meditating now?"

Scott nodded affirmatively, and said, "I'm just glad that Ron hasn't shaved his head yet. Not that that would be a big job," he added as a dig.

"Well, I think it's really interesting. We should try it, Scott. Brandi's been telling me that it's really helping her calm herself." Looking around to make sure there weren't any minors around, she added, "And the sex is…how did you put it Brandi?' she asked, looking at her.

"More spiritual."

"More spiritual!" repeated Elise. "What's not to like about more spiritual sex?"

"I'd be happy with just *more* sex," dryly responded Scott, receiving a shoulder punch from Elise for his effort.

"Keep that up and the tap will close completely, mister," she threatened.

Scott's eyes rolled. He shook his head and slowly responded, "Concerning their meditation, it's not for us, my love. They've been sworn to secrecy by their Yogi not to disclose, to the unwashed masses, the mystical techniques they've been taught. That would be us. We'll just have to suffer through the same old unspiritual ten minutes of obligatory weekly conjugal commune whether we need it or not."

Elise narrowed her eyes and shot Scott an evil glare.

Ron said, "Actually, Brandi seems to be a quick study compared to me. I seem to have a lot of trouble staying focused."

"That reminds me," interjected Scott, "the ceiling in our bedroom needs painting."

Elise recommenced her evil glare at Scott, this time even more committed to the gesture.

"Joking," exclaimed Scott, reaching over and hugging his now unresponsive wife. "You know those are invariably the best ten minutes of my week." He kissed her repeatedly on her cheek until she surrendered, smiled, and relaxed.

"Actually, Scott, I don't think this type of meditation *is* for everyone," Ron said. "Meditation is in general healthy, but *Tummo* has specifically been developed for facilitating Tantric practices. Dr. Fiona thinks, and Yogi Kukuraja agrees, *Tummo* is a natural extension to our resolution."

"How does that work?" inquired Elise.

"Well," Ron replied, "Dr. Fiona believes that an unintended consequence of the resolution is the diminishing influence of the primal core of our brains on our actions. We can now better access the more sophisticated parts of our brain to gain better, or even full, control of our bodies through this meditative technique. The 'harmonizing' of our brains through the chemical conditioning caused by constant sex has, apparently, had the equivalent effect of a lifetime of dedicated meditation. Yogi Kukuraja has suggested this uncommon state of harmony not only allows, but is a requisite for, the successful mastering of *Tummo*. At least in theory that is."

"So we wouldn't have a chance at being able to master *Tummo*?" asked Scott.

"What the hell do I know? But that's what we're hearing from Yogi Kukuraja," replied Ron.

Turning to Elise, Scott stated as sincerely as he could, "Honey, after hearing what Ron and Brandi have to say, I'm all for meditation."

"Really?" Elise replied, her brows raised optimistically.

"Absolutely," he replied. "I suggest we start by harmonizing our brain chemistry with a daily sex routine, starting immediately."

Pausing while sipping her wine, Elise quietly and unenthusiastically responded deadpan into her glass, "Can we at least wait until I finish my wine?"

Both Brandi and Ron erupted in laughter.

Using the lull in the conversation, Elise broached the subject of the "mole." "Have you guys figured out who's responsible for the leaks yet?"

Brandi and Ron simultaneously shook their heads. "Not yet," Brandi answered. "It's either Dr. Fiona herself—which would be a major breach of confidentiality—or, more likely, a lucky guess by someone following #resolutionottawa on Twitter. Or maybe the details have slipped out some other way we haven't considered. We're planning to talk to Dr. Fiona about it the next time we see her, but we're pretty sure it isn't her."

"And we know it isn't you guys," Ron commented, attempting to keep the atmosphere relaxed.

Both Scott and Elise smiled back at their friends appreciatively, but behind Elise's smile was a growing seed of doubt and guilt. When she had asked about the identity of the mole moments earlier, she'd been hopeful the perpetrator had been identified—the reason being she had been, under the sternest promise of confidentiality, and unbeknownst to anybody else currently at the table, keeping her sister in Winnipeg abreast of resolution developments in their weekly Face-Time calls. Typically discreet, and Elise's closest confidant, her sister had never, as least to Elise's knowledge, ever betrayed the trust of anyone who had confided in her. So why would she now? Still, however improbable it was that her sister was the individual responsible for the ongoing leaks, she knew that her actions would be considered a breach of trust by *everyone* at this table.

Upon hearing that the mole remained unidentified, Elise made the decision, as she smiled back at the Lees, to cease the weekly updates to her sister. With the damage already done, it being unlikely that her sister was the source of these leaks, and not wanting to weaken any of these relationships, she didn't see the point of bringing up her indiscretion to the table.

As these thoughts swirled behind Elise's smiling face, Scott was also disguising his disappointment at learning that the identity of the mole had not yet been discovered. Similar to his wife, he was currently suppressing a blossoming guilt borne of a few cryptic—and then-believed innocuous—tweets he, under his 'anonymous' Twitter account, had contributed to the on-line conversation in support of his friends. Now, in hindsight, he thought this *might* have been the seed commentary for the ongoing shit-storm. The most recent being one had been in late June: "*#resolutionottawa* the resolution is taking marital sex to places it's never been. Keep your eyes open and you will learn!" Although it wasn't a direct straight-line back to him and this comment, provenance of the tweet discussing the resolution couple having public sex *could* be tracked back to its vicinity. As he smiled back at the Lees, Scott made a decision to delete this Twitter account and to cease and desist with any further tweets on the subject. With the damage already done, it being unlikely that his tweets were actually the source of the leak, and not wanting to look like an idiot in front of his friends, he decided against bringing up this indiscretion to the table.

As Brandi nodded and returned the Hartwell's smiles, she too was repressing an uncertainty as to whether she had been inadvertently responsible for the current leak. Near the end of June she hadn't been able to resist scrolling through recent tweets attached to *#resolutionottawa* during a short break at work. The tweetversation had innocently and ambiguously turned towards the resolution going places most couples would never go. She thought that was intriguingly proximal to her and Ron's actual activity during the previous weeks, and couldn't help herself, teasingly tweeting from her *nom-du-plume* account, "*#resolutionottawa* coming soon to a grocery store in your neighbourhood." In hindsight, she thought that careless tweet *could* have been ground zero for the ongoing online speculation. *How ironic would it be if I'm the mole?* thought Brandi. But, with the damage done and no way of truly knowing if her actions did catalyze the current leak, she decided not to act recklessly again, and keep this event to herself.

"Not a chance," added Ron, with an assuring smile.

Saturday, July 18

The day was unfolding a bit slower than usual. Tommy and his girlfriend, Amanda, had shown up late on Friday evening, but somehow were the first up, and sitting on the wrap-around balcony enjoying the morning birdsong over a cup of coffee when Brandi made it downstairs. The rest of the adults had over-indulged the previous night, and were prolonging their somnolent convalescence for medicinal reasons. The girls typically didn't stir until close to noon, so it was just the three of them for now.

"How did you two sleep?" asked Brandi, joining them with coffee in hand.

"Great Mom, thanks," replied Tommy.

Amanda added, "I usually have trouble sleeping with any noise, but my last memory before I fell asleep was listening to a chorus of loons against a background of frogs croaking. This place is amazing."

Just then, they heard some banging around in the kitchen. "Sounds like your father's up," Brandi said, looking at her son.

About a minute later, Ron shuffled through the screen door and, clutching a cup of coffee, sat, without a word, at one of the chairs on the balcony. He took a sip from his coffee, and mumbled into his mug, "That's the last time we invite Scott Hartwell for an overnight visit."

"So is Elise part of that, and are we throwing them out today?" Brandi asked him, playing along.

"Elise can stay, but I want him gone by noon," replied Ron, with a "final word on the matter" severity.

After a few seconds of silence, Ron slowly turned his head to look at Brandi, who stared back, with a deadpan expression. Tommy was smiling, but Amanda had a concerned look on her face.

Ron attempted a look of defiance. "You know the rules. I only have to make one decision a day when I'm on vacation. And that was it. Any other decisions today are yours."

"Since you've evoked the vacation-rules protocol," Brandi said, "I'm here to remind you that, under these extreme measures, I have veto rights, and I'm over-ruling you. Scott will not only be staying, but you'll also be mixing him his first drink tonight at exactly five o'clock this afternoon. So get yourself straightened out, mister." The last comment was delivered with drill-sergeantesque severity.

Ron moaned, and loudly slurped his coffee, much to the amusement of his son and Amanda, who had by now figured out the act. "Thank God it's only a weekend," he woefully added.

There still wasn't anybody else up about an hour later, Tommy and Amanda had left to find breakfast in Almonte, so Brandi and Ron took the opportunity to shower and meditate before making brunch for the remaining crew. Ron found that the meditation left him with a much clearer head, and an energy he hadn't expected, given the severity of his hangover. When he opened his eyes, he met Brandi's blissful stare.

"I don't have to ask you how *that* went," commented Ron. "You look positively radiant."

"And may I say you look way better," said Brandi. "Any progress?"

"I'm able to focus better now, but still no core warmth or visualization of a growing energy in my as-of-yet-not-hollow body. How about you?"

"Every day seems a bit different," Brandi pensively replied. "Today, I was able to move my energy from my core to my hands just by visualizing it. I also pictured myself floating in a dark empty space with my hands glowing red. Feel them." Brandi leaned forward, offering them to Ron.

"Holy shit!" exclaimed Ron as he touched Brandi's fingertips. Brandi's fingers felt hot, so much so that Ron actually involuntarily recoiled, like someone would when grabbing an ember or touching a hot element. "That's ridiculous!" he added, looking perplexed.

"Isn't it?" Brandi agreed, smiling broadly.

Ron didn't smile back. He wasn't too familiar with Buddhism or meditation, but he was pretty sure that this wasn't normal. "You realize that you're able to do this after just ten days? What are you going to be able to do after a month or so?"

"I have no idea. You know what I know about this, and we both only know what Yogi Kukuraja's told us. But I can tell you that I feel more alive now than I ever have."

Ron felt a growing sense of trepidation, and was contemplating what it meant when Brandi spoke again. "How about we use this small window of opportunity to satisfy both today's resolution and ourselves with some post-meditative physical therapy?"

In his current state, and with guests in the house, Ron was about to gently decline—but then he was captured by Brandi's salacious gaze. With the planned words caught in his throat, his eyes moved to Brandi's breasts at the same moment he registered a primal, musky scent emanating from his wife. He gulped and stared helplessly at his growing erection. It was the second time today that he had been overruled. And it wasn't yet noon.

Monday, July 20

With the weekend guests departed and the teenage girls still hours from consciousness, Brandi and Ron were enjoying an extended reprieve from the chaos of the weekend, and a quiet morning on the balcony. The morning warmth, agreeable birdsong, good coffee, and complete lack of competing civilization had, in effect, extended their morning meditation.

"Do we have to go back to Ottawa?" asked Ron

"I'm sure you haven't forgotten that we have full-time jobs. And I'm also sure you'll recall it's our twentieth anniversary next Wednesday, and we're throwing a fairly big party on the August long weekend that still requires a bit more planning."

"Yes, there is that," said Ron, with exaggerated resignation. "I guess there's no getting out of this relationship now."

Brandi stared at Ron. "Nice try. You keep forgetting I can read your mind. I agree; I am the best thing that's ever happened to you."

Saturday, July 25

Brandi, Sam, and Caroline sat in the screened deck chatting, with good-humoured morning radio banter from a local station playing in the background. It was a rare morning, with everyone having breakfast together. Not voluntarily, of course. Since they were due to depart by noon, the girls had had reveille forced upon them at the ungodly hour of eight, to allow them time for sustenance, showering, packing, and cleaning. As the morning ripened, the girls' claims of permanent psychological damage from this premature arousal were being discredited, with both of them enthusiastically engaged in discussion with Brandi. Ron stood in wonder of his wife who, in a matter of about ten minutes, had transformed the two moaning shipwreck victims into their normal vibrant selves. With multiple plates balanced on his arms, Ron entered onto the deck, announcing breakfast was served.

As the girls hungrily tucked into the breakfast fare, Ron thought that Brandi was looking different these days. He pondered what exactly it was that had struck him. Physically she looked the same, though definitely a bit browner after the two weeks spent on the lake, but it was more than that. As he stared at her, it came to him. She appeared more serene. Her face had a permanent peaceful glow about it that never left her, regardless of the circumstances. As this thought came to him, Brandi slowly turned her attention from the girls, and stared into Ron's eyes, smiled, and appreciatively winked at him.

Ron nearly fell off his chair. If there were any doubts that Brandi was capable of comprehending his thoughts, they were, at that moment, dispelled. This was not the educated-guess kind of knowing that couples are capable of, using physical clues or the spousal predictability that comes with decades of living with and loving someone. No, this was different. Brandi was actually strolling around in his brain, registering his thoughts as surely as if he were verbalizing them for her.

Brandi turned back to the girls, who were hungry for her attention. They had opened up about topics that Ron had never heard Sam previously discuss, certainly with him in the room. After a few minutes hearing about cute boys, what makes a boy a good kisser, hopes for long and fulfilling romances, and how many children they wanted, Ron excused himself, collected the dirty plates, and retreated back to the kitchen to clean up.

Later that day, with the sun still high and warm, the entire family, including Ron's parents and Brandi's mom, Megan—who had just arrived in town—gathered in their backyard in Centrepointe. The Redwoods was close enough that Abby and Tommy Sr. had walked over, but his dad was already complaining about his sore knees, hinting that a drive back would be appreciated.

As they all sat around the large patio table, Ron noticed that every person was particularly focused on Brandi. It reminded him of the sycophants at his office who would sit, backs straightened and ties over-tightened, breathlessly focused with hushed anticipation on every word that EllisDon's CEO Geoff Smith would speak at his town-hall gatherings. Whereas those corporate-climbing toadies would declare their commitment to the company, for all adjacent management to witness, with the fervent nodding of heads and too-loud, well-timed laughs, the current group around the table, to a person, was genuinely interested in what Brandi had to say. Ron thought he should listen as well.

When she spoke, Ron noticed that he, too, was curiously imbued with a sense of peace and contentment that he hadn't previously recalled experiencing when Brandi spoke. The conversation shifted to his mother, and the spell was broken. *What the hell was that?* he asked himself. At that precise moment, Brandi momentarily diverted her attention from Abby and smiled at Ron, which only served to further freak him out. Brandi's smile broadened, and she turned back to the conversation with Ron's mom.

As the sun slipped below the roof of their house, Abby declared she was getting a bit tired, so Ron drove his parents back to The Redwoods. When he returned he saw that the kids had dispersed, so Ron joined Brandi and her mom in the backyard. They were conversing over an award-winning Magnotta Winery 2013 Shiraz that Megan had acquired on a recent trip to Vaughan, north of Toronto. Ron slipped in beside Brandi, and poured himself a glass. He let his palate absorb the dark-berry fruit and chocolate flavours as he caught up with the conversation between the two Fuller ladies. As he locked onto the discussion, he was sure he had misheard his wife as she spoke to her mother.

"If you completely relax, there's really no limit to how many times you can orgasm."

In response to this comment, Ron stopped swallowing, and froze with his wine glass pressed against his lips. Brandi turned to him and cheerfully stated, "I was just telling Mom about our resolution, Ron."

Unfortunately, upon hearing this unanticipated declaration, he involuntarily inhaled a good portion of the volume of wine in his mouth into his trachea which, regardless of the quality of the wine, was not appreciated. An intense laryngeal spasm was immediately triggered, which expelled, at near sneeze-like speed, the offending liquid. Fortunately, this all happened so quickly that his glass was still poised in front of his mouth and effectively served as a shield for Megan, and helped to limit the damage on Brandi to a few splatters on her one side.

"Oh my, Ron. Are you all right?" Megan asked, her query barely audible over Ron's coughing and sputtering.

Dripping red wine from his hair, ears, nose and chin, Ron excused himself from the table, and said he'd be right back after he cleaned himself up. Still in shock as he towelled the wine from his face in the downstairs bathroom, he wondered what his wife was thinking, telling her mother about their resolution. He was so flabbergasted and embarrassed that he couldn't bring himself to go back and confront his mother-in-law. He stood at the patio door and asked, with a broad affected smile, "Brandi honey, could I speak with you for a second please?"

"Sure, Ron," she said and slid away from the table.

Ron had receded around the corner. When she entered the house she found Ron near-hysterical, sporting a full-out, open-handed "WTF?" look. Upon seeing this, Brandi cautiously asked, "Is this about me telling Mom about our resolution?"

Without a word, Ron expertly switched his look over to a highly animated "duuuhh" look.

"She brought it up after your parents left. Apparently Mags let it slip about a month ago, and she's been following our 'progress' on Twitter. I wasn't going to lie to her." Brandi calmly delivered this explanation with an "it's not that big a deal" look on her face.

Ron had entered this exchange with Brandi with no intention of being placated, but strangely, the angst and discomfort he had just experienced were now melting away. In about three seconds, he found himself fully understanding Brandi's position.

"Why don't you go change your shirt and come join us outside," she added. "Mom is curious about how someone of your age and fitness level has actually managed to keep up with the resolution."

Ron nodded, and headed upstairs for a change of clothes. While he was ascending the stairs he was already formulating an answer to his mother-in-law's query.

Sunday, July 26

Their last day of their holidays started with a sleep-in, an extra-long meditation session, and some spirited lovemaking. Ron felt much more centred after the meditation, and some of it was actually spent thoughtlessly for a change. After they showered, Ron asked Brandi, while she was dressing, "So, can you read everybody's mind, or just mine?"

"You're easy. So don't even *try* lying to me," she joked, then paused a second. "Everyone else is a bit different. I can sense what they're thinking, and know what emotion they're feeling, but it's not like hearing—like it is with you."

Oh great, thought Ron.

"Well, not all the time anyways." Brandi continued; her lips slightly pursed while she searched for the right words. "I can 'hear' Sam and Tommy Jr. every once in a while when I don't concentrate, but even with your parents I know the essence of what they're thinking and what they're feeling." She let this comment hang for a couple of seconds. "You'll be happy to know they're very happy at The Redwoods and are especially pleased at being so close to us."

"Did they tell you that?" asked Ron

"Not in so many words," admitted Brandi.

"So when did this start, and is it the resolution or the meditation that's causing it?" asked Ron

"Well, you'll recall, it started with the resolution. We were starting to read each other's mind in early summer."

Ron nodded.

"But since I started *Tummo* meditation, it's gone to an entirely different level. And it has to be the meditation, since it's been getting more frequent and 'clearer' the more I meditate. And..."

Ron felt a growing anxiety at what Brandi was about to say next.

"The last few days, I've been able to float."

"Float?" Ron exclaimed. A further explanation was implicit.

"Not physically, but mentally. During the deepest part of my meditation, I can actually feel myself lift out of my body and float above it. I can see myself meditating below, and I can see you, and look around the room."

Ron stood speechless, processing what Brandi was telling him.

"I can see you taking peeks at me, by the way," she added.

Ron felt a crimson tide of embarrassment start to imbue his face. Before he could say anything in his defense, Brandi continued. "Don't be embarrassed, Ron. I think it's sweet. You are my husband, after all. And I've noticed lately that you're actually meditating part of time. Congratulations!"

Ron sat on the bed, suddenly feeling overwhelmed.

Brandi sat down beside him and held his hand. "It's nothing to be concerned about," she whispered. "We shouldn't be surprised that this is happening. It's what Dr. Fiona and Yogi Kukuraja were hoping would happen."

Monday, July 27

It had been over two weeks since Yogi Kukuraja had met with Brandi and Ron, and he was curious as to their progress, so he had requested a short visit updating him upon their return to Ottawa. Ron had to work late to catch up on his workload, so it was close to eight o'clock when they finally settled into the low bench in front of the good Yogi's desk. Niceties were exchanged and the obligatory vacation highlights were discussed before they got down to business.

Ron started, and explained how the meditation was providing some positive changes, including sleeping better, experiencing more joy in everyday situations, and being calmer and generally happier. When he explained he hadn't yet got the hang of the "visualize yourself as a hollow vesicle filled with a glowing core" thing, the Yogi smiled and assured Ron that mastering *Tummo* can take years of devotion, to not be discouraged, and to keep trying.

He turned to Brandi, and asked how she was progressing. Her download took a bit longer than Ron's. She went through the various stages that she had experienced in the short time since they had last met with him. As her discourse progressed, the smile on Yogi Kukuraja's face slowly faded away, and was replaced by a stern look that neither Ron nor Brandi had previously seen on him. Brandi stopped and asked if everything was OK. Yogi Kukuraja said it was, and to please continue.

After a few more minutes Brandi finished. They were now sitting across the table from a very serious-looking Yogi.

He sat silent for the better part of a minute, simply staring at Brandi. Finally he asked, "You're sure that everything you've told me just now is completely accurate?"

"Yes, I'm sure," Brandi replied.

"Very good," nodded the Yogi, looking even more severe. "In that case, can I ask that we reconvene in a few days? I'd like you, Brandi, to meet with someone, and recount your experiences. Would that be possible?"

Ron and Brandi looked at each with a perplexed look. Brandi replied, "I guess so, but it'll have to be early next week since we're planning for and celebrating our twentieth wedding anniversary later this week and on the weekend."

"Congratulations," the Yogi cheerfully offered, then immediately switched back to his more serious self. "Then how about next Tuesday evening at seven o'clock?"

Brandi and Ron looked at each other, did a mental check of their calendars, and nodded. "I think that'll work for us," Brandi replied.

"Good. In the meantime, Ron, please continue with your meditation as I've instructed you. Brandi, can I speak to you alone for a moment?"

Surprised at the request, Brandi looked at Ron to gauge his reaction. Although as perplexed as she was, he nodded that he was OK with leaving the room. She then nodded. "Sure."

Ron sat on one of the cushions surrounding the main chamber containing the shrine, losing himself in the incense-thick atmosphere of the dimly lit room. He drifted in and out of a calming meditation, and lost track of time. When he glanced at his watch, he realized it had only been about fifteen minutes. Just then Brandi and Yogi Kukuraja emerged from the door adjacent to the main altar, shook hands, and separated, with the Yogi retreating into the back rooms.

Looking around and allowing her eyes to adjust to the darker setting, Brandi spotted Ron sitting nearby against the wall, and walked over and sat down beside him. "That was interesting," she said.

"Well, let's get out of here, and you can tell me what the Yogi's cooking up for you while we drive home."

Later that night, Ron lay awake in bed. Yogi Kukuraja's comments to Brandi had dug a groove in his consciousness, and he was having difficulty crawling out of the rut.

The Yogi had said that, for a layperson, she was exhibiting a very high level of innate spirituality, especially given the short period of time she had actually been meditating. Because of her strangely swift progress, he wanted her to meet an accomplished female monk, or *Bhikkhuni*, at their meeting next week. To assist in Brandi's ongoing spiritual ascent, he had also instructed her on the next level of *Tummo* meditation techniques, and made her swear to secrecy, as he initially had done with both of them when introducing *Tummo* a few weeks ago.

This was the primary reason for Ron's current concern. Their journey through the resolution had been, to this point, a shared experience, bringing them closer together as a couple. This was the first development related to the resolution that was exclusive to one or the other of them, which was counter to the fundamental intent of the resolution.

Ron's mind buzzed as he lay in bed. *What will be the consequences of Brandi's new Tummo teachings? Could this next stage drive us apart? Should I suggest stopping this Buddhist experiment? Why can't I focus during meditation? Why is my hairline receding while my father still has a full head of hair?*

As he drifted off to sleep, the last thought he had was, *maybe it's time to admit defeat and surrender to the resolution.*

Tuesday, July 28

It was the hottest day of the year so far. Even though he had worked until almost six, and his walk home wasn't until after the warmest part of the day, Ron arrived home soaked, with his shirt and pants slick against his skin.

Megan and the kids had met up with his parents at The Redwood for happy hour and supper to give Ron and Brandi some "uncrowded anniversary time," so he wasn't surprised there wasn't anybody around when he arrived home. He figured Brandi had had to work late as well.

He jogged upstairs to change, and upon entering their bedroom saw Brandi sitting naked and lotus-style on their bed, deep in meditation. Leaving her to it, he quietly changed into a T-shirt and shorts and headed back downstairs.

After about ten minutes Brandi came downstairs in loose shorts and a T-shirt of her own. Her sheer T-shirt sent the message to Ron that she was interested in advancing the resolution. Ron, on the other hand, had been sitting and fretting over a beer about recent developments, and his priority was discussing them with Brandi.

As Brandi sidled up beside him at the island in the kitchen, he could feel her warmth. It was more than temperature—it was like an aura had enveloped him. He stayed strong and turned to confront her.

Just before he could speak, she tenderly asked, "What's wrong, Ron?"

While Ron was composing himself and formulating his response, Brandi answered for him. "You're worried about me taking advanced *Tummo* while you've been held back, aren't you?"

Ron nodded, and was clearing his throat in preparation for his response when Brandi continued, "And you're uncomfortable with me doing something that you're not part of. Especially as an extension of the resolution."

Ron nodded again, and drew in a breath to support his imminent comment, but Brandi again intercepted him. "You're worried that my expedited learning of *Tummo* may drive a wedge between the two of us and, it's bothering you so much that you're thinking that we should stop the meditation, or maybe even the resolution."

Ron nodded a bit faster.

"Oh, Ron—that's so sweet that you're willing to give up the resolution for *us*." She grabbed his face in her hands and kissed him passionately on the lips. "Knowing that just makes me more determined to complete it." She paused briefly, looking deep into Ron's eyes. "You don't have to worry honey, we got this."

Feeling somewhat relieved that he'd gotten that off his chest, his shoulders relaxed, and he could feel the tension drain from his chest.

After a few seconds, Brandi added, "Now, concerning the resolution…" She slowly moved away from him towards the stairs, looking back with an exaggerated "come-hither" look. As she ascended the stairs, he was hypnotized by the rhythmical swaying of her beautiful bottom in her flimsy short shorts. All his worries forgotten, he followed her up the stairs.

Wednesday, July 29

Brandi and Ron were surrounded by their family in their favourite local Italian restaurant. With a larger, more inclusive, party planned for Saturday, today's anniversary celebration was limited to the immediate family currently in Ottawa. Tommy Sr.'s birthday was tomorrow, so that celebration had also been layered into tonight's fete. Due to the blazing heat, and in consideration of the grandparents attending this evening, they had driven over, and Tommy Jr. had offered to drive back. Mercifully, the kids had planned this for a few weeks now, and they got a prime table inside, where the air conditioning made for a more comfort-able mealtime.

After a couple of bottles of wine, some excellent homemade pasta, and tiramisu, the mood was festive and the conversation boisterous. Romano—the proprietor of the restaurant—caught wind of the anniversary celebration, came over and congratulated Brandi and Ron personally, and insisted that the table enjoy a round of his personal stock of Grappa. And when the first round was complete, Romano insisted that it would be a personal insult to him, his family, and his deceased ancestors if all the adults didn't enjoy a second round of Grappa—since there were two participants in the anniversary celebration. Romano of course joined them for both rounds. Someone then mentioned that this was also Tommy Sr.'s birthday celebration and, following a boisterous cheer led by Romano, a final compulsory round of Grappa was consumed.

The post-Grappa glow was evident upon the faces of those who had partici-pated, and a number of simultaneous conversations erupted around the table, periodically interrupted by the percussion of a spoon on a wine glass and the raising of a wine glass in further toasts. Tommy Sr. was grinning ear-to-ear at one point, lost in his own thoughts. Then a lightbulb went off, his eyes lit up, and his dessert spoon started clanging a bit too hard against his wine glass, signifying his proposal for yet another toast, while gathering the table's collective attention.

The table quieted, along with a fair portion of the curious rubber-necking patrons in the restaurant, and then Tommy Sr. raised his glass a bit too high, and loudly exclaimed, "To the resolution!"

The smile on Tommy Sr.'s face faded when the table collectively gasped—not the expected response. Ron felt the colour drain from his face as he sat, mouth and eyes agape, staring in shock at his father. In the matter of a few silent seconds, the flow of blood in Ron's body reversed tide, and coursed back into his face with a vengeance. His face, frozen in a stunned expression, and his cheeks and ears bright crimson, suggested to his father that, perhaps, Ron didn't consider the resolution an appropriate subject for a toast.

Abby just rolled her eyes and slowly shook her head, with a look of unsurprised exasperation on her face. Megan looked around confused. Sam had buried her head in her hands and was slowly sliding off her bench and under the table. Tommy Jr. had registered the quiet in the rest of the restaurant, and was looking around gauging who had heard what, and their reaction to both the toast and their table's reaction. Tommy Sr. whispered a barely audible, "Uh-oh," and Brandi just sat, there smiling at Ron's father.

"Sorry about that, guys. I thought everybody knew," Tommy Sr. sheepishly explained.

Abby responded, "Well if they didn't know before, they know now."

Tommy Jr., whispered, anxiously looking around at the numerous prying eyes locked on their table, "I think a few more people in this restaurant also know now."

Sam just groaned as if she was going to be ill.

Ron sat glowing, his mouth slowly opening and closing.

Brandi said sincerely, "Don't worry about it, Tommy. Not a big deal." Looking at Ron, she added, "Ron's face is just overreacting."

With the bill quickly paid and Ron's parents dropped off at The Redwoods, Sam and Tommy Jr. eagerly disembarked at their Centrepointe home and retreated to their rooms, as did their dad, while Brandi and her mom grabbed a cleansing glass of white wine and relaxed outside. A case of Kismet Estate Sauvignon Blanc had been purchased for the coming weekend, and Brandi and her mom were enjoying the crisp complex peach and citrus overtones as Megan asked the obvious question. "Why was Ron so embarrassed at the restaurant, Brandi?"

"I think it was mostly because of the kids, mom. He was hoping that they were still in the dark about our resolution. But, in actual fact, they both knew and were keeping it to themselves so as not to embarrass us, or themselves—at least in Sam's case. But they've known for at least a month now. I decided not to tell Ron so he wouldn't fret about it. In hindsight, I probably should have told him to avoid…well, to avoid what happened this evening."

"Do you think he'll be OK?" asked Megan.

"Oh, for sure, Mom. He's resilient. Once he gets his head around the fact that everybody in his house is now aware that he is having sex with his wife on a daily basis, he'll be fine."

At that very moment, Ron was in his bathroom, staring into the mirror while brushing his teeth, his mind whirling. *How can I look my kids in the eye now? I can't believe both my parents know—boy, does that suck the fun out of sex. How can I have sex with Brandi knowing that everybody in my family knows? Are they imagining what we're doing? How many people in the restaurant connected us to the resolution? I'm really not in the mood tonight. I hope Brandi doesn't expect me to have sex tonight. I'll pretend I'm sleeping. We did drink a lot tonight, so she won't be suspicious.*

On and on it went, until sleep finally rescued him.

When Brandi finally did call it a day and bid her mother good night, she found Ron curled up under the covers, snoring softly. Fully aware that Ron, in his agitated state, had purposely retired early to avoid the possibility of disappointing Brandi in bed tonight, Brandi smiled at her husband, and was overwhelmed with a sense of contentment for this man with whom she had spent twenty years living and raising a family. She marveled at his innate humanity and zest for life, grateful that his obsession with resolutions had fortuitously taken her to this place in which she currently resided, a place she knew she would have never intersected without him. A place so unique, so awe-inspiring, that an appreciative tear of pure joy rolled down her cheek as she stood over her sleeping husband.

Thursday, July 30

Fortunately for Ron, Dr. Kaur had just returned from vacation, and was available to meet with Ron on short notice. After the events of the previous day, Ron needed to talk to someone other than his mindreading wife, and Scott was out of town on business. Ron hadn't been feeling himself lately, so he justified his trip to the doctor's with that excuse, but in reality he simply needed counsel, and this burden defaulted to the available Dr. Kaur.

As was typical, Ron was his last patient of the day. Ron figured he had been tacked onto his full docket out of curiosity as to how the resolution was progressing. Dr. Kaur had already sent his receptionist home when he surged into his waiting room and cheerfully requested Ron to follow him into one of his examination rooms.

Once sitting, he brightly commented on the wonderfully warm weather, and praised his parents' choice of Ottawa as their immigration destination in Canada. "Weather like this is good for the soul and the body, Ron. Sweating helps flush out the body toxins. It reminds me of growing up in Raipur—except without the constant smell of sewage, the lack of any air conditioning, and the cattle roaming the streets, of course," he added, with a broad smile and a faraway look.

After a few seconds of gazing at Ron, shaking his head dreamily, he released himself from his reminiscences, placed his hands on his knees, leaned forward, and asked, "So then, what can I do for you today Ron?"

About two seconds later, while Ron was formulating his response, a light bulb went off in Dr. Kaur's brain, his eyes lit up, a schoolboy smile spread across his face, and he asked in a salacious raspy whisper, "It's about the resolution, isn't it Ron?"

Ron nodded that indeed it was.

Before he could say anything, Dr. Kaur interjected, "My wife and I have been following your progress on Twitter. Last I heard you were taking testosterone supplements and having sex in public places. Is that all true, Ron?"

Dr. Kaur had finally stopped talking and leaned forward, fully paused and focused in anticipation of Ron's response.

Fairly confident now that the floor was his, Ron replied, "Yes, it is."

"I knew it," the doctor exclaimed, as he jolted upwards in his seat, slapping his thighs. "I knew you could do this, my friend," he continued, wagging his finger at Ron. "My wife said, way back in February, you didn't stand a chance." He scrunched up his face, as if in response to some unpleasant smell. "But *I* said there was something determined about *you* Ron. I said to her that this man has a rare gift of intelligence, but without introspection. Not common, I can tell you, Ron."

With Dr. Kaur smiling and bobbling his head, Ron assumed that was meant as a compliment, so he replied, "Thanks, I think, Dr. Kaur."

"So what is it, Ron? You're looking a bit down, if I can be totally honest with you."

Ron provided Dr. Kaur with a condensed version of his and Brandi's activities over the last almost half-year, including the counselling with Dr. Fiona, their prescribed supplements, the strategies deployed and, most importantly, the recent developments related to their introduction to Buddhism and meditation.

"So, tell me if I'm correct, Ron," Dr. Kaur asked Ron after his briefing. "You're feeling as if Brandi has taken a different path than you?"

Ron nodded in agreement.

"And this new development has left you feeling anxious?"

Ron nodded again.

"And confused, and possibly feeling a bit inadequate?"

Ron thought about this for a second, shrugged, and nodded in agreement.

"Interesting," Dr. Kaur commented.

He paused pensively for a few seconds, and then restarted. "Well, I'm no psychiatrist, Ron, but I think you're worried that you and your wife Brandi are not as perfectly matched as you have, through all the years you've been married, believed you were. Most disturbing, however, is you are now realizing just how exceptional Brandi is, and are worried she, too, will realize this, and possibly look elsewhere for a spousal upgrade."

Ron thought about what Dr. Kaur had just said, and although he hadn't previously considered this to be the root of his recent malaise, this theory resonated with him. He nodded back at Dr. Kaur, encouraging him to continue.

"If this is the case, Ron," Dr. Kaur accommodatingly continued, "you are not alone, my friend. That is the situation with the majority of my friends and family—including myself! It is the sign of a healthy and happy marriage that the wife is recognized as the more capable, more cerebral, and more spiritual member of the partnership. That said, Brandi appears to be even more exceptional."

He let that comment hang while he considered his next comment. "But I don't think this should be cause for concern, Ron."

Ron took the bait and asked, "Why do you say that, Dr. Kaur?"

"Simply because, if you are accurate in your summary of events, she is becoming or even has become a very spiritual being, and as such, she will embrace *all* your abundant shortcomings. Each and every one of them."

He raised his eyebrows, slowly bobbled his head, and let this comment sink in before he continued. "She will accept them as part of who you are. That is the face of compassion and understanding in all religions. I may have been born a Hindu, but the basic tenets are the same in my old religion as they are in your new one."

Ron lifted his hand, index finger extended, and was opening his mouth to correct Dr. Kaur about his misconception concerning Ron's "new religion" when the doctor continued. "Those, and the fact that you two are already the parents to two young adults, are past your prime child-bearing years, are both employed, with good-paying jobs, and engage in mutually gratifying daily sexual activity. Those things also contribute to marital happiness and continuity."

Ron sat for a few seconds absorbing Dr. Kaur's words before he spoke. "So, you're saying this is all in my head?"

"Most likely, Ron. Given your wife's exceptional skills, I would suggest you now devote yourself to assisting her on her journey going forward. This isn't a competition, Ron. And if it were, you'd have already lost, my friend. Surround her with joy and happiness and encouragement, and you may be witness to a rare and beautiful metamorphosis as she moves from the confinement of her human cocoon and spreads the wings of her spirituality. Some of it may even rub off on you if you're lucky."

The doctor paused for a couple of beats, and then said, "That doesn't mean you should abandon your resolution. No, not at all. You should redouble your efforts to make sure you get to the finish line. Towards that end, can I help you with renewal of any of your prescriptions?"

His gaze drifted upwards from Ron's eyes to his forehead, and he added, "And since you're here, maybe something to reinforce the northern front?"

CHAPTER 9

WHEEL OF LIFE

Saturday, August 1

Ron took a break from socializing to watch a few summer clouds drift by. It was a weather-perfect afternoon celebration, and their backyard was spilling over with family, friends, and co-workers. Ron and Brandi's siblings and their children had also made the trip, and were somewhere in the crowd.

What a rare moment, Ron was thinking—then he noticed Scott making a beeline towards him. Scott was sporting an evil grin, and Ron knew that this brief moment of bliss was about to end.

"Hey buddy," Scott started, as he came in for an embrace. "Congratulations. Twenty years is quite the achievement."

"Thanks, man. With Brandi, it really wasn't that hard."

"Probably true to some degree, but still, twenty years is hard work. So again, congrats," Scott said as he raised his beer. Then he added, "That's the good news."

In response Ron stopped his imbibe, slowly swallowed, and waited for the other shoe to drop. "Here's the bad news," Scott continued. He brought his phone from his pocket, and spun it around so Ron could read it. It was a tweet tagged to *#resolutionottawa*.

"Best anniversary wishes to the resolution couple. Happy twentieth!"

Ron felt the blood drain from his face. He scanned the crowd for his boss, Nigel Hewitt, as well as his co-workers. He knew that the crack in the dam had now grown past repair. Their exposure as *the* resolution couple was now likely inevitable.

"Sorry to be the bearer of bad news, buddy, but I thought you should know ASAP," Scott said consolingly.

Ron nodded at his buddy, while snatching his phone. He went in search of Brandi to give her the news.

It wasn't hard to find her. She was surrounded by about half a dozen women, gleefully chatting amongst themselves. Although the conversation was moving around the circle, the participants would periodically glance at Brandi as if to recharge their happiness quotient. Ron wondered if this attention was solely because of today's celebration.

While he silently stood about six feet to one side of Brandi, assessing the group dynamics, she slowly peered around one of the women in the group and caught Ron's eye. Excusing herself from the confabulating clutch, Brandi walked over to Ron. He was sure a couple of the ladies shot him a disapproving glance for being the cause for Brandi's departure.

"Well?" Ron asked Brandi.

"Well what?" replied Brandi, playing along with him.

"The magnificent Carnac is unable to read my mind?" asked Ron.

"Ron," Brandi patiently replied, "your mind is the equivalent of spaghetti at the moment." She let that comment sit for a couple of seconds, then continued, "But to answer your question, I do know you're upset about something."

Ron nodded.

"And I know that it's something about the resolution," she whispered.

Ron nodded faster.

Suddenly Brandi, looking uncharacteristically troubled, commented. "Oh my God! Really?"

Ron nodded even faster, and gave her Scott's phone.

༁

Later, with the sun setting, only family remained as remnants of the much bigger daytime celebration. The kids were engaged elsewhere in the house, and just Ron and Brandi and their parents and siblings were left in the backyard.

Since learning that social media was nipping at their heels, Ron had done his best to appear cheerful, but his insides were roiling, and he couldn't wait for the guests to disperse so he could talk to Brandi about recent developments. Somehow, however, Brandi appeared to be untroubled, and was again the centre of the conversation.

Ron knew that at least some of the family members around the table had been following their progress on Twitter, thanks to their mole, but from the upbeat exchange around the table, and the lack of both searching stares and whispered queries, Ron assumed none of them had checked the recent tweets concerning *#resolutionottawa*. This was fine with Ron. He wanted to formulate a strategy with Brandi before confronting the masses. In the meantime, Ron had decided that getting drunk was the best strategy.

The light toasts ubiquitous throughout the day had now grown into full-blown "let's get shitfaced" offerings, at least for Ron, his brother, Stewart, and Mags's husband, Bernie. Ron had made the unfortunate decision of buying a bottle of Grappa for the party, and was now liberally dispensing it to all willing participants around the table. All three of them. Things were starting to get messy. Unbeknownst to the three "brothers," the rest of the table was taking note, and concerned looks were being cast at the three men, with the general conversation becoming considerably less free-flowing than the Grappa.

After another half hour of progressively more obnoxious behaviour by the three guys, Mags leaned over to Bernie and suggested that maybe it was time to call it a day. Sam had agreed to move into a kid's commune downstairs with her visiting cousins, freeing up some space for her aunt and uncle, so Bernie's sleeping quarters were mere feet away and Mags was hoping for a quick getaway.

"Sorry, guys," exclaimed Bernie sadly, gazing at his fellow inebriates. "It looks like I'm getting the hook."

In unison, Ron and Stewart both groaned their disappointment.

Bernie, emboldened by the support of his two drinking partners, insisted that first he make one last toast for the table in celebration of this "thpecial effent." With arms crossed and eyes firmly rolled back into her head, Mags impatiently waited for her husband to articulate his final toast of the day.

After some time steadying his swaying head, Bernie pinched his face, mustering up the focus for his crowning salutations. With his words now successfully structured, his eyebrows unfurrowed, and in as dignified a manner as he was currently capable, he raised his glass of Grappa and called out, "To the resolution!"

Brandi's younger sister, Debbie, audibly gasped.

Stewart and his wife, Kristine, looked at each other, perplexed.

Mags lowered her face into her hands out of embarrassment, and started shaking her head.

Tommy Sr. looked at Abby and said, "See, it's not just me."

Brandi smiled and raised her wine glass.

Ron replied, "To the ffffuckin' resolution," as he loudly clinked glasses with Bernie.

Sunday, August 2

Around eleven o'clock, with the smell of a hearty fried breakfast almost fully dissipated, Ron and Bernie were the last to rise. When Bernie rounded the corner into the kitchen, he found Ron at the island, silently pointing towards the coffee maker. After collecting his cup, he joined Ron at the island and asked, "Am I in trouble?"

Ron shook his head, but added, "I'm pretty sure I am, though."

He glanced into the backyard, and noticed Stewart and Kristen sitting there, looking intently at their phones. He knew that they were examining the #resolutionottawa tweets, and accepted that part of today's hell would be fielding questions and absorbing innuendos and jabs from his brother. But that wasn't his main concern. He needed to talk to Brandi, to make amends for his behaviour last night, and talk about their being outed. Just then, Tommy Jr. entered the kitchen.

"Whoa! You two look like you had a rough one last night."

Both men raised their eyebrows, and subtly nodded in agreement.

Ron asked, "Do you know where your mom is?"

"Yeah. She's out having coffee and shopping with Grandma Fuller, Aunt Mags, and Aunt Debbie. She said she'd be back around lunchtime."

"Thanks, Tommy."

"I'm heading over to Amanda's place. See you guys later," Tommy added, loud enough so his uncle and aunt outside could hear him. He waved over his shoulder while bounding out the front door.

The noise and commotion were too much for Bernie. He groaned, got up from his stool, and beat a retreat back to his bedroom, coffee in hand. Ron looked around, noting that it was just him and his brother and sister-in-law in the immediate area. With nowhere to hide, and resigned to the inevitable unpleasantries of the imminent conversation, he shuffled out the back door into the backyard, and sat down at the table with his brother.

Stewart looked up and said, "Good morning, bro. Quite the party yesterday."

Ron nodded patiently, waiting for Stewart's query concerning the resolution. Kristen was looking down, avoiding any eye contact with Ron.

A few silent beats passed while Ron held his brother's gaze.

Recognizing this as an invitation to raise the subject that was at the forefront of his mind, Stewart began. "That's one ambitious resolution you and Brandi have undertaken this year," he said with a chuckle, nodding slowly, with eyebrows fully raised, to emphasize the comment.

Looking at his phone, he added, "and it appears that you and Brandi are about to become local celebrities." He laughed out loud at this comment, and shook his head. "I'll bet you didn't see this coming back in January."

With the subject broached, and Ron still calm and unperturbed, Kristen cautiously glanced up and took in her brother-in-law's reaction.

Ron nodded his head matter-of-factly, with a closed mouth smile, and then replied, "No, that's for sure, bro. But I'll tell you, regardless of what happens, it's all been worthwhile. If that's the price we have to pay for this experience, then so be it. We'd do it all over again in a heartbeat."

Not having yet talked to Brandi after discovering last night's tweet, Ron wasn't completely sure that Brandi would agree with the last comment, but he wasn't going to show his brother any weakness and encourage further, possibly meaner commentary from him.

Listening to Ron, Stewart's demeanour instantly changed. The smirk on his face faded, and a sincere expression took its place as he leaned in, glancing around.

"To be honest with you, Ron, Kristen and I are sort of interested in how you guys have managed this. You know, to get this far. And both of us have noticed a big change in Brandi. She's... I don't know exactly. For the lack of a better word, she's radiant." He said looking at Kristen, who was nodding in agreement.

She spoke. "I've recently been dealing with some anxiety issues, and when I'm around her I *feel* better Ron. When she talks to me, I actually feel good. It's been a while since I've actually felt *good*."

Wow, Ron was thinking. He hadn't seen this coming, either. The dreaded conversation with his brother concerning their resolution had just become an unprecedented plea for help from him. He was taken aback, and sat there speechless.

Just then, he heard the front door close and the voices of the three Fuller sisters and their mother, as they effervescently flowed into the adjacent kitchen. Brandi walked to the open door by the patio and smiled. "He lives!" she exclaimed with mock incredulity. "How are you feeling, honey?" she added as she came over. She rubbed his head and gave him a kiss on the lips. "I don't think we should have Grappa in our house. That stuff is dangerous!"

Phew! Ron thought. *Dodged that bullet. Now, we just have to come up with a plan to deal with the resolution going public.* Ron could feel his headache intensify as he thought about some of the worst-case scenarios.

Mercifully, by about seven that evening all family had departed back to their primary residences and, aside from the kids, Brandi and Ron once again had their house back to themselves. As they sat soaking in a cool bubble bath, Ron looked worriedly at Brandi and asked, "It appears we're not going to be able to keep this a secret from the curious, sex-obsessed masses much longer. Do you think there's anything we can do to stop this?"

Brandi pensively paused, then shook her head. "Someone very familiar with the resolution wants details to be public. There are so many people who know about it now I don't think we're going to be able to stop this from getting out. It's probably damage-control time, Ron. I think the best we can do is to get out in front of this. I'm going to talk to my boss, Julie, and I suggest you have a confidential chat with Nigel, as well, so you can control the messaging. Better he hears it directly from you that we're the "resolution" couple than hear it for the first time on the evening news. He's a reasonable guy and hopefully, if he's forewarned, he'll downplay it to the exec, and display an indifference in the office that'll mute the response of your co-workers. That would be the plan, anyway. I'm really more worried about Sam. She's going to get a hard time at school and not like us very much for a while."

Ron hadn't even thought about Sam since he first saw the text last night. As soon as Brandi brought her up, he knew that was going to be a problem.

"We should give her a heads-up as well, then," Ron suggested.

Brandi nodded in agreement. "I'll do that sometime this week."

Ron was more than happy that burden again fell to Brandi. He considered himself totally unprepared to have that discussion with a fifteen-year-old girl with a bit of a mean streak.

Brandi added, "That means that you'll have to warn Tommy that this may be coming down the pipe."

Ron nodded. Although he was sure that Tommy wouldn't be happy about being known as the eldest child of the resolution couple, he was also sure Tommy wouldn't be dramatic about it, and would be able to spin it in a positive light within his circle of friends and at work. "I wish I knew who was responsible for all this. It's really beginning to bug me."

"We may never know, Ron. But one thing's for sure now, I'm more determined than ever to finish the resolution. If it's the intention of this 'mole' to have us fail, he or she is going to be disappointed."

Ron involuntarily shivered when he heard Brandi's last comment. Ron knew that her recent transformation had made her a force of nature not to be underestimated or purposely maligned.

Brandi noticed Ron's shiver, and said, "The water's getting a little cool. How about we dry off and check today off the calendar?"

Ron wasn't going to argue. He had been feeling "hungover horny" all day, and was looking forward to progressing the resolution at the first available opportunity.

As Ron slowly towelled himself off, he wondered about what exactly caused this phenomenon, which, based on frank discussions with his buddies and Brandi, appeared more prevalent in males than it was in females. A world of riches awaited the person who could, using this naturally produced compound, provide that level of sexual invigoration without the hangover.

Brandi called out to him from the bed. "Instead of wondering why it happens, Ron, you should just enjoy it."

Tuesday, August 4

As he and Brandi made their way to the temple on Bank Street, Ron reflected on the events of the day. Following a morning group meeting, Ron had asked his boss, Nigel, for a few minutes to discuss a "personal matter." Back in Nigel's office, Ron had tensely sat opposite his serious-looking boss, and inquired if he had heard about the "resolution" that an Ottawa couple had undertaken. When Nigel nodded that he had, Ron, red-faced and nervous, explained that that couple was indeed himself and Brandi, and that it was likely that they would soon be publically exposed.

Once Nigel was convinced of the veracity of Ron's claim, a smile spread across his face. He confided that he and his wife had been following their progress via Twitter, and had started some of the "routines," detailed in the Twitter feeds, that Brandi and Ron had been using to successfully execute their resolution. Ron didn't ask which ones.

For the next ten minutes, Ron had fielded questions about the resolution from his usually staid and conservative boss. The last thing Nigel said to Ron when he was leaving was, "Don't worry, Ron. I've got your back," which did momentarily relieve his general feeling of anxiety.

Unfortunately, the anxiety soon returned when he thought about tonight's meeting with Yogi Kukuraja and the "guest" monk. Although a quick evening meditation helped to alleviate some of his tension, he was still on edge when he walked into the temple on Bank Street.

After removing their shoes, they shuffled cautiously into the incense-rich atmosphere of the main hall, the elaborately festooned surroundings and gilded statues slowly emerging as their eyes adjusted. Ron breathed deep, and felt completely relaxed for the first time that day. Yogi Kukuraja was nowhere to be seen, so they sat on some cushions against one of the walls, and waited.

"How're you feeling, Ron?" Brandi quietly inquired

"I'm glad my talk with Nigel is over with. Hey. Did you have yours with Julie today?"

"Sort of," she replied.

"What do you mean by that?"

"She already knew it was me." Brandi took Ron's puzzled look as a cue to continue. "Remember, she was at the party, and was aware that it was our twentieth anniversary."

Ron nodded.

"Well, she must have put two and two together."

"What did she say?" inquired Ron.

"Nothing, actually."

The puzzled look once again took up residence on Ron's face.

"I was about to corral her, when she walked by my office, stopped for a couple of seconds, and winked at me."

"That was it?" inquired Ron.

"Well… Ron, I *knew* that's why she had stopped by and winked at me."

"You *knew*?" asked Ron, feeling a bit resentful that she had gotten off so easily.

Brandi nodded. "Listen. Consider the time you and Nigel spent today as a bonding experience. How many other of his managers have talked sex with him?" she asked rhetorically, knowing the sum total was one.

Ron's pouty face slowly relaxed as he realized that Brandi was right.

Just then, Yogi Kukuraja emerged from the door by the shrine, and looked around while his eyes adjusted to the lower light. After a few seconds they focused on Brandi and Ron, and his face lit up. As they got to their feet, Yogi Kukuraja made his way over to them. "So good to see you both again," he greeted them. "I've been looking forward to this meeting for quite a few days now."

"Us too, Yogi Kukuraja," Brandi replied effusively. Ron mustered a weak smile, while nodding politely. His emotion had been more that of trepidation.

"Please follow me," Yogi Kukuraja requested. "There's someone I want you to meet."

They exited the main hall through the side door, and walked the few steps to Yogi Kukuraja's office. To their surprise, there were two women waiting there. One, wrapped in a dark burgundy robe, they had never met; the other was Dr. Fiona Xanthopoulos, whom they hadn't seen in over a month.

"Good to see you both," Dr. Fiona gushed, as she came in for hugs. "I understand that things are going well. I'm so happy to hear that."

Yogi Kukuraja interjected, "I'd like you both to meet Acharya Jetsunma Kusho Chödrön. She is a famous *Bhikkhuni* and author, and director of Gampo Abbey in Nova Scotia. Last week, after our meeting, I relayed your experiences to her, and she informed me that she was going to be in the region this week, and was interested in meeting you both." Yogi Kukuraja had said "both," but he was looking at Brandi when he said it.

Ron had no illusions that this famous Buddhist nun was dropping in just to chat. Nor was she there to see Ron. He knew Brandi's newly developed skills had caught her attention, and she was here to see Brandi for herself.

After the introductions, Ms. Chödrön explained that she had been friends with Yogi Kukuraja for a few years, and had met Dr. Fiona through the Yogi. "Our original founder, Chögyam Trungpa, was one of the first lamas to expose the more esoteric practices of Vajrayana to the west. As you may already know, Yogi Kukuraja has dedicated his life to these practices, and this commonality has brought us together. I reside in Gampo Abbey, located in Pleasant Bay, Nova Scotia. Gampo Abbey is a western monastery based on the Shambhala warrior tradition, which attempts to align enlightenment with the realities of modern western life. Chögyam Trungpa realized that there were many paths to enlightenment, and his Shambhala vision applied to people of any faith, not just Buddhists. We may identify as Buddhists, but first and foremost, we are humanists."

Ron inquired, "Does Chögyam Trungpa also reside at Gampo Abbey?"

"No," Yogi Kukuraja replied, "Chögyam Trungpa succumbed to cirrhosis of the liver in 1987."

Seeing the confused look on both Ron and Brandi's face as they tried to reconcile alcoholism with a Buddhist legend, the Yogi added, "Even lifelong Buddhist practitioners fall prey to common human shortcomings. We are all human, and it was through his expansive humanity that he understood that the pursuit of enlightenment should be made available to every person. He saw his radical representation of Shambhala Buddhism as the best way to achieve this goal. Shambhala emphasizes a belief in the goodness of all people, and teaches a fearless and uncompromising approach based on wisdom, dignity, and compassion."

"So you're now in charge of Gampo Abbey? Ron asked, looking at Ms. Chödrön.

"It's complicated, Ron," she replied. "Think of me as the head teacher."

"So why is the head teacher from a Nova Scotian monastery interested in Brandi and myself?"

"Although we are interested in enlightening all people, Ron, I'm here to corroborate what Yogi Kukuraja has told me about your wife."

With this comment she pivoted her body square to Brandi's, and offered a brilliantly joyful smile, which Brandi mirrored back at her.

Oh-oh, thought Ron.

This time, Ron was allowed to stay and participate in the conversation concerning their resolution and the recent developments stemming from their meditation. Dr. Fiona supplemented the discussion with her take on the changing of their brain chemistry throughout the resolution, and particularly, managing it under her counsel. Ron basically sat and listened, chipping in here and there as required, but Brandi was the individual of interest, and it was her story they were after. As she described her rapid ascension through meditative techniques and consequences, Ron noted the three listeners were holding their breath, leaning forward, and hanging on Brandi's every word. Near the end of her narrative, she explained the most recent phenomenon that she had experienced; Ron himself was hearing it for the first time.

"Whereas I've been able to detach from my physical body and float above it for some time now, during the deeper meditation sessions of the past couple of days, I've been able to move my 'spirit', for the lack of a better word," she half-embarrassingly proffered, "throughout the house. And I can do this instantaneously. I can almost be in two places at once."

Ron and Brandi had been sitting on some cushions in the main hall for about ten minutes now. After Brandi completed her account of events, the learned audience sat there motionless for the better part of a minute, apparently stunned by what Brandi had told them, and then Yogi Kukuraja had asked if they could have a moment alone. Ron was pretty sure that what Brandi was capable of was special, but from the reaction of the three listeners, he apparently hadn't yet grasped just *how* remarkable.

He and Brandi silently sat holding hands until Ron quietly asked, "So when did your spirit get *mobile?*"

"Sunday evening after you fell asleep," she responded, half lost in thought.

"How did it feel? Weird?"

"The only weird part is that it felt completely normal—like I've been doing it my whole life."

"Wow. Do you think it's actually happening, or is it all in your head…so to speak?"

"I know what you're saying, and I'm pretty sure it was real."

"Why's that?" Ron cautiously asked.

"Because I actually saw Tommy watching TV in the basement. *Sportsnet.* Jays won five to two. Sanchez was ejected from the game."

While Ron was absorbing this new reality, Yogi Kukuraja poked his head out from the door by the shrine, found them, and motioned for them to come back into his office.

Once they were seated, Ms. Chödrön was the first to speak. "Brandi," she said, paused, then perfunctorily turned her head towards Ron and nodded. "Ron. I'd like you both to come visit me in Gampo Abbey for a one-week spiritual retreat later this month. We've created meditative programs to accommodate the western lifestyle, and we think that you both may benefit greatly from an immersive program." When she said "both," she was looking directly at Brandi.

Dr. Fiona spoke up. "Brandi, you've made amazing progress in a very short period of time. I think your resolution, and our managing of your brain chemistry, has facilitated your rapid development. You're experiencing phenomenon that only the most skilled Buddhist practitioners are *sometimes* capable of after a lifetime of devotion. All of us are astounded. We think Ron should accompany you as well," she quickly added.

Ron thought he saw a look of distaste flash across Ms. Chödrön's face at this last comment, but he couldn't be sure.

Ron and Brandi looked at other. He shrugged. "Let us think about it," Ron requested.

Brandi added, "Can you forward us some information concerning Gampo Abbey, what our agenda would be, possible dates, and cost?"

"I'll do that over the next few days," replied Ms. Chödrön. "But don't worry about the cost. I won't be charging you for the week, and Dr. Fiona has graciously agreed to cover your airfares."

Friday, August 7

"I feel like a drone," Ron whined to Scott between sips of his beer. Ron had needed to download, so he and Scott had walked over to the Bassline Pub after work. "It seems as if they're reluctantly tolerating me so I can continue servicing Brandi and maintain her chemical harmony while she transforms into this spiritual oddity."

"Sounds like a first-world problem again, my friend," responded Scott. "That said, your situation really isn't analogous to a drone. If that were the case, Brandi would have a cadre of males lined up behind you to keep the train on the track, so to speak. That's called 'polyandry', and although the shape of the penis suggests we humans have evolved from that particular social activity, you'd be more accurately described as a servant or a sex slave."

"What are you talking about?"

"If you're asking about us males having a penis tooled specifically for polyandrous activity, have you ever wondered why the old soldier is wearing a bishop's tuque?"

Ron shook his head in disbelief. Scott took it as a negative response to his question and proceeded to educate his friend. "Do you remember seeing the pump jacks out west?" Scott didn't wait for a response. "It's exactly the same thing."

Unwittingly, Ron had been drawn into Scott's disquisition. "How are they the same thing?"

"I'm glad you asked," seamlessly replied Scott. "Think of the rod connecting the surface pump to the oil column as your penis. Except infinitely longer of course," he added matter-of-factly. "Now imagine that the oil being pumped out of the ground at depth is actually the jism recently deposited in your present *amor*'s vagina by your tribal competitors. Let's assume, not unreasonably given your paltry physical stature and dull intellect, every other male in the tribe has already had his way with your date, and due only to extreme fatigue and total indifference to your very presence has she has allowed you to mount her. Don't despair, however. Last doesn't necessarily mean loser here. Despite your laundry list of genetic deficiencies, evolution has provided you with the great equalizer—the shape of your penis! The helmet-shaped glans capping your lovestick combine with copulatory action during sex to actually suction your competitor's sperm back away from the cervix of your sweetheart, clearing the path for your own man seed to, against all odds and natural intent, inseminate the unfortunate girl."

Ron furrowed his eyebrows. "And what does this have to do with *my* current situation?"

"You're more accurately a sex slave, Ron, not a drone."

"That, somehow, doesn't make me feel better."

"Sorry. I really should be more sensitive, given that you're having sex with a goddess on a daily basis, have been offered an all-expense paid trip to Nova Scotia, and have the blushing admiration of your boss as we approach bonus time," replied Scott, with a "you've got to be kidding me" look.

"It doesn't sound so bad when you put it that way," replied Ron, lightening up a bit. "But don't you think the resolution has sort of gotten out of control?"

"The resolution hasn't. This Buddhist meditation is the source of your angst. I hate to say I told you so but…" Scott offered a benevolent smile and open palms.

"And now that Brandi's awakened her spiritual side, there's no going back, or even stopping this as far as I can see," lamented Ron.

"Unintended consequences, my friend. You've opened up a Pandora's Box here, and God only knows where it's going. All *I* know is it's going to be good entertainment." Scott raised his glass in a toast. "And I'm enjoying my front-row seat."

Ron drank some beer but, deep in thought, didn't return Scott's salutation.

Thursday, August 13

"Well, you don't *look* good," Brandi commented to Ron, who was sitting beside her at the kitchen island. "And you do realize I do know what you're thinking."

Despite doing his best to be supportive of Brandi, Ron was struggling with spending a week of his precious vacation time holed up in a monastery at the eastern edge of North America. There were about fourteen thousand other destinations that he had on his travel list in front of Pleasant Bay, Nova Scotia.

"You're not looking at this the right way, Ron," said Brandi.

Ron looked up and gave Brandi a "well how *should* I look at it then?" look, which was redundant since Brandi knew that question was coming before he could offer the pose.

"You've never been to Nova Scotia," she held up one finger, "Pleasant Bay is just outside of the Cape Breton Highlands, which are supposed to be beautiful, especially in the summertime," she held up a second finger, "we can go to the Halifax Urban Folk festival," she held up a third finger, "and they have very freshly brewed Keith's beer there." She held up a seal's fin worth of fingers after listing the last benefit.

Ron looked into the pleading eyes of his wife and his resistance melted away. All those points raised by Brandi were, he had to admit, pluses. It was the week of meditating and chanting and being calm that was vexing him. And the inevitable fawning over Brandi. Not so much that, but his exclusion from that attention. He realized *that* was really the source of his angst. He then recalled Dr. Kaur's words of advice—"*I would suggest you now devote yourself to assisting her on her journey going forward*"—and he immediately felt selfish and ashamed. "OK, OK, enough. I'm sold. Let's do it."

"I always did like Dr. Kaur," Brandi added with a broad smile.

"Jesus," Ron muttered through the hand now cradling his shaking head.

Saturday, August 22

They weren't due at Gampo Abbey until Tuesday, and wanted to use this opportunity to explore Halifax and the Cabot Trail, so they flew in late Friday night. About an hour later, they were in their hotel room on the city's waterfront. Although tired from the journey, both of them were inspired by the ambient lighting and energetic sounds of the Halifax waterfront. With the room darkened, they made love with the curtains and windows open and the salt air enveloping them, while watching the nearby, but oblivious, nightlife go about its own pursuit of pleasures.

Ron awoke Saturday morning to Brandi softly humming an Irish ditty in the bathroom. Bright light was streaming into the room around the edges of the window curtains, suggesting that, because of the time change, it was at least mid-morning, and time was a-wasting. Be that as it may, he lay silent, listening to Brandi's rendition of "Black Velvet Band." There was something so pure and genuine about it that he was unexpectedly filled with an intense sense of joy and contentment. He was disappointed when it abruptly stopped and Brandi came back into the bedroom.

"Sounds as if we'll be tracking down some live Celtic music tonight," intuited Ron from the comfort of the bed.

"*Now*, who's reading minds?" replied Brandi as she walked over to him. "How did you sleep?"

"Too damn long by the look of it," replied Ron, throwing his covers off and popping out of bed. "Let me have a quick shower and let's get out there."

When he opened the curtains, the mid-morning sun exploded into the room, which overlooked the harbour, with Dartmouth visible about a kilometre away, on the far side of The Narrows. Ron instinctively brought his hand up to shield his eyes, then spun, and jogged to the bathroom. "I'll be ready to go in about ten minutes," he called to Brandi as he entered the bathroom.

"Take your time Ron," Brandi countered. "I'll be meditating."

Oh yeah, Ron thought as he turned the shower on. *Now I remember why we're here.*

They spent the day on the waterfront, taking in museums and markets and seemingly endless galleries and shops, and a guided tour of the Keith's brewery, complete with a kitchen-party atmosphere. There was singing, dancing, and beer-tasting, after which they grabbed some pub food at the brewery. They finished off the afternoon touring the timber-and-stone warehouses of the Historic Properties near their hotel. Brandi noted it was also called the Privateers Wharf, since they had been built in the late 1700s and early 1800s as storage facilities for the ill-gotten booty obtained by the "legally" sanctioned pirates, called privateers, contracted by the British to disrupt the ocean-going commerce of their newly independent neighbours to the south.

"Stan Rogers sang a song about them that my dad used to sing," Brandi commented. "As I recall, the poor bugger ended up legless on this very Halifax pier."

"I wouldn't mind getting legless tonight," Ron added with a goofy smile, still feeling the effects of his beery lunch.

"Not this kind of legless, you wouldn't," added Brandi. "Permanently. Apparently the mast fell on him."

"You don't have to be a mind reader to know that I'm in full agreement with you on that point. But are you picking up what I'm thinking now?" asked Ron.

Brandi nodded, and they sauntered off for an early happy hour at the nearby pub.

ولا

After an extended happy hour, a fine waterfront lobster meal, and some raucous live Irish music, the two of them made it back to the hotel room close to midnight, fully sated. Well, *almost* fully sated. Although Ron was lying on the bed drifting in and out of consciousness, Brandi was still wound up from the live music, and she danced the jig in front of Ron with only her skimpy undies on, prodding Ron, and singing until he and his Celtic sword awoke.

With Brandi well and properly slain, Ron leaned over to Brandi and whispered, "Do you know how much I love you, girl?"

"Actually Ron, I do," she responded, just as sleep overtook her.

Tuesday, August 25

After departing Halifax late Sunday morning, Brandi and Ron had made their way up to Cape Breton Island via Antigonish and the Canso Causeway. Over the next two days they travelled counterclockwise around Cape Breton: across the gently rounded and heavily forested Precambrian granitic spine coring the Cape Breton Highlands, onto the rugged east coast, and eventually to Sydney and the now defunct coal mines—those desiccated remnants of the immense Carboniferous swamps and forests that once extended across present-day western Europe and eastern North America.

The Sydney mines provided feedstock for one of the largest steel plants in the world during the first half of the twentieth century, and were the commercial lifeblood for the people of Cape Breton during that time. The coal and steel industries declined steadily during the latter half of the twentieth century, gutting the local economy and sending Cape Breton diaspora across Canada in search of gainful employment. These days, it seemed everybody knew a Bretoner, regardless of where you were in Canada.

Early on Tuesday morning they continued north on the Cabot Trail to the northern tip of Cape Breton, and westward back across the ancient spine of the island, getting into Pleasant Bay around mid-day. During a seafood lunch at a local eatery, they struck up a conversation with Stan, who was owner, cook, waiter, and chief bottle-washer of his seafood shack by the ocean.

"So where youz two heading after ya done with dis fine cuisine?" Stan asked in an accent that was reminiscent of that heard in the Ottawa Valley.

"We're actually on our way to the Gampo Abbey monastery. Do you know it?" replied Ron.

"G'way wit ya. Youz serious now? Dem lot are as crazy as a bag of hammers, dey are. Every year on de last day of lobster season, end of June, a bunch of dem come down here all ceremonious and such, and buy de entire catch from de lads, rent demselves a boat—and I'm not shittin' ya—release dem back into da water. And I'm not talking a few here. Like dozens of dem. Can youz believe dat? Cost dem a fortune!"

Brandi and Ron assumed the question was rhetorical, so they sat quietly while Stan loaded up his thoughts, seeding his imminent verbal pearls.

"Dat said," he continued in a conciliatory tone, while scratching his head, "deyz harmless as a bunch of kittens, dey are. And Christ knows we can use any business here, even if it's da business of making peace with ya maker." He paused for a couple of seconds, then added, "I s'pose we could all use a bit more of dat, eh? Well den anywho, safe travels and enjoy the rest of youz time on the Island and wit dem Buddhists. Give dem my best too, eh? Tell dem Stan has a nice juicy lobster burger waiting for dem when dey had 'nough of eating plants," he concluded, laughing and walking away.

Gampo Abbey was about five kilometres north of Pleasant Bay, and Brandi and Ron drove the distance in silence along the cliff adjacent to the calm Atlantic Ocean. A couple of kilometres from the monastery, the road swung inland and climbed up the steep shoreline in a series of switchbacks. It wasn't long before they came up to a side road with a bright sign announcing Gampo Abbey: "A Monastery of Shambhala International. Tours Mon. through Fri. Hours 1:30 & 2:30."

"I do believe we've arrived," muttered Ron, stating the obvious. "And apparently, right on time for the 1:30 tour."

They drove a couple of hundred metres into the compound, and parked adjacent to the largest building, which looked like an administrative headquarters. The entire compound appeared to be about a half a kilometre wide, and was built on a cliff-side terrace about sixty metres above the Atlantic. The grounds were busy with people going about their business. Most were wearing a short-sleeved deep-burgundy robe, some wore a lighter-coloured red robe, and some residents had either a yellow sash or a yellow undershirt. There were a few dressed as they were, in civilian clothes. Everybody who walked by gave them a hearty "Namaste!" and a genuine smile. *So far so good*, thought Ron.

The entrance to the main building was modest and understated, and that theme continued inside. Not knowing what to expect, Ron was surprised by the plainness. It was hard to rival Yogi Kukuraja's temple for bling, and that was the only other Buddhist structure they had previously been in.

A small young man approached them, introduced himself as Anzan, and asked if he could be of assistance.

Brandi returned his "Namaste," then said, "Nice to meet you, Anzan. We're here for Jetsunma Kusho Chödrön. She's expecting us."

"Please have a seat." Anzan gestured towards a couch. "I'll see if I can track her down. She's likely working in the gardens."

About ten minutes later Ms. Chödrön entered the waiting room, wiping sweat from her brow. "Sorry I was so long. I was tending our vegetable gardens at the other end of the complex. It's a bit of a walk." She removed her gardener's hat, exhaled exaggeratedly, and fanned herself with the hat. It was another hot day.

Brandi had looked into Jetsunma Kusho Chödrön's background. The lady was close to eighty years old, but didn't look anywhere near that.

"I'm so glad you both could make it out to our humble monastery at world's end. I've been looking forward to working with you," she said, looking directly at Brandi. "And once you get settled, I'd like to start right away, if that's fine with you?"

Both Ron and Brandi nodded.

"Good. But first, I have to brief you on the ground rules for this place. For the time you're here you must take some vows regarding your behaviour."

Oh-oh, Ron thought. *Here we go*. Brandi's gaze remained fixed on Ms. Chödrön, but she squeezed Ron's hand a little.

"Everybody staying at Gampo Abbey has to agree to these rules. These are: Refrain from taking life."

Ron figured that should be easy enough, but he could also envisage a scenario over the next week where he would suffer a nervous breakdown and, while temporarily impaired, commit a homicide for which he would be not criminally responsible. Brandi squeezed his hand a little harder.

"Refrain from stealing."

What in the world could I possibly want here? Ron thought, barely suppressing an ironic smile.

"Or more accurately, do not take what is not offered to you," Ms. Chödrön amended, then continued with, "Refrain from lying."

As long as nobody asks me if I'm having a good time, Ron mused. Brandi squeezed his hand tighter still.

"Refrain from taking alcohol or drugs,"

Oh my God, thought Ron. *This is going to be the longest week of my life.* Brandi's pressure on his hand had now cut off his blood supply, and his fingers were rapidly blanching.

"And finally," Ms. Chödrön concluded, "refrain from all sexual activity."

Brandi's hand went limp. Ron's fingers immediately started tingling with the resurgence of blood into them.

"We of course agree with the first four vows," Brandi replied, looking at Ron, who was nodding in concurrence. "But Acharya, the reason we're here is *because* we have sex on a very regular basis."

She paused. Ms. Chödrön said nothing, so Brandi continued to plead her case.

"To maintain my...sorry, *our* chemical balance, we require regular sexual activity. I thought Dr. Fiona was very clear about this in Ottawa. She's very confident that it's the current unrestricted access to the higher functioning regions of my brain that is enabling my accelerated 'spiritual' progress. Frankly, I'm not prepared to risk disrupting that at this time when things are developing at such a rapid pace."

Ron quietly sat back and let his wife argue for the cause. *Best if this is woman to woman,* he mused.

Jetsunma Kusho Chödrön sat quietly for a moment, her face passive, while seriously considering Brandi's words. She exhaled audibly through her nose, her mouth still prudishly pinched closed. "We may be able to compromise on this issue. You are here for only a short time and under exceptional circumstances."

She said the last sentence as if to herself. She paused for a moment, and then finally said, "We do have a cottage that we keep open for visiting dignitaries. There are no such visits planned this week. Other than yourselves."

Ron wasn't sure if the last comment was delivered ironically or not.

"I'm prepared to allow you to stay there for the duration of your stay, and engage in sexual acts, if you do not mention this to anybody else in the compound, do so discretely only after lights-out and before morning chants and medita-tion, and please, wash your own sheets." The last comment was delivered with visible disrelish.

Brandi looked at Ron. They shrugged and nodded in unison at Ms. Chödrön.

"Good. I don't want your presence to be a disruptive influence in the monastery, so I appreciate you both rigorously adhering to these conditions. Additionally, we have a strict vegetarian diet here, and when the craving for meat hits, and it will, there's no popping down to Stan's in Pleasant Bay for a burger. Understood?"

Ron felt a rising tension in his chest as he nodded in agreement. He could use a week of healthy eating and no alcohol in any case. *This'll be just like a fitness camp*, he rationalized, still feeling a bloom of anxiety in his chest.

"OK, then. Let me get you settled in your cottage, and then we can start with your daily routines."

Their cottage was offset about a hundred metres from the main compound. Although modest, it was comfortable, and had a spectacular view of the Atlantic. They found two sets of red robes their sizes waiting for them on their bed, along with three yellow T-shirts each. While getting settled and changed, Ron watched Brandi strip down to her undies, and felt a wave of lustfulness engulf him.

Brandi stopped what she was doing, turned around, and said, "Ron, she was willing to compromise, and we agreed. We're not going to break our promise ten minutes after we made it," then turned back to the bed.

Summarily chastised, Ron mopishly commenced changing into his robe as well. It appeared that Brandi was taking this retreat more seriously than he was. The week had just got a bit longer in his mind.

Ms. Chödrön had asked them to find her in the gardens after they had settled and changed. It was about a five-minute walk along the trails and access roads to the garden complex at the opposite end of the compound. The short journey was filled with numerous deferential "Namaste"-endowed encounters along the way. Ron felt far less self-conscious now, being dressed for the part.

"There you two are," exclaimed Ms. Chödrön, noticing them walking up to the edge of the garden. She was elbow-deep in the soil, with a young woman working alongside her. "Ron, you're going to need a hat today, I'm afraid," she said, glancing at his head. "You too, Brandi. This is Nima." "Namastes" all around. "Nima, can you please grab a couple of hats and some work gloves for our guests?"

"Absolutely, Acharya," replied the young lady. She took off for the nearby house.

"I don't know how familiar you both are with gardening," Ms. Chödrön said, "but the premise is simple. Nurture the plants you want, and weed out the ones you don't." She gestured over the expansive garden. "It's a lot like life in that way. Nurture your compassion, while defending against your ingrained selfish tendencies."

Ron realized he had just received the first lesson of his week, and suspected there were many more to follow.

Once Nima returned with the hat and gloves, Ms. Chödrön pointed to the far end of the garden and said, "That section is particularly prone to weeds, and a bit unruly at the moment. Ron, why don't you start there? Brandi, come work with me on this patch."

After a couple of grueling and backbreaking hours, at least for Ron, Brandi finally came over to rescue him. "Acharya suggested we head back to the cottage to clean up and meditate for a while, and join everybody back here for dinner at six-thirty."

"I'm good with that. My back is killing me. How about you?"

"Yeah, I'm sore too, but we'll get used to it quickly, I'm sure," Brandi replied, smiling positively.

Encouraged by Brandi's attitude, Ron felt better as they started their walk back to the cottage. He asked, "Well, how is she?"

"Calm."

"That's it?"

"No, not *just* calm," Brandi amended. "But in one word, yes—calm. She told me that after dinner tonight, she'll start working exclusively with us during our meditation periods to optimize our time here. I think she's quite curious about what I'm experiencing. I even sensed a bit of something else."

She paused, searching for the right words. "Hope! Yes, that's it—hope. She's hoping that she can learn from me. And she's hoping that I can learn from her, as well. I also sensed desperation from her, Ron. She's been a Buddhist nun for more than four decades, and I think she wants more."

"More?" Ron parroted, confused. "More what?"

"More understanding, I think. More answers."

"No pressure on you, is there?" Ron replied. "Here's a famous and published woman who's spent the majority of a long life pursuing enlightenment, and she's looking to you—a neophyte at best—for help. Don't you find that just a wee bit unusual?"

"Yes and no, Ron," Brandi replied as they got to their cottage.

Once they'd entered and started changing out of their sweaty clothing, she continued. "It's a lesson in itself, Ron. Everybody has something to offer, and everybody can learn something from anybody else."

After a few beats, she added mischievously, "There may even be hope for you, Ron," in response to which he automatically commenced a tickle offensive that had her begging for mercy in no time at all.

His victim fully subdued, he added with *faux* severity, and for reasons known only to him, with an East Indian accent, while sternly wagging his finger "When those lights are out you are going to get such a rogering, that I can promise you."

They arrived at the communal dining hall just before six-thirty. The place was already packed with forty or fifty men and women of all ages and colours. The majority of them had their hair cropped to the scalp and all of them looked, well…happy to be alive.

The quiet but celebratory atmosphere instantly infused Ron with a sense of wellbeing. They sat beside a number of monks and nuns in training, and a few "visitors" there on shorter retreats—none, however, as short as theirs.

Although curious as to Ron and Brandi's situation, which allowed for both an abbreviated timeline and habitation of the VIP cottage, their dining mates didn't press too hard, and Brandi deftly turned the conversation to where everybody was from, the weather, and the excellent food.

Although Ron enjoyed the conversation, he found the food wanting. Not that the butternut squash bake and bean enchiladas weren't tasty. They were, but he was already jonesing for some meat. Beef was preferable, but chicken would also do. Neither, not unexpectedly, was available. Brandi, of course, picked up on this even while juggling three other conversations, and suggested that eating more should sate him. It was code that she was looking forward to lights-out later, and it was enough to distract him from his digestive cravings. That, and the extra large portion of blueberry grunt he had for dessert.

Enthusiastic conversation continued until all the plates were cleared and a bell chimed. Abruptly, everybody sitting around them went into a quiet meditative state. Ron and Brandi looked at each other, shrugged and joined in. This went on for about a half hour, until another chime signalled the end to that activity, and everybody quietly got up from their chairs and left the dining hall to head back to their residences, leaving Brandi and Ron sitting there alone.

But not for long. Ms. Chödrön soon appeared and gestured them to follow her, which they did. Outside, although the sun had already set, the evening was still warm, and the western sky to their right still beautifully coloured with a red twilight glow. They silently followed Ms. Chödrön to her personal dwelling, where she sat on the floor of her small shrine. Incense was already burning, and she lit a few candles to light their immediate area.

"After supper we have quiet time until lights out. Typically, most of our residents have already departed for their residences by then, but they were obviously enjoying the novelty of your presence and conversation tonight, so they meditated with you at the dinner table as a gesture of respect. It was beautiful to see.

"Given the brevity of your visit, we're going to skip a few quiet times after dinners, and use the time after supper and before lights-out for teaching and exchange of ideas and views." Again a pause. "If that's all right with you both, of course?"

"That's fine with us," Brandi replied, knowing that Ron had resigned himself to making the most out of his time at Gampo Abbey. "We're here to learn as much as we can over this week, and we very much appreciate you committing your time to us."

Ms. Chödrön nodded peacefully. "Very good then. Let's begin." She paused for a few seconds, took a deep breath, and then spoke.

"Buddhism is very complicated. I believe it is more layered and unstructured than any of the other major religions. If you have a million Buddhists, you will have a million interpretations of what it is to be a Buddhist. A million different *reasons* for pursuing enlightenment as an earthly goal. A million different *ways* of approaching the path to enlightenment.

"Buddhism doesn't herd people onto a single path, then prod them forward single-file towards a distant light. It asks only one thing of you: compassion and respect for all living things. From this compassion will flow enlightenment.

"We express this simple goal in a very complex symbolic visual tool called the *Bhavacakra*, or the 'Wheel of Life.' This wheel demonstrates that enlightenment is gained by liberating oneself from the selfish primal core that exists in all of us, rising through the various realms of life experience until, ultimately, one can escape all human suffering and earthly bondage. *Enlightenment* by another name. Sounds simple enough, but human beings are complex creatures, and typically need *many* lives to fully appreciate and adopt life's lessons. An individual who has eventually risen through the earthly realms will have fully eschewed ignorance, envy, indifference to suffering, anger and, yes—physical desire."

Brandi and Ron stole a glance at each other at her final comment.

"But the journey doesn't end there. To attain true enlightenment, one must fully appreciate the impermanence of life, and fully accept the cyclic nature of life: birth, old age, physical infirmity, and death. Then, and only then, is enlightenment possible. Again, it sounds easy enough, but I can tell you—it's not."

She looked down upon saying these last words, and Ron saw her real age for the first time, and a person struggling with her own mortality. He couldn't help himself: tears welled up in his eyes.

After she collected herself, Ms. Chödrön looked Brandi in the eyes. "I'm interested in you, Brandi, since you have somehow attained the skills typically, and exclusively, exhibited by one who has attained enlightenment. It is the goal of all serious Buddhist practitioners. A goal almost never reached."

She took a deep breath, appeared to steel herself, and continued. "Given our time together is short, it's essential that our discussions are genuine. Brandi, I'm ashamed to say that I am envious of your achievements. What you're capable of is nothing short of miraculous, but to have achieved this in such a short period of time and so… so *unconventionally*, is frankly disconcerting to me. Once this becomes public, these achievements will also be distressing to the Buddhist powers-that-be. My objective this week is to reconcile your shortcut path to enlightenment with the longer-term, more conventional route by which half a billion people worldwide currently govern their life."

A lightbulb went off in Ron's head. *Brandi's been perceived as a threat by the Buddhist establishment!*

"This 'modernization' of a legacy objective has the potential to destabilize the entire foundation of our religion. *We*," she emphasized the word, "*must* find a way forward that doesn't allow that to happen."

She let the gravitas of the comment and situation sink in for a few seconds. "On a more selfish note, I'm realizing, for the first time since my ordainment almost fifty years ago, that true enlightenment may not be in the cards for me this lifetime." She lowered her head again, searching for her composure. "And it saddens me. I'm looking to you, Brandi, to help me towards that goal if possible."

Brandi looked serenely at Jetsunma Kusho Chödrön. "Acharya, I think we both have something to learn from each other this week."

Monday, August 31

Ron pondered the events of the previous week as he weeded around the yellow beans in the massive garden. After a few days of this backbreaking and monotonous work, his body and mind had quietly adapted, and now he actually looked forward to the four hours of work in the garden every afternoon—even in the unrelenting heat.

Pausing to lift the hat off his head, he wiped the accumulating sweat from his skull. And skull was a good word for it. Last Friday, he had walked over to one of his garden buddies—Chimon, who he knew was also the *coiffeur* for the compound—and asked if he could find time to trim Ron's hair later in the day. Under the summer sun his locks had become a sweat-laden, tangled burden, and Ron was becoming a bit self-conscious that he was the only male in his friend group with hair longer than a grain of rice. Chimon was an absolute expert at the buzz-cut—just enough hair to provide a bit of colour on an otherwise pasty crown, but short enough to merit neither maintenance or vain thoughts concerning physical appearance. Ron had felt the act cathartic, and had no intention of growing it back anytime soon.

The gardening had turned out to be a physical manifestation of what he had been doing for most of his waking hours at Gampo Abbey—meditation. During the last week, he and Brandi had actively meditated for about six hours a day. Counting the time in the garden, it was about ten hours a day. The main difference, as he saw it, was the audible group chanting associated with meditation in the compound. Ms. Chödrön had introduced them to chanting mantras and controlled breathing on the morning of their first full day and, much to Ron and Brandi's surprise, it immediately helped them focus during their practice. The chanting had quickly become an integral part of their meditative exercise, and Ron found himself softly chanting *"hom vajrapani, hom vajrapani"* over and over as he toiled in the garden. The calming throaty vibrations accompanying the baritone chanting seemed to have dug a rut up his spine, facilitating deeper access into his brain. Ron wasn't sure, but there was a distinct possibility that the chanting was generating a low-level pleasure response that helped reinforce the activity.

Brandi and Ms. Chödrön had, after their initial meeting last Tuesday, agreed to cloister themselves for the morning meditation and practice period, leaving Ron to fend for himself in the wilds of the main practice hall. He had been quickly assimilated into a group of aging monks in training, whose company he enjoyed during discussions and whilst sitting quietly meditating.

During the last week, he had experienced a blossoming contentment, and with it, a steady decline of his lifelong anxiety disorder. His body had adjusted positively to the vegetarian diet and the hard daily physical work, and he felt as fit and well as he had in at least a decade. As amazing as all that was, it was his "spiritual" changes that really caught him by surprise. About four days into the grueling meditation schedule he visualized his core warming and glowing red-hot. It had startled him so much the first couple of times that he lost focus, but on the third time, he remained calm, maintained his slow rhythmical breathing and chanting, and allowed the experience to fully play out. He didn't know how long he had been in that vacuous state—it could have been a nanosecond or the full three hours—but when he re-entered the physical world, he couldn't stop smiling. When he met up with Brandi for lunch, she took one look at him and exclaimed, "You did it!"

As amazing as his days here had been for him, Brandi's experience had been even more remarkable. Her discussions with Ms. Chödrön had allowed Brandi to understand and intellectualize the spiritual side of her rapidly evolving skillset, giving her more command over her gifts, and an emerging ability to "focus them outward." Ron didn't fully understand what that meant, but he was sure he soon would. Brandi had also confided in him that Ms. Chödrön's anxiety concerning leaving this world unenlightened had been, for the most part, assuaged. They both realized that Brandi's backdoor access to the spiritual skills that lifelong practitioners acquire through endless dedication and persistence was akin to being helicoptered onto the top of Everest. Brandi harboured no guilt about these gifts, however, and her Acharya came to respect her acquisition of them as simply having happened through an avenue not available to herself; her lot was to tirelessly trek uphill to an unattainable pinnacle—grateful for the opportunity to live her life the way she had chosen, and to be a humble and accepting link in the chain of lives along the path to ultimate enlightenment.

It sounded to Ron like their time together was a win-win.

The night before, just before turning off the lights, Brandi had lain in bed, neutrally passive for an unusually long time, prompting Ron to ask what was on her mind. She'd said she now understood what Gampo Abbey was all about. It was a sanctuary. People coming here for visits and retreats, and those who resided within the monastery, were looking for answers, as all sentient humans have since their first self-aware breath was drawn a couple hundred thousand years ago. The chaos, uncertainty, and lack of compassion in the outside world not only terrified them, but also disappointed them. They knew there was more to being sentient, and they'd come here in search of a safe environment conducive to their personal exploration of this belief.

Then it had come to Ron like a light bulb turning on: the connection between what he and Brandi were doing and Buddhism. Why they were here in the first place. It was all about being human. He and Brandi had circumvented the arduous lifelong meditative process of training your primal core to behave so you could access the more "human," less self-serving, and more compassionate parts of your brain. They had been feeding meat to the beast—essentially keeping it at bay. Same result, but whereas religion had domesticated the primal beast using skill and tact and patience, they had fattened the beast into submission; and might have inadvertently made it stronger and more dangerous.

As he sat motionless, mulling these thoughts over, Brandi, reading his mind, said that possibility had occurred to her as well, but meditation and religious fervour also stimulated the pleasure centres. Not with the intensity that sex produces, but then again, they didn't make love for ten hours a day either.

Ron fell asleep wondering which activity generated more dopamine—ten hours of meditation and chanting, or a brief sexual encounter.

CHAPTER 10

EVOLUTION...

Tuesday, September 1

It seemed as if the entire compound gathered to see them off, just after the morning group chant. There were plenty of "Namastes" and hugs, and Brandi was sure she saw tears in Jetsunma Kusho Chödrön's eyes. Although their flight didn't depart until after five that afternoon, this early departure allowed them to travel back to Halifax at a leisurely pace, and besides, they wanted to stop at Stan's in Pleasant Bay to enjoy some coffee on the way out. A week of caffeine deprivation was enough, they had agreed.

They pulled into Stan's just after seven-thirty. They were the only ones in the parking lot, and wondered if Stan's was even open yet. Testing the front door and finding it unlocked, they entered with bells jingling, and sat at the same table they had occupied the previous week.

In short order, Stan came around the corner from the kitchen, wiping his hands on a dish towel. "Good morning, good morning," he called out, looking more at his task at hand than at Brandi and Ron. When he did finally look up and focus on his first customers of the day, he exclaimed, "Well, if it isn't the two of youz again! Couldn't stay away from my haute cuisine, could ya?"

Taking a squinty second look at Ron as he closed the distance between himself and their table, he continued, "Jesus, Mary, and that ne'er-do-well Joseph, would ya look at yer head, boy. Did dey hold ya down and force demselves on ya, or did ya drink the Kool-Aid?"

Judging from how quickly he launched into his next line of questioning, he really wasn't expecting an answer. "Youz got to tell me all about dat place," he said, as he slid a chair over to the table and sat down with them. "Does dey just sit around all day and chant 'ohm ohm ohm' in some kind or another of a trance?"

"Good morning, Stan," Brandi said. "Yes, there is a lot of chanting and meditation going on. But that's only part of it. There's a lot of discussion about why everyone is there, and how to make yourself a better person. And they're pretty self-sufficient, so they spend a lot of time tending to their gardens."

Screwing up his face in an expression of understanding, whilst nodding, Stan asked, "So, have ya both emerged better people from de experience?"

Ron believed it was a sincere question. "Without question, Stan."

"Even wit dat hair-do of yers? Looks more like a hair-don't, if ya ask me, buddy."

Ron smiled, and said, "Yes Stan. Even with this haircut of mine."

"Tell me den," Stan continued, his eyes now filled with sincerity. "What in God's good green earth is dey looking for up dere on dat cliff?"

Brandi responded. "Stan, they're just trying to understand how they fit into…" she paused, swept her hands in a circular motion while looking around, then added, "all of this."

Stan quietly nodded his head for a few seconds, absorbing this pearl. "Well, den, I must be a lucky man, 'coz I knows dat *I'm* living my dream—in all dis." He waved his arms and looked around in mimicry of Brandi.

She couldn't tell if he had misinterpreted the scale of her gesture or not.

"One plate of perfectly seasoned lobster and toast at a time. Which brings me to my next question. What are youz two having for breakfast dis fine east-coast morning? And as my first customers dis September, it's on me, I'll have ya know."

They finally hit the road close to nine. Stan had sat with them and drank coffee while they ate, making the most of this opportunity to learn as much about Gampo Abbey as he could. Glancing at his watch and realizing they'd lost track of the time, Stan shooed them out the door, reminding them they had a flight to catch in Halifax in about eight hours.

He stood in the drizzle by their car, removed his cook's cap, and scratched his head while saying, almost to himself, "Ya know, dat enlightenment ting seems fine and all, but I tink I'll stick wit my beer, my big-ass HD TV, my burgers, and de odd stray lass who finds de smell of boiled lobster... *intriguing*. Youz two have a safe drive back to da city and flight home, and make sure youz tell dem Haligonians dat Stan sends his best. Come back to visit when ya can."

The drive back to Halifax took about five hours, and presented Brandi and Ron with an opportunity to have a fulsome discussion about their Gampo Abbey experience.

"Acharya Chödrön asked if we'd consider not attaching our resolution to the Gampo Abbey monastery, and more generally, to Buddhist practices," Brandi mentioned just outside of Pleasant Bay.

Ron was expecting a request along these lines. "I think I know why sex is incompatible with existing fundamental religious practices."

"I'm listening," said Brandi.

"All living things, including us humans, are hardwired to search out positive reinforcement and, of course, the chemical reward associated with that action. You and I both felt *pleasure* while we were chanting and meditating this last week. This means that praying, which is in essence what we've been doing, and appreciative adulation of one's maker, actually stimulates the pleasure centres of the brain, and conditions the practitioner to repeat the activity. But as we know, there are plenty of ways to tickle the pleasure centres, so, to limit rivalry, religions typically require disciplined abstinence from the things in life that provide those physical rewards—alcohol, drugs, gambling, masturbation, extra and premarital sex, and even music in some cases; basically anything that gives you pleasure. Sex for the purpose of procreation is begrudgingly tolerated to keep the numbers up. For the serious practitioners, such as monks, priests, and nuns, total sexual abstinence is required, but the premise is the same in all cases—get rid of the competition, and create an environment that conditions the practitioner and promotes a reliance on his or her worship to fill the pleasure void. Think of how important *that* chemical reinforcement is to an individual whose primary vehicle for pleasure is prayer. "Praise the Lord!" indeed.

"I'm not, in any way, saying that developing your spirituality through devout religious practices is negative. Religion, at its core, provides structure and sanctuary for those requiring assistance dealing with their world. But the current major religions now behave like large corporations, and they do what they have to in order to ensure customer loyalty. It seems like spiritual enlightenment is an oft-forgotten byproduct."

"Acharya Chödrön and the Gampo Abbyites aren't your typical religious practitioners, however," suggested Brandi. "I think they're all there in the single-minded pursuit of enlightenment, whatever that means individually to each of them."

Ron nodded. "They certainly seem genuine."

"Which brings us back to your comment on the incompatibility of sex and religion," Brandi continued. "What we're essentially demonstrating with the resolution is that *doesn't* have to be the case."

"So are we breaking new ground here?"

Brandi laughed, and said, "Ron, in the history of our species there's been one hundred billion human beings of equivalent intelligence and curiosity. Do you really think we're the first ones to realize this? Especially since we're dealing with *sex?*"

Ron realized her question was delivered as a rhetorical rebuke, so no answer was necessary.

"There have been sex cults around since humans started organizing themselves into tribes. I'd bet you that every civilization in the history of mankind has explored sexuality as a path to…if not enlightenment, then to something like immortality, developing extraordinary powers, or just as a clever way to have as much sex with as many people as possible. Look at the Maenads of ancient Greece. Or the Gnostics, who began in ancient Europe and lasted in one form or another into the nineteenth century. Closer to home for us, Tantric Buddhism is one of the longest-lived and most successful sex-related sects, but new ones are still popping up. I just heard that the Raelians are becoming more popular in Canada."

"Who the heck are the Raelians?" asked Ron.

"I'm surprised you've never heard of them. They were founded in 1974 by a French race-car driver previously known as Claude Vorilhon, now known as Rael—the last prophet—who believed that sensual pleasure was programmed into humans by aliens as a way to find enlightenment. I heard there were about one hundred thousand members worldwide, with more than five thousand in Canada—and growing."

"Aliens, eh?"

"That part may be a little strange, but they are big on sensuality, peace, pleasure, meditation, nudity, and gender equality. I know of at least a couple of global religions that could be schooled with the Raelian playbook."

"That I get. Hard to get past the aliens thing, though."

"The point is, we're not the first to use sex to open the door to enlightenment, Ron."

"Listen. I was just asking. I can assure you that from my perspective, the less publicity we get, the better."

He could see Brandi nodding in his peripheral vision as he kept his eyes on the winding road.

"But," Ron added, "if we were to form a sex-cult, with you as our goddess leader, what would you call it?"

Brandi laughed, thought for a couple of seconds, and said. "How about 'Brandiism'?"

"Not bad," replied Ron. "I was thinking 'Her Lady of Perpetual Fornication' is pretty catchy," he added, at which they both had a good giggle.

"You know, there's really nothing special about what we're doing, Ron."

"On one level I agree, but then, there's the issue of your evolving mystical abilities, Brandi. You have to admit that's not normal. That's the whole reason we're, at this moment, driving on this road in Nova Scotia. Ms. Chödrön, Dr. Fiona, and Yogi Kukuraja all saw something special in you, and they're all pretty impressive people."

Brandi sat quietly for a couple of seconds, and then responded, "Oh yeah, there is that. I've been looking for an opportunity to update you on that subject. There've been some further developments."

Ron did divert his eyes from the road then, and looked directly at Brandi. "I'm afraid to ask."

Friday, September 4

The last long weekend of the short-lived Canadian summer was not to be squandered. In accordance with Canadian tradition, campfires were to be built, requisite praise for warm bug-free evenings lavished upon Mother Nature, ample amounts of alcohol consumed and, inevitably, with forlornness gestated in the memories of many cold, dark winter days, and prompted by a progressively sleepy inebriation, a communal bemoaning of summer's end, pronounced through gnashing teeth and pensive faces lit by the glowing embers of a fading fire.

This year was no different. Scott and Elise had secured a week in a cottage/mansion (Scott's words) on "Millionaire's Row" on Lake Rosseau in the Muskoka region, and had invited the Lee family up for the Labour Day weekend. Normally, the five hour drive would have been a major deterrent, but given Tommy was heading back to university in Toronto on the Monday, the location actually helped with the logistics of depositing him back at school, and allowed Brandi and Ron to enjoy their son's company as long as possible.

Ron, Brandi, Sam and Tommy had taken Friday off, and the five of them, including Amanda, left Ottawa after an early breakfast. They beat the typically heinous long weekend traffic with their early departure, and made it to Lake Rousseau for lunch.

Scott wasn't lying about the mansion part of his description. From the driveway, the waterfront "shack" looked like it was four thousand square feet.

"Closer to five thousand," Scott clarified shortly after they were settled. "Six full bedrooms with ensuites. And take a look at this view."

Ron shaded his eyes from the intense sunlight, and stared out at the lake. He had to agree it was spectacular.

"There's Steven Spielberg's place across the lake. Tom Hanks is just around the corner to the south."

Spielberg's house dwarfed the one they were currently standing in. "How'd you get your hands on this place?" asked Ron.

"Luck of the draw, really. We had our pick of dates this year with our timeshare, and this place was available in the rotation. Can I get you a beer?"

"I thought you'd never ask," replied Ron.

ॐ

It was a spectacular warm, calm, and clear late summer's day, and the entire weekend was forecast to be more of the same, only hotter. Being by the water was almost a necessity on these weekends, and they spent the rest of the day on the beach, and swimming back and forth to the offshore dock.

Later in the afternoon, after an extended session of "king of the dock," the siblings and Amanda joined Brandi and Elise on the beach. Scott and Ron had already adjourned to the deck, up at the house.

Sam cuddled up with her mom, both to help herself warm up and just because. "Tommy was trying to drown me," she moaned to her mother when Tommy and Amanda headed back into the house to change.

"Well, I for one am glad he didn't succeed," replied Brandi, kissing Sam on the forehead and rubbing her back to warm her up.

"He sprained my wrist," she whined, holding up her right hand. "Ow!" she exclaimed as she flexed it for her mom to see.

"Let me see that," Brandi asked, and proceeded to gently rub it.

After about thirty seconds, Sam retrieved her wrist, and flexed it to test Brandi's handiwork. "Wow, Mom. Where did you learn to do that? I don't feel anything now. Thanks." She leaned over and kissed her mom on the cheek, then exploded up the beachfront to the stairs and into the house.

"Where *did* you learn to do that?" queried Elise, sitting on the other side of Brandi.

"She just needed a little motherly attention," replied Brandi, then added with a smile, "Hey, isn't it happy hour? How about we get out of the sun, get cleaned up, and join the boys on the deck?"

"Sounds good to me, girlfriend."

As Brandi walked past the deck toward her room, she gestured to Ron to join her. "Do we have time?" Ron asked, entering their bedroom while Brandi was changing out of her swimsuit.

"Let's save that for later. We shouldn't leave Scott and Elise out there by themselves."

"OK. So what's up?" asked Ron, sensing some consternation in Brandi.

"I just freaked myself out, Ron," she replied, looking as serious as Ron as seen her look in ages.

She had his full attention. "Tell me what happened?" Ron sat beside her on the bed, his hand on her arm.

"I think I just…just… *healed* Sammy." Brandi explained the event to Ron.

"What? Healed? Oh, was it Sam's wrist just now? She mentioned that you 'fixed' her wrist on the way to her room. Are you sure she wasn't exaggerating?"

"No, Ron. She was really hurting, and was actually being a bit brave about it in front of Elise. When I started rubbing Sam's sprained wrist, I could feel my core heat focus into my hands, and I *saw* the heat transferring to her wrist. I think I was rubbing it for only a few seconds, but it could have been much longer. I lost track of time. Then I remember Sam saying it was better."

She paused a couple of seconds, looked directly at Ron, and added, "I'm pretty sure I *healed* her…"

Ron just sat there, absorbing this new development. If this was real, and he had no reason to believe that it wasn't, given the events of the last few months, Brandi's preternatural capability had just expanded to the next level. This new "gift" followed closely on the heels of one she had developed with Jetsunma Kusho Chödrön during their stay at Gampo Abbey. Although Brandi had already experienced numerous out-of-body experiences, at Gampo Abbey she had been able to project her consciousness into Ms. Chödrön's mind, and truly look at the world from another person's perspective. It had been a profound and life-changing experience. Brandi had confided that it was like nothing she had ever previously experienced, or could have even heretofore imagined, and allowed her to truly appreciate how varied our individual interpretation of shared experiences can be. She embarrassingly realized that her empathy and compassion for her fellow human beings had been, to that point in her life, well-intentioned and perfunctory at best, and more commonly ambivalent and begrudging.

Brandi's stroll in Jetsunma's mind was only possible with deep "connected" meditation, and her teacher's unconditional consent and acceptance. Jetsunma admitted afterwards that having Brandi in her consciousness was more intimate than sex—which she gave up decades ago, upon being ordained. Brandi had also felt an intimacy akin to her sexual interaction with Ron.

In return for the experience, Brandi had worked hard with Jetsunma for the rest of her stay, guiding her to her first out-of-body experience the day before their departure. *Who's the teacher now?* Ron had mused, perhaps a bit jealous.

"Would that be a 'laying on of hands' kind of healing, or more Reiki-style?" Ron finally asked, trying to introduce a bit of levity.

"Thanks for trying, but this is really weirding me out," Brandi seriously replied. "I've been brought up with the biblical tales of Jesus and his band of pietistic pals doing exactly what I did for our daughter about fifteen minutes ago, so you can understand my anxiety."

Ron replied, "I'll have you know that the whole laying-on-of-hands thing originated from the Old Testament, which was based on The Hebrew Bible, so you can partially blame your anxiety on us Jews—again. That said, the Christians did take it to an entirely new level."

Brandi looked at him and flatly commented, "Not helping, Ron."

"OK. Bibles aside, if you put this into context with your out-of-body experiences and projection of consciousness skills, it's not too much of a stretch—don't you think?"

Brandi inhaled slowly. "My out-of-body and consciousness projections are like party tricks compared to healing, Ron. Can you imagine if people found out about this?"

Ron could, and he had to agree, that would change everything.

"Everything I've read about healing with touch suggests that it's actually just channeling the will or power of a divine entity." She paused. "I can tell you that, to the best of my knowledge, I have not been in direct contact with God or the Holy Spirit, or any other deity, creator, or supreme or immortal being—so what's going on here?"

"It's got to be the resolution, Brandi. What else could it be? It's just too coincidental that you can do this just after developing your other skills."

Brandi nodded in agreement.

"Jesus Christ!" Ron suddenly exclaimed, startling Brandi. "Who's to say that others before you didn't have this healing ability, as well? And to keep it as otherworldly as possible, made themselves out to be the hands of God Himself, claiming to channel His power directly and exclusively. Talk about making yourself bulletproof."

Brandi finally registered Ron's hypothesis.

"It would definitely be quite a selling point for the masses if, say for example, you were launching a new religion, and needed to entice the skeptical multitudes into the fold. 'Find salvation *and* do away with your bothersome leprosy.' There would be some long, unwashed line-ups at the registration table. But I digress," Ron continued. "The point is, I agree that it's a powerful gift, Brandi; maybe partially responsible for the meteoric rise of the world's most popular religion. We should *absolutely* keep this new development to ourselves. Not one word to anyone."

&

"Seriously. Let Brandi have a look at your tennis elbow, Scott," Elise helpfully suggested after supper and a few too many drinks. Scott had yelped when he went to put down his wine glass, and offhandedly remarked about his nagging tendinous ailment. "She seemed to know what she was doing with Sammy," Elise added.

"It can't hurt, Brandi," said Ron, glancing over at Brandi, who was sternly glaring at him with a "what the hell are you doing?" look. "What? He can't get rid of it. Six months already. It's killing his golf game."

Brandi narrowed her eyes further.

"Good God, Brandi. He's even tried acupuncture! Throw the man a bone."

Brandi sighed heavily, smiled at Scott, and replied, "It's just a little massage thingy I do that works sometimes."

"Hey, I'm willing to try anything. Ron even beat me at golf a couple of weeks ago," Scott said. He sidled up next to Brandi, holding the offending elbow out to her.

"Well, now, that really does sound desperate. Let me have a look." Brandi started massaging his elbow.

"Wow. You sure generate a lot of heat with your technique, Brandi," exclaimed Scott. "I don't remember the physiotherapists doing that."

After about a minute Brandi stopped, and said, "How does that feel, Scott?"

Ron and Elise were watching intently. Ron had a dumbass smile on his face.

"Six months," Scott started. "Six months going to my doctor, physiotherapists, an acupuncturist, watching my diet, ice packs, hot baths, and even a Reiki prac-titioner and…nothing."

He was repeatedly extending and retracting his arm as he spoke. "One minute with you… and the pain is gone. I mean *totally* gone. *It's a miracle!*" he exclaimed, his arms raised in a halleluiah.

He leaned in to hug Brandi. "That's amazing! You should go into business. There're plenty of us old buggers around who could benefit from this service."

Ron was smiling proudly at his wife as she slowly turned away from Scott and looked him in the eyes. Ron's smile melted away under her gaze. *Oops,* he thought. *I've done it again haven't I?*

Brandi nodded at him.

A short while later, with Brandi in the bathroom, Ron lay in bed preparing his case. In his defense, he hadn't initiated the discussion, but on the other side of the argument, he didn't exactly try to dissuade Elise either. Actually, he had encouraged her—which in hindsight was pretty impulsive, given they had just a few hours earlier agreed to keep Brandi's newfound ability resolutely secret. *Damn that alcohol,* Ron thought.

As Brandi crawled into bed, Ron said, "The good news is they haven't connected the dots back to the resolution, or even know that this ability of yours is anything other than a learned physio technique." He offered this with a sheepish, conciliatory tone, and framed it with a face to match.

"I know it was well-intended Ron," evenly replied Brandi. "But this has the potential to be a Pandora's Box. Did you happen to catch Scott's comment? 'It's a miracle!'" She pondered further. "We can't un-ring the bell, so I guess all we can do is follow Margaret Atwood's advice."

"Which is?" asked Ron.

"The best way of keeping a secret is to pretend there isn't one."

Sunday, September 7

Ron, Brandi and Sam arrived home late after dropping Tommy Jr. off at the U of T, and Amanda at her nearby house in Ottawa. The day had been another scorcher—too hot even to drive with the windows down after they left Toronto. A weekend of long drives and longer nights had worn them both out, so a fulsome meditation and lovemaking session was required to clear their minds and refresh their spirits; after which they relaxed in their backyard, in the dwindling light and cooling September evening temperatures.

"Cheers," Ron proffered, holding up a crisp citrusy glass of chilled Konzelmann Estate Pinot Blanc from the Niagara region. "We made it through another summer."

"And what a summer it's been." Brandi leaned in to kiss her husband on the lips. "I can't help wondering what the fall's going to be like this year."

"God only knows," replied Ron. "Unless, of course, you already have an idea?" he added sardonically, which earned him a flick on his ear from Brandi. He continued, "I have to admit, on the drive back today I was thinking about your new 'healing touch' thing, if you're interested?"

"Why not?" resignedly replied Brandi.

Ron smiled. "Well, it's the Jesus Christ, laying-on-of-hands, God-connection thing that's been bugging me. Let's assume that JC really did have the gift of healing, as you appear to have. He was unquestionably extraordinary, so I can believe—especially now," he gave Brandi a "you're living proof" look and gesture—"believe that it's at least possible he had the ability to heal, too. Christian doctrine repeatedly states that healing is the channeling of God's will. As an atheist, I've naturally got a problem with that." He paused for effect. "So here it is. I think you've changed my view on God."

"What? I have? How?" Brandi looked mightily perplexed.

"So many questions," Ron quipped. "Whereas before I was resolutely atheistic, I'm now agnostic. The transformation that you've undergone with the resolution suggests that maybe, just maybe, there may be a higher power—but it doesn't exist outside of us as an entity. It exists within us—all of us. You can call it whatever you want. The supernatural; the Almighty; God—just a name, really. We just have to allow ourselves to freely access it."

Ron took a sip from his wine, looking smug. "What I really like about this is that we've done this using sex and, may I add, thanks to my knuckleheaded resolution. Talk about an unintended consequence!"

Friday, September 11

Ron patiently waited for his friend to recover his composure.

He and Scott were at the Bassline Pub having a quick beer after the workweek. For some reason, Scott couldn't stop laughing after looking at Ron's head.

"You've seen it for a week. Why are you hacking me about it now?" Ron finally asked.

"To be completely honest with you, buddy," Scott answered, his shaking shoulders now subsiding, "when I saw you last Friday after your Monkish retreat, I was worried that you had actually converted to Buddhism, and I didn't want to insult you. I am Canadian after all."

He then added, with most of his composure regained, "Or I thought, more likely, you had suffered a psychological breakdown and I didn't want to exacerbate your delicate and declining mental state. *Now*, however, I know you're simply trying to save money on shampoo. Quite logical really. Except," he added, running his hands through his freakishly thick hair while doing his best Daniel Craig/James Bond impression, "it would be a crime against nature for me to shear *these* locks from my head."

"So it took you three full days together in Muskoka, and the better part of a week at work, to reassure yourself that I was neither?"

Scott looked deadpan at Ron, nodding. "Better safe than sorry. You *are* a good friend, after all. But don't worry, buddy. I'll make up for it over the coming months."

"Well, that's good to know. By the way, how's your elbow?"

"Still one hundred percent. It's like I never had an issue with it. That wife of yours is a keeper, Ronny."

Ron nodded in exaggerated agreement while having a sip of beer.

"She obviously didn't want to talk about it last weekend, but where *did* she learn to do that?"

Ron took a deep breath, fortified himself with another pull of draft, and replied, "She doesn't actually have any training, Scott."

"You're kidding? I find that hard to believe, Ron." Now it was Scott's turn to take a sip from his mug as he pondered Ron's reply. "Nothing at all?" he pressed.

"Nope. Nada. Zilch. Nothing. Also zip."

"Then the girl's got a gift," Scott seriously responded, as he tried to reconcile this understanding with his ligamental patch-up a week earlier. A few seconds later, he slowly shook his head in disbelief as his eyes opened wide above the top of his mug. His epiphany had occurred as he was unconsciously drawing especially deeply from his mug—a mechanism he had developed as a child for coping with perplexing topics that had been raised during mealtime conversations with his family. Over the years this behaviour had evolved into an effective cognitive tool for focusing, and over his professional career it had aided his problem-solving abilities. Whereas as a child his focused deliberations where conducted over a glass of milk, and in the office with a mug of coffee, today's insight, unfortunately for Ron, occurred with his mouth filled with exactly three (fluid) ounces of premium-quality Kokanee Gold draft. This beer had been created twenty-one days earlier—about the time they were embarking on their Gampo Abbey adventure—at the Columbia Brewery in the heart of the Kootenay's in British Columbia. Following a five-week brewing process that included malting, milling, mashing, lautering, boiling, two separate fermentations, filtering, and packaging, the amber ale had been driven 3,769 kilometres to the outdated Ontario beer monopoly distribution centre about ten kilometres to the east of where they currently sat, from which it was delivered to the Bassline Pub as part of the establishment's attempt to provide a wider variety of beverage for its patrons. A total of fifty-four people had been involved in the production, transportation, and serving of this amber nectar to Scott's mouth. But the effort and intricacies of this modern-day marvel were lost on both of them, as the magnitude of Scott's realization prompted him to attempt to inhale a lung-full of air, as the preferred medium for the vocal communication of his new-found revelation. Normally, this action would have been seamlessly executed, but today there was a three-ounce barrier lying between the desired air and Scott's lungs. Less than one ounce of beer was respired before a violent gag reaction was triggered.

Ron sat at his stool dripping in beer, an untimely fate for the lovingly crafted liquid, which no one, especially Ron and those immediately adjacent to him, or anyone along the supply chain from the farmer's field to the lady who had delivered the keg earlier in the day, had they foreseen it, would have been pleased with.

"It's the resolution!" Scott sputtered. He cleared his throat as a few nearby patrons reacted with queries about his mental health.

Ron used his sleeve to wipe his face, and stared neutrally back at his friend.

"It is isn't it? I can tell by your reaction," Scott whispered excitedly.

"Why do you keep doing that?" Ron asked, continuing to wipe away at the deeper nooks and crevasses on his face.

"Come on, Ron. This is huge! You'd have been offended if I hadn't reacted that way." Not waiting for the likely rebuttal, he continued, "This is exactly what Dr. Fiona hypothesized could happen."

Knowing he was a terrible liar, Ron abandoned any thought of attempting to otherwise dissuade Scott. "OK. We think it is, but we need to keep this quiet. Can you imagine the shitstorm this could quickly become if it got out? Desperate people are more than willing to believe in spiritual healing. There are fifty active registered faith healers in the Philippines alone. And I would bet the majority, if not all, do not have skills anything close to what Brandi has. In North America the whole healing thing is shrouded in charlatanism and is mostly financially motivated. These are dangerous grounds, Scott."

"But we know that Brandi is legitimate. Just think of how much good she can do."

"She's been struggling with that, too. Knowing Brandi, I don't think she's going to be able to *not* use this ability to benefit more people. I'm just hoping that she can do it without bringing the world to our doorstep."

At that exact moment, Brandi was talking with MN Deborah Shillington at the CHEO (Children's Hospital of Eastern Ontario); coincidentally, located just north of The Beer Store warehouse that had earlier in the day supplied the beer currently coating Ron.

Nurse Shillington was going through the details of Brandi's application as part of the interview process for an evening volunteer position at the hospital. Nurse Shillington had conducted hundreds of these interviews over the years, and she immediately knew that Brandi was a good candidate. In fact, the more she talked with Brandi, the firmer her positive opinion of her became. By the end of the twenty-minute interview, she felt as if it was *she* who was being interviewed, and desperately hoped that Brandi held a favourable view of her, and would still want to volunteer at the hospital.

"Thanks for coming in, Brandi," she said. "Assuming, as I'm sure will be case," she smiled in a motherly fashion at Brandi, "your references check out and your background check is clean, we can likely get you into our volunteer rotation as early as next week. If that suits you, of course?"

Brandi nodded.

"Excellent. Is there any role or program that you have in mind?"

"Actually, there is, Nurse Shillington."

"Please call me Deborah."

"Deborah, I'd like to spend time in long-term care with the terminally ill kids."

Saturday, September 12

They were debriefing Dr. Fiona concerning their trip to Gampo Abbey, and had just informed her about Brandi's new healing touch.

"Well. I have to say, in all honesty, I didn't expect *this*," Dr. Fiona finally commented, still wide-eyed and stunned after hearing about Brandi's recently acquired skills. "You'll recall, we did talk hypothetically about publicizing the results from this 'experiment' before we started. The world needs to know about the power of the mind and, specifically, how these abilities *can* be attained through structured sexual activity. Something at the fingertips of virtually every human—no pun intended."

She looked at Ron. "At least for those who are innately gifted," she added consolingly. "This doesn't mean that eventually you, too, wouldn't be able to develop similar skills, Ron. It's just that Brandi has been able to achieve this within a shockingly short period of time."

Ron spoke up. "I know we agreed to that as part of your *pro bono* service, Dr. Fiona, but if word of this got out, our lives, as we know it, would be over."

"I agree, Ron. That's why your identities will be strictly withheld in the publication. I think it's far more likely that any leak will come from you two. Brandi has decided, for reasons of conscious and compassion, that she will share her gift with the most vulnerable and needy amongst us, and I would never counsel against that." She now looked directly at Brandi. "But you must realize that you'll risk exposure through your actions at the CHEO."

"I have," replied Brandi, "but it's a risk I'm prepared to take. How could I even consider not helping?"

"I would expect nothing less of you, Brandi. This is, after all, a test of what humanity is capable of, and it starts with and evolves through compassion. I would, however, strongly recommend that you tell no one about this."

She looked sternly at both Brandi and Ron. Then her gaze fixed suspiciously on Ron. After a few seconds she asked, "Ron. Do you have something to tell me?"

Ron hadn't yet informed Brandi that Scott had "outed" her yesterday evening during their tête-à-tête. Now he slowly turned his head towards Brandi, sporting an exaggerated apologetic look. "Scott figured it out on his own," he said in a pleading tone.

Brandi visualized one of Ron's favourite T-shirts, which had the words "IT WASN'T MY FAULT" boldly displayed on the front. "That means Elise likely knows as well."

Ron shrugged that he didn't know, but in fact, he could sure provide a solid guess.

"As I said," Dr. Fiona continued, with a thinly veiled look of disappointment at Ron, "there's a greater risk of a leak from your side."

"So what happens next?" asked Brandi.

"You two keep going with the resolution. And Brandi, I want you to keep a record of your interactions with the kids at the Children's Hospital. Anything you can tell me about the child's condition, the timeline of your interaction, and changes in your patient's illness, if any, would be helpful. This will assist me in framing and quantifying the extent of your ability.

"As for you, Ron, I recommend that you resist further dissemination of Brandi's talent to the general public, and ask the same from your intuitive buddy."

Before they departed Dr. Fiona's office, Ron thought about bringing up the issue of the identity of the mole publically leaking details about the resolution; but given Dr. Fiona's unequivocal plea for secrecy, in his mind it was now clear that she wasn't a suspect.

❧

Once Ron and Brandi had left the office, Dr. Fiona pondered the unexpected direction in which her experiment had gone. Whereas initially she had hoped there would be *some* positive developments involving Ron and Brandi's resolution, this most recent development was transformational. Unbeknownst to Ron and Brandi, she had expanded the experiment a few months ago, secretly gauging public reaction by leaking their resolution out to Twitter via *Marny@gogirl*, using the hashtag *#resolutionottawa*, but she now knew that had been a mistake. And there would be no further leaks. Brandi's wellbeing depended on keeping her new skill completely secret. *Marny@gogirl* would disappear. She now hoped *#resolutionottawa* would follow.

Sunday, September 13

Ron's parents came over for Sunday supper. They had happily settled into their new, nearby residence, and the stress-free living environment was starting to feel like home. The rich social environment was re-invigorating both of them; the trepidatious, gloomy aura that they had been lugging around with them all year was nowhere to be seen. Much to Ron's surprise, they actually looked relaxed.

It was a rare cool and wet weekend, so they were inside around the dining room table. Talk had mostly been about their recent trip to the monastery in Nova Scotia.

"I'm still having trouble adjusting to your Buddhist-style haircut, Ron," Abby commented, staring directly at Ron's head and shaking her head slightly in motherly disapproval.

Ron was getting used to being the subject of such looks, and replied, "Mom, don't think of it as a Buddhist haircut. I'm just proud of the shape of my head, and want to share it with my friends and family."

"I'll get used to it eventually," Abby responded. "Just not today."

"Tell us what the highlight to your trip was," asked Tommy Sr.

Brandi replied, "There were a bunch of highlights, Tommy. Halifax and the Cabot Trail are amazing, and the Bretoners are hilarious. But for me, anyway," she looked at Ron, "it was the genuine and humble nature of the residents at Gampo Abbey."

"I admit, they were great," Ron agreed. "And I especially liked the whole feel of Halifax."

"Well, it sounds as if it was time well spent," Abby concluded. "Did you find what you were looking for at the monastery?"

"Oh, yeah," replied Ron. "We found things we didn't even *know* we were looking for."

Tommy Sr. thoughtfully nodded his head.

Wednesday, September 23

A spectacular September was, thankfully from Ron's perspective, uneventfully rolling along. Ron and Sam had adjusted to Brandi's volunteering schedule at the Children's Hospital, and Twitter chatter concerning *#resolutionottawa* had died down to a few tweets a day, most of them inquiries as to how the couple was progressing. *Dodged a bullet there,* Ron thought.

He was watching the Blue Jays beat up on the Yankees when he heard Brandi come home from her volunteering stint at the hospital. *She's home early,* he thought. Pausing the game, he went up to say hello.

When he got upstairs he found Brandi sitting pensively over a glass of white wine. It was one of Ron's favourites—a 2013 Ensemble from the La Frenz Vineyards north of Penticton. But she looked so distracted she might as well have been drinking turpentine.

Ron stopped cold. "Oh-oh." Sitting down beside her, he asked, "What's up, Brandi?"

Ron could see her trembling as she sipped her wine, staring straight ahead. She put the wine down and slowly turned her head towards Ron. Trying to speak, she broke down, started crying, and leaned into Ron.

After a moment or two, she regained her composure, wiped her cheeks, and said, "I think I cured a child of her cancer."

She explained that there was a particularly sick young girl, about whom the nurses had solemnly whispered to Brandi that the best they could do was to make her remaining days a bit more enjoyable. Brandi had been spending a lot of time with her over the last week, and thought she had seen improvement after a few of her inconspicuous healing sessions.

She hadn't seen the girl for a couple of days, and today, when she got to the hospital, she found the terminal ward unexpectedly charged with a positive energy, and the nurses, who typically walked around in a state of perpetual despondency, animated and smiling. Deborah, the nurse who had initially interviewed her, had practically run to Brandi when she spotted her. She excitedly explained that Haniya, the young girl Brandi had been spending so much time with, had made a miraculous recovery, and the doctors had confirmed today that the rare form of brain cancer that had been ravaging her and ebbing away her life-force had completely disappeared.

Brandi had realized immediately that it was no coincidence, and was shaken by the gravitas of the event. Doing her best to hide her anxiety, she shared the excitement of the moment with the staff, briefly joining in with the energetic group encircling Haniya, then informed Deborah that she wasn't feeling well and was heading home.

"I know this was what I was intending to do, but I'm having trouble believing that all this is real."

"So what's your plan now?" asked Ron.

She took a deep breath. "I guess there's no going back now. I'll be showing up for my next shift tomorrow evening, and keep doing whatever I'm doing." She paused for a couple of seconds. "There's this sweet little boy named Timmy, whose immune system is so compromised that his parents can't even hold him. He's someone who could really benefit from some human touch. It'll take a bit of planning, but he's definitely next on my list."

Saturday, September 26

Sam was overnighting at a friend's place, so Ron and Brandi had the place to themselves. Brandi pondered the events of the past few days while Ron cooked up some kabobs on the barbecue.

The emotional shock of her actions had quickly been replaced with a stubborn determination to fully embrace her furtive task at the Children's Hospital. She had managed to get alone with Timmy on Thursday evening and, while sponge-bathing him, slipped off her rubber gloves and gave him an intense five minutes of her healing touch. Brandi could feel his energy returning by the end of the session, a silent smile of thanks by the withered lad confirming her sentiment. She was anxious to get back to the hospital tomorrow morning and check up on him.

"Done to perfection," Ron suggested, placing the kabobs on the table in the backyard. His smile faded when he saw that Brandi had hardly even noticed his culinary work of art. "I, unlike you, my dear, am not proficient at reading minds. But I'm pretty sure I know what you're thinking about."

"Sorry Ron. It's hard for me to think about anything else. It's just so…well… overwhelming, if you know what I mean."

"I think I do, Brandi. But even prophets deserve a night off once in a while, so why don't we focus on ourselves tonight? It's why we're *here* in the first place."

Brandi offered her wine in a toast to his suggestion. Tonight they had decided to celebrate Brandi's healing miracle of the past week, and were sipping on an earthy, full-bodied, dark, and fruity 2012 Holy Moly Petit Verdot from the Blasted Church Winery on Skaha Lake in BC. As she returned her glass to the table, she commented, "Ron, along that line of thought, I'd like to try something a little different tonight."

Ron froze mid-sip, and nodded for her to continue.

"You remember when Jetsunma Kusho Chödrön and I transferred our consciousnesses at Gampo Abbey?"

Wondering where Brandi was going with this, Ron continued nodding, the glass still against his lips.

"I was thinking; why can't *we* do that?" she asked rhetorically.

Ron kept nodding, glass glued to his lips.

"But *we* could do it while having sex."

Ron stopped nodding, but the glass remained in place. After a few seconds of considering Brandi's proposal, he half asked, half stated, "Let me see if I've got this right. You mean be in each other's bodies while having sex; so essentially, we'd be watching ourselves have sex with ourselves?"

"Yes and no," replied Brandi. "Yes, we'd be watching ourselves have sex, but no, we wouldn't be having sex with ourselves. The experience would be physically filtered through each other's body so we'd get to experience how each other feels during sex...with each other?" she finished, furrowed brows conceding her confusion.

"So," Ron replied while slowing exhaling, "I, you....we..." He pointed pointing first at himself, then at Brandi, then, gesturing back and forth, finally conclude, "would get to experience each other's orgasm. Right?"

"Yes...I think so," Brandi cautiously replied.

Ron's eyes widened. "Or in your case...I mean in my case, *orgasms*. I'm liking the sound of that already, but it might be a little weird watching yourself. A bit like masturbating in front of the mirror, I'd imagine."

He continued after a short thoughtful pause. "But what if I just want to play with your, I mean *my*, boobs? I've always wanted to have my own boobs to play with. What if we don't know what we're doing? It's going to be like losing your virginity all over again. What if..."

Brandi held up her hand, stopping Ron mid-speculation. "I guess we're just going to have to give it a go and see what happens." She picked up her knife and fork and pointed at the cooling kabobs. "Come on, our food is getting cold. Let's finish up here and take the party upstairs. I'm dying to find out what it's like to pee standing up!"

Sunday, September 27

When Brandi made it to the Children's Hospital at around 10 a.m., all seemed normal, which meant that Timmy's healing session probably hadn't gone as she had planned. She changed up and started her rounds, cheerfully greeting the kids as she found them in the hall or in their rooms. When she got to Timmy's room, he was apparently still asleep, his back turned to her. But just as she was about to move on, he sat up in his bed and stared directly at her.

"Hello Miss Brandi," he said.

Brandi adjusted her mask, went into his room, and sat down at the base of his bed. "How are you doing today, Timmy?" she gently inquired.

"I'm doing *much* better, Miss Brandi," he said with a growing smile. "I want you to wash me *every* day!"

Holding back tears, Brandi responded, "If it makes you happy, I'll wash you up for as long as you're here."

CHAPTER 11

AN AGENT OF CHANGE

Friday, October 2

The boys were at their local haunt, wrapping up their workweek. "Ron. I never, *ever*, thought I would ask you this question." Scott paused for dramatic effect. "How *did* Brandi's orgasm feel?"

Ron put down his glass of beer, swallowed, inhaled pensively, and replied. "Weird." He nodded, as if he had found the exactly correct word.

Scott stared disappointedly at Ron, and replied, "That, I'm afraid, doesn't really help me a whole bunch, Ron. This whole thing is *weird*." He delivered the last word with jazz hands. "From the resolution, to your meditation, to your Buddhist retreat, to Brandi's new abilities, it's all *weird*," again with the jazz hands. "I'm asking about one particular *weird* aspect of your completely *weird* life. Can you try and help me with *that*?"

Ron pondered Scott's comment for a while, taking a sip of his beer while looking pensively back at Scott, thoroughly enjoying his friend's anxiety and this brief moment of leverage over him. "Well, weird at first."

Scott silently stared expressionlessly at him. He exhaled loudly, and replied, "OK, I'll play along. Why was it weird *at first*?"

"Mainly because you're …I mean I…was being penetrated by my own penis."

Unfortunately for Ron, he made this rather improbable comment just at the moment Scott had reflexively attempted to settle his growing frustration with Ron with a sip of his beer. Fortunately for Ron, however, the day had been cool, and he was wearing a waterproof windbreaker, which he hadn't bothered taking off when he arrived at the Bassline Pub. Consequently, the clean-up was a bit quicker today. As he wiped his face off with a paper napkin, to the sound of Scott gagging and clearing his sinuses, he wondered whether they had unconsciously chosen the corner table with Scott facing towards the wall, just in case. He also marveled at how easy it was to dry his head these days.

"You deserved that, Ron," Scott responded, quickly regaining his composure. He chuckled and added, "I was instantly reminded of that old lewd limerick, 'There once was a man from Nantucket…'"

"If you're finished regurgitating fluids on me, should I continue?" asked Ron.

"Absolutely. And I won't drink while you're talking. As a safety measure, given the topic."

"So, as I was saying…the penetration thing was entirely weird, but after a while I got used to it and started to relax and enjoy the experience."

"What was it like to be…you know…penetrated? Never mind by your own penis?"

"My own penis aside," Ron said, "It actually felt normal…ish. It's not like it was first time for Brandi, so there wasn't any physical stress. And may I say it was a rather fine penis that was doing the penetrating," Ron added with a smile.

"After a while I actually saw Brandi when I looked at her…um… I mean me… and when that happened, I actually got into it. And, I think, so did Brandi, judging from the look on my… I mean her…face, and her comments afterwards."

"What did she say?" asked Scott.

"Not to go into too much detail…"

"Too late," Scott said.

"She said what her experience lacked in *quantity*, it made up in *quality*."

"Sounds as if she enjoyed having a penis. Probably wasn't much of a stretch, since she's been wearing the pants in the family for a couple of decades."

Ron threw back his head, feigning hilarious laughter, then said, "Good one," straight-faced.

"So," Scott continued, "the 64,000-dollar question. How did the orgasm feel?"

"Which one?"

"Bastard. OK, the first one."

"Well, don't laugh…"

"I can't promise anything," replied Scott

"I actually felt a wave of emotion and affection towards myself…I mean… Brandi. And I'm not talking about your standard, run-of-the mill spousal affection. It was a walking-into-a-sauna full-body kind of effect." He paused for a couple of seconds. "It's the first time in our marriage—no; in my entire life—I've totally understood how a woman's mind works, and the fundamental difference between men and women."

"And what's that?" asked Scott, sitting up straight.

"Women not only have a greater capacity for love and compassion than men, they access it more often and more effectively than men can."

Scott let his comment hang for a couple beats, and then seriously asked, "How did it feel having boobs? Did you get distracted?"

ॐ

Meanwhile, back in Centrepointe, Brandi and Charlene were sitting at the kitchen island over a glass of Quails' Gate Estate Pinot Noir. Its light and cheerful demeanour was perfectly paired with the ongoing conversation.

"I don't think I could walk around with all that extra stuff in my pants, but it was sure fun to throw it around in the privacy of my own bedroom." Brandi was continuing their discussion of her and Ron's recent "experiment."

When Charlene stopped laughing, she asked, "So it was similar to when your clitoris swells, but more like a clitoris on steroids?"

"And then some. It was like having a fifth appendage. No wonder guys can't stop fiddling with it. It's front and centre. Your hands and eyes are naturally drawn to it. *I* couldn't stop playing with it!"

"So how was the orgasm?"

"It was sort of like climbing a mountain, but not as physical." She paused, looking for more and better words to describe it. "It was like...like the objective was to get to the top of the mountain, and when you got to the top, there was an incomparable rush of exhilaration, and I instantly knew why I was hurrying to get there. But as soon as I got to the top and took in the view, I needed to descend the mountain as quickly as possible, and while I was tumbling down the slope, the beauty of the view I had just enjoyed didn't even occur to me again."

"But overall, was it OK?"

"Definitely. But I don't think I could get used to the one-and-done thing. And frankly, I would miss the feeling I get after making love. You know. That warm afterglow feeling of contentment you get?"

Charlene nodded in agreement.

"I sort of feel bad for guys. I *know* Ron loves me with all his heart, and still there wasn't much of that outflow of emotion that I have for Ron after making love."

"Poor buggers," Charlene agreed. "But tell me. Did you get a chance to pee standing up?"

Wednesday, October 7

Brandi had been volunteering at the Children's Hospital now for a little less than a month, during which three kids she had "worked" with had been discharged due to dramatically improved health. She had also seen the mood of the ward markedly improve. In vivid contrast to the somber shuffling by which the adults previously conducted their business, the nurses and volunteers now more often than not had smiles on their faces and a bounce in their steps. Brandi believed the recent "miracles" the ward had experienced was the reason for the current optimism and hope in a setting that was typically only familiar with stoic courage, despair, death, and grief.

Brandi knew these were just the first green shoots of hope in a tragic desert landscape. Although she felt a spiritual joyfulness concerning the children she *had* helped, this feeling was often quickly quelled with the reality that the ward was still filled with sick and dying kids, and the beds that she had helped vacate had been immediately filled with equally sick and desperate children. At times, she had felt completely overwhelmed, and had recently been relying more and more on Ron's support to keep herself positive and focused.

She was becoming concerned that this distress she was feeling would erode her newfound abilities; in effect, self-limiting them. Additionally, her performance at her paying job was now suffering, and she was progressively becoming less interested in those mundane duties that neither satisfied her nor cured heartbreakingly sick children. It was under this pall she and Ron were talking this evening.

Ron was stroking Brandi's head as she leaned into him on the couch. "You can't cure them all, Brandi. There are simply too many sick kids in the Children's Hospital, let alone Ottawa, let alone the rest of the world."

"Practically, I know this, Ron. But emotionally, I'm conflicted. How can I spend hours of my day managing property issues while kids, that I could be helping, are dying a few kilometres away?"

"You know it's not that simple. We have to manage this or it *will* get out of control and no one will benefit. You have to be content with the good that you actually *are* doing, not worrying about everything that you *haven't* done. There are an infinite number of possible realities available for everybody every single day. The best we can do is to *contribute* to positive change on a daily basis." Ron paused. "That's it. That's all. No person can or should shoulder the problems of the world. That includes you. I'd suggest that in one day at the Children's Hospital, you are able to effect more positive change than some people do in their entire lifetime."

Brandi shrugged, enjoying Ron's consoling words.

"I suggest you take solace in this fact, and stay focused on helping the *extremely* fortunate kids that you *can* help. Think of the difference you are making in *their* lives. It may be an isolated event in a concrete building in a small city in Canada, but all these events will have a ripple effect, that I can promise you. You're actually changing the world for the better with each one of these acts."

"How so?" asked Brandi.

"Imagine that you drop a single pebble in the middle of a calm ocean. Although the visible effects of that event are soon lost in the enormity of the endless water, the energy from it spreads out in all directions—theoretically forever. How this event ultimately effects change we can only guess at, but its energy will live on well past the location and time of the initial event. You drop enough of these pebbles, and maybe they'll combine into a wave, which may combine with other similarly formed waves to form a tsunami of change. The point is, keep dropping these small pebbles of positive change and bigger things will eventually happen."

"Even though all that sounds ridiculously Buddhistic, it does, somehow, make me feel better. I knew I married you for something other than your sexual prowess," Brandi said, and leaned in for a deep kiss.

At that exact moment Sam was walking past the living room, and involuntarily belched out a heartfelt "Yeeeeech!"—immediately followed by a, "Please don't do that."

Monday, October 12

After a weekend spent with family, and in intense lovemaking and meditation, Brandi felt rejuvenated and centred again, and was back at the Children's Hospital volunteering on the evening shift. Even though it was Thanksgiving, Brandi, Ron, and the rest of the family had celebrated the official end of summer the night before.

Nurse Shillington noticed her, and walked over purposefully. "Happy Thanksgiving, and congratulations, Brandi!" She offered her hand, sporting a broad smile.

Brandi shook her hand instinctively, but stared back at her, confused.

"It's been one month since you started volunteering here," Nurse Shillington exuberantly explained.

"Thanks, Deborah. I really appreciate you remembering," Brandi replied with a smile, relieved Nurse Shillington was referring to her short tenure at the hospital.

Looking around to confirm they weren't near any children, Nurse Shillington whispered, "You know we've had a stretch of good fortune since you've been volunteering here."

She paused to let the comment sink in. "I don't want to sound pessimistic," she continued, "but that isn't typically the case." She shook her head slowly, now wearing a morose expression. "We can go months or even years before we see a child, against all odds, recover like the three children who fully recovered over the last month. I've been working this ward for eight years and, although I hope with all my heart this trend could continue, it likely will not. My advice is to enjoy these miracles when they happen, but don't expect them."

Brandi nodded with a solemn expression, but was thinking, *If you thought last month was unusual, you haven't seen anything yet, Nurse Shillington.*

"Well, enough said. Enjoy your shift tonight, and keep on doing good."

As she walked away, Brandi was already looking for her next "mark." Over the last couple of weeks, an eight-year-old girl named Liz with a deteriorating congenital heart condition, waiting for a suitable donor, had been dying in front of Brandi's eyes. Brandi knew she wouldn't last the wait, or possibly even the week. She walked over to where the girl sat watching the other children play, sat across from her, and asked, "Lizzy, would you like to play a special game with me tonight?"

With what looked like a Herculean effort, the girl rotated her head towards Brandi, a smile growing on her bluish lips, shifting the paper-thin grey skin of her face ever-so slightly. "Yes, Miss Brandi. That sounds like fun."

Monday, October 19

Brandi and Ron cuddled on the couch while watching the federal election results roll-in. "I guess it doesn't really matter who gets in," Ron said. "It's my experience that no matter how idealistic and energetic a person is, a thankless job like Prime Minister will wear anybody down. I'll bet you that within a year he'll be acting as arrogant and entitled to power as the last one. This one even looks a bit more self-absorbed than usual. We've never had a narcissistic GenX Prime Minister, so it should be good entertainment, at least."

"Wow. Sour grapes or what? You make it sound like we can expect Trudeau to now publically perform singing duets with his wife, or demonstrate his yoga proficiency for the press." Brandi chuckled at the absurdity of this visual. "And speaking of wearing someone down, do you know we only have seventy-three days left in the resolution?"

"I knew we were getting close, but I hadn't actually calculated the days. Seventy-three does sound manageable, doesn't it?"

"Manageable? Sounds like a good long weekend," Brandi replied.

"Pff," Ron replied. "Maybe for you. You know that's more of a challenge for me having, now walked a mile in my shoes… so to speak."

"So are you starting to get bored with me, or just plain worn down?" Brandi playfully asked.

"It's just that I'm not forty-seven anymore. That said, I don't foresee any problems humping this old ass over the finish line."

Just then Brandi's mobile pinged, and she had a peek at it. "It's from Charlene," she said. She opened the text, read it, then said, "Oh-oh," and turned the phone to Ron

It was a tweet from one of the groupies calling him or herself *@lovejunkie*. A small group of devotees obsessed with the whole resolution concept, including and especially *@lovejunkie*, had helped keep the conversation about the resolution alive through the summer and into the fall.

The tweet said, "*Identity of Ottawa resolution couple discovered. All will be revealed soon.*"

Ron turned back to Brandi and said, "Oh-oh is right."

Tuesday, October 20

It was about eight-thirty in the evening when Brandi returned from volunteering at the Children's Hospital. Ron greeted her at the front door with a kiss, and helped her out of her coat while asking how things had gone tonight. He was particularly interested in one of the kids that she had spent time with the previous week. He recalled her name was Liz.

Sitting at the kitchen island, Brandi updated Ron. "You should see her Ron. It's like…" She paused, looking for the right words. Ron noticed that her eyes were moistening as she thought about the girl. "She's like a different person. They're keeping her in the ward for a while longer for further assessment, but she's a little pink-skinned, high-energy chatterbox now."

"And what's the reaction on the ward?"

"They're walking around like they won the lottery. What they don't know is they think they've won 6/49, but actually they've won the Lotto Max! I've been working with a couple of other kids suffering with terminal cancer, and I expect that over the next couple of days they'll be showing some 'miraculous' improvement as well."

Ron now seriously asked, "I wonder if people will look back at this resolution a thousand years from now and muse that the originator was a genius?"

Brandi guffawed, and said, "More like an idiot savant, I'd imagine."

Ron responded by successfully executing a midsection tickle offensive, to which Brandi quickly submitted.

Just then the front doorbell chimed. Ron and Brandi looked at each other, puzzled. They weren't expecting anyone, and it was getting late. Ron popped up, and said over his shoulder, "Now who could that be?"

He opened the door. There stood a thirty-something lady with jet-black hair and an overall gothic appearance. "Hi. Can I help you?" Ron politely asked.

"Hi," the lady replied. "I'm *lovejunkie*."

A few minutes later, *lovejunkie*, who's actual name was Vanessa, was sitting in the living room with Ron and Brandi. "So why do you think we're the resolution couple?" queried Brandi.

"I was at the restaurant when you two were celebrating your wedding anniversary in July, and heard the elderly gentleman at the table make a toast to the resolution that fell flat. I had already been following the resolution on Twitter and I found that event peculiar, but I didn't put it together. I have to admit, I absolutely love the idea of what you guys are doing. It's *soooo* romantic, especially at your age, and having been married as long as you two have."

Vanessa gazed lovingly at both Brandi and Ron, then after a few seconds of silence, refocused on her story. "Like I said, I didn't put it together—at first. A few weeks ago I revisited the *#resolutionottawa* tweets, and noted that someone had wished the resolution couple a happy twentieth anniversary. I still didn't connect the dots. But last week over my morning coffee I had a flash recollection of *that* toast in the restaurant. You guys fit the demographics perfectly, and I knew right then you were the resolution couple." The loving smile returned, this time augmented with clutched hands supporting the chin of her tilted head.

Brandi looked at Ron and they held a silent conference. After a minute or so, Brandi turned towards Vanessa. "So, after your epiphany, it was just some detective work to find out where we lived?"

Vanessa nodded. "I hope that doesn't sound like I was stalking you guys. I look at it as something I had to do."

"What's really concerning to us, Vanessa," Brandi said, "is the tweet you posted yesterday announcing your discovery of the resolution couple's identity, and your intention to publically announce the identities of the couple 'soon.' You have to realize that it would be very disruptive to have our names published as *the* resolution couple."

"I realized that last night *after* I had sent the tweet," Vanessa said apologetically. "Part of me wants the world to know about what you're doing so you can inspire more people to try it themselves. But another part of me realizes this isn't *my* decision to make." Vanessa delivered this last comment with genuine contriteness. "That's why I'm here now."

"Well, Vanessa," Brandi said, "we both appreciate you being sensitive to our position. I think we may have a way forward where *we* can keep our anonymity, and you can get the word out about what we're doing in a more complete and objective fashion."

In response, Vanessa reassumed her reverent pose, this time with a broad smile, confirming her excitement at this proposal.

Wednesday, October 28

During Brandi's short drive home from the Children's Hospital, she pondered recent developments. They had asked Vanessa if she would be interested in creating and administrating a blog, which she could link to Twitter and Facebook, to disseminate the sanctioned word concerning the resolution. She had enthusiastically agreed. Once Vanessa had pinkie-sworn an oath to keep their identities secret, they'd agreed they'd set some time aside to discuss details of their resolution, including the challenges they had encountered and how those had been overcome. If all went well, eventually they would inform Vanessa and her followers about the potential for enlightenment using their structured sexual regime—but that was down the road a ways yet.

Both she and Ron had still harboured a desire to share what they had learned, and were still learning, but not at the sacrifice of their personal life if at all possible; so Vanessa as a middleman was a perfect solution.

Brandi's thoughts drifted back to her volunteer work at the hospital. Over the last ten days, three more "terminal" kids had been discharged, and the feeling of optimism in her ward had now morphed into a kind of stunned disbelief. The last couple of times she had showed up to volunteer, the ward had been teeming with doctors she hadn't previously met, or even seen on that floor. Some of them sounded and looked, by their physical presentation, distinctly foreign. The most senior doctors in the entire hospital were commonly by their side, uncharacteristically deferent.

Nurse Shillington, who seemed to exactly reflect the mood of the ward through her facial expressions, invariably looked intoxicated and confused, a small cache of incredulous looks now her primary form of communication with co-workers. During tonight's shift, though, she'd cornered Brandi, and demonstrated she was still capable of verbal communication by suggesting that what was happening on the ward was nothing short of a miracle. As Nurse Shillington stood there shaking her head, having thereafter instantly reverted back to non-verbal communication, sporting a textbook mystified look, Brandi thought she saw a lightbulb go off in the nurse's brain. She slowly turned her head towards Brandi, the mystified look melting away into a rare neutral expression. Brandi had been around Nurse Shillington quite a bit over the last couple of months, and was capable of intuiting this woman's thoughts whenever she wished. What she heard tonight was, *all this started when Brandi showed up!*

Brandi knew this wasn't great news, but didn't know what she would, or could, do about it. She'd discuss this development with Ron when she got home. She assumed Nurse Shillington would now be keeping a very close eye on her while she was volunteering on the ward, looking for a correlation between the kids she spent time with and those whose health markedly improved.

When she got home, Ron was sitting in the kitchen, focused on his laptop. "What you up to, my little studmuffin?" Brandi asked as she closed in on him.

"Just checking out Vanessa's blog. She's been live for only a week, and she already has 17,000-plus followers. Can you believe that? But the way she's writing it makes me sound a bit bumbling and inept, don't you think? I'm not like that, am I?"

Brandi leaned in and kissed Ron on the forehead. "Of course you aren't. She's just capturing your honest nature, Ron. You're not inept." She paused a couple of seconds, and then added, "You're not Black Ops-capable either, but certainly not *entirely* clumsy or graceless."

Brandi sensed an attack, and as Ron lunged from the stool, she had already started to sprint a retreat, squealing in anticipation of the imminent onslaught.

Saturday, October 31

Brandi sat in Dr. Fiona's office, silently staring at her, waiting for her response. She had just spent the last twenty minutes relating her activities over the last month or so at the Children's Hospital.

Brandi had detailed the children's ages, specifics of their maladies, the time she had spent with each child, the techniques she had used, the changes in the children's conditions, and her state of mind while she conducted her ministrations.

Ron had accompanied Brandi primarily out of curiosity. He was becoming more and more fascinated with Brandi's current activities, and hadn't yet heard a concise summary like what Brandi was now providing for Dr. Fiona.

Dr. Fiona finally looked up from her notes, slipping her glasses down her nose as she did so. "Holy shit, Brandi," she said in stunned elation. "I've never come across anything quite like this—and since our last discussion, I've been scouring the literature. There's nothing out there like this that can be scientifically corroborated. Plenty of debunked shysters and frauds, sort of like what you see concerning UFO sightings, but nothing where this healing touch you have can be unequivocally proven."

"So what's next?" asked Ron.

"Frankly, the peer-review board for the *Journal of Sex Research* will be skeptical of these claims. Any professional publication of these assertions will have to be thoroughly vetted. And there will only be one way to do that." Dr. Fiona took off her glasses and looked directly at Brandi.

Brandi nodded knowingly. "What exactly will that in-person vetting entail?"

"Let me check into it, and I'll get back to you. But most likely we'll have to meet with a quorum of their board, and…" Dr. Fiona didn't bother finishing the sentence, knowing Brandi already knew how it finished.

Ron, a bit exasperated with the exchange, spoke up. "Ladies, *I* don't read minds, so can you tell me what's being considered here?"

Brandi turned to Ron and said, "Dr. Fiona wants me to demonstrate my healing ability for the Editorial Board of the *Journal of Sex Research*."

Later that evening, as Ron and Brandi prepared for the trick-and-treaters to start arriving, they discussed the pros and cons of Dr. Fiona's proposal. They had been switching around in their debate roles over the last hour, and, currently, Brandi was playing the role of the protagonist. "I'll…we'll…remain anonymous. Dr. Fiona guarantees that."

Ron, in his current role as the antagonist, replied, "Do you really think something like this can remain completely secret? This is the stuff of ancient religious folklore. The masses used to walk for weeks across deserts to gather within earshot of healers. Cripes, people still travel halfway around the world for the chance to be 'cured.' Can you imagine to what extent the rich would go to survive just a tiny bit longer?" He paused. "Have I ever told you the story about the 'Heart Man' of Qatar?"

Brandi shook her head.

"Apparently, the Emir suffers from a bad and degenerating heart condition. The Qatari royal family employs someone who is known as the 'Heart Man.' This fellow is extremely well paid, and lives the most luxurious and healthy lifestyle imaginable. He is also a perfect blood and tissue match for the Emir. The Heart Man's only job is to have his healthy heart available for the Emir if the Emir's heart were to give out. Can you imagine how many 'Emirs' there are around the world, and to what lengths they would go to you to have you perform your services?"

Brandi pondered this while Ron organized his next thought.

"All it would take would be one off-handed whisper from one member of the Board to start unravelling this supposed cocoon of secrecy," he said.

"But Ron," Brandi countered, "broadcasting the incredible potential of the resolution to a wider audience could really make a difference. How often do everyday people like us get to make a difference of this magnitude? This may be our one and only chance. Do we really want to pass on it?"

"You are already making a difference at the Children's Hospital, Brandi. Remember, dropping small pebbles in the ocean?"

Brandi smiled and replied, "This may be the best way to drop millions of the pebbles of change in the ocean, Ron."

Just then, the doorbell signaled the arrival of the first Halloweeners. They answered the door to an enthusiastic chorus of "Trick or treat!" One of the kids in the group was a girl of about eleven in a wheelchair. Her parents stood off to one side, smiling proudly at their daughter's courage and determination to participate in this event.

Ron was doling out candy when he caught a look in Brandi's eye. Between his comments regarding the costumes, and queries about how much candy the revelers thought they deserved, he was whispering out the side of his mouth, "Don't do it, Brandi. Brandi. Not here. Brandi..."

CHAPTER 12

WHEN ONE DOOR CLOSES...

Sunday, November 1

While Brandi was in the kitchen preparing supper, her phoned pinged with the arrival of a text. It was from Dr. Fiona. "Brandi, would you be prepared to travel to Whitehall, Pennsylvania, a few weeks from now? The *Journal of Sex Research Board* is extremely excited about meeting with you. Don't worry about the costs. I'll cover it. Get back to me and we can work out the details."

Wednesday, November 4

News of something miraculous happening at the Children's Hospital of Eastern Ontario had leaked out to the press on Monday.

Details of recent events in the terminal ward couldn't be indefinitely suppressed, and on the weekend a junior nurse from the ward had mentioned to a friend, who happened to work at the local television station, that there had been a series of remarkable occurrences at the CHEO.

It was the type of human-interest story that checked all the boxes, so it wasn't surprising that both social media and traditional news agencies in Ottawa and around Canada aggressively ran with the story. The public, always susceptible to a feel-good narrative, was instantly transfixed, and wanted more. Some social media sites were suggesting a causal relationship between the optimistic "Sunny Days" guiding philosophy of the new Liberal government and recent events at the CHEO.

With news of the "miracle" cures came the wave of desperate parents, pleading with the hospital administration to admit their child so they, too, could be inexplicably cured. A flood of requests for admittance came not only from the Ottawa area, but from all over North America, and even Europe and Asia. The press had parked themselves in front of the hospital, and security was needed to keep unwanted reporters and random story stalkers out of the ward.

Consequently, when Brandi arrived for her evening shift, the temperament in the ward was decidedly more defensive. As she was hanging up her windbreaker, she heard an approaching pair of size-nine Faxon soft soles beating out a muffled *allegro* tempo, suggesting Nurse Shillington was not only in a talkative mood, she also immediately desired Brandi's ear.

When Brandi turned to greet her, she saw that the nurse had reverted back to her officious puckered public persona. "The bloody reporters have been relentless today, Brandi. So far, the kids are unaware of all the hoopla, and let's keep it that way, OK? We don't want them unduly agitated," Nurse Shillington loudly whispered, her flustered tone revealing her anxiety and, Brandi thought, a hint of indictment.

Nurse Shillington spun and reversed her direction at the same pace as she had made her entrance without waiting for either acknowledgement or agreement from Brandi.

"Good evening to you too," Brandi quietly commented, when she knew her agitated ward-matron was out of earshot. Personnel in the ward were clearly overwhelmed with the publicity and the ramped-up pressure from an increasing number of distraught parents requesting admission of their children to the hospital. She knew Nurse Shillington was simply reflecting the ward's mood, and couldn't help herself.

As Brandi walked around the ward, greeting and talking with the kids, she could almost pretend that nothing had changed. But it had. She knew this was the tip of the iceberg of unintended consequences that Ron had warned about. She would have to be more circumspect in her ministrations, and needed to talk with Ron about a forward strategy. Tonight it would be prudent if she only provided basic comfort for the children.

It was forty minutes into her shift when seven year old Aliya wheeled herself over to Brandi and asked, with a soul-penetrating smile, if Brandi could read to her. She had a freezer baggy clipped onto her pediatric walker, and inside it Brandi could see the book she was hoping to have read—Sam McBratney's *Guess How Much I Love You.*

Oh, what the hell, thought Brandi. She reached down, scooped up the girl, and made for a nearby sofa.

Friday, November 6

Tonight had been designated pizza-movie night. As they waited for the pizza delivery, Sam was bringing Ron and Brandi up to date about her classes, her teachers, and the drama that seemed inevitable whenever and wherever fifteen-year-old girls gathered.

They tried not to laugh as Sam seriously recounted the many misadventures of these dynamic young adults in life's transition. She also had her fair share of sad stories concerning various emotional traumas some of her friends were going through with their families, and in few cases, themselves.

It was a poignant reminder (not that Brandi needed one these days) that, even in the relative sanctuary of modern-day Ottawa, the face of tragedy was only suppressed, not vanquished.

When the doorbell rang, all three of them in unison said, "Pizza!"

Ron popped up, bounded to the front door, and flung it open. "What do I owe you?" he said as he dug out his wallet from his back pocket.

Then he stopped cold, his hand still in his back pocket, as the small, well-dressed, be-hatted grey-haired woman of about seventy standing on his doorstep said, "Actually, you owe me nothing, but I would appreciate it if I could talk to a Mrs. Brandi Lee."

"Brandi. It's for you," he called out, and invited the lady out of the cooling night air into the hallway.

&

Brandi had been talking with the elderly woman behind closed doors in their office for over a half hour. The pizzas had arrived, and both Sam and Ron had had their share, and were now just enjoying the physical contentment of full bellies while continuing their discussion in the kitchen.

The presence of the woman at their home, her request to meet alone with Brandi, and the subsequent time they had spent talking all seemed very unusual to Ron. Given how out of the ordinary it was, he sensed that it must have something to do with Brandi's new skills.

After a quick query concerning the identity of the uninvited stranger, Sam had all but forgotten about her, and became re-absorbed in the details of her life. Currently she was playing some of her favourite YouTube videos for her dad, over which they were sharing some laughs.

Ron heard the door to the office open, and Brandi and the woman's voices moving towards the front door. He went to join Brandi. Her curiosity rekindled, Sam followed behind him. They all arrived at the front door at the same time.

"Ron, Sam. I'd like you meet Deheune. Deheune, this is my husband, Ron, whom you met earlier, and my daughter, Samantha," Brandi said.

"I'm so sorry to have come over unannounced, and in the middle of your family night. I wouldn't have done either if I hadn't thought it important," Deheune said, shaking their hands. While sliding her coat on she added, "It was a pleasure to meet you all." Then she spun on her heels and receded into the evening.

Ron closed the door, looked at Brandi, and said, "We've been keeping your pizza warm. While you're eating you can tell us who that lady was and what she wanted."

Ron's instincts proved correct. Deheune *had* been there to talk to Brandi about her abilities, but they couldn't openly discuss those details in front of Sam, so Brandi's initial explanation focused on the Children's Hospital connection that

Deheune had brought up. She told Ron and Sam that Deheune was affiliated with the CHEO, that they had noted her good work, and that they wanted her to commit further time and effort to the cause.

That partial explanation appeared to satisfy Sam, but as soon as she left for a nearby friend's house, Ron immediately said, "OK. What's really going on?"

"Something quite amazing, actually, Ron," Brandi replied. "Let me grab a glass of wine and I'll fill you in."

Twenty minutes later, following Brandi's summary of her meeting with Deheune, Ron sat dumbfounded beside his wife. "So, let me see if I've got this right. Deheune, no last name—just Deheune—represents an international organization that is on the lookout for people with your special talents?"

Brandi nodded.

"And their organization is on constant global alert, via social networks and media, for any indicators of people demonstrating abilities such as those you've been employing at the CHEO?"

Branded nodded again.

"And somehow they've gained access to the hospital files concerning the recent spate of miraculous cures, and concluded that these events were very likely not a coincidence?"

"Yup." Brandi nodded one more time.

"OK. I can see all that. What I don't understand is how they tied these events back to you."

"Like I said, these guys, somehow, have access to the hospital files, and noted that these 'miracles' began just after I started volunteering in the ward. And also, apparently, Nurse Shillington suggested this correlation in her most recent weekly operational summary, which, by the way, Deheune's organization also had access to. In their minds, they were fairly certain I was somehow related to these events."

"But not *yet* sufficiently sure enough to set loose a mononymous septuagenarian emissary to directly confront you."

"Correct."

"And there's something about your *ancestry* that convinced them?" Ron asked.

"Well, unbeknownst to me—and possibly even to my parents—my mother's Irish lineage can be traced back to sometime in the early seventeenth century, where it connects directly with a famous faith healer named Muireen Ni Hiongardail from the coastal village of Eyeries in West Cork. Although that information was intriguing, what got them off their chairs was the fact that Muireen was the seventh daughter of a seventh daughter."

"And how's that significant?" asked Ron.

"Well, according to Deheune and the organization she represents, anybody demonstrating healing abilities is, invariably, directly related to the seventh daughter of a seventh daughter. That's seven girls in a row. Both times in successive lineages."

"Who knew?" commented Ron. He thought for a minute. "Hold on. If everybody directly related to Muireen is a healer, why isn't your mom a healer? Or your sisters?"

"I asked the same question. Apparently, this 'gift' has to be triggered by a profound external force, event, or activity. Otherwise, it lies latent for the entire life of the individual."

"The resolution was *your* trigger," suggested Ron, nodding knowingly.

"Most likely; but probably in combination with our meditation."

Ron said, "What's really impressive is that these guys have put all this together just since Monday, when the news broke; have unrestricted access to the hospital's records; and traced your ancestry back to a specific individual in the early seventeenth century. They must have some pretty extraordinary support."

"Deheune did mention that they were backed by some very rich and powerful philanthropists. She also mentioned that the original backers founded this secret organization with the sole intent of protecting a small group of healers from commercial exploitation, while most effectively and humanely utilizing their skills to the benefit of everybody, not just an entitled few."

"Wow," muttered Ron, pondering the implications.

"And you'll never guess the name of the organization."

Ron shook his head: no, he didn't even have a guess.

"The Salvation Army!" Brandi exclaimed. "But it's not your mother's Sally Ann, so to speak. This is the covert and highly secretive arm that no one will ever hear about. Except, of course—you. By the way, you have to swear to absolute secrecy about this or..."

"Or *what?*" asked Ron, a wave of apprehension rising in his stomach.

"Well, she said they would categorically deny any such claim, and..."

"And *what?*" Ron inquired, his anxiety growing.

"Well, I don't know if I read her correctly, but her organization is determined not to be exposed, and has the means to protect themselves. Let's just say, you wouldn't want to get on their bad side." Brandi purposely made the last comment sound ominous.

"And you're OK with this?" he asked. "When do you have to decide if you want to get involved with these guys?"

Brandi stared at Ron for a second, and realized she had left out a fairly important bit of information.

"Sorry I didn't make this clear earlier, Ron. I don't *have* a choice. Apparently I am part of this secretive group of healers *now*. I joined when I admitted to Deheune that I was the person responsible for curing the kids in the terminal ward."

Tuesday, November 10

Brandi found Ron in his upstairs office, and cheerfully asked him if he could join them downstairs. Deheune had returned to the house after supper, and had been meeting with Brandi behind closed doors for the last hour.

After Ron was seated, Deheune smiled sympathetically at Ron. "Brandi has informed me of your discomfort with Brandi being 'conscripted' into the 'Organization.' I understand that having us foisted upon you and Brandi will seem at first as a violation of your free will, but I can tell you that eventually everybody comes to realize that this is a small sacrifice, measured against the enormous positive effect that our small group of healers has on the world."

She paused, then said, "In the interim, as we demonstrate to Brandi what this group is capable of, all we ask of you is that you keep our existence quiet. *Completely* quiet. Do not tell your parents, children, best friends, co-workers... secret lover...?"

She looked at Brandi, who shook her head, blew a raspberry and chortled.

"Well, you get my meaning, Ron," Deheune said, turning her attention back to him. "Can you do that?"

Ron looked at Brandi, who was very obviously on-board, giving him that "come on Ron—you can do this" look of hers.

"Oh. What the hell." He sighed. "This thing's clearly bigger than me. What does this mean for Brandi…and me, I guess?"

Brandi answered. "To start with, I'm handing in my notice at work tomorrow."

Ron's eyes opened wide in surprise.

"Don't worry though, Ron, the 'Salvation Army' will now be paying me *twice* what I make at the Kanata Research Park, and all I have to do is keep volunteering the odd evening and some weekends at the CHEO."

"And during the days?" Ron queried.

"Well, for the first month Deheune will be mentoring me, and I'll be taking short trips to meet and integrate with other members of the 'healing team.'"

"Mentoring?" asked Ron. He looked at Deheune. "So you're a healer as well?"

"Yes. But apparently not nearly as powerful as Brandi. You guys seemed to have tapped into something very potent with your resolution." She shot Ron a lewd look that caused him to blush. "Additionally, I'll be teaching Brandi the art of deception and exfiltration, so she can operate unnoticed in a variety of situations and circumstances."

Ron frowned. "That all sounds a bit…clandestine."

"Yes, it is, Ron. You *are* a quick study. Our work has to be done surreptitiously or we risk exposure, and with that, the full force of a diseased and desperate world and the highly entitled crashing through our front door. Neither of which would be helpful to our cause."

Ron nodded his head, starting to get the point. He had been very concerned about what would happen if Brandi's skills became common knowledge. These guys had been dealing with this issue, and apparently successfully managing it, for years. "So how long has this 'healing team' been around?" he asked.

"Since 1865, Ron." She paused to allow Ron some time to appreciate this date. "The Salvation Army was actually created as the public front for our secretive healing group, and was based on the same tenets of compassion and provision for the sick and needy amongst us. Think of the Salvation Army, as you know it, as the storefront, and what Brandi and the healing team do as what goes on in the back room. As the public Salvation Army has evolved over the last century and a half, so have we. We are extremely well-funded, and limited only by the number of gifted individuals who are capable of healing ministrations." She paused for a couple of seconds, and then added, "As well as various other gifts."

She then lovingly turned to look at Brandi. "That why Brandi's discovery is so important to us. Our numbers have been diminishing over the last few years, without any truly capable recruits, such as Brandi, to replace them."

"And what's my part in all this?" asked Ron

"You," Deheune replied, "just have to sit there and look good. And keep Brandi 'happy', if you catch my meaning?"

He did, and could feel the crimson blush of embarrassment returning to his face.

Saturday, November 14

"No. I'm sorry. We've made up our minds," Brandi replied in response to Dr. Fiona's pleas to reconsider making the trip to meet with the peer-review panel at the *Journal of Sex Research* in Whitehall, Pennsylvania.

Dr. Fiona had been more than a little disappointed by the news that Brandi had decided against meeting with the *JSR* board. Over the last half hour she had repeatedly queried Brandi and Ron about the reasons for the change of heart, without getting any explanation from them other than "we just can't," which only served to frustrate her further. Finally she offered to bring the *JSR* panel to Ottawa to accommodate them. To this concession, Brandi simply shook her head no.

The reality was, from the moment Brandi signed onto the secret arm of the Salvation Army, there would never be any further dissemination of Brandi's skills, either informally amongst friends and family, or formally, such as that which Dr. Fiona had proposed with the *JSR* panel in Whitehall. The name of the game now was uncompromising, absolute discretion, and total secrecy. The consequence of which, at this moment, was Dr. Fiona being dumbfounded and exasperated.

"Well, that's the best I can do for you guys," she said to Brandi and Ron. "You've obviously made up your mind on this. Good luck to you both, and remember— I'm here if you need any help with the resolution, or even afterwards." She stood and shook hands with them in farewell.

After Ron and Brandi had left, Dr. Fiona sat pondering their unexpected change of heart. Something just didn't feel right to her. As recently as last week, Brandi had been on board with the proposal, and had even agreed on the date and travel plans. No, there was more to this than newly discovered cold feet. Clearly, they were being evasive as to the actual reasons for their change of heart, and that really bothered Dr. Fiona since, up to this point, they had enjoyed a very open and productive relationship.

She had been dumped. She figured it was somehow tied to Brandi's work at the CHEO and the recent publicizing of the miraculous events she knew Brandi was responsible for. But what exactly had happened?

Then she suddenly realized that someone else must have connected the dots. She'd been supplanted, and from the determined resolve with which the couple had just dismissed her, the supplanter *must* be a formidable force. But were these forces directed by personal and selfish motives, or were they benevolent and altruistic in nature?

The uncertainty fueled a growing anxiety in her, to the point where she couldn't take it any longer. She picked up her phone and called Brandi.

Brandi picked up on the first ring. "Hi, Dr. Fiona. Is something wrong?"

"That's what *I'm* calling about Brandi," replied Dr. Fiona. "I've figured out that someone or some organization has contacted you over the last week or so." She let that comment hang for a second, allowing Brandi an opportunity to refute her hypothesis. She did not, so Dr. Fiona continued. "I have to know. Are you and Ron OK, and are these people looking out for you? I mean… you're not being forced to do this, are you?"

Brandi considered her response. "Dr. Fiona. You can rest assured, Ron and I are in good hands." She left it at that.

"I'm so relieved to hear that, Brandi," Dr. Fiona responded, tears welling-up in her eyes. "Good luck to you and Ron, then. I'll be looking out for your work—as discreet as it's likely to be."

"Thank you Dr. Fiona." She hung up, and looked at her curious husband.

"Well?" Ron asked. "What did our disappointed advisor have to say?"

"She just called to wish us good luck."

Thursday, November 19

"Ron! It's so good to see you again." Dr. Kaur smiled enthusiastically, and executed a two-handed shake with Ron. "Come in, come in. Tell me what brings you here."

Not waiting for a reply, the doctor continued his conversation as Ron entered the examination room and sat. "I have to tell you, I've been following you and your lovely wife's journey on *@lovejunkie*'s blog. Most fascinating, and, may I say, uplifting and inspiring as well. My wonderful wife follows it like a soap opera." The doctor paused, and a lewd smile grew on his face, complete with waggling eyebrows. "I can tell you that, without even one single doubt, sexual interaction with my darling spouse has not only increased in frequency, but the level of enthusiasm with which the act is conducted has materially improved as well. I owe you and your wife some most heartfelt thanks."

He stood beside Ron, smiling affectionately down on him, for about ten seconds; then he snapped out of his euphoric state, and asked, "So then, what can I do for you today, Ron?"

Ron waited the requisite few seconds, making sure Dr. Kaur was finished speaking, before he started answering. However, much to his surprise, when he tried to explain, he had trouble getting the words out.

After a couple of his false starts, Dr. Kaur nodded, and solemnly stated, "It's the penis again, isn't it Ron?"

Ron nodded.

"OK then. Let's have a look at the overworked old boy."

Ron turned his back to Dr. Kaur, undid his belt, slipped his pants and undies down below his crotch and turned back to the doctor.

"Good God, man!" Dr. Kaur exclaimed, with a look of incredulity. "That is the worst case of contact dermatitis I have ever seen! How in the world did you get it on your penis? What have you been in contact with? Tell me you're not using a trendy new poison-ivy scrub or lubricant as part of your normal sexual practices?"

He snapped on a pair of blue latex gloves and went in for a closer examination. "Does it hurt? It certainly looks painful," he asked, glancing up at Ron with an aggrieved look.

"It's itchy to the point of burning."

Dr. Kaur nodded his head, and tsked-tsked a few times in response. "So tell me how you got, this Ron."

Ron explained that he had started experiencing a rash about a week before, and hadn't thought much of it at first. He just figured he needed to change out his workout gear more frequently, and shower immediately after exercise, instead of waiting until he got home that evening. Or maybe he needed to buy a new jock for hockey. But it had gotten worse...and so, here he was.

(He didn't tell Dr. Kaur that, initially, he had mentioned the rash to Brandi, and she had offered to "fix" it for him, but he had declined, and had attempted to "play through the pain" for the first few days, until the condition had worsened to the point that intercourse was virtually impossible. With the resolution on the line, Ron had swallowed his pride and gone back to Brandi with hat in hand, requesting a healing ministration. He'd woken up as good as new the next morning, and he and Brandi had immediately made up for lost time, catching up on the small arrears in which, because of Ron's affliction, they had found themselves concerning the resolution. However, by mid-afternoon that same day Ron had felt a familiar itching once again emanating from his groin, and was horrified to see that the rash had returned, and was literally spreading before his eyes. That had been yesterday.)

"So nothing out of the ordinary? No new lubricants or anything like that?" asked Dr. Kaur.

Ron shook his head.

"And no contact with anything unhygienic?"

Ron shook his head again.

Dr. Kaur pondered this information. Eventually he looked at Ron and said, "Well, Ron, my friend, I hate to be the bearer of bad news, but you have apparently become allergic to your wife."

After Ron had ceased with his sputtering and single-word questions, Dr. Kaur explained. "You see Ron, contact dermatitis doesn't happen immediately. There must be sufficient contact to change the properties of the outer layer of skin." The doctor paused and looked over his glasses at Ron. "And there has been a *lot* of contact, Ron." He nodded his head for a few seconds, and continued. "Once the skin has been sensitized to a particular allergen, it will remember it, and activate the immune system whenever you come in contact with the allergen again."

Ron quickly saw the implications of what Dr. Kaur was suggesting. "You mean I'm *always* going to be allergic to Brandi?"

"Maybe yes, or maybe no. These late-life allergic sensitivities can disappear after a period of non-exposure, and can be partially controlled with antihistamines."

"But...but, what about the resolution?" whined Ron.

"My friend, I am already way ahead of you on that front. I shall provide you with a most effective topical agent for you to apply immediately and liberally. That should speed your recovery. When the old boy is back in fighting shape, I also have the ways and means for you to carry on and succeed with your noble quest."

Ron looked at him, somewhat relieved to hear the doctor's supportive words.

While Ron sat waiting for further details, Dr. Kaur evacuated his seat and the examination room. He came back about a minute later. "I hold in my hand the key to your successful completion of the resolution, Ron," he said, and held it up for him to see.

Ron involuntarily groaned. He hated condoms.

&

Later that night, after explaining Dr. Kaur's prognosis and suggested remedy to the problem, Brandi, trying to stifle her laughs, commented, "Come on, Ron, it won't be that bad."

"Maybe not for you," he sulked.

"Look at the bright side of this."

"There's a bright side?"

"You won't have to wait a couple weeks for that...that whatever-that-is to heal before you can get yourself back in the game. I'll take your matter into my hands again, and you'll be as good as new tomorrow."

That brought a smile to Ron's face.

"And maybe tomorrow you can break-out a blue pill and we can have a nice romantic evening," she added, kissing Ron on the mouth. "Complete with massage and a hot bubble bath. I'll even throw some dancing in for you."

"Topless?" shyly asked Ron.

Brandi nodded.

"With your sexy undies that your husband bought for you?"

Brandi nodded again.

Ron pursed his lips and furrowed his brow, *faux*-seriously assessing Brandi's offer. "OK" He nodded, and then offered his hand to shake on it. "It's a deal."

As he was rolling off the bed, Brandi called from behind him. "Hold on!"

Ron stopped a few steps from the bed and spun around. "What?"

"*You* may be out of commission, but I'm not. You get yourself back into this bed and see to your woman's needs."

Sighing loudly, he bowed his head, and started shuffling back towards the bed.

"All I ask is, *please*, keep your underwear on."

Sunday, November 22

Deheune had been spending some serious time with Brandi over the last couple of weeks, and a bond between them had quickly grown. Tonight Deheune had been invited over to the Sunday family meal to meet Ron's parents for the first time.

They sat around the dining table, with Abby grilling Brandi and Deheune as to the specifics of Brandi's new job.

"Well it certainly does sound like an interesting job, Brandi," Abby finally said. "You won't mind the travel?" The question was meant for Brandi, but Abby was looking at Ron when she asked the question.

"No, not at all," replied Brandi. "I'm looking forward to it, actually. I haven't travelled that much, and now having the opportunity to do so with work is a bonus."

Abby cast a slightly veiled disparaging look at Deheune, and then looked at Ron.

"I'm fine with it, Mom. It's a great opportunity for Brandi. I'm excited for her."

"So Reykjavik this Wednesday; for how long?" Abby asked Brandi, some of the fight having gone out of her.

"We'll be about four days. Back late Sunday evening."

"And what is it you'll be doing?" Abby inquired, not yet willing to drop the issue.

"Maybe I can answer that better," Deheune volunteered. "Our international managers meet fairly regularly to globally coordinate our programs, and I'm training Brandi to eventually take over my position as our Eastern Canadian International Manager. I thought it would be worthwhile she travel with me to these meetings to meet the players and get a feel for the inner workings of the international division."

"You make it sound like the Salvation Army is an international organization. How many countries does it operate in?" Abby inquired, her curiosity temporarily overriding her interrogative mood.

"We're in 127 countries, Mrs. Lee. Brandi has joined a truly international organization. Our mandate is to help all people, no matter where fate has landed them. Brandi has a unique opportunity to benefit people around the world, in ways that most couldn't even imagine." She turned slightly towards Brandi, and surreptitiously offered her a wink.

Thursday, November 26

Brandi and Deheune arrived in Reykjavik just after six in the morning, following a five-hour redeye flight that had departed the night before from Toronto. It was still dark when they arrived, so she spent the majority of the forty-five-minute drive into downtown Reykjavik napping.

She was rousted out of a light sleep at their destination—the Salvation Army Guesthouse, located in the middle of downtown. She noted the tidy, geometrically uniform Icelandic architectural style of the surrounding buildings. The Guesthouse was an imposing four-story classically styled building, bearing the word *Hjálpraedisherinn* emblazoned within the Salvation Army shield. She assumed it meant Salvation Army. The inside of the Guesthouse stayed true to the simple and clean utilitarian style she had noted outside.

Much to her surprise, Deheune spoke the local language fluently, and checked them both in with a twenty-something clerk whom she obviously knew. After the paperwork was completed, the young lady behind the desk smiled at Brandi, welcomed her, and wished her a pleasant stay.

The Guesthouse had reserved the entire top floor for the members of Deheune's group, to provide them with the required privacy for their meetings during the next few days. As they walked up the main stairway, Brandi guessed, "Fifty rooms?"

"Close," replied Deheune. "Fifty-eight, with a ninety-person capacity. It's the only Salvation Army Guesthouse anywhere in the world, and our 'healing group' gathers here at least once a year. We typically book the entire top floor, and sleep and meet there for the three days we're here. You'll love the view when the sun eventually rises. It overlooks the downtown and our *Tjornin*—that means "the pond"—which lies at the centre of downtown."

"So, I'm going to meet the other members of the 'healing group' over the next few days?"

"Indeed you will, Brandi." Deheune looked her in the eyes. "You will, in fact, meet every other healer affiliated with our Organization *today*."

"And how many are we?"

"Including you and myself, Brandi…" She paused. "We number seven."

Brandi couldn't hide her surprise at hearing how few healers from around the world there actually were.

Deheune noted her surprise and said, "Yes, Brandi. There are precious few of us in the world. This should give you a better appreciation for how rare your talent is, and how valuable it is to us. And a feel for the extremes those who desire power would go to to control you and your fellow healers."

Upon reaching the fourth floor, Brandi and Deheune found their rooms, and fumbled with their keys to open the doors. As Brandi was entering her room, Deheune shouted out that they would be meeting in about an hour, at nine o'clock, in the conference room at the end of the hall. Brandi swung her head out into the hall and nodded so Deheune could see she had heard.

She turned the lights on in her room, and found, not surprisingly, that it was small, boxy, and drab, with a single bed off to one side. The good news was it had a washbasin and toilet, but she'd have to track down the outside showers before nine o'clock to wash the travel grime off her.

After a few minutes she grabbed a towel and her toiletries and went searching. She found the showers at the end of the hallway, opposite the conference room. There were no gender signs, so she assumed they were unisex. When she entered, she encountered a large, older, black woman, fixing her substantial hair in front of one of the small aged mirrors in the changing area.

When Brandi entered, the woman spun around and smiled, revealing the brightest set of perfect teeth Brandi had ever seen. "You must be the Canadian girl we've heard about," she stated, more than asked, in a deep, rolling central-African accent that sang the words as much as spoke them.

Brandi smiled back, and nodded. "I'm Brandi Lee from Ottawa." She offered her hand as she advanced towards the lady.

The lady shook her hand and said, "I'm Muteteli Manishimye. Pleasure to meet you." Her smile was transfixing. "I'm very much looking forward to spending some time with you over the next few days, Brandi."

"Me as well, Muteteli," Brandi replied, involuntarily smiling more broadly than usual.

"I guess I'll see you at nine. Ta ta for now, then, dear," Muteteli chirped as she headed for the door.

Following a reinvigorating shower, Brandi used some down time to read emails from Ron, and write back her initial thoughts of her travel so far. She didn't expect Ron to be up, since Ottawa was four hours behind, but he would enjoy the read when he woke. Absorbed in her emails, she hadn't realized she was late for her first meeting until there was a knock on her door. Glancing at her watch, she jumped up and opened the door to her room, to see Deheune standing there.

"Why don't you join us, Brandi? Everybody's anxious to meet you."

Trailing Deheune, and muttering apologetically about her unpunctuality, she entered the conference room, which had seven chairs in the middle, and five faces staring back at her. Recognizing Muteteli, she smiled and waved at her. Brandi noted there was only one male in the group.

"Sorry I'm late, everybody. I'm not used to this international travel and I'm a bit slow this morning."

"Not to worry, Brandi," replied Deheune. "Please grab yourself a muffin and some coffee," she gestured at a table stocked with foodstuff and various morning beverages, "and join us in the circle."

Fortified with some food and a black coffee, Brandi sat in the one open seat, directly to the right of Deheune, who then called the meeting to order.

"Today I'm very happy to introduce Brandi Fuller Lee to you all. I know you've heard a lot about her, so I'm sure you'll be pleased to be able to put a face to the name and get to know her. And vice versa," she added, looking at Brandi.

Brandi nodded.

"But before we get going, I think it's important that I discuss the reason for this meeting, and for Brandi's benefit let everybody introduce themselves, and recount their own narrative of how they find themselves sitting here today.

"You see Brandi, the fact that we're all here today is a bit of a miracle," she giggled at the use of the word, "and a positive testament to the effectiveness of the Organization to promptly recognize and protect 'healers' anywhere in the world—before darker forces can become involved." She paused, and looked around the small group. "And I can assure you, Brandi, there *are* darker forces at work.

"Our objective over these next few days is for you to better understand the goals of our Organization and become familiar with all the skillsets within our healing group, to discuss short, medium, and long-term strategies and targets for our deployment, and to share techniques that can augment our existing skillsets.

"But before we get going, I think it's very important that each of you introduce yourselves and your background, describe the event or events that awoke the 'gift' within you, and the extent of each of your abilities.

"As we discussed earlier, Brandi, as a common thread, each one of these individuals either is, or is hereditarily related to, the seventh daughter of a seven daughter. But each has had her or his gift uniquely activated by a profound event."

Muteteli was sitting to Deheune's left. Deheune turned to her to begin.

"First of all," Muteteli said, "I've already met Brandi, in the showers this morning, and I can tell you she radiates the 'gift.' On top of this, she's a lovely and polite young lady. Just what you'd expect from a Canadian." The group chuckled. "I can tell we're going to be good friends. Most of you have heard my story, so I'll stick to the most relevant aspects if I may?" She looked at Deheune to gain approval for this approach. Deheune nodded.

"I was born in Cellule Kanatome in Central Rwanda in 1948," Muteteli began, "and lived there, peacefully farming and tending our herds with my family, until about twenty years ago, when the Rwandese Patriotic Front invaded my village and began killing all the Tutsi they could find. I'm of Tutsi ancestry, so my family and I were targeted. There was much tragedy that day, but the one event that I think likely triggered my gift occurred after the militia had broken down the front door to the church, in which we had locked ourselves, and were systematically hacking everyone inside to death with machetes. While these men were taking turns raping me, they made me watch as they killed and decapitated my mother and my youngest daughter. At that very moment, I *felt* a flash of light consume me, and something far greater than me awaken within me. Once everyone else lay dead, these men mercilessly hacked at me until they believed me dead, too, and then left to continue their homicidal carnage elsewhere.

"I should have died there and then, but somehow, I survived and healed quickly, my scars now only thin lines where gaping wounds previously existed." She held out her arms, which were crisscrossed with thin scars. "I knew I had irrevocably changed from that moment, and quickly realized I was able to help heal people, and, consequently, have been doing just that since that day."

Brandi sat transfixed, and only after Muteteli's extended silence, signalling the end of her story, did she become aware that she had tears streaming down her cheeks.

"Thank you, Muteteli," Deheune said. "I know you gain strength every time you recount that story, as painful as it is. So you know, Brandi, Muteteli join our Organization in 1999. It took us a little longer to track her down in Rwanda."

Deheune now turned to the young honey blonde sitting beside Muteteli, and motioned to her to impart her story to the group.

"Hi Brandi," the blonde said. "It's good to meet with you. My name is Leana Hansen, and I was born in 1990 in a small town called Firgårde, in central Denmark. It's the lake district of Denmark, which is ironic, since I'm here today because I drowned." She chuckled as she recalled this. "It was a warm July day in 2006, and I was repeatedly diving to the bottom of the lake to see what I could find and retrieve to the surface. While I was at the lake bottom, looking up into the brilliantly sunny day some thirty feet above me, all the colours went brilliantly white. I could make out the definition of everything around me with a sharpness that hurt my eyes; but still, everything was brilliant white. I couldn't tell at the time how long I gazed upon this wonder. In my mind it could have been ten seconds or the rest of my life, but when it ended I was on the beach, surrounded by a crowd of people hysterically yelling, with the normal colours of the summer's day having returned. I recall people exclaiming, 'She's alive!' and, 'It's a miracle!' I felt completely normal and fine.

"From that day I started to realize that I was particularly sensitive to the emotions of everyone around me, and when I focused—which I'm still learning to do, since I probably suffer from ADD," she smiled sheepishly as she said this, "I can precisely read people's minds. I was in Oslo in 2012, and had just won my third international WPT open poker tournament, when Deheune approached me and convinced me to join the Organization."

After Leana nodded, signalling the end of her story, the only man in the group, to Leana's left, spoke up.

"Pleasure to meet you, Miss Brandi," he said in a thick Asian accent. "Please excuse my English. Still learning. Is not very good, but I will try to tell story." He smiled politely. "My name is Hiroto Tanaka. I am now thirty-four years old. Both parents were accidentally killed when I was only three years old. Because of no money, my family relatives could not help me, so I become youngest monk in Shingon Koyasan Buddhist Temple on Mount Koya, near Osaka. Since beginning, every day was filled with meditations and hard work. My mentor—Yukei Matsunaga, now head priest—want to protect me. He become my new father. He saw that by when I am twelve I could..." he paused, looking for the correct words, "...help sick plants to be better. By time I was eighteen, I was able to cure big old trees that surround our temple when they become sick. When I am twenty-three, I can wake up birds that fly into temple windows. After the venerable Yukei Matsunaga saw me many times help these birds, he called me to his office and tell me that I have 'gift.' He said this 'gift' could grow bigger, so I can help many more things in world. He said it was his and my *duty* to grow this 'gift.' A week after we talk, the venerable Yukei Matsunaga again called me to his office where I meet Deheune," he nodded and smiled at her, "for first time." He exhaled loudly, took a deep breath, and continued. "Since then I have worked with this healing group and have become much stronger."

"Thank you, Hiroto," Deheune said, taking over the conversation. "Hiroto's mother was the seventh daughter of a seventh daughter, and his trigger to becoming a healer has solely been his meditation. Over the last decade he's used his meditation to advance his skills, and can now sometimes help heal people. That said, he remains the undisputed champion gardener within the group." The entire circle erupted in laughter.

After a short pause, the small older lady to the left of Hiroto began telling her story. "My name is Yatzil of the Wixáritari people from central-western Mexico. I was born in 1952, so that makes me..." she looked up and started to do some math concerning her age. Unable to do the calculus on the spot, she emphatically stated "Old!" When the laughing died down, she continued. "There has always been a tradition of woman healers in my family. My grandmother, my auntie, and my mother were all healers. We believe this power comes from the peyote plant that grows in our territory. How do I know this? Because every year my people journey back to a sacred place called Wirikuta, where we regenerate our souls. This is where the peyote plant grows, and we use it to speak to our ancestor's spirits and the Gods who control our fate, and have our questions about life answered. It was after my first peyote ritual when I realized that something had changed in me. The power was there from that beginning, but as I learned more about this power and my confidence grew, the full potential of this gift was revealed.

"I had been quietly healing people from my tribe for about thirty years when Deheune rode into my village and told me about how I could use my gift more effectively and to the benefit of all people. It was an offer I couldn't say no to."

"And that was nearly twenty years ago," commented Deheune, smiling lovingly at Yatzil. "To be clear, Brandi, Yatzil doesn't heal the physical body. She heals the spirit."

Over the last twenty minutes, the conversation had moved clockwise around the small circle, and now shifted to the very tall thirty-something blond directly to Brandi's right. Having arrived late, and immediately diving into the proceedings, Brandi hadn't yet had the chance to appreciate just how striking this woman beside her was. Although she was sitting down, Brandi estimated she was well over six feet tall; maybe closer to seven. She smiled at Brandi. Her features were remarkable, with sharply defined, prominent cheeks, a long, slender nose, and an elongated face unlike any she had ever seen. Curious to hear this person's story, Brandi sat up in her chair, her eyes locked on this strange beauty beside her.

"My pleasure to meet you, Brandi," the woman said, her accent unmistakably Slavic. Her voice was strangely musical, and incongruous against her imposing physicality. "My name is Snežana Bogdanovic. My friends call me Sneezy," she added, casting Brandi an affectionate look. "I was born in southern Serbia, in a small town called Leskova. Beautiful but boring. What's a girl to do? Move away, of course! So, when I was seventeen, I moved to the big city of Novi Pazar, where there were many people, thriving businesses, and a nightlife. Everything a young girl needs to properly develop—yes? I settled into a good job working at a popular nightclub in the downtown, eventually found a man brave enough to date me, and created a very comfortable life for myself. And there I would have stayed if it wasn't for my death." She let that comment hang for dramatic effect.

"I attribute my death to my height. I was the only one on staff who could reach a burnt-out bulb without dragging a stool over. As it turned out, the bulb was fine. It was the wiring that was faulty. And I had been padding around in the bar barefooted—so people wouldn't have to crane their heads so much upwards to talk to me—and we had just cleaned up from a rainstorm the night before; so the floor was still damp and…well…you can guess how that story ends. The unusual part was that I lay dead for about twenty-five minutes, and resisted any and all attempts to revive me—so I am told. It was when they were trying to wrestle my body into the body bag—this was the second attempt, since the first bag they used was too small for me—that I suddenly awoke, sat up, and desperately drew in a lung full of air. This is the part from which I do remember. All these people were standing around me open-mouthed and speechless. I've always evoked strange reactions from people, but *this* was over the top!"

She paused again, absorbing the attention of her fellow healers. "I certainly felt a bit off for a few days afterwards. A kind of dizziness that wouldn't go away. It got to the point where I went to a local doctor in search of remedy. While waiting in his examination room, I noticed a large beetle lying dead against one of the walls. I've always been obsessively clean, so I picked it off the floor to throw in the garbage." As she said this, she unconsciously demonstrated the act of picking the beetle up. Brandi was surprised at just how long and slender her fingers were. "But before I could release it into the bin, it resuscitated in my hands. I dropped it to the ground, and it skittered under the examination table. *How odd*, I was thinking to myself just as the old doctor entered the room. He was a particularly wizened ancient individual and, I thought, probably needed help worse than I did. He examined me, and said this was a normal response to being electrocuted. Eventually, he gave me some tranquilizers to get me through my recovery period.

"I was already out the door when I heard a scream coming from his office. I ran back in to find his nurse and a terrified older lady standing over the rigid body of the old doctor I had just visited. His colour was chalk, his eyes were open, and he was clutching at his unmoving chest. I had no first-aid training, but thought that shifting him from the floor to his examination table seemed like a reasonable course of action. This, I did by myself. After I placed the old physician on his table, I noticed some colour had come back to his face, and his death grimace had softened. I looked down to see I was still holding his arm, and when I looked back up at his face he had improved further. Seconds later he blinked, drew a short breath, and started to stir. Within minutes he was sitting up, still dazed, but speaking again.

"This was the moment when I first realized that things were not as they were. And that I may have the ability to reverse death itself." She stoically looked around the circle. "I had become a necromancer.

"Over the course of the next six years I intersected death a number of times, and if I'm honest with you all, searched it out, so I could disappoint the Grim Reaper whenever possible. I might or might not have continued in that manner, but, as fate would have it, Deheune tracked me down and convinced me to join the Organization seven years ago." She paused again before delivery of her final admission. "If only my friends from Leskova could see me now."

"But of course they won't, Sneezy," Deheune interjected, signalling the end of her loquacious compatriot's narrative.

Deheune now looked at Brandi. "Brandi, perhaps you could now tell your story about how you have ended up here within this small circle of exceptional people today."

Brandi knew this was coming, but she was still overwhelmed with a sense of inadequacy after hearing the stories of her fellow healers, and was now a bit embarrassed by the manner by which her gift had been triggered. She noticed that it was getting lighter outside, and, glancing out the slanted windows to her right, glimpsed the tidy low-rise rectangular buildings of downtown emerging from the greyness of the night. She took a deep breath, smiled at the group, and began.

About fifteen minutes later she finished up with her narrative. Part of Brandi had felt like she was bragging when she stated the laundry list of skills that she had quickly developed over the last few months: astral projection, mind reading, consciousness transfer, and, most significantly, healing of very sick people. But the practical side of her knew this was the one gathering where it wasn't bragging. Everybody in this group *had* to be fully aware of what their peers were capable of. That knowledge was integral to the effective planning of future interventions.

"So, what started out as a simple couple's challenge has inadvertently led to the triggering of *my* 'gift'," she concluded.

"I knew there was more to sex than a good time and procreating," Snežana commented. "I'm very anxious to learn from you about this, Brandi," she added.

"Since our first encounter, Deheune has been working with me to help fine-tune my 'gifts', and develop a strategy that would allow me to continue volunteering at the Children's Hospital without being exposed," Brandi stated, winding up her story.

As she waited for Deheune to intercede, she noticed for the first time that the interior wall was filled with photographs of women, each with a small plaque which appeared to indicate the year of birth and death. It was obviously a memorial wall.

Deheune saw Brandi scanning the wall of photographs, and said, "Those are memorials to all the healers from this group who have passed. It is the one vanity that we allow ourselves, since it is in tribute to those who gave so much of their lives to the benefit of mankind." She paused briefly. "Mankind may not be the most appropriate word since, as I'm sure you've noticed by now, 'healers' are overwhelmingly female. There have been precious few males like our Hiroto," she gestured at him, "who have ever been gifted. There appears to be a fundamental difference between the minds of men and woman, and it's been our experience that it takes an *extra* extraordinary man to develop the 'gift'." She glanced again at Hiroto, who acknowledged her compliment with a modest nod.

"But enough of that. Let me finish the introductions by imparting my story. I don't think any of you have ever heard it, and it will add an extra dimension to the discussions we've been having today."

She looked around at the gathering. "I was born in the Eastern Townships of Quebec in 1943." She paused, and turned to Yatzil. "If you're old, what does that make me?" Everyone around the circle smiled, and visibly relaxed. "I can trace my lineage back to the Abenaki First Nations, who inhabited these lands before the British and French colonized the region. The Abenaki originally sided with the French, and the 'greatest' grandmother in my traceable lineage was born from this union. When the Irish Catholics immigrated to Lower Canada in the 1820s, these two pedigrees intertwined, and flourished in the rich farmlands south of the St. Lawrence River.

"In true Catholic tradition, the families that followed consisted of no fewer than a dozen children in *every* subsequent generation of my immediate family tree. In these families, the proportion of female children born was peculiar and, given the need for sturdy hard-working bodies on the farm, a stubborn source of frustration for my lineal ancestors. So typical were female births that during the five-generation period from when my Irish descendants landed to when I was born, only four males had ever been born in an overall tally of seventy-six births.

"As you can probably guess—since it is the one common thread that binds us all today—this lineage did in fact experience the improbable occurrence of having two successive generations where a seventh daughter was born of a seventh daughter. Although rare—as we all have experienced—it is not unheard of. What makes me different, however, is that *I* am an unbroken *third*-generation seventh daughter—a seventh daughter of a seventh daughter of a seventh daughter. *This* was my trigger event.

"I was *born* with the 'gift', and remember having it from my first memory. I have always been extremely sensitive to people's emotions, and able to read minds. Under certain circumstances, I can reverse death in animals and heal people. But I am a generalist; a Jill of all trades, so to speak. My gifts are nowhere as developed as each of you are in your own 'specialties'. And my gift came with a cost. I was born sterile. It appears that the genetic process at work is, by nature, self-limiting."

Deheune paused for a moment to collect her thoughts. Looking up and around at the small group, she tenderly stated, "You all here today are my family."

After a short pause, while Deheune regained her normal stoic composure, she added, "I think that's a great place to take a break. I've got things to attend to, so why don't you all take Brandi for a quick tour of downtown so she can stretch her legs and shake off the jet lag. Let's meet back in about a half hour and we'll continue on with our agenda."

Friday, November 27

"Why don't you go see your doctor if it's bugging you that much?" asked Scott.

He was sitting with Ron at the Bassline Pub downloading the events of the week, but Ron's distraction with his "ailment" was a persistent interruption to their conversation.

"I did," replied Ron. "About a week ago." He stopped, and surreptitiously scratched his groin.

"So, what's the problem?"

"It appears that I've developed an allergic reaction to Brandi."

"What? Can that even happen?" incredulously asked Scott.

"Apparently it can. The worst part is that I have to use condoms now."

"You're joking. You poor bastard," replied Scott, uncharacteristically sympathetic. "It's a good thing you can see the finish line for this resolution, or I bet you'd be having second thoughts about finishing it."

"That did occur to me, to be honest with you. But you know me and finishing my resolutions. I wasn't going to let this stop me."

"But if you've already been to the doctor and are using condoms, why's it still bugging you?"

"That's a good question. Given I have an in-house healer, I only had to wait a day to remedy the situation after I got back from the doctor. As undesirable as the condom fix was, it kept the resolution on track. Problem was, around Wednesday the rash came back with a vengeance, and being without access to my healer, I've been generously applying the cream the doctor gave me last week—to absolutely no avail."

"Sounds grim, mate. What's next?"

"I'm back to see Dr. Kaur later this evening. I don't know what else to do." He took a sip of beer. "The beer seems to help, though."

"Beer makes everything better, my friend," Scott proclaimed, lifting his mug in a toast. Then he quietly added, "Hey. Brandi's becoming quite the *shadow* celebrity. I've been following the story about the miracles at the CHEO. And Ron," Scott paused here for emphasis, "it took me about six nanoseconds to figure out Brandi was responsible for these 'miracles.'"

"Well, no one else knows about Brandi's skills—other than you and Elise and Dr. Fiona. And we're going to keep it that way. OK?"

"Absolutely, Ron. It doesn't take a rocket surgeon to figure out how things would quickly go pear-shaped if this became public knowledge. By the way, how's Brandi's new job with the Salvation Army working out? It looks as if she's hit the ground running already, travelling with her position. Where is she this week?"

"She's in Reykjavik, Iceland."

"Wow. They must have really liked what they saw in her."

"I can tell you, they certainly appreciate her skillset," Ron replied, nodding his head.

As Scott was sipping his beer, Ron saw his eyes widen, and him connect the dots again concerning Brandi, her newfound skills, and the recent change of employment. Ron looked seriously at him and said, "Don't even go there, Scott," while shaking his head.

ॐ

Ron pulled into Dr. Kaur's office a bit later than usual, but the hardworking physician still cheerfully greeted him in his waiting area. "Ron, so good to see you again. But your return is sooner than I would have hoped for. I can only guess that things have not improved as expected?"

Ron nodded.

"Oh my," muttered Dr. Kaur. "Well, come into the examination room and let's see if we find some relief for you."

Once they were both seated in the examination room, Dr. Kaur began. "So, Ron, has the cream not worked on your rash?"

Ron had to measure his response, since he couldn't bring Brandi's quick-fix approach into the discussion. "The cream worked great, Dr. Kaur. The rash cleared up to the point where I could resume the resolution again using a condom after a few days. But even using the condom, the rash has returned. This time it feels worse than ever."

"OK, let's have another look at your tuckered-out tallywhacker, Ron," Dr. Kaur asked, as he went searching for some latex gloves in the adjacent drawer.

Ron carefully slipped his pants down around his ruined member and waited for the doctor to examine it. Dr. Kaur, unable to find any gloves where he was looking, called out behind him as he exited the examination room that he'd be "right back," leaving Ron with his thoughts and his almost-unrecognizable phallus, airing out in the still and stuffy tiny room. *How in the world did I ever end up here? Pants down, with my exposed penis a pustulent, crimson, wrecked remnant of its previous glorious self. Forced to use condoms with my spouse of twenty years. Reduced to the status of a sex slave, while my wife now travels first-class around the world, supported by billionaire backers. I can't even keep any secrets around her anymore. For God's sake, I can't even pee without it hurting anymore.*

Ron's piteous musings were abruptly terminated as Dr. Kaur returned to the examination room. While simultaneously snapping on the blue latex gloves and closing the door with his foot, he cheerfully stated, "OK, let's have a look, Ron."

When his gaze did finally take in Ron's hurting member, he actually jumped back, and exclaimed with a look somewhere between revulsion and disbelief, "Sweet Baby Jesus, man!" He stared at Ron's nether region. "I may have to phone the hazmat team." He cautiously approached Ron, and reluctantly inspected his penis. "Ron, I sincerely hope we won't have to amputate!"

Ron recounted all the events of the past week, except those concerning Brandi's quick fix, and waited for the doctor's prognosis.

"Ron," Dr. Kaur began, "it appears that you have now become allergic to latex. Yours is a particularly bad case, however. *This* is now officially the worst case of contact dermatitis I have ever seen." He squinted, and his head edged closer to Ron's penis, his face pinched as if he had just encountered a particularly noxious fart. "You must stop using latex condoms immediately, my friend. Secondly, you must freely use the cream I gave you. Otherwise, keep it dry. That means avoiding all forms of moisture. And unfortunate for you and your most noble resolution, you will have to take a hiatus from your loving ways until your old boy is fully recovered. That could be weeks, my friend—but be patient. It will get better, I promise you."

Ron was trying to reflect an appropriately glum mood, but he knew that he would be back in the saddle early next week, immediately after Brandi's return. *What then?* he thought. "After I've recovered, what do you recommend? You know...so I can complete the resolution."

"That's the spirit, Ron!" Dr. Kaur exclaimed. "There are a number of latex-free options, including polyurethane or polyisoprene, but..." Dr. Kaur paused, and quietly thought further. "But you know, Ron, given the extreme reaction you've suffered using latex, and given the limited time and the current setback that you've suffered concerning the resolution, we should not even risk you contacting anything chemically derived that starts with 'poly.' I'm going to recommend natural skin condoms for you. They're 100-percent natural, and will do the trick for sure."

"What are they made of, Dr. Kaur?"

"Well, they are made from lambs," the doctor cautiously explained.

"Lambs?" queried Ron. "Lambskin?"

"Not exactly, Ron. They are made from the intestines of lambs." He noted the growing look of disgust on Ron's face and quickly added, "But don't dwell on that, Ron. The important thing is getting you better, and able to complete the resolution, my friend. You are so close. The fact that a few lambs must be sacrificed for the cause is inconsequential. You must remember the bigger picture."

Ron visualized a flock of colostomy bag-wearing sheep despondently grazing in an open field. He sat rather deflated across from Dr. Kaur. The thought of slipping on lamb's intestine every time he wanted to have sex felt more like punishment than pleasure.

"Cheer up, Ron," consoled Dr. Kaur. "You are almost there."

Sunday, November 29

Ron and Sam were at the airport to welcome Brandi back home. They were both excited to hear how it went. Ron knew there would be one story for Sam, and a much more interesting one for him.

Brandi's flight arrived just before eight in the evening, and she quickly made her way to the meeting area by the luggage carousels. They greeted each other with a chorus of "Hey!", "Hi, Mom!", "Hi Babe!", and a round of hugs and kisses.

"How was Iceland, Mom?" asked Sam. "It's so cool you get to travel with your new job. I want to travel with my work when I grow up."

"It was amazing. I'll tell you guys all about it in the car on the drive back home."

After about an hour at home, Brandi pleaded exhaustion to Sam, and headed upstairs with Ron in tow. Once alone, Ron immediately commented, "I'm anxious to hear what you were really up to, Brandi; if you're not too tired, that is."

"I tell you what. How about I fill you in with some of the details, and you can help me relax with a little bit of resolution catch-up?"

Ron stood there shaking his head.

"What's wrong, Ron?" Brandi asked, knowing Ron never turned down sex; especially this year; especially after a multi-day hiatus.

Ron slowly unzipped his pants and exposed his wounded pride for Brandi to see.

"Yikes!" she exclaimed. "On second thought, maybe just I'll just tell you about the healing group. What the heck happened there?" she inquired, her eyes darting back and forth between Ron's eyes and his dermatologically damaged dink.

"Well, as it turns out, I'm also allergic to latex."

"When did that happen?"

"Recently, or maybe twenty years ago. I don't know for sure, but as you can see, I'm sure allergic to it now."

"Well, first things first. We've got to get Mr. Happy better, and quickly. So, let me wash up and change, and I'll give him some attention."

Afterwards, they lay in bed and talked about recent events.

"So how do you feel about using an all-organic condom for the rest of the year?" Brandi asked.

"I guess it's better than nothing, Brandi, but it'll be a challenge not to think about slipping lamb's gut on my willie every time we have sex," Ron replied.

Brandi nodded sympathetically.

"But I'll guess we'll find out tomorrow if I can get my head around as well as into it."

Brandi nodded again.

"So, do you want to hear about the healing group and their stories?" she excitedly asked. "They're the most amazing people. Really, Ron."

"Absolutely," he replied.

Twenty minutes later, after Brandi had given him a summary of each healer, Ron asked, "So you're the only one who's used sex as a trigger for your gift?"

"Yup. Sex and meditation, more accurately. The other triggers in the group were severe emotional and physical trauma, death—by drowning and electrocution, at least—intense meditation, drug-based spiritual awakening, and three contiguous generations of a seventh daughter."

"That is a rather esoteric group you've joined, Brandi."

"Esoteric and extremely gifted, Ron. We spent part of the time discussing and sharing techniques to enhance our gifts, and, surprise—everyone wanted to learn about how to use sex to get to the next level, and possibly learn some of my skills, as well."

Ron nodded appreciatively. "Well, if I'm ever needed to help out for the betterment of mankind…"

Brandi looked at him, then his groin, then back up at his face. "Ron, if *anyone* of those ladies ever saw that mess, they would become instantly and irreversibly celibate."

The boyish smile on Ron's face melted away into a shameful look.

Brandi let that comment sink in a bit more, and then continued. "Hiroto worked with me concerning some meditation techniques, but he said that I was already a 'master.' How about that?"

Quickly recovering from his shaming, Ron asked, "So who's your favourite in the group?"

"They are all amazing, Ron, but I have a special bond with Deheune, who you know; Sneezy, who blows my mind every time I look at her; and Muteteli, who is the physical embodiment of strength and optimism."

"Will I ever get to meet them?"

"Don't know, dear. Still early days."

Ron nodded, appreciative of her situation. "So what else?" Ron asked, to keep Brandi talking.

"Oh, speaking of Sneezy, and I guess Leana and Muteteli—their triggers were a one-off occurrence. They've done nothing since to nurture, retrigger, or enhance their 'gift'—but regardless, their 'gifts' haven't changed since that singular event."

Ron shook his head that he didn't understand.

"It appears that once the 'gift' is triggered it stays 'on.'"

Ron shook his head again.

"That means we probably don't have to keep up with the resolution to support *my* 'gift.'"

"What are you saying, Brandi?" Ron blurted, clearly upset by her comment. "The resolution is sacrosanct. You know that. It is beyond reproach or compromise. It is its own entity, and a *raison d'être* of the most grandiose and noble nature. And in this case, completely independent of your new life. Whether it does or does not have utilitarian value to your higher calling is completely irrelevant. We will continue and succeed, regardless of all that conspires to defeat us."

Brandi looked down at Ron's groin again. "I was just giving you a way out—if you wanted it. You know I'm good to go, Ron. I'm just worried about you. You're looking a bit beat up these days."

"I'll be good as gold tomorrow, and right back on the horse, my dear. Not to worry," Ron said with exaggerated bravado.

"OK then. Let's get a few feet of lamb's gut lined up for tomorrow, because we've got some catch-up to do, laddo. And baby, nothing... I mean *nothing*... screams sex like animal guts!"

With that, Ron rolled off the bed and took a few steps towards the bathroom. Brandi called out, "Hold on!"

Ron stopped and spun around. "What now?"

"*You* may be out of commission, but I'm not. You get yourself back into this bed and see to your woman's needs. I shouldn't have to have to remind you about this every time, Ron," she said, shaking her head in disappointment.

"What am I? Your sex slave?"

Brandi nodded.

Sighing loudly, Rod shuffled back, head bowed, towards the bed, and crawled onto it.

"All I ask—again—is, *please*, keep your underwear on," Brandi added.

Later, as Ron was falling asleep, Brandi leaned over, kissed him on his shut eye, and said, "By the way, Ron, I'm scheduled to go on my first mission later next week. Goodnight."

Monday, November 30

Ron woke early, well before Brandi was planning to get up. He quietly walked through the dark bedroom into the bathroom, anxious to see the results of Brandi's ministrations the night before. He turned on the lights and checked his groin. *Yeah, baby! Pink and perfect!* he almost said out loud. *Priceless: a MasterCard moment*, he thought, disrobing completely for the shower.

As he walked to work in the cold predawn air, he smiled, and reflected on the journey over the last eleven months.

This damned resolution had turned out to be much harder than he ever could have expected when he had originally proposed it in an attempt to spice up their love life. He knew that his fearless, maybe even reckless, approach to challenges had been his strength and weakness his entire life. His inherent optimism and enthusiasm had often distracted him from fully assessing the harsh realities that opportunistically lurked around the periphery of any unconventional action or novel idea—waiting, like wild animals around a dying fire at night, for their opening to re-establish the status quo. Still, he understood that analytical paralysis deterred innovative thinking. It was his perspective that it was better he take an impetuous risk than be deterred by fear of the unknown, look back in his later years, and wonder what could have been.

Just look at all the good that has come from the resolution, he mused. *Brandi and I are closer than we've ever been. There are thousands of people following us and copying our resolution, and Brandi has developed a miraculous healing ability. We're saving marriages and lives. And I have an excellent new haircut. None of this would have happened without the resolution.*

With the physical setbacks of recent weeks behind him, a mitigation strategy in place, and only a month to go, he was more enthusiastic now about the resolution than he could remember being in recent months.

Just as he got to work he remembered something that Brandi had said to him as he was falling asleep last night. *Something about going on a mission,* was all he could recall.

He'd talk to her about it that night.

CHAPTER 13

TAPPED OUT

Friday, December 4

Brandi had left with Deheune for Sao Paolo, Brazil, late on Thursday evening, and wasn't expected back until Monday or Tuesday. With Scott busy and Sam at a friend's house for the evening, this left Ron alone with his thoughts, which, truth be known, were not his preferred company. He was so desperate that he invited Vanessa, aka *lovejunkie*, over, to update her on the resolution progress.

Ron was relieved to hear the doorbell ring just after seven, and hurriedly answered it, expecting to find the always-delighted Vanessa standing there. But when he opened the door, his polite smile melted away. Instead, a pale blonde giantess was gazing benevolently down on him. Familiarity quickly replaced his shock. From Brandi's recent description of her fellow members in the healing group, this had to be Sneezy.

"Snežana?" he tentatively asked.

"Yes! And you must be Ron. I knew that Brandi would have told you about us. That does make this much easier. How very good of you to have remembered my name."

At that exact moment, the head of a small elderly woman about a foot and a half shorter than Snežana poked out around from behind her compatriot's big body, and smiled brightly at Ron.

"And you must be Yatzil?" guessed Ron.

Her smile grew even wider, indicating Ron was correct again.

"Well, what a pleasure meeting you both. Please, come in."

After Ron settled the two ladies in the living room and had fetched them drinks, (Snežana asked for a glass of room-temperature vodka, while Yatzil requested an herbal tea) he asked the obvious question. "Well, what brings you two ladies around here? You do know that Brandi and Deheune are currently in Brazil?"

"Yes, Ron, we are aware of that. Deheune runs a very tidy ship, and we're aware of everyone's coordinates, and travel plans for all group members, at all times," Snežana replied.

An awkward pause followed when she didn't continue and answer Ron's main query; so once again he asked, "So what brings you two here, to Ottawa? To our house?" He made the question as specific as possible this time.

"This is our first time in Ottawa, Ron." Snežana looked at Yatzil, who nodded enthusiastically at him, "And we are very impressed."

Ron nodded back at them both, an insincere grin growing on his face. He continued nodding.

Eventually Snežana spoke again. "Is it always this warm in wintertime?" she inquired.

Ron now realized that he was not so much in a conversation as he was in a process. Having lived in a government city his entire life, and forced to deal with civil bureaucracy on almost a daily basis he, however, was not unprepared.

"Not always. This fall *has* been unseasonably warm," he replied

Both women nodded appreciatively.

More silence.

Ron held his ground, nodding and smiling.

Yatzil spoke next. "What a lovely house you and Brandi have."

More nodding, and looking around the room.

"And what a lovely neighbourhood."

"Yes, it is," Ron agreed, smiling proudly.

"You still have a daughter living at home. Is she here tonight?" Snežana asked.

"No, she's at a friend's place tonight."

"Good. That's very good," Snežana commented.

After a further pause, Snežana shifted gears and started to get down to business. "So, Ron," she began, "you're probably wondering what we're doing here tonight?"

Still in bureaucratic discourse mode, he dug deep, suppressing a reflexive sarcastic response while keeping his expression neutral. "Yes, I had wondered that," he replied evenly.

"We're here at the request of Deheune," said Yatzil. "She asked us to lead an intervention, Ron."

That got Ron's attention. "An intervention? For whom?"

"Well," Yatzil replied, smiling broadly at him, "for you, Ron."

As Ron's face compressed into a textbook WTF expression, Snežana cheerfully added, "And I thought that we could take the opportunity to talk a bit about your and Brandi's sexual practices. We're both very curious to learn more about them."

With a now impressively contorted face, Ron, rendered not only speechless but effectively soundless, was only able to glance back and forth from Snežana to Yatzil.

Just then, the doorbell rang.

"Oh God. That must be Vanessa," Ron muttered, his ability to verbalize restored. He stood and unconsciously started spinning on the spot while planning his next course of action.

Snežana asked, "Who is Vanessa, Ron?"

Leaving the living room and making his way to the front door, Ron answered over his shoulder, "She's the lady who's blogging about our resolution. She's here so I can update her."

When he opened the door, sure enough, a smiling and clearly excited Vanessa was standing there, rocking back and forth on her feet, barely able to contain her exuberance.

"Hi, Mr. Lee. Thanks so much for having me over tonight. I really do appreciate the opportunity to get updated on the resolution," she blurted before Ron could say anything.

Ron's face reset into one of unfortunate regret. He said, with as much empathy as he could currently muster, "Vanessa, I'm *so* sorry. But some...family has, just now, unexpectedly showed-up and, unfortunately, I won't be able to sit and chat with you tonight."

In response, Vanessa's eyes widened, and her head craned upwards and behind Ron.

"Ron, don't be silly and change your plans on our account. Invite Vanessa in," Snežana calmly suggested over Ron's shoulder. "It would be rude not to after she's come all this way to meet with you."

Before Ron could respond, he felt himself being effortlessly shifted off to one side, as Snežana moved forward to grab Vanessa's hand and draw her into the front hall.

The situation lost, Ron sputtered, "Vanessa, this is Snežana." He felt a poke in his ribs, and glanced around to see Yatzil smiling and also looking for an introduction. "And this is Yatzil."

Vanessa shook hands with both of them.

"They're cousins..."

Vanessa looked back and forth, and up and down, from Snežana's face to Yatzil's a couple of times. The physical contrast could not have been greater.

Thinking on his feet, Ron added, "On Brandi's side." He thought it more likely that Vanessa would accept that explanation, without Brandi present for direct corporeal comparison. He waited a few seconds, and then suggested, "OK, then. Why don't you come in, Vanessa, and maybe we can find a quiet place to talk."

"Nonsense, Ron," Snežana interjected. "We are both well aware of details of the resolution, and would be happy to hear any updates that you and Brandi might have." She moved her long arm around Vanessa's shoulder, and steering her inwards, said, "Come into the living room, my dear." Calling back over her shoulder, she added, "Ron, maybe you could get Vanessa something to drink."

About a half hour later, Ron sat red-faced and alone on one couch, looking at the three ladies looking back at him from the other. He was beyond embarrassed.

He had just summarized the "progress" he and Brandi had made over the last couple of weeks concerning the resolution. The normal awkwardness he usually felt discussing his sex life had been amplified by the presence of two complete strangers, not having Brandi to tag team with and defer to during discussion of the more intimate aspects of their activities, the growing lascivious smiles on both of Brandi's "cousins" faces, and, worst of all, the recounting of his two recent allergic episodes and the dreadful dermatological effects on his penis, and, finally, the need for lamb's gut to support their ongoing sexual activities.

The only way this could have been worse, he thought, *was if I'd had this discussion standing naked in front of these three women.* Just as he formulated this last thought, Snežana's smile broadened, and her eyebrow lifted slightly. *Shit; mind-readers!*

"Well, that's quite the two weeks you've had, Mr. Lee," commented Vanessa awkwardly, still recovering from Ron's narrative, and feeling his discomfort. "I do appreciate your honesty," she added.

"We did have an agreement, Vanessa," he replied. "And I'm sure you will write about it in your usual positive manner." He wondered how she could possibly make the last two weeks sound like anything other than an unfortunate series of events.

Vanessa smiled at the other ladies, stood up, and announced, "Well, I'll get out of your hair so you can continue with your visit."

"Pleasure to meet you, Vanessa," the other ladies sung out in unison.

When Ron returned from seeing Vanessa out, he reoccupied his seat on the couch opposite the two ladies, bowed his head, exhaled loudly, and asked, as calmly as he could, "So why do I require an intervention?"

Yatzil chuckled. "Ron. It isn't an intervention like those for self-destructive behaviour. No, not at all. It's because Deheune detected a certain 'fatigue' in you when you last met, and recent events dealing with your allergies made her realize that you could benefit from some spiritual healing. That's why I'm here."

Ron nodded, and then looked at Snežana.

"I'm here for the sex, Ron," she replied with a mischievous smile.

Shaking his head, he turned his attention back to Yatzil. "So, what does that entail?"

"Just a few quiet minutes alone with me, Ron. You're in need of an 'adjustment', not full repair. Deheune has offered this to you as a reward for your contribution to Brandi's development. She's aware that completion of your resolution is important to you, and this process will serve to recharge your batteries so you should be able to sprint to the finish."

Ron had to admit that recent events had been wearing him down, and putting some spring back in his step did sound appealing.

"And Deheune wants to keep Brandi in top form for some challenging operations that she's planned for later in the month."

Ron's eyebrows reflexively furrowed upon hearing the word "challenging."

"Brandi will tell you about it, Ron. Not to worry. Deheune meticulously plans every operation, and we do have the backing of some very impressive resources and people," Yatzil replied reassuringly. "But now, if we could begin with our intervention?"

"Yes, and afterwards, Ron, I have some questions concerning optimizing female orgasms," Snežana added.

Two hours and a bottle of vodka and one of wine later, the three of them were bent over, recovering from a particularly funny story Snežana had just told them about meeting a man through an online dating service. The poor fellow hadn't been adequately prepared for her. In her written description, she had described herself as a tall blonde, while he described himself as average height. Following the agreed meeting instructions, she found the only man in the bar wearing a bright-red Serbian football jersey with Milošević stenciled across the shoulders, and introduced herself to him. The five-foot-five middle-aged man looked up at her, the blood drained from his face, and he turned and ran out of the bar with, according to Snežana, surprising speed, considering his age and physical condition.

Wiping the tears from his eyes, Ron sympathetically looked at Snežana and asked, "Has it always been that difficult for you to meet men, Snežana?"

"Please, call me Sneezy," she replied. "Unfortunately, it has been, Ron. All people see is my physical presence. Not my inner sensual self. And I suppose it doesn't help my cause that I've become a necromancer."

"You know, Sneezy," Ron said, "a lot of guys would consider that a plus."

Snežana nodded gratefully. "Thank you, Ron. By the way, do you happen to have any single male friends?"

Ron instantly thought of Gerry. "Maybe one or two, Sneezy. Leave that with me."

She smiled so genuinely that Ron's heart almost broke.

༄

After the ladies had left, Ron sat on the couch, pondering the strange events of the evening. What a fortunate man he was to have somehow intersected these exceptional people, and personally benefit from them. Since Yatzil had worked her magic on Ron, he'd been feeling completely rejuvenated, and ridiculously contented.

She said that all she did was allow him to think freely and positively, like he used to be able to do as a child, and now that he had been reacquainted with his younger self, it should be easier for him to recapture that state of mind, should he ever regress. Really, *when* he regressed. Yatzil had informed him that this state was unfortunately not permanent, and would likely slowly diminish as Ron encountered and dealt with his typical daily hassles.

However, with less than a month to go in the resolution, he now felt that its completion was all but certain. All he needed now was his wife.

Sunday, December 6

The phone rang at the Lee residence.

It hardly ever rang these days unless it was a toll-free number, an unknown caller, a charity that either Ron or Brandi had previously donated to, or one of their service providers, all wanting more money from them. In this case, Sam saw the caller was Scott Hartwell, so she grabbed the phone.

"Hi, Scott," answered Sam. "What's up?"

"Hi, Sam. Nothing major…really," Scott said, trying to keep his voice even and calm. "It's just that your dad hurt himself playing hockey tonight, and he's gone to the Civic Hospital to get looked after."

"Oh my God!" exclaimed Sam. "What happened?"

"Well, he got hit by the puck."

"Is it bad? Is he cut?" she asked.

"I didn't see any blood. From the way he was acting though it was apparently pretty painful, but I don't think it's anything too bad. Well, not life-threatening, anyway. In any case, he'll likely be a couple of hours late tonight, and he asked me to call you. And he said not to worry.

"Oh, yeah," Scott added. "He also specifically said to tell you not to tell your mom. He doesn't want her cutting her business trip short because of this. OK?"

"OK," replied Sam. "Are you sure he'll be fine?"

"For sure. You know your dad. Not to worry. He'll likely be home before midnight. Just lock the doors and don't worry. OK?"

"OK, Scott. Thanks for the call. I probably won't be able to sleep until Dad gets home, but thanks for the heads-up. Bye."

ॐ

Sam heard the side door connecting to the garage open. She had fallen asleep on the couch waiting for her father to get home. Glancing at her phone, she saw that it was almost two in the morning. She jumped up from the couch and called out. "Dad?" When she came around the corner she saw her father standing at the door, hunched over, in obvious pain.

"Can you help me take my boots off, Sam?" he whispered.

"Sure, Dad. Are you all right? You look terrible. What happened?" she asked, as she carefully helped her dad out of his boots.

"I blocked a slapshot," he replied.

"Where did it get you?" she inquired.

Ron slowly and silently looked down towards his crotch.

"Ouch," responded Sam.

"And wouldn't you know it. I just chucked out my old jock and bought a new one, and…"

Before Ron could finish with his story, Sam finished it for him. "You forgot it at home, but played anyways without one," she correctly guessed.

Ron nodded. "Can you help me up to my room? It's going to be a long day."

Monday, December 7

Ron woke up late, and phoned into work to say he'd be taking a couple of sick days. The painkillers the hospital had given him weren't doing the trick, and he thought the swelling had somehow increased overnight. He phoned Dr. Kaur's office to book an "emergency" appointment, and was told the doctor's schedule was "completely full." Ron persisted, and after the receptionist consulted directly with Dr. Kaur she said he'd be able to see Ron at the end of the day.

ॐ

After several restless and uncomfortable hours, Ron drove the few blocks to the doctor's office, shuffling his way through the entrance around six that evening. The doctor must have heard him come in, and swung around the corner into the waiting room with a smiling exuberance that suggested he was looking forward to seeing Ron. He was about to welcome him with a quip, as was his custom, but stopped before he said a word. His face dropped into a concerned look. "What in God's good green Gaia has happened to you, my friend? You look like you've been hit by a truck. Tell me that you weren't."

Ron shook his head and started to reply, but was cut short by Dr. Kaur.

"Well, at least that's something. Come. Follow me."

Once in the examination room, Ron gingerly sat on his usual chair and looked back at a concerned Dr. Kaur.

"Ron. By the way you're moving I can't help but think that you once again have a problem with your penis..."

Ron nodded.

"Oh, no. Not again, my friend. And by the looks of it, this is worse than the other times." He paused, and unsuccessfully attempted some math. "*All* the other times."

Ron nodded again.

"I'm actually a bit reluctant to ask you to do this, but I'm obliged by the rules of my profession and the fundamental tenets of the Hippocratic Oath: please drop your pants and let's have a look at your unfortunate fellow."

As Dr. Kaur was digging out some gloves, Ron delicately started undoing his belt and started slipping his pants down. The pain was agonizing. To the sound of the gloves snapping onto Dr. Kaur's hands, he finally exposed his bruised and battered todger.

Dr. Kaur turned to Ron. "*Are baap re!*" he involuntarily exclaimed in his native tongue. "Ron! What have you done this time? It looks as if you were using your genitals to open coconuts. Tell me—what could possibly cause that? Because I want to make sure it never, ever happens to me!"

"I got hit by a puck playing hockey."

"I can't believe the damage, Ron. Lucky you were wearing your protective gear. I can't even imagine the trauma if you weren't." Dr. Kaur looked genuinely shocked.

Ron's face slowly shifted into a "well actually" contrite expression.

Dr. Kaur shook his head. "Tsk, tsk, tsk," was all he could muster. Looking severely at his patient, he asked, "Ron. Would you say that your tired old tugger has served you well over your years?"

Ron nodded.

"Would you also agree that, in your adult years, your babymaker has been a dependable and valuable ally in life's journey?

Ron nodded again.

"And during this last year, hasn't *old reliable* risen to the formidable challenge of the resolution; above and beyond all reasonable expectations?"

Feeling the effects of the doctor's shaming, Ron lowered his eyes and nodded once more.

"Yes. On all three accounts. Yet, as your thanks to him, you recklessly take him, unprotected, into a violent arena, and expose this valiant soldier to extreme danger. Can you tell that I am very, very disappointed in you, Ron?"

His head bowed, Ron mustered a low amplitude nod.

"Mainly because now there is a distinct chance that you will not be able to finish the resolution. And so close, too!" Distraught, he looked at Ron, and Ron thought he saw his eyes water up.

"Dr. Kaur, I can promise you that it will take more than a puck to the pills to deter me from completing the resolution."

"Ron, I appreciate and admire your determination but…" he gestured towards Ron's swollen junk, looking like he had just swallowed something foul.

"Dr. Kaur," Ron started, "I heal very quickly, so do what you can with painkillers and anti-inflammatories to get me on my feet again, and I'll do the rest."

Over the course of about ten seconds, Dr. Kaur's face morphed from the picture of despair to one of growing hope and optimism. "Ron, you truly *are* a warrior. OK. Let's do this!" He offered a high five to Ron who, immediately regretting it, met his hand with a hearty smack that painfully resonated through his core.

Tuesday, December 8

Fueled by stubborn male pride, Ron made it to the airport to pick up Brandi upon her return. Sam was swamped with homework, so had to pass.

It was close to 9 p.m. when Brandi exited from the terminal into the meeting area. The moment she saw Ron waving back at her she knew something wasn't right. He was slightly stooped, and a grimace had his smile in a headlock and was winning the battle. As she grabbed Ron's head in her hands she asked, "Honey, what happened?"

Ron looked into Brandi's eyes. The smile submitted fully to the grimace.

Brandi looked at him and shook her head. Before Ron could speak she chided him, "You weren't even wearing a cup?"

He shook his head.

"Why didn't you tell me earlier?"

Ron started to speak, but Brandi reprimanded him. "You didn't want me to worry? Ron. I'm a big girl." She stared at him. "I can decide if I have to come home early or not."

Ron's was now sporting a "wounded sheep" look.

Brandi took mercy on him. "The main thing is to get you home so I can have a look at that," she said sympathetically, as she glanced towards Ron's damaged groin.

After they got home, and Brandi quickly debriefed Sam about her trip to Brazil, she went upstairs to find her husband lying on the bed in his underwear, still in obvious discomfort, his arm draped across his head.

"Let's have a look at that and get you fixed up, baby." She carefully slid Ron's underwear down a bit. "Jesus Christ, Ron!" Looking up, she added, "How can you even walk with that?"

She paused for a couple of seconds, looking as if she was having trouble reconciling what lay in front of her with her husband's normally tidy package. "It looks like a ruptured octopus!"

"Not helping, Brandi," muttered Ron.

Shaking her head, and unsuccessfully suppressing a shiver, she softly began her ministrations. After a few minutes she said, "That should do the trick Ron. Hard to believe, but you should be good to go in the morning."

With that Ron started to gingerly roll off the bed, but Brandi called out. "Hold on!"

Ron stopped, and slowly turned around. "What?"

"*You* may be out of commission, but I'm not. You get yourself back into this bed and see to your woman's needs. And tonight…your woman needs to hold her man."

Sighing loudly, he rolled back towards her.

"But *please*, can put your underwear back on?"

Wednesday, December 9

When Ron woke in the morning he held his breath as he opened his eyes, slowly moving his hand downwards to assess his groin. He involuntarily let out a "Whoop!", which woke Brandi. "I'm assuming that's a happy sound?" she sleepily asked.

"You bet your beautiful booty it is," he said, as he slid over and kissed her on the cheek. "You know," he added jubilantly, "I think I'm going to keep you around."

"Jeez, thanks," Brandi muttered, her face still in her pillow. "But can you do that quietly so I can get some sleep?"

He let loose another "Whoop!" as he made his way to the bathroom.

Now he was walking—no, *bounding*—home from work. Whereas yesterday the constant agony had vanquished all forms of optimism, today he was the exact opposite. *What a difference a day makes*, he thought, now truly understanding the expression.

He knew that it wasn't only Brandi's touch at work here. Yatzil's "intervention" had allowed him to recover his positive mindset with a child's alacrity and unjaded perspective. With about three weeks left in the resolution, he was again feeling infused with an irrepressible sense of reverential love of life and his wife. Yes, there was some work to be done tonight. They had fallen a few days behind because of Brandi's travel and his personal misfortunes, but that was all behind him. His groin now ached, not with the pain of injury, but in anticipation of an enthusiastic renewal of the resolution.

Bathed in sweat and breathing heavily, Ron rolled off Brandi. "One time?" he moaned in disbelief. "You've been gone for five days and all I've got is a single effort? These damned goat guts aren't helping either." He removed the prophylactic and tossed it onto the floor, thus ending the highly improbable utilitarian rebirth of that particular organic material.

"Ron. Don't be so hard on yourself. You've been through some trauma lately, and regardless of how healed you may feel, there's likely some residual physical and/or psychological effects. Have you been taking your supplements?"

Ron nodded.

"Meditating?"

He nodded again.

"Exercising, etc.?"

"Yup."

"Then just be patient. It'll come around soon enough," Brandi advised.

"Brandi, I...I mean, *we* can't afford to be patient. There's only three weeks left. And we've got some ground to make up."

"Ron..." Brandi replied reproachfully.

"Brandi..." Ron responded in a "don't even" tone, eyebrows raised.

Saturday, December 12

Scott and Elise were over for drinks and dinner. The weather had been unseasonably warm the last few days, and in celebration of the fine weather both couples had agreed to make an offering of a notable white wine to the "gods of unseasonably warm inclinations," in an attempt to encourage and prolong the agreeable weather. Memories of the previous winter were still fresh in their minds.

Ron and Brandi led with a sub-twenty-dollar 2012 Pinot Gris gem from the CedarCreek winery in the Okanagan Valley. The ripe fruit and honey overtones subconsciously transported them back to a hot late summer's day, sugary juices from plump peaches and pears, just plucked from the trees, running down their chins to the ambient drone of foraging bees.

Scott was the first to emerge from his daydream. "Nice, guys. Reminds me of summer when I was a kid."

He allowed a short pause for the others to refocus on the here and now. "Speaking of being a kid," he continued when he had everyone's attention, "Ron, the only thing that hasn't happened to your old boy yet is get it caught in your zipper. You do know, of course, that without Brandi and her 'help'," he paused to make sure those present understood his code, "you guys wouldn't stand a chance of finishing the resolution?"

Ron nodded. Scott wasn't even aware that he had also been mightily assisted with an equally important part of the resolution: a renewal of his positive mindset.

"Notwithstanding, however, since you *are* in good hands, Ron, I assume completion of the resolution is essentially a *fait accompli?*" Scott queried, as only a best friend could, would, or should.

This was a sensitive topic these days in the Lee household. Ron was still dealing with some sort of block that Brandi couldn't fix, and Yatzil's spiritual rejuvenation wasn't completely remedying. The situation was exacerbated by the fact that, with less than three weeks to go, they were almost a week's worth of loving in arrears, and Ron was beginning to feel anxious again.

Ron inhaled deeply, and cast Scott an "I don't know—it could go either way" look.

"No possible way!" exclaimed Scott. "So close, and you're telling me it's not in the bag? That's completely unacceptable, and not at all like *you*, Ron." He paused a second. His eyes widened as if he were experiencing an epiphany, and he asked seriously, "Who are you, and what have you done with Ron?"

Ron smiled. "It's really me, I can assure you, Scott. Should I prove it by recounting the story of you losing your underwear during a walk home from the bar during our South Carolina golf trip?"

Scott lifted his arm and tilted and dipped his head in concession. "That won't be necessary, Ron, I'm convinced."

Ron allowed Elise a few more seconds to glare at her husband before he continued. "I think I'm getting a bit worn out. I feel great, but it's just—I don't know—I think I've become de-sensitized or something."

Scott just looked at Ron, shaking his head.

"What?" asked Ron.

"Ron. You are such a dumbass," Scott replied. Everyone looked at him in anticipation of his next volley. "First of all, are you guys still using that goat-gut condom thingy?"

Ron nodded.

"Get rid of it, and damn the consequences. Brandi can quickly repair any dermatological consequences that may arise. I can promise you that using that thing has destroyed your spontaneity. You guys may be superhuman, but you're still human.

"Secondly, I recommend some very good reading concerning how to sexually spice up your relationship. It's a blog by *@lovejunkie*, who's writing about *#resolutionottawa*; this amazing couple right here in Ottawa. They're attempting to make love every day of the year this year, and have experimented with a number of techniques and behaviours that have enhanced their already solid relationship and allowed them to, so far, successfully achieve that goal."

He let that comment hang for a moment, and then continued. "Ron. You've already forgotten what you've learned this year, and it's time for a refresher course. No one—not even you guys—can take this relationship stuff for granted. I'm guessing that you've both unconsciously settled into some sort of comfortable rhythm, and just assumed that you could ride that wave into shore. Wrong. Now for the sake of the resolution, take the time to rediscover how you got here and pick up your game. There's less than a month to go, for God's sake."

In a few seconds, his demeanour changed from stern to cordial. "Now, can I open our bottle? It's called The Rusty Shed. It's a 2013 Chardonnay from Flat Rock Cellars in the Niagara. I've heard great things about it."

Sunday, December 13

Ron and Brandi spent the morning reading through Vanessa's blog. It was the first time they had sat down and read about themselves together. Afterwards they silently lay on the couch holding each other, lost in their thoughts.

"Thank goodness for Vanessa," Ron eventually suggested.

"No kidding."

"It would break her heart if we gave up on the resolution, or even if we didn't successfully complete it," Ron added.

"We can't let that happen."

"No, we can't," Ron agreed.

"So, can I suggest that we go to supper tonight?" Brandi asked.

"Are you craving Italian?" Ron suggested, eyebrows raised.

"I am. And I've got this little skirt with a zipper up the side that I'd like to wear."
Ron waggled his eyebrows.

"And you know those cute green undies?"

"The ones that weigh about four nannograms?" Ron asked.

"Those are the ones. Well, I'm not going to wear those. In fact, I think I'm not
going to wear *any* undies."

"I have to admit, I do like the sound of that," Ron answered. He realized his
heart was pounding, and he was sporting a full erection.

Brandi looked down at Ron's constricted groin, and said, "But you'll have to
wait until this evening, my love. I've got to meet with Deheune at noon to discuss
our next mission." And with that, she got up from the couch.

Feeling a case of blue balls coming on, Ron called out defiantly, "Well, that's
fine with me, because I've got to go to work anyways, I'll have you know."

"Tell you what, though," Brandi added, as she was climbing the stairs to the
bedroom, "I'll meet you at the restaurant at six o'clock tonight. Hopefully I don't
have to remind you to wear very baggy pants and no underwear. Ta ta for now,"
she added, as the bedroom door closed.

Ron had trouble concentrating at work. It had been quite a while since he'd spent
the better part of the day fighting an erection at his desk, but he soldiered through
with a seventy/thirty split between effectiveness and erectiveness. When he got
home just after five, only Sam was at home. Brandi had informed her that they
would be going out to supper, so Sam was warming up a pizza and then heading
over to her friend's place to study. By the time Ron had cleaned up and changed
into his loosest cotton pants it was about a quarter to six; just enough time to
walk over to the local Italian restaurant.

When he arrived, there was no line-up, and the young Italian girl at the door
suggested he could sit where ever he wanted. As he looked towards their *special*
corner table, he saw it was occupied by an exotic-looking redheaded woman
who, Ron noticed, kept staring at him.

He looked around the place. Brandi wasn't anywhere to be seen, so he texted her as to her whereabouts, and chose a table that, he thought, would be the next best option for tonight's activities. As he made his way to the table, the lady in the corner table called out.

"Excuse me," she said, with an air of familiarity that immediately got his attention. "Are you Ron? Ron Lee?"

Ron offered the lady a polite, surprised smile and replied, "Yes, I am. Do I know you?"

"No, not really. Your wife Brandi asked me to get here early and make sure that I got *this* table. She said it had *sentimental* value."

Ron could feel his face start to redden. "I'm sorry. I'm confused. Brandi specifically asked you to come early and sit at *this* table?"

The lady nodded.

"Why would she do that?"

"She said you'd ask that question." The lady chuckled and smiled at Ron. "She also said that she'd explain everything to you later."

After a brief pause she patted the bench beside herself. When Ron didn't move she said, "That was an invitation for you to join me, Ron."

Ron slowly walked over to the stranger, taking off his coat while he did. When he got to the table, she patted the bench again, and smiled broadly at Ron. He noted that she was an extraordinary beauty. From what he could tell she also had an exceptional body, and much to his surprise, he felt his crotch start to heat up. He sat down quickly before the unwanted effects of this unconscious redistribution of blood could manifest itself in obvious changes to regions which happened to be right at her eye level while he was standing. The loose pants didn't help either.

"Nice to meet you," Ron politely said, offering his hand in greeting.

As she shook it, he continued with his inquiry. "So, who exactly are you, how do you know Brandi and *why* are you here?"

"So many questions, Ron. All will become clear soon enough. But first, let's order some wine. I assume red?" she asked, waving to get the waiter's attention.

Once the wine had been ordered and the waiter was out of earshot, Ron turned his head towards the woman and said, "So your name is…?"

"Rubellan Fielder. Pleasure to meet you, Ron." She offered her hand formally to Ron. "You can call me Ruby."

As he shook her hand for the second time, something about the woman seemed familiar, but he couldn't put his finger on exactly what it was. "So how do you know Brandi?" he asked.

"We both work at the Organization."

OK. Now it's starting to make more sense, he thought. He had recently met some interesting characters who worked with Brandi. Ruby was somehow related to that esoteric group. "Oh. How long have you been working there?"

"I started only very recently, actually." And she left it at that.

Ron knew the importance of secrecy in the Organization, so he didn't inquire further.

Just as the wine arrived, Ruby shifted slightly, and her hand moved against Ron's thigh. Ron felt the energy of her touch jolt through his body like electricity. The hair stood up on the back of his neck. He instinctively turned to look at Ruby. She was staring neutrally at the waiter filling the glass in front of her. Ron thought the touch could have been accidental, but his body thought otherwise. In response to her subtle physical stimuli his confused parasympathetic nervous system made an executive decision and released nitric oxide into his circulatory system, causing the spongy muscles in his penis to involuntarily relax, which in turn allowed the primary arteries running down the length of Ron's tallywhacker to dilate. The result was a pressure void. Nature, so the story goes, deplores a void, so individual corpuscles, tripping over themselves and elbowing their brethren out of the way, rushed forward to equilibrate Ron's vascular system. By the time the wine was poured, Ron's system had fully rebalanced.

"Cheers," Ruby said, looking Ron squarely in his eyes and raising her glass.

He raised his glass in return, while assessing his situation. Checking his phone and seeing Brandi had not responded to his text, he said, "I really should find Brandi."

"Ron," she said coyly, "we both know that you're not going anywhere in your current condition." She glanced at his lap.

For the second time in the matter of a couple of minutes, Ron's parasympathetic nervous system unilaterally decided on a course of action to help him cope. This time it led with a pulse of adrenaline that dilated the capillaries in his skin. Amazingly, there was still sufficient superfluous blood lying around Ron's body to amply redden his neck and cheeks.

Embarrassed that he was so transparent, he sat there red-faced, sipping his wine for a moment, willing his erection to dissipate. Unfortunately for Ron however, given the events of the morning and his anticipation for the events of this evening, his body was not in the mood to be reasoned with.

With the passing of a few moments, and no change in the status of the southern front, Ron accepted his situation, and asked her, "So tell me. Why *are* you here, Ruby?"

"Ronny, I'm here for you, of course."

When Ron had regained his composure, he asked, "Are you saying Brandi's arranged for you to meet up with me tonight?"

She nodded. "It's her idea that I'm here, Ron."

He nodded, and cautiously asked, "And what, exactly, were her instructions, Ruby?"

"Ron, what am I wearing?" she asked.

Ron leaned back to get a better look at Ruby's legs, and realized that she was wearing a skirt. A very short one, at that. The lady appeared to have great legs, as well.

"What did Brandi say she would be wearing to the restaurant?" Ruby probed.

After a brief recollection of this morning discussion, he answered, "A short skirt."

Nodding seductively, Ruby added, "And not even one underwear to be seen."

Ron's parasympathetic nervous system was having a busy day. It once again defaulted to its earlier strategies, this time with an added vigor, which required an increase in heartrate to accommodate the various vascular requirements in his extremities. Ron could feel the vein in his temple pulse.

"I've clearly made you uncomfortable, Ron. Please don't be. I assure you that Brandi is completely fine with this. How about we drink our wine and get to know each other better?" she said—and moved her hand onto Ron's thigh, subtly searching for his erect penis.

Ron thought he was going to pass out. He grabbed the wine glass, to cover his face more than anything, and started gulping the wine. After a few seconds he felt that familiar gathering of energy in his groin; the wonderful full-body tingling sensations that herald an imminent orgasm began to increase in intensity, and he knew he was past the point of no return. His will now relegated to observer status, he kept the wine glass pressed against his lips and stared straight ahead, waiting for the imminent explosion in his pants. It was an orgasm reminiscent of when he was a teenager; the kind of all-in, world-melting-away, one-with-the-universe climax that wipes the blackboard clean of all your problems.

After a period of time of indeterminate length, he exhaled like it was his last breath, opened his eyes again, and looked at Ruby.

Only it wasn't Ruby. It was Brandi.

As he sat wide-eyed and speechless, his mouth involuntarily agape, Brandi commented, "Well, sailor, that didn't take long," and smiled brightly at her husband.

After the better part of a minute, Ron's heartrate settled a bit, and he felt himself relaxing. "But how...?" was all he could muster.

"Well, Ron, this is part of my ongoing training. I've been learning how to disguise myself by projecting a different physical presence into the mind of someone I'm interacting with. Deheune thought the perfect test would be with someone who knew me intimately. It was my idea to present to you as someone who I knew you would be very sexually attracted to."

She paused again. When Ron didn't respond, she added, "You're welcome."

"Brandi, I don't know if I'm angry at you or not."

"Typical man," she playfully replied. "Once he gets what he wants, the loving shuts off like a tap. Let me help you decide. Did you enjoy Ruby's company?"

He nodded, looking a bit sheepish.

"Was she physically exceptional, sexy as hell, and good with her hands?"

He nodded again.

"Would you like to spend some more time with her? Like tonight? This time not feeling awkward and guilty?"

Ron was beginning to see the upside of Brandi's newest skill. His simmering anger was hurriedly nudged to one side by his blossoming lust.

"I recognize that look, and yes, I can also read your mind, you horny old bugger. Stop that! *I'm* going to blush now," she said, fanning her face with her hand. "How about we finish this wine and take this *ménage à trois* home?"

Ron nodded again.

Thursday, December 17

Ron reflected on the last few days during his walk home from work.

Brandi's introduction of "Ruby" into their love life had been a stroke of genius. Her preemptive ministrations to avoid the expected allergic reactions following their daily sexual activities had proven effective; so without condom or fear of allergic reaction, and Ruby in their bed, Ron had experienced a sexual resurgence. And as Ron rationalized, the integrity of the resolution hadn't been compromised. Having Ruby in bed with them was technically just a form of roleplaying. A very sophisticated and effective form of roleplaying; but role playing all the same.

He had chuckled when he found out that Ruby's name was an anagram derived from Brandi's full name. She and Deheune had thought it was so clever that Brandi had made Rubellan Fielder her "professional" name for future missions, and somehow she had already been issued a Canadian passport, an Ontario driver's license, and a Costco credit card under that name. Ron had learnt not to underestimate the Organization or anybody who worked for it, but the issuance of official documents under a false identity in a matter of a few days still surprised him. Brandi had explained they'd need it for their next mission, which had been planned for just after Christmas. He wasn't too pleased to hear about the timing of this next mission, but she had promised to be back for New Year's. Good thing, too, because Scott and Elise were planning for a New Year's party this year. Not just any party, but a resolution-celebration party in their honour.

Ron had calmly suggested that Scott was out of his frigging mind when he suggested this, but Scott assured him that the only invitees would be people who knew about Ron and Brandi's resolution, and he and Brandi would be in charge of the invitation list. It took some convincing, but eventually he came around to the idea, and was actually looking forward to it now.

With two weeks left in the resolution, they were actually a bit ahead of schedule. Not that it mattered. Ron couldn't wait to get home and spend some quality time with Brandi and Ruby.

When he got home he found the girls in the kitchen, talking as they prepared supper. Only much to Ron's surprise, it wasn't Brandi and Sam, it was Ruby and Sam. He was momentarily taken aback, but realized that only he was seeing Brandi as Ruby; Sam was oblivious to the persona Brandi was projecting for her husband.

"Hello, honey," Ruby called out when Ron entered the kitchen. "How was your day?" She made her way over to him for a smooch. Ruby was a signal from

Brandi that he could expect another fulsome evening of lovemaking; the intent manifested with a particularly passionate welcome-home kiss.

"Ugh." Sam commented. "Can't you guys act your age? You can be arrested in twenty-three countries for doing that in public, you know."

"Well it's a good thing that we live in Canada and are currently in our kitchen," replied Brandi to her daughter.

"What's for supper?" asked Ron.

"Shrimp pasta," replied Ruby. "And I have something special for you for dessert," she added lasciviously.

"Ick!" exclaimed Sam, rising from her stool, having had quite enough, thank you very much.

Sunday, December 20

Tommy Jr. had finished his semester and was home for the holidays. He, Amanda, and Ron's parents had joined the rest of the family for the Sunday meal. With the house fully decorated there was an unmistakably festive feeling in the air, despite the lack of snow or cold weather outside.

"This weather is a miracle," exclaimed Tommy Sr.

"Why's that?" asked his granddaughter.

"Just think of all the hips that haven't been broken and hearts that are still beating with the lack of cold and snow and the related shovelling," he replied.

"I hadn't thought of that," Sam replied.

"What's really a miracle is what's happening over at the Children's Hospital, where Brandi's volunteering," Abby suggested. "There have been another four terminally ill kids cured over there this month already." She shook her head in disbelief. "Brandi—that's pretty amazing, isn't it?"

Brandi replied. "It is pretty special, but I don't know if I'd call it a miracle. Rumour has it that the doctors are trying out some new procedures that are working better than expected, but most likely, it's just an extreme occurrence. You know; improbable, but still statistically possible."

"The odds must be one in a billion in that case. A miracle is more likely if you ask me," Abby countered.

Tommy Sr. spoke. "This has been a special year. You know I'm not religious, but I'm betting that we haven't seen the end of whatever's happening over at the Children's Hospital. Mark my words on that."

Ron stole a quick glance at Brandi. He was sure he saw a mischievous look flash across her face.

Thursday, December 24

The Lee family Christmas Eve tradition was to walk over to the nearby St. John the Apostle Catholic church, be turned away, and walk home. There was limited seating—this mass was by far and away the most popular service of the year—and priority for midnight mass on Christmas Eve was given to regular parishioners.

The Lee family wasn't bothered by this. In fact, as devout atheists, they expected it. It was the walk they were after: the unbroken procession of decorated homes along the route, both tasteful and over-the-top, all helped to encourage those ephemeral blissful Christmas feelings, while at the same time distracting them from unpleasant world realities.

Their group pilgrimage this year was larger than normal. Brandi's mom, Megan, was in from Toronto to spend Christmas with them and attend the special resolution New Year's party. Ron's parents also joined them, since Tommy Sr.'s knees were feeling remarkably good after Brandi had massaged them the other night, and the sidewalks were completely free of snow and ice, given the record-high temperatures they had been experiencing.

Bedazzled by the kaleidoscope-like array of colours and characters, both ecclesiastical and secular, they didn't even notice the lack of snow as they wound their way towards the church, arriving at the back of the building via the residential roads to the south. The parking lot was packed, as usual.

After a brief pause at the edge of the parking lot, Ron, Sam, and Tommy Jr. turned and started the journey back home. "Hold on!" Tommy Sr. called out, genuinely surprised. "We haven't even been denied access yet, and you're heading back?"

Ron stopped and turned back, looking confused. "But we never get in, Dad. I thought we'd skip this last part and just get back to the eggnog and the gifts."

"Gift," his mom corrected him.

"How can we be sure we won't get in unless we try?" his father persisted.

"Dad, you're not even religious," Ron said, shaking his head, visibly perplexed.

"That's not the point, son. This is a Catholic holiday. Regardless of our spiritual leanings, our entire family has, for as long as I can remember, benefited from this celebration, and since we just happen to be standing outside of a Catholic church on the eve of its most important day, don't you think we owe it to ourselves to make sure there's no room before we recede back into our secular ways?"

Ron stood silently.

"What's the worst that could happen?" Tommy Sr. offered.

Tommy Jr. spoke. "By the time you guys make a decision, it'll already be midnight. I'll run over and make sure that they're at capacity." And he sprinted off.

About a minute later he returned. Ron gave him an "I told you so" smug smile and pose.

"Well, for some reason, they saved seven seats at the back tonight. The priest met me at the door and said that he was expecting us."

As Ron stood dumbfounded, Tommy Sr. grabbed Abby's elbow and started marching towards the church, calling out over his shoulder. "Well, we shouldn't keep them waiting, should we?"

Once they were sitting on the backbench, Ron nervously looked around at his surroundings. In all these years living in Centrepointe and he had never, not even once, been in this church. The entire interior was finished in dark, lacquered pine slats, which, combined with the neo-eclectic A-Frame design and detached curved support beams, gave the undeniable impression of sitting in an overturned ship's hull. Besides the smell of wood, Ron detected smoky incense, more spicy than floral. The soft lighting added to a venerable ambiance, and the total silence that emanated from the nearly three hundred people in the closed space gave the moment an otherworldly feel. The entire group sat staring straight ahead, spellbound, as the priest at the distant pulpit finished his preparation, smiled, gazed over the silenced crowd, harrumphed, and readied himself to sermonize.

"We gather here tonight in celebration of our Lord Jesus' birth, and the ultimate sacrifice he made for us while amongst us on this Earth."

Ron felt his sense of awe start to melt away with those words. *It's going to be a long hour*, he thought. Brandi moved her hand over his and subtly gave him a stern pinch in response.

The priest continued. "And why do you think he made this sacrifice?" he asked rhetorically. "Because of his love for us, and as an example of what true love and sacrifice can look like," he said, answering his own question.

With Brandi's hand still resting on his, poised to mete out punishment, Ron did his best to keep his mind blank.

"And because of Jesus' love for us, God our Father looks down upon us as His children, and teaches us as any father would. In His wisdom, He makes us labour for our happiness, for without challenge and sacrifice to know the face of pain, how can we truly measure, understand, and appreciate our joy?

"He rewards our sacrifices with our loving families and beloved friends, and the freedom to live in a world that can be as beautiful as it is challenging."

After a brief pause, the priest continued. "These challenges can seem cruel at times, creating unimaginable pain and suffering. We can never hope to fully understand why we must endure such pain, but I believe that this is His way of making His children on Earth even stronger; as any parent would endeavour to do for their children.

"Imagine the pain and sorrow, if you will, of watching a loved one wither away and die weak, speechless, and incontinent in front of your eyes. Now imagine that same person as your own child. One who has yet to enjoy the fullness of life's journey; yet to steal their first kiss; yet to develop and understand the range and richness of emotions that God has granted us; yet to have stared into the eyes of their own children and know the profound love that most intimately connects us with our God."

The priest had Ron's attention now. He was currently blinking furiously to avoid from tearing up. He could see a number of people in front of him, mostly woman, but some men, discreetly move their hands up to brush a tear away from their eye.

"Can you imagine a deeper sorrow? No. I imagine you cannot. But the Lord is good; and as he takes with extreme dispassion, he also gives with equal passion. Tonight in Ottawa, the Lord has used this venerated date to remind us of His magnificence and His benevolence. Although not public knowledge, until this moment, I have recently learnt that on this day, three terribly sick and terminally ill children at our nearby Children's Hospital have, miraculously, gone into full remission."

The entire church simultaneously gasped, and the majority of women involuntarily moved their hand to their mouth. Ron noticed that Brandi did not.

"Not one of them was expected to live past the end of this year."

The crowd gasped again.

"A miracle?" asked the priest. "If this event, occurring on the eve of the anniversary of our Lord's birth, is *not* a miracle, then what, if anything, could ever be considered one?"

After a pause to let the collective murmuring die down, he continued. "This miracle is a reminder that not everything in the world need be hopeless, sorrowful, or impossible. As long as there is one glimmer of hope, one kernel of something greater than ourselves—we should build on that. No, we *have* to build on that. We owe it to ourselves, to our families, to the *entire human race* to build on that: to use this one brick as the foundation for building something filled with hope; something filled with possibilities; something that literally breeds compassion and happiness; something which all humans can look upon and say—this is just the start!"

The entire congregation stood and exploded into applause.

Ron leaned into Brandi and whispered, "Now you've done it."

Friday, December 25

Always on the look-out for feel-good stories, the press had enthusiastically latched onto the "miracle" and its auspicious timing, cleverly calling it the "Christmas Mass Miracle" to capitalize on both the site of the announcement and the multiple number of children simultaneously cured; even though three was hardly massive, the "miracle" had had nothing to do with the midnight mass at St. John's church, and the "miracle" hadn't even occurred on Christmas Day. But rather than let details get in the way of a good story, they were altered to make for a cleaner narrative, and wouldn't you know it—the storybook simplicity of the "Christmas Mass Miracle" went viral, and despite the near-ubiquitous absence of newspaper copy on Christmas Day, the internet lit up with the story, and eighty-seven countries carried the story on their Christmas Day evening television newscast. Ottawa was officially on the map. If the CHEO had had difficulty dealing with the unwanted local press due to the earlier spat of improbable cures in the children's terminal ward, the imminent flood of international attention would soon have them reminiscing for those good old days.

Of course it was Brandi who had informed the parish priest of the CHEO goings-on of the day, and in return for her providing some inspirational material for that night's mass, he had set aside the seven seats for the Lee family, and delayed commencement of the proceedings until they had arrived. As clever as Brandi was, she hadn't received Deheune's permission for her timely and generous hospital ministrations, nor considered her reaction. Not surprisingly, Deheune was none too pleased, and made an unexpected early-morning Christmas call to their home and, following a terse and perfunctory salutation to the household, quietly chatted with Brandi about it behind closed doors. Brandi emerged from the office as if she had just had a good dressing down by the school principal.

After the gifts had been opened and she found herself alone with Ron, he was informed that she would be indefinitely suspending her volunteer work at the hospital, until the current brouhaha died down. Her defiance still intact, however, she said it was worth it.

It certainly *was* worth it for Tommy Sr., who, upon arrival at the house on his newly re-functioned knees, had commented for all to hear that he *had* told them this was a special year and there was more to come; vicariously and subconsciously taking partial credit for the event. Ron wondered how many people out there were doing exactly the same thing as his father, attributing the "Christmas Mass Miracle" at least partially to their good behaviour, prayers, and positive feelings. Ron had learnt to never underestimate a person's ability to make any situation or event about themselves.

He thought that wasn't such a bad thing in this case. It would likely encourage more positive behaviour in the future. And if this act by Brandi had gone worldwide, as he suspected it had, how many thousands or even millions of people would carry out an act of kindness of their own because of Brandi? He recalled his earlier discussions with Brandi. *One ripple in the ocean combining with other ripples to make a tidal wave of change.* Maybe this was how that happened.

When he looked at his wife, she looked nothing like the agent of change he was currently musing about. Mostly recovered from the bollocking Deheune had given her, she was now simply enjoying being around her family, folding back into the palpably loving atmosphere in the house. Ron was overcome with love, respect, and admiration for the woman he had chosen to build a life and family with.

He put his arm around her, looked her in the eyes, and quietly asked, "Any chance Ruby might come out to play later on?"

Monday, December 28

The weather had taken a sudden turn for the normal, and the inescapable cold and snow Ottawa was known for had returned with a vengeance, as if it was trying to make up for lost time. Ron had left early for the airport to allow himself ample time, but Brandi's flight from Toronto had been delayed twice now due to snow and bad weather. It was nearly eight o'clock, and he had already been at the airport two hours.

Earlier in the day, Ron had received a text from Brandi that her trip had been cut short and she'd be home two days early. She didn't say why.

Just as he had resigned himself to an indefinite stay, his phoned pinged with an "ARRIVED!" from Brandi. About ten minutes later he watched Brandi descend the escalators down to the baggage area. His smile slowly morphed into a concerned look when he saw that Deheune was standing beside and casually supporting Brandi. His wife also looked decidedly unwell.

As she and Deheune came off the escalator, he ran to Brandi's unaccompanied side and asked, "Honey, are you alright?"

She offered him a weak smile, and Deheune answered for her. "She's just tired, Ron. This was a difficult mission, and she overextended herself. I've seen it before. She'll be fine after a couple of days of rest. If you have her, I'll hand her off to you now, and come by tomorrow morning to see how she's doing."

She then turned to Brandi and said, "Regardless of what happened, Brandi, remember you've changed a lot of people's lives for the better over the last couple of days." She leaned in and gave her a hug and a kiss on the cheek. "I'll see you tomorrow sometime, my dear," she said, and departed with her usual crisp quick pace.

Ron gave Brandi a concerned hug, hooked his arm solidly into hers and said, "Let's get you home. You look like you could use a good night's sleep."

Tuesday, December 29

Ron was working intermittently during the period between Christmas and New Year's, and got home after lunch to find Brandi, still in her housecoat, sitting at the kitchen island sipping coffee.

He walked over, put his arm around her, and kissed her on the cheek. "How are you feeling today my sweet?"

Looking much improved from the previous night, she smiled lovingly at him and replied, "Still a bit tired, but way better than yesterday. I was toast when I got on that plane in Guatemala."

This was the first Ron had heard about Brandi's destination for her most recent mission. "Can you tell me what happened, Brandi?" he asked.

She looked pensively at Ron, considering his request for a few seconds, then said, "I guess, this once, under the protection of marital confidentiality—but don't tell Deheune. OK?"

"Scout's honour," Ron replied, holding up the three middle fingers of his right hand as assurance.

Brandi took another sip of coffee, and then began. "The Organization has been looking at Central America for some time now, because of a particularly bad strain of measles working its way through the region. Death rates amongst children have been greater than twenty percent in urban regions. Still, the overall numbers of deaths have been low in these urban centres, due to the established vaccination programs in place there.

"It's been a different story for the poor indigenous rural northeast province of Peten. These people there have been largely ignored by the central government. They have virtually no medical system, and a complete lack of systemic vaccination programs. Because of that, the poor kids there were extremely susceptible to this outbreak. By mid-December, it became a full-blown epidemic. When the mortality rate for children in Peten approached forty percent, Deheune and the Organization made the mission call. They believed that we could potentially end the outbreak with a few days of focused 'attention', and they laid all the groundwork in advance of our arrival.

"They flew me, Deheune, and Muteteli into Guatemala City on their private plane via Houston. We all travelled under our aliases; I was travelling as Rubellan Fielder."

Ron felt, and immediately suppressed, the sexual warmth spreading through his body at the mention of her name.

"Since both Deheune and Muteteli are fully qualified medical doctors, our 'humanitarian' mission was approved on short notice by the Guatemalan government. It didn't hurt that we were flying the Salvation Army banner. Ms. Fielder was documented as medical assistant.

"After an eight-hour road trip to Sayaxché, where sick people from the region had been collecting for a couple of days in anticipation of our arrival, we started our clinic. The Organization had, apparently, very effectively got the message out to the surrounding area that the Salvation Army International Mobile Medical Team was coming.

"Ron, I can't even start to describe the chaos and agony we encountered when we got there. The large tent that the Organization had set-up for us was packed with dozens of very sick children and, to a lesser degree, adults as well. It wasn't just measles, there were people suffering from everything—AIDS, advanced malnutrition, cancer—you name it. We got there just before midnight on Saturday, and, following an intense triage, worked right through the night until morning; still, the lineups didn't seem to get smaller. If anything, they appeared to be getting longer.

"Deheune has some ability to cure people, but I think she was mainly there as a medical doctor. Muteteli was pulling double duty as far as I could tell. I was following orders from both of them and 'comforting' whomever I came across. We did what we could, as quickly as we could, and freed up beds for those waiting outside the tent. I passed out around noon on Sunday from exhaustion, and was woken a couple of hours later and got right back at it. I honestly don't remember if I had anything to eat. Oh my God. That was only two days ago!" Brandi exclaimed, surprised at how much had transpired over the last forty-eight hours.

After a few seconds of quiet contemplation, she continued. "We worked through the day until dark, stealing an hour of sleep here or there when we could. By about midnight the line of people outside had disappeared, and I noticed, for the first time, some empty cots. By dawn on Monday, about half of the cots were empty, and only the sickest kids remained. I went over to those who remained and gave them a little more TLC.

"Just after breakfast we heard a commotion outside. A very excited and animated mother was wailing, 'Es un milagro. Dios bendiga a estas persona.' over and over—'It's a miracle. God bless these people.' I looked at Deheune, and she mouthed an 'Oh-oh' at me, and then went out to meet the woman and accept her enthusiastic thanks, as a curious crowd gathered around them. Deheune remembered the woman had brought her very sick little daughter in the previous night. The little girl was dying from a secondary pneumonia infection. What had really impressed this emotionally overwhelmed mother was that this morning her daughter woke up right as rain. Clearly, she was quite pleased.

"This in itself would have been fine, but a few minutes later another couple showed up, adding to the clamour, alternatively chanting, '*Estamos entre los santos*' and '*Esta personas son santos*'—'We are amongst saints; these people are saints.' At about this time, it seemed that all of humanity burst forth from the forest, arms filled with sick children, pleading for assistance from the visiting 'saints.' Word of the 'miracles in the jungle' had gotten out, and those who, for whatever reason, had remained at home during the first wave were now determined not to miss out on any miracles being doled out at the Salvation Army tent in the jungle.

"We handled this new wave as best as we could, but by about nine o'clock the increasingly desperate growing crowd started to get unruly, and bumping escalated into pushing, then into shoving. Our small security group was being quickly overwhelmed, and it became obvious, even to me, that we had lost control of the situation. I looked over at Deheune, and she was already on her phone. When she got off, she signalled for Muteteli and me to grab our stuff and follow her. She made her way to a small exit flap I hadn't previously noticed at the back of the tent. A jeep was already idling there, and within seconds the ruckus at the tent faded into the background as we sped down the road, dodging even more people coming to join the fray at the tent.

"The Organization must have pulled some strings—easily enough done with some monetary incentive in Guatemala—and got clearance to land their private plane at the nearby municipal airport. When we arrived about ten o'clock, the plane was already on the tarmac, door open and ladder down. We hopped on, and were in the air about five minutes later.

"I didn't realize how drained I was until I relaxed on the plane. Deheune wasn't surprised. She said that my ministrations do require significant amounts of personal energy and, not unexpectedly, I have a finite amount available. After the intense day and half in the jungle, I was tapped out."

Ron rubbed her shoulders and sat quietly.

She smiled at him and said, "Don't worry. I'm already beginning to feel more like myself. I'm new at this and it was a good learning experience for me. I'll be more cautious in the future."

She saw Ron's expression, and determinedly continued. "Yes, there *will* be more Ron. Our work is too important. Remember, I'm still a rookie and have lots to learn about the Organization."

At that moment, the doorbell rang. Ron answered the door and found himself face-to-face with Deheune, who smiled broadly. "How's our girl today, Ron?" she asked while walking uninvited into the hallway and removing her coat.

"Much better," replied Ron, trying his best to look ignorant of the details Brandi had just revealed to him. "She's in the kitchen."

As she entered the kitchen and saw Brandi, Deheune happily exclaimed, "My, you *are* looking much better. As I knew you would be," she added. "Let me make you some of my medicinal tea and we can do a mission debrief. I'll have you know that, although we had to perform an emergency egress, the early numbers reported to me this morning suggest our mission was an unqualified success. The Organization believes we saved between forty and fifty lives with our short visit. And, just as important, we created a firewall against the further spread of the epidemic in the Peten area."

She paused for both their benefits, seeing the concern on Ron's face. "You both should be very proud of what was achieved there."

A further pause. "I know this was all a bit scary and hectic, but this was your first mission. Not mine. We have extensive contingency planning in place on all our missions, and it's far more common that we have to improvise than everything comes off without a hitch. You'll get used to it, Brandi." She looked at Ron. Nodding her head, she added, "And you will too, Ron. Now, where are your herbs and spices?"

Thursday, December 31

Brandi's condition had improved markedly since her return from Guatemala. By New Year's Eve, she had fully recovered. She and Ron had now settled back into their normal daily rhythm of meditation and lovemaking. It was near noon, and they quietly lay in bed, breathing heavily after their recent session.

"I do believe *that* it is one of my favourite human characteristics," Ron mused.

Playing along, Brandi asked, "What's '*that*', Ron?"

"Our steadfastly renewable intense desire for sex. Regardless of the season, weather, or time of day or night, it's our constant companion. It's the dynamic spoke in the wheel of physical human needs; growing aggressively like a bamboo shoot between encounters, only to be chopped down and regrown over and over and over again. If left untended, its priority will surpass everything except your next breath."

"Why do you say it's 'human'?"

"Well, whereas animals have evolved seasonal strategies that optimize survival rates for their offspring, we humans procreate with reckless abandon all year round."

"That's mainly due to environmental factors, Ron. Winters aren't what they used to be for the average person now."

"Agreed, but I'm claiming it as human because of our unique intelligence and adaptability. I'm not saying that before we sidelined the influences of our environment we didn't have similar strategies to ensure the survival of our progeny. What I *am* saying is, subsequent to the taming of our environment, we've uniquely adapted our sexual practices into a 24/7, 365-days-a-year free-for-all activity."

"I'll concede you that," Brandi said, "but I'm more interested in the human characteristics that transcend the environment."

"I was getting there," retorted Ron, giving Brandi a "be patient" look. "It's all interconnected. The taming of our environment has freed us to be able to direct our intelligence toward the pursuit of things altruistic and spiritual. However, as we know, we come with *a lot* of genetic baggage programmed to survive in a dog-eat-dog world, which makes accessing any higher plane difficult."

Brandi nodded.

Her silence prompted Ron to continue. "What we stumbled upon this year, quite by accident, may I say, was that to truly understand what it was to be human, we had to accept and embrace where we came from. You can't deny what you are; you can't fight city hall, as the saying goes. To get anything done, you have to work with that which controls the system. Again, completely by accident, that's what we did. Instead of denying what the primal-core region of our brain craves, we worked with it; gave it what it wanted, placated it, and ultimately moved beyond it to explore our true 'humanity.' And we just have to look at what you've become to see what enormous potential there is there."

"So you've concluded that sex is *the* bridge between our physical and spiritual world?" asked Brandi.

"Not *the* bridge. *A* bridge. And, most likely, the quickest way to get there from what we've seen this year." Ron chuckled. "With their external physical needs satisfied, a significant portion of humanity is now casting around for a *raison d'être* that comes with our intellectual gravitas. There's a certain irony that the means to attaining it is right there in front of you. That ubiquitous burning physical desire is like a cat bell. Everything we do, everywhere we go, our sex bell is jingling. People get numb to the constant drum of it, and learn to work around it. We decided to dance to it.

"If there is a God—and I'm not by any means suggesting there is—it's as if He's made spirituality as easily attainable for us as is divinely possible. I can see Him pulling at His hair, shaking His head, and lamenting, 'How much more obvious do I have to make it? If I make you people any more oversexed, things are going to get out of control down there.'"

Brandi laughed, and said, "By the way, that was the 365th time we've 'felled the bamboo' this year, my dear. We successfully completed the resolution. Congratulations." She leaned over and kissed him. Then she gave him a loving look that took Ron aback.

"What?" he inquired.

"Want to make it a leap year?" she suggested.

Thursday, December 31, 11 p.m.

Ron and Brandi looked around Scott and Elise's kitchen. It was packed with revellers, most of whom they knew well, but a few they hadn't met until tonight. This was a little disconcerting, given that the theme of tonight's New Year's Eve party was a celebration of the resolution, and they had handpicked the guest list to include only those individuals who explicitly knew about it. Yet there were at least three people in the kitchen neither he nor Brandi had met until this evening. There were a few more in the living room.

Those few people aside, there was a surprisingly big crowd on hand tonight to help celebrate his and Brandi's successful completion of the resolution, including Brandi's entire family from Toronto, and Stewart and his family from out west. Ron and Brandi had maximized their overflow sleeping arrangements to accommodate all of them.

Deheune and the rest of Brandi's "healing group" were also in attendance. Ron had met Leana, Muteteli, and Hiroto for the first time, and found all of them magnetic and compelling individuals. Yatzil had given him a heartfelt hug when she arrived, and was now proceeding to get quietly drunk. Brandi had met Deheune's boss – Mr. Messervy - for the first time tonight: he was a small, cheery, older fellow with intensely intelligent eyes who, after initial introductions, had expertly mixed in unnoticed with the rest of the crowd.

Scott had also invited their mutual friends Gerry and Ian, and Ian's wife, Kelly. Gerry had confided to Ron that since their resolution had found its way onto Twitter, and more recently on @*lovejunkie*'s blog, he had been closely following their progress. Although Gerry's long-distance love affair with Trish across the border hadn't worked out, that appeared water under the bridge at the moment. He was currently engrossed in a very intimate conversation with Sneezy, who periodically looked over at Ron, smiled, and enthusiastically waggled her eyebrows at him.

Dr. Fiona was also there with her female partner, one of the people they had just met for the first time tonight. Dr. Kaur was in attendance with his wife, who, whenever Ron noticed her in the crowd, smiled broadly back at him. He couldn't tell whether it was a friendly, deferential, or lascivious smile.

Ron noticed his parents sitting at the small table in the breakfast nook, mingling with Megan and some of the in-laws. His father must have sensed his gaze, because he smilingly looked directly at Ron, and raised his glass in toast. Abby followed her husband's action to its objective, and waved lovingly at Ron. When Abby shifted over to wave, Ron noticed a familiar smiling face beside her that he hadn't seen for a couple of years—Aunt Colleen. She too smiled and waved at Ron who, to Aunt Colleen's delight, couldn't hide his surprise at seeing her.

Yogi Kukuraja, also in attendance, floated serenely through the crowd, engaging everyone he came across with his genuine nature. The most surprising of all the guests present was Jetsunma Kusho Chödrön, who had travelled all the way from Nova Scotia to be with them on this special night. She wore her most inconspicuous robes, and was the embodiment of peace and grace. Cassandra waved to him and Brandi from the other side of the kitchen. Ron whispered into Brandi's ear. "Discounted sex toys for life. Yeah, baby!"

Brandi's closest group of friends, including, but not limited to, Charlene and her husband, Kevin, were also present. Vanessa wouldn't have missed this for the world, and had requested to bring her beau with her, on the promise of confidentiality. *Right*, thought Ron. There was no way they were going to be able to keep this under wraps. The best he could hope for was to get through the party without local reporters showing up.

Ron looked at Brandi. "How did so many people find out about our very intimate resolution? There must be fifty people here tonight."

"Closer to seventy, I think."

"Did you notice that Aunt Colleen's here?"

"I talked to her earlier. She said, 'I told you you had the gift.' Seemed pretty pleased with herself, too."

Just then Tommy's girlfriend, Amanda, walked up to them and said, "Congratulations Mr. and Mrs. Lee. This is quite an accomplishment. Especially at your age." Then she bounded away.

Ron looked at Brandi, and shook his head. "I guess we really *were* a bit old for this resolution."

"Just a number, Ron. And if we were much younger, it wouldn't have been as much of a challenge. And aren't you the one who loves a challenge?"

Ron smiled and nodded in agreement.

"That brings me to my next question. What's the resolution going to be for next year? Or is there even going to *be* a resolution? Has this year's effort finally dissuaded you from attempting similarly ridiculous undertakings?"

Ron screwed his face up in mock flabbergast. "Who..." he paused for effect, "... do you think you're talking to? You're talking to the resolution king himself, I'll have you know." He delivered this in his 'best' Scottish accent, to which Brandi rolled her eyes.

"There will *of course* be a resolution for 2016. It will be as challenging as this year's, if not more so." He added the last with an indignant flourish meant to extract further inquiry from his wife.

"OK then. What's it going to be?" she asked.

Ron looked around to make sure everyone else was out of earshot. He leaned into Brandi and whispered. Brandi's eye's opened wide, her face drained of blood, and she stared, open-mouthed, at her husband. "You're joking, of course?" she asked.

Ron shook his head. "No, my dearest love, I most certainly am not," he said in the most dignified manner which he imagined a rural Scottish gentleman could possibly muster.

"Ron, have you thought this one through? Are you sure this is a good idea?"

"I have not only given this the benefit of my extended ponderance, I have decided that this is exactly the right resolution for this moment in time."

Brandi glanced away from Ron, sighed heavily, shook her head, and muttered, "It's going to be a long year."

Over the din of multiple conversations, and Marvin Gaye crooning "Sexual Healing" in the background, Ron noticed his wife, Brandi, chatting with a group of friends across the room. *My God, she looks gorgeous tonight,* he thought. As midnight approached, Ron gazed across the room in appreciation of all he had. His friends, his family, and, most of all—his loving wife.

Sporting a wide purple-toothed smile, tastefully accentuated with a red-wine mini-mustachio, Ron initiated a shuffle through the congested room towards her. Halfway there Dr. Kaur intercepted him and, pumping his hand with a two-handed shake, enthusiastically exclaimed, "I knew you would do it, Ron." Ron smiled, and noticed Dr. Kaur's wife smiling broadly at him over the doctor's shoulder.

He continued on his path to Brandi. Mere feet away from her, Gerry intercepted him. "Well done, buddy. Who knew? BTW, thanks for setting me up with Snežana. She's amazing!"

When he finally made it to Brandi, he wrapped his arms around her. "Do you know how much I love you?" Ron whispered in her ear.

She leaned into him and kissed him. "As you know by now, I do. And we're going to need all that love to successfully get through next year's resolution."

Just then, Scott sidled up to them. "Hey, guys. Can I suggest that you both say a couple of words to the appreciative crowd before midnight?"

Brandi and Ron simultaneously shook their heads and tried to dissuade Scott, but he wouldn't take no for an answer. "Just a few words to mark the event," he cajoled.

Brandi looked at Ron. He nodded. "Oh, what the hell."

"Excellent," exclaimed Scott. He sprinted off to find a microphone.

Upon his return he checked the microphone, but waited for Marvin Gaye to finish before he spoke. "Hello, hello. If I could get everyone's attention for a minute."

The murmuring in the crowd progressively diminished.

"We all know why we're here tonight. I mean, other than it's New Year's Eve. Actually, it really is because it is New Year's Eve—and anybody who knows Ron, knows where there's a New Year's Eve, there's always a resolution. And last year's resolution was a doozy. But anyone who knows Ron knows how stubborn he is. Right from the beginning I thought, if anybody could complete *this* resolution, it would be him and Brandi." This comment met with boisterous cheers from the crowd. "But enough of me droning on, let's get Ron and Brandi to say a few words."

Standing beside Ron, Brandi overtly deferred to him to be their spokesperson and, typically loquacious in proportion to his blood-alcohol level, Ron was more than happy to oblige.

"A year ago, I would have thought it improbable, if not impossible," he started, "that I'd be standing up here unembarrassedly discussing my sex life with a large group of friends and family." Pausing, he squinted at the few strangers he saw in the crowd. "But that's the joy of life, isn't it? There are so many things that are completely unpredictable and out of your hands, that there's no telling where our journey will bring us. I *can* tell you however, that this year has been the most profound of our lives." He looked at Brandi. "Together, we've discovered so much about ourselves and grown as close as any two people could ever hope to be."

More cheers and applause.

"This wasn't a resolution for the faint of heart," Ron went on. "Or, for that matter, someone with a bad heart."

He waited for the ripple of laughter to die down.

"As it turned out, this resolution was not only an affirmation of our love, but an adventure into what that resolution could create. We're both changed forever, and for the better, from the experience. We want to take this opportunity to tell everyone here tonight how much we appreciate you all being in our lives."

Everyone cheered.

Someone in the crowd called out, "What's the resolution for next year, Ron?"

Ron smiled lovingly at Brandi, whose eyes inadvertently rolled as her head dropped.

"My resolution," he paused for effect, "is to embrace celibacy for the entire year."

The crowd instantly went quiet. Brandi looked at them with a long-suffering 'what's a girl supposed to do?' look on her face, and Ron's grin grew even wider at the thought of a new resolution. Someone in the crowd guffawed and called out, "Good luck with that!" just as Elise started counting down to midnight.

"Ten, nine, eight…"

Ron hugged Brandi as everyone started pairing up in preparation for the moment. "This will be a real test of our love," he whispered into her ear.

"Seven, six, five…"

"For once, I'm actually hoping that you won't succeed," Brandi replied.

"Four, three, two…"

"It'll be over before we know it. And who knows what good will come of it?" Ron replied, with the enthusiasm only someone who's a child at heart could possess.

"One. *Happy New Year!*"

And they kissed.

ABOUT THE AUTHOR

J. J. Sykora lives in Calgary, with his wife of twenty-three years and the youngest of their three children. His scientific background, inquisitive nature, relentless search for humour in any situation, love of a good yarn, belief that we humans are more than the sum of our parts, and (most of all) true love of his wife, led him to write The Resolution, his first novel. He's currently working on a sequel.

CPSIA information can be obtained
at www.ICGtesting.com
Printed in the USA
LVHW03s0618120718
583518LV00001B/68/P

9 781525 523090